I0639561

GILMAN OF REDFORD

GILMAN
OF REDFORD

A STORY OF BOSTON
& HARVARD COLLEGE
ON THE EVE OF THE
REVOLUTIONARY WAR
1770-1775

BY

WILLIAM STEARNS DAVIS

✳

Fredonia Books
Amsterdam, The Netherlands

Gilman of Redford:
A Story of Boston and Harvard College on the Eve
of the Revolutionary War 1770-1775

by
William Stearns Davis

ISBN: 1-4101-0797-3

Copyright © 2005 by Fredonia Books

Reprinted from the 1927 edition

Fredonia Books
Amsterdam, The Netherlands
http://www.fredoniabooks.com

All rights reserved, including the right to reproduce
this book, or portions thereof, in any form.

In order to make original editions of historical works
available to scholars at an economical price, this
facsimile of the original edition of 1927 is
reproduced from the best available copy and has
been digitally enhanced to improve legibility, but the
text remains unaltered to retain historical
authenticity.

TO THE MEMORY OF

ISAAC DAVIS

Numbered among my ancestors:
Captain of Acton Company and first to fall
at the Bridge at Concord.

TO MY FATHERS' FATHERS

I who once turned afar an idler's glance,
Dreamed of dim wars and paladins of France,
Of Rome, of Athens, Allemaine, Byzance,
From old New England summon the romance.
Stern were her sons and simple all their ways,
Simple their college in those loftier days
When in tall youth America began.
Yet in their breasts glowed warm the dauntless fire
Brooking no thralldom; keen intense desire
To mould a nobler realm of God through man.
Lords of decision, masters of their fate,
They dared their vision,—made the Republic great.

ADVERTISEMENT

TO THE ALWAYS GENTLE READER

THE author of this narrative was of course the well-known Boston merchant (founder of the State Street firm of Gilman, Slater and Peabody) who at the close of the Revolution did so much to solidify the commercial prosperity of Massachusetts. As is herein suggested he served through the War for Independence, rising to the rank of colonel, and if his ambitions had carried him into politics he might have advanced far. As it was he served three times in the State House of Representatives and twice in the State Senate. He was counted a very moderate member of the Jeffersonian Republicans, probably on account of his marriage and a natural sympathy with France, but he always retained the good will of the Federalists, and enjoyed the personal friendship of John Adams during that veteran statesman's long retirement at Quincy. During the later part of his life Colonel Gilman was a valued member of the Harvard Board of Overseers, and was also a very active deacon of the Old South Church.

This story of his life during the years 1770-75 was apparently written during the presidency of John Quincy Adams, at the instigation of Colonel Gilman's gifted daughter Deborah. It will be recalled that her husband was the distinguished jurist, Justice Peltiah Gridley of the Massachusetts Supreme Court, and that her second son, General Roger Gridley, commanded a Union division in the Five Forks-Appomattox campaign and subsequently had a conspicuous part in the building of the Union Pacific Railroad.

Colonel Gilman speaks frequently of the town of Redford, which, it may be complained, cannot be found upon modern maps of Middlesex County. It is certain, however, that it cannot have been far from Lexington, Concord and Billerica, and indeed it may perhaps be identified with a town known at present under a slightly different name.

In preparing this manuscript the editor has sometimes modernized the diction slightly, also he has omitted certain theological observations, which Colonel Gilman probably introduced for the benefit of his own family. Otherwise Roger Gilman is allowed to tell his own story, as a vivid reminder of "The times which tried men's souls."

W. S. D.

CONTENTS

GILMAN OF REDFORD

GILMAN OF REDFORD

CHAPTER I

THE HOUSE ON SUDBURY STREET

THE evening of Sunday, March 4th, 1770, I shall always count among the turning hours in my life. The reason for this I suppose I ought to explain.

As everybody knows, I had been living with Uncle Peleg Fifield (my mother's younger brother) at his house on Charter Street, while attending Master John Lovell's Latin School—our Redford school not comparing with Boston, and I still lacked a year and some months of being ready for Harvard—if means could be found to send me. That afternoon, however, I had come over to Uncle Eleazer's (Peleg's elder brother) on Sudbury Street. I was feeling somewhat happy, for Darius, my own younger brother, had trundled down from Redford in the chaise along with father; and it had been a proud pleasure for sixteen to marshal awestruck eleven around to see the sights and wonders of the great town of Boston. The fact that it was the Lord's Day, and the need of attending two long services had indeed interfered with this pleasure, as well as had the necessity of avoiding the watch which patrolled King Street and the Mall to prevent ungodly philandering and promenading; nevertheless our satisfaction had been inordinate.

Father had been brought to Boston by the funeral of a high personage, the famous Reverend Dr. Coburn. A great man had fallen in Israel, and father as his chief clerical

1

friend had been summoned to preach the funeral sermon. Uncle Eleazer had claimed his brother-in-law as his guest, but to my great satisfaction Darius was going home with me to Uncle Peleg's to spend the night.

That afternoon I had marched my brother past the grandeurs of Faneuil Hall, the Town House, Province House, and most of the churches. We had even peered most unorthodoxy through the doors of King's Chapel, and Darius had actually seen the Church of England altar with its embroidered linen and the cross above it—something which made him draw back with an anxious mutter: "I don't think, Roger, that mother would like to have you get me into prelacy."—Then we had, with worldly mind, gone out on Long Wharf and viewed the harbor and a couple of black frigates riding significantly at their moorings. We had watched the regulars change guard with pomp and circumstance at the head of King Street:—and now I was meditating upon all the sophisticated speeches with which I was to favor Darius, when I had him back in my room at Uncle Peleg's and we were undressing for bed. An older brother will always collect his perquisites.

These speeches I studiously meditated.—But alas! I fear my aspect late that afternoon was consciously hypocritical. I was seated on a high, stiff chair in the waning light from the window, with a big octavo in front of me, and was trying desperately to give my betters the impression that I was reading Wigglesworth's *Day of Doom*. Darius, sitting close by, as a concession to his youthful frailty was permitted to turn over (and therefore presumably to read) an elegantly illustrated copy of *Paradise Lost*. My cousin, Hope Fifield (Uncle Eleazer's sole offspring), a small, remarkably homely, brownish girl of fourteen, with snapping eyes and a temper smart as a whip, was ostensibly keeping company with Law's *Treatise of Christian Perfec-*

tion—a book which I trust did her good, for she assuredly partook of the earth earthy.

These books were before us while we sat and tried not to let our eyes wander nor our bodies fidget—for we were in the collective presence of both of my uncles, of my father, Dr. Jonathan Gilman, and of his fellow minister, the Reverend Elnathan Hirst.

The four gentlemen sat around the big fire of hickory logs that was snapping upon the brass dogs at the lower end of the long white-wainscoted room. It was still daylight, although the fading sunbeams seemed cold and promising another winterish day to follow. Being Sunday the talk, as was proper, ran all upon matters theological, or the pious virtues of the deceased, a well-known figure in Boston.

"So far as carnal wisdom can scan," Uncle Eleazer was affirming, with his wonted dry solemnity, "it seems proper to maintain that it was freely predestinated and liberally foreordained that Dr. Coburn should be numbered among the elect."

"I concur," spoke my father in his best ecclesiastical manner, moving the white lace at his wrists, and slightly shaking his white full-bottomed wig. "By all human judgment New England has lost one of her wisest saints at a time when there is sorest need of his counsels."

"Right, Jonathan; very right," began Uncle Peleg in his brisk, desultory manner, but the Reverend Elnathan Hirst moved his large jaws slowly:

"I am grieved, Dr. Gilman—ahem!—to be moved to differ from a fellow minister of your acceptance. Neither do I forget the proper maxim, *De mortuis nil nisi bonum.* Nevertheless my opinion being now by inference invited, I am sorry to say that our late brother seemed dangerously tinctured with Arminianism, and even Socinianism, although I trust not with actual Arianism. His sermons betrayed his unsteady convictions and I fear lest he sowed tares among his congregation. We should not be too confident therefore of the plans of the Almighty concerning him.—No doubt the uncovenanted mercies——"

"I tell you," rejoined father, more testily than was his wont, "I knew Coburn better than did you. One clearer in logic and stauncher in Calvinism never breathed."

Father's attitude in fact betrayed that there was not the best of feeling between Hirst and at least many other members of the local clergy. Hirst had come recently from a small Connecticut parish to assist old Dr. Byles at the Hollis Street Church, and everybody knew that Byles was a high Tory. But then Uncle Eleazer, his best parishioner, was a Tory too, and it was probably just because Mr. Hirst held firm royalist principles that he had been given first his appointment, and then his invitation to-day to Sudbury Street. However, the talk soon drifted over to the question of what psalms should be sung at the funeral, and whether the departed would have desired the new Watts version or the old Bay Psalm Book.

As the four talked I watched abstractedly their group seated between the gleaming fire and the waning light through the windows. It was a long, pleasant room with good if rather black Smibert portraits looking down from the walls, which otherwise were covered with a French paper showing lilac rivers and boats, along with villas, mountains and shepherd scenes. The mahogany shield-back chairs might have been Hallet or Chippendale: there was a handsomely inlaid spinnet, a similar desk, several cases of solidly calf-bound books on divinity (Uncle Eleazer was a firm Calvinist like his fellow Tory, Hutchinson), the Turkey carpets were luxurious, the carving and beading on the wainscoting were excellent, and on one side of the door, framed and glazed, there hung a large coat of arms of the Fifield family. Is there need to say that the master of such a house was a great merchant, to whom Hancocks and Faneuils would take off their three-cornered hats, as to an equal?

In the gilt pier mirror I could see a good part of the room and incidentally notice myself,—seated very stiffly. My own person did not interest me. Hope, doubtless, would have said that I was a large, overgrown boy, with manly height but not with a manly breadth, copiously freckled, with reddish brown hair clubbed behind, and that I wore a fairly spruce Sunday dress. I trust she could have added that my face was clean and honest, and was not that of a fool.

But Roger Gilman was a very familiar individual to me personally. I liked better to study the others. Father of course was father—the solid incarnation of fifty-five years —years now of clerical dignity, learning and command. "The great Dr. Gilman" people always called him, and with added respect because he had gained his leadership among the Middlesex clergy notwithstanding the fact that he was settled over a poor country parish whence no summons to a Boston pulpit could seduce him. His black silk gown, spotless bands, and black gloves all bespoke his mighty office of justifying the ways of God to man. Of course I was in vast awe of him: of course I devotedly loved him—but that is another part of the story. He sat now stately and benevolent, like an anchored ship-of-the-line, portholes closed,—yet ever ready, when called to action, to unloose the thunders against false opinion or godless malpractice: and even Uncle Eleazer, who differed from him violently in politics, listened almost obsequiously when father laid down a doctrinal point, or quoted his "Thus says Willard" or "Thus says Doddridge."

Father sat in the biggest armchair as became a chieftain in the church militant. Uncle Eleazer was at his right and Uncle Peleg with Mr. Hirst upon his left. You would hardly have taken my two uncles for brothers, despite the same dark eyes and cast of features. Eleazer was slim, Peleg was round. Eleazer's glance was sharp, Peleg's was shrewd. Eleazer never cracked a jest, Peleg (even in his most serious moments) seemed struggling to hold back some witticism.

At this moment furthermore their costumes differed remarkably. Being in the citadel of his home Eleazer had thrown off his heavy wig, and a part of his shaven crown now shone from under his blue silk dressing cap, while he had exchanged his coat for a plum damask "banyan"—a dressing-gown which covered all his body down to his silver shoe buckles. Peleg, having officiated as deacon at the Old South a little earlier, was in his brown coat of fine broadcloth, deeply ruffled, and his satin embroidered waistcoat. His small clothes were of blue silk, stockings of white ditto, his heavy knee and shoe buckles alike of silver, and he wore an elaborately craped and powdered wig. His rings and the great seals on his fob also proclaimed the great merchant—very respectable.

As for Mr. Hirst, his costume was strictly clerical, black and decent, albeit a bit rusty. He was a widower and the women were already speculating as to "how soon he would warm his heart again." Like many of the inland clergy, he was spare and looked perpetually undernourished, although he had had his digestion ruined by hospitable dinners since joining Dr. Byles' work. His face was long and red, his eyes dullish blue, and he wore his own hair unpowdered and falling down his back in a long, greasy, brown queue.—I had already decided that I did not like Mr. Hirst apart from his being a Tory.

The conversation of the four was presently interrupted by the door opening and by Nero (most good natured of Africans) resplendent in blue coat, silk ruffled shirt and gold buttons, announcing that one of Dr. Coburn's relatives was without, desirous of asking Dr. Gilman something about the funeral. Father rose and presently my uncles joined him in the hall. I gathered the question was concerning how many persons would feel entitled to funeral gloves, and how much port and sherry had better be ordered for the dinner at the Salutation which would follow the obsequies. Being left for some time, Mr. Hirst at length let his eyes wander over toward me. The chance of catechising the son of a fellow minister upon a Sunday afternoon was no doubt irresistible, but my heart rebelled when I saw him hitching his chair in my direction.

"My worthy lad," he began with his most ministerial smile, "you of course realize that you are the heir of a great inheritance. You are a Gilman and a Fifield. The Fifields are of excellent stock, but the Gilmans—am I not correctly informed that the founder of the family was the peculiar friend of the first Winthrop and the foster brother of the sainted Dudley?"

"That is said of my great-great-grandfather, sir," I answered respectfully.

"A great inheritance," he pursued, *"very respectable:* nevertheless, already to you, young as you are, a heavy responsibility. You will recall the Scripture 'Unto whom much is given, of him much shall be required.' Therefore even to the son of so eminent a pastor, I can address a question I trust you understand, *Have you indulged a hope?"*

Probably my face grew a little red when I replied, "My parents, sir, have taught me to be hopefully pious."

"Take care, my good youth," returned Mr. Hirst, with slow, icy accents, "that this is not a false peace."

But here Hope ("Hope" of a very different kind) always my friend in need, charged splendidly to my rescue. "Oh, Mr. Hirst," spoke she, with perfect soberness, "there's a question in divinity which I want to ask you. Uncle Peleg said it was too deep for him." He turned with a benevolent beam toward the heiress of his patron as she pursued, "Why was Dr. Franklin blamed when he was a boy, because he urged his father to say grace at once over a whole barrel of salt beef in the cellar, so as to avoid the need of blessing each separate piece upon the table?"

The countenance of Hirst was a study. The damsel's lips were solemn as a tombstone, though I just caught the profane gleam from the corner of an eye. What he might have answered history recordeth not, for even as the minister's lips began to move slowly, preliminary to a very considered reply, my father and uncles reëntered the parlor. To my infinite relief they at once beckoned Mr. Hirst back toward their chairs and resumed the discussion of Jonathan Edwards' theory of Divine Sovereignty. As for Hope and myself, both conscious that we had harbored unholy imaginings, we devoted ourselves to our books. The big text of Wigglesworth spread out before me, I was reading how the bard of Malden made the justified Saints rejoice upon the Last Day, when they beheld their non-elect relatives adjudged to the fiery pit:

"One natural brother beholds another
    In his astonied fit,
Yet sorrows not thereat one jot
    Nor pities him a whit.
The godly wife conceives no grief
    Nor can she shed a tear,
For the sad state of her dear mate
    When she his doom doth hear.

> He that was erst a husband, pierced
>   With sense of wife's distress,
> Whose tender heart did bear a part
>   Of all her grievances:
> Shall mourn no more as heretofore
>   Because of her ill plight,
> Although he see her now to be
>   A damned, forsaken wight."

I was just permitting myself the sinful luxury of speculating whether my father could ever conceivably witness my
mother being "damned" and have no regrets about it, when
suddenly we all heard the dull boom of a gun at the distant
battery. Uncle Eleazer literally jumped from his chair.
"Sun-down!—Sabbath's over!" he exclaimed spryly. "We
can talk secular.—Well, Peleg—if you've brought those
papers I'll consider that Barbados venture. You're to find
the ship and I'm to find the rum.—Yes, I guess it can be
managed."

The Day of Doom, Paradise Lost and *The Treatise of
Christian Perfection* had closed with three simultaneous
snaps. Hope was over at the spinnet rustling a great pile
of music. My father was at the fire making sure that the
big iron loggerhead for the flip was heated red hot. Peleg
was producing a roll of business papers from his coat-tails.
Eleazer was tugging the bell-cord, an act which instantly
brought in Nero (expectant of the summons) to take his
master's orders for "a good pitcher of flip with plenty of
beer and sugar in it, and a big platter of doughnuts." Only
Mr. Hirst sat solemnly immovable, muttering something
about how at Hartford they believed that both Saturday
and Sunday evenings should be kept apart for the Lord's
service.

"To everything there is a season, and a time for every
purpose under heaven!" quoted father, unmoved, approving
the redness of the flip iron. "If the service of God begins

Saturday night, Providence will forgive us now for a little
rest from dogmatics.—Would you like Eli to give you a
stiff punch instead of the flip, Brother Hirst?"

Here, however, I lost track of their conversation because
the spinnet began to tinkle, and I had to hold the two-
horned phœbe-lamp over Hope's shoulder while she began
to play off "Maid of the Mill," "Roslin Castle," and other
worldly songs which doubtless made Mr. Hirst sigh within.
I caught, however, Uncle Eleazer urging Uncle Peleg not to
be content with a voyage to the West Indies, but to join
on a venture to the Gold Coast after "black ivory."

"Good money," Eleazer was saying: "only one nigger in
four's likely to die if you get the right captain, and I always
give thanks in church when I hear a slaver's made Jamaica,
just for knowing that another cargo of benighted heathen
is brought within the blessings of a gospel dispensation."

"Aye, I know there's guineas in it, Eli—sometimes,"
Peleg was rejoining. "That is if your fresh water holds out
and you don't lose the whole cargo as Fayerweather did
last summer. But I've doubts whether the Lord selects that
particular road to conversion: in fact I'm one of those that
suspicionate the piosity of the whole business. It's an old
story now how I voted with the majority in town meeting
to petition the General Court to abolish slavery in Massachusetts outright; and then your big friend, Tom Hutchinson, blocked the way. But your Medford distillery has
turned out a powerful lot of rum, and my *Polly and Rachel*
needs a cargo. So we'd better get together. She can lade
two hundred hogsheads."

More music: with Hope singing in a clear and vigorous
if very untrained voice, while I made shift to join her. We
forgot all about the four gentlemen until suddenly father
beckoned me to come down to their end of the room.

"Roger, my son," father said a little formally, "your

uncles have been conversing with me about you. Your
Uncle Peleg has received good accounts of you from the
Latin School."

"I am very glad, father," I replied with suitable modesty.

"It has been my hope," father continued, "that you, like
your elder brother Ephraim, now settled over Camperfield,
would feel a summons to imitate so many of your ancestors
and prepare for the Christian ministry. Of course your
mother and I have often talked with you concerning this.
Our hopes are known but the decision is yours. We do not
force you: for as the calling of the ministry is great, great
also is the error in mistaking parental wish for inward
summons. You have thought on this, my son. Are you still
convinced that you are not fitted for the pulpit?"

I felt tongue-tied and sheepish enough, with all four of
them looking straight at me, but I had been preparing long
since for some such dialogue.

"Father," I said directly, "you know that I despise not
the ministry, but I can never be an orator or do the work
of a parish."

My father sighed, but not with surprise. "I had feared
as much, Roger. My own cool judgment, as against my
natural wish, has agreed with yours. You have decided.
Providence has assigned too great a work to pious and
devoted laymen for me to cavil at this leadership. But
now I have to tell you of the proffer of your uncles. Many
there are who say that he who does not seek a learned pro-
fession needs no liberal education. Your uncles reason differently. Between them they agree to pay for your charges
through college."

Now this proposal had long been in the air, but there is
a wide difference between strong hope and certainty. I
trust that I seemed suitably "overwhelmed," and "unspeakably grateful," etc., etc., going on and on, boy fashion, until

Uncle Eleazer cut me short with, "Well yer see, nevvy, since Jonathan *will* stick to that barebones of a Redford and won't come to a Boston church, we're rather called upon to fish down in our small-clothes."

"Don't put it that way," thrust in Peleg, "since we've no sons of our own we're glad to do it. When Sabra up and vowed she'd marry a minister and a Gilman, we told her the Fifields recognized the honor and would act accordingly."

"In any case," remarked father, calmly ignoring this family cut-and-thrust, "Roger is grateful, I am grateful, of course his mother is grateful. Roger will go through college mindful of the obligation laid upon him."

Here my three relatives paused, and in the silence Mr. Hirst somewhat deliberately interposed himself: "I have been touched, I repeat I have been touched, by this avuncular generosity. But permit the sober query of a friend? The college to which this promising youth is to be sent has not been named. What with his gospel bringing up——"

"Harvard of course:" asserted Peleg, not waiting for Hirst to finish.

"Ah, my dear Mr. Fifield," pursued the younger clergyman, "it is as I apprehended. Here in Boston local pride has perhaps closed your eyes to those charges of unorthodoxy sorrowfully plentiful against the Cambridge institution. What did once that man of God, Cotton Mather, say? What have so many following after him said concerning the lax doctrines for years there tolerated? I am even informed that Harvard students have been permitted to attend, if they wished, the Episcopal services at that iniquitous building in Cambridge called Christ Church. Be persuaded: no such evil deviation is endured in the straiter and godlier atmosphere of Yale whereof I may claim to be an alumnus. And I fervently recommend——"

But here father shook his great wig and frowned like the clouds about Mt. Sinai, and even Uncle Eleazer scowled in warning. "Mr. Hirst," spoke father austerely, "this is a family matter and not a clerical conference. Your expostulations are uninvited. Since the colony was, when a Gilman went to college that college was Harvard, and to Harvard Roger shall go."

It did me good to see Hirst redden to the roots of his ill-combed hair. Peleg chuckled audibly. Eleazer muttered something about, "Even a sound Tory can be otherwise a perfect ass." As for Hirst, after a moment of awkward coughs and excuses, he suddenly remembered that he was due to read Scripture at the bedside of a sick old lady. He left quite abruptly, not even waiting for the refreshments, and Hope, Darius and I all felt the room grow three shades warmer. Uncle Peleg nudged his brother and congratulated him ironically upon "the next pastor of Hollis Street," and I saw a glint of satisfaction even in father's normally passionless eyes.

Nero, however, soon brought in a tall pewter pitcher, whence came the unmistakable whiff of strong beer and divers spices. Uncle Eleazer tasted the concoction with a silver spoon, slowly stirred in a quantity of cut sugar, and was just opening a panel in the wainscoting, and taking thence a glass decanter of choice rum, when we heard the outside knocker again, and an instant later Nero, with a very queer grin, was throwing back the parlor door and announcing: "Two gemmen to see Mis'r Fifield—and they say their business's important."

And before Uncle Eleazer could do more than touch up the peak of his dressing cap, the two gentlemen entered and I saw my father's and Uncle Peleg's countenances become wondering and quizzical.

The two gentlemen had nothing ungenteel or repellent

about them. In fact their whole appearance was very respectable. The elder, the shorter and the worst dressed of the twain, was a man of some eight-and-forty though perhaps he looked a few years older. He wore a decent, well-brushed red coat the least bit darned and rusty; in his hand was an equally decent, yet well-worn dark cocked hat. His face was one to command attention with its high broad brow, away from which swept his own abundant hair streaked with gray. The blue eyes were full of light and force, the nose prominent, the lips and chin spoke determination. His strong well-knit figure in fact made one think that it came from that Quincy granite, on which his ancestors had planted themselves when they migrated to America. For a very familiar figure in Boston had now entered Uncle Eleazer's parlor—Mr. Samuel Adams himself, the "grand incendiary" of the Tories, who already had given King George many a headache.

The person beside him was very smartly dressed in dark blue: everything about him being scrupulously neat. The lace upon his shirt front and wrists was spotless and costly. He was not over nine-and-twenty, but his broad ingenious countenance made you forget the first impression of youth. Every step and gesture was that of a man of elegant address and thorough culture. He wore his own hair clubbed back and heavily powdered, the white setting bringing out the full brilliancy of a pair of penetrating eyes. You instantly thought of him as an acquaintance absolutely to be trusted, easy to confide in, and promptly to be welcomed as a friend. No wonder his practice was already the largest and most fashionable of any physician of Boston. For this was Dr. Joseph Warren.

The two visitors came well into the room, then halted, and bowed a little stiffly, while Uncle Eleazer's face became a study for a great artist. I heard him mutter something

under breath—some mention it seemed of "the devil:" but
after all he was a Fifield, and quickly he bowed himself
ceremoniously. Peleg and my father were content with
less formal nods. And next as the proper host Uncle
Eleazer offered his formal: "You do me honor, gentlemen.
It is not often that Mr. Samuel Adams and Dr. Warren
call here on Sudbury Street. Nero states your errand is
important: but not too important I trust for you to join us
in the flip which is just ready, for I fear (he added with
the least trace of a smile) I cannot urge upon you
any *tea!*"

The visitors laid down their hats, threw back their coats
and Adams warmed himself peacefully by the fire. "I need
not tell Mr. Eleazer Fifield," he said in a voice peculiarly
rich and pleasant, "that I don't dismiss personal esteem
merely because of differences in politics. If without imposi-
tion, we can intrude, we are most happy——"

And so the ice was thawed: Dr. Warren asked father a
question about the Coburn funeral: Mr. Adams asked if I
was the lad he had often seen going down Tremont Street
toward Master Lovell's: Dr. Warren assured Uncle Peleg
that old Mrs. Leverett was a great deal better; and Uncle
Eleazer asked Mr. Adams whether a mutual cousin had
returned from Antigua, Mr. Adams being a Fifield on his
mother's side, although the two wings of the family were
rather separate.

Then the flip iron, white hot at last, was duly seized from
the fire by Eleazer and plunged in the great pitcher. Forthwith the liquor began to bubble, foam and give out a delicious odor, being charged now with that burnt bitter taste
wherein true New Englanders delighted. The glasses were
filled, the beverage was sampled and praised; one could
have imagined that five old friends were drawing about the
fire for a comfortable evening; and yet I knew that Uncle

Eleazer, Mr. Adams and Dr. Warren were really watching one another as cats watch mouseholes, and that Uncle Peleg and father were watching the three, themselves very amused and puzzled. At last my eldest uncle put down his glass and cleared his throat: "Well, gentlemen. You honor my hospitality—but I'm not vain enough to hope that you came solely to praise my flip and talk about relations."

Adams shifted his elbows thoughtfully. "You are correct, Mr. Fifield. I told your servant that our business was important. Dr. Warren can best explain."

The doctor hitched his chair a little closer to the fire. "Mr. Fifield: of course you know our principles: and we know yours. We are not discourteous enough to try to mend them in your own parlor. We have come to ask of you a great public service."

Eleazer smiled ironically: "And what 'public service' except turning Son of Liberty have I the privilege of performing?"

"Mr. Fifield," continued Warren: and I for one sat fascinated with his genial, ingratiating manner, "it is well known that you above any other man in the colony have influence with the Lieutenant Governor. Not the Olivers, not Flucker, not the Vassals carry as much weight with Tom Hutchinson as do you. He must be reached. You may despise our principles, but you cannot deny that we know the condition of Boston. A serious situation exists."

"I concur!" rejoined Eleazer resolutely.

"I do not mean the weightier, standing issue with England. We are not here to argue taxation and rights of Parliament. I mean the state of peace up and down this great town of twenty thousand people. It is now nigh eighteen months since the troops came here to Boston: and what have they done save to make for brawling, tumult and ill-feeling? I'll not speak of the earlier backbiting: but with the present winter you know well matters have become infinitely worse. It was as Dr. Franklin said, 'They will not find a rebellion, but they be only too likely to make one.' "

Uncle Eleazer hemmed loudly: "I know all about that Richardson business of ten days ago. He was being mobbed in his own house for tattling against the smugglers, and so he shot out and killed a dirty lad called Chris Snyder—no-account German I believe. Well—poor Richardson's in jail, but he never belonged to the military."

"Then you've *not* heard of the affair at Grey's?" spoke Adams, in his turn.

"Something recent? I was out at Milton Friday and Saturday."

"It was at Grey's ropewalk. There was almost a battle. The soldiers of the twenty-ninth had brawled earlier with the ropemakers. They were driven off: then when off duty they came back in platoons with clubs and cutlasses. Grey's men used their wolding sticks. Thank heaven not a man had firearms. When the affair was over nobody could count the broken heads. Both the soldiers and the rope-makers claimed victory—and prepared for another tumult. The shipbuilders and idle sailors are on the ropemakers' side. It's a foul prospect."

"Agreed," said Eleazer calmly: "but I neither command the twenty-ninth nor own Grey's ropewalk. Why come to me?"

Warren leaned forward in his chair, his fine face lit with earnestness as he resumed: "Because unless the troops are withdrawn very soon there will be blood on the stones of Boston. The King's ministers have been like boys playing with loaded pistols. The troops have nothing to do but to polish their gun barrels and curse the town folk. Not one farthing more is paid on tea, or on any of the Townshend

imposts because of their presence. They have not detained
one smuggler nor quelled one riot. Our 'Sons of Liberty',
our 'mob' as you please to call them, has its share I grant
of men who are not angels. This ropewalk affair is an
earnest of what may come. We'll restrain our friends as
we can, but human nature is human nature. If things pass
from bludgeons to firelocks, don't say that all of the blame
is ours."

"Then what do you wish?" Eleazer still impassively
inquired.

"To-morrow," continued Warren, "the council will meet
and voices will be raised that the Lieutenant Governor forthwith withdraw the troops to the Castle down harbor. At
the least sign of insurrection they can be recalled. The
undisciplined character of the men of the twenty-ninth is
confessed by their own officers. But whether Tom Hutchinson sees this depends not on what our friends say, but on
what *his* friends say. If you will tell the Lieutenant Governor that without forsaking the principles which you and
he sincerely hold, for the public quiet the troops should be
at once withdrawn, you will do a service for which all Boston, Tory and Whig, will rise to thank you."

"And if you will do this thing, Mr. Fifield," Adams added
in his deep clear voice, "let me in turn say this. So far as
Warren and I can speak for the Whigs, in order to avoid
sullying this long quarrel with blood, if the troops will go
voluntarily, we engage to review the larger debate with the
ministry and see if some honorable compromise can possibly
be found."

The manner of Warren had been ingratiating, of Adams
impressive. I saw father and Uncle Peleg nodding approval
at their words. It seemed (in my ignorance) impossible that
Uncle Eleazer should fail to consent immediately, but there
was a warning flash in his eyes when he rose suddenly from

his chair: so suddenly that the silk cap tumbled from his shining poll. He made his visitors an ironical congé.

"I've not sought this interview, gentlemen:" his words came gratingly: "Peleg and Jonathan are witnesses as to that. I know nothing about this Grey's affair. I'll ask Colonel Carr, next time I see him, to keep his men more in the barracks. But this I'll say—since you drive me to it: the last time I met Tom Hutchinson I told him, 'Let them explode as they will, the troops must stay in Boston if only to show that Massachusetts Province is under the Hanover and not the Adams dynasty.'"

The color of the other three men heightened, but Adams never flushed. "I told Warren," he remarked quietly: "it would do no good: but he thought the appeal worth trying. Of course I don't blame Mr. Eleazer Fifield for saying to my face what his friends are writing every day to the Tory papers or back to England."

Warren had turned to my father and Peleg: "Have you gentlemen no influence here? You know as well as we, how matters stand to-night in the town."

Peleg shrugged his shoulders: "Eleazer and I agree perfectly because we've agreed to disagree. We never talk politics, except when we slam one another in town meeting. Jonathan and I can't help you."

The doctor returned, however, to the fray with many earnest arguments, yet they were all lost on his host, who continued darting dry sarcasms, as he paced to and fro before the fire. At last Adams reached for his hat. "We've done our duty, Warren," he remarked, "as we see it, and so Mr. Fifield must do his. The case is with the Almighty— and we have other calls this evening."

But as the two were bowing at the parlor door, Eleazer raised a detaining finger: "Mr. Adams?"

"Your servant, sir," said the other politely.

"You made me a request unsolicited, now unsolicited I'll make one of you."

"More easily granted than was ours I trust," said Adams, good-humoredly.

"Have a better care to yourself, Mr. Adams. After all your mother came from our family. Your bitterest foes acknowledge your sincerity and wish you well personally. Did you know that more correspondence about you has lately passed with Lord North?"

"I understand my name is sometimes mentioned in dispatches," said the visitor coolly, putting his thumbs in his pockets.

"Of course you know Parliament passed the resolve last year that seditious persons in Boston could be sent to England to be tried under the statute of Henry VIII before a picked commission."

"And of course Mr. Fifield knows," interposed Warren, with a keen flash, "that the highest law officers of the Crown instructed ministers that no sedition had been committed and that the bad old statute could not be enforced."

"Anon!" observed Eleazer, his head on one side. "We'll not argue that. What I *do* know, Mr. Adams, is that you are said to skate on very thin ice: that new affidavits sworn before Hutchinson have lately gone to England against you: and I've seen myself a letter from a man very close to Lord North, 'Do you write me word that Adams and his friends are seized and I'll write you word that they've been hanged.'"

Adams continued gazing mildly at the carpet, but Warren made a motion with his gold-headed cane: "Mr. Fifield will observe that if the power of Government is not equal to keeping the peace between its own troops and a gang of ropemakers it is not yet equal to shipping the first Whig of Boston for trial beyond seas without a struggle calculated

to shake the British Empire. Good evening, gentlemen."
And out they went.

. . . A moment later, having received father's blessing
and taken farewell of Uncle Eleazer and of Hope, I started
out with Darius for Uncle Peleg's house on Charter Street.
It was quite dark but I knew the way very well. We had
hardly turned the corner from Sudbury into Hanover
Street, when, before the Orange Tree Inn, I saw Dr. Warren
and Mr. Adams halting in the light from the tap-room windows and deep in conversation. Of course in politeness we
pulled our caps and said our "Good evening," whereupon
Mr. Adams in a most friendly manner motioned, "Come
here, my lads." Then he put one firm hand on my shoulder
and the other upon Darius' head.

"Did you hear all that we and all that your uncles said?"
he asked.

"Oh, somewhat, sir." (Somewhat?—We had drunk in
that talk as a cat laps cream.)

"And do you agree with Uncle Eleazer or Uncle Peleg?"

"With Uncle Peleg, sir, everybody does in Redford."

"Good news, Warren," chuckled the older gentleman,
"then Middlesex can be trusted!—Now, my boys, go home.
But remember this: when you grow to be very old you'll
still recall the warning which was given your uncle Eleazer
and how he made answer. God bless you then—good night."

Away he went. And for the first time in my life it somehow came over me that the much discussed quarrel with
England might imply more than merely going without tea,
wearing homespun on week-days, deriding the King's ministers and singing the Liberty Song.

CHAPTER II

"WHEN in the course of human events" (to quote a document that was, at the time whereof I write, still six years in embryo) some very important thing happens in your life, gentle reader, have you not often found that the same great thing was apparently caused by happenings so trivial as to set you speculating about chance, ruling Providence and all the other deep matters that weigh down the big tomes of philosophy? Certain am I in any case, that my whole life would have been ordered far differently, if, after we quitted Uncle Eleazer's, Darius had not wanted to go by the Town Pump.

Darius of course had been too young for much flip and was thirsty. The night was cold, but not too nipping for two lively boys turned loose on the streets of Boston. The selectmen had not yet put in the system of street lights which came three years later, but many public minded citizens hung out lanterns at their doors, there was a small moon, and what with the snow the ways were reasonably clear going. The deep strokes of the Old First clock told us that it was only seven, somewhat earlier than I had imagined, and Aunt Mercy would hardly be expecting us. So we took another turn around the streets, swinging back toward Province House where a great chandelier was flashing through the tall windows of his Excellency's reception room, and we could glimpse red uniforms, gold brocaded waistcoats, silver hilted swords and every manner of deeply

22

powdered wigs gathered in social knots together. Then we turned down Hanover Street and were nearly at Union near the Blue Ball chandlery shop, when Darius announced he wanted a drink—and that meant a detour back into Cornhill where the Town Pump stood near the north side of Queen Street.

For a Sabbath evening the streets were fairly full of people. Soldiers off duty had wandered out of Murray's barracks near the Brattle Street Church; they had been visiting the taverns freely and if they hated Whig politics had not the slightest aversion to Whig punch, hard cider and rum. We passed several squads of infantrymen, decidedly unsteady, who shouted things after us. Also the "townborn" were abroad: swinging young fellows from the North End ship yards, sailors from the wharves and a good many more quiet folk from the houses of quality. Nothing happened, however, until we reached the foot of Queen Street, and here for a wonder (I suppose because all the shops were closed and no tavern directly handy) there was a remarkable solitude and calm: in fact so complete a desertion that Darius and I felt summoned to fortify our courage first by whistling and then beginning the Liberty Song— just to show any lurking red coats that we were not in the least afraid of them. We reached the pump. All around us loomed the sober brick shop fronts and offices, with the pinnacles of the Town House frowning across the gloomy square. I took the handle while Darius hunted the dipper, and we both sang together our lusty,

> "Come join hand in hand, brave Americans all,
>   And rouse your bold hearts at fair Liberty's call;
> No tyrannous acts shall oppress your just claim,
> Or stain with dishonor America's name.
> In freedom we're born and in freedom we'll live,
>   Our purses are ready,
>   Steady, friends, steady,
> Not as slaves but as freemen our money we'll give."

But just as I was giving the handle a mighty swing, to match up with the music and we both were trying to quaver into the second verse, Darius dropped the still empty dipper: "Hark, Roger!" And I did hark—for a voice, unmistakably a woman's voice, was coming from one of the dark little alleys off Queen Street. "Oh, Mons'r, Mons'r let go!—Stop!"—And I caught the glint of brass buttons with dark forms behind them: next a man's voice, "I must buss you, lass." Then a real scream, *"Au secours!* Help!"

Never had I read about St. George, the maid and the dragon, but the saint never flew over cobbles as then did I with Darius loyally at my heels.

Everything took place in much less time than it takes to recite. In the darkness I sensed rather than knew that two soldiers were trying to force some woman down the alley: that she was struggling, and that a second woman, apparently older, was clinging to their great coats, buffeting, and howling with all her might. This howling I dimly realized was in French. I was still a raw lad but I had already part of my strength, and Bill Allen had taught me his wrestling tricks. Instinct, rather than reason, made me send the hindermost soldier down with a thud on his crupper upon the bare stones. His comrade—reeking with brandy,—had one arm around the woman when I drove my full fist against his jaw. Being very tipsy he toppled like a log.—Then for a moment more I recall nothing but feminine squalls, moans and adjurations, in bad English and incoherent French: and next I knew we were out again in Queen Street and I had a young woman on one side of me and an old woman on the other, and the first was crying *"Les bêtes! Les bêtes!* Take me away."

"The beasts," however, although both very drunken, were picking themselves up, and following us out upon the pavement.

"Make him pay for this, Jem," one was calling to the other: and although Darius stood manfully by, proud to fight at his brother's side, I was considering whether discretion if not valor did not warrant my shouting "Town-born turn out!" the accepted summons for assistance against the regulars: when with a clatter of scabbard, and the moonbeams glittering on his gilt epaulets, a very fine, straight officer came down the way, evidently from Madame Apthorpe's where the command of the twenty-ninth was billeted.

A very fine, tall officer he seemed, and I assumed him to be at least a major, and only presently learned he was merely an ensign. He bore straight toward us, and at sight of him the two drunkards pulled themselves together and their hands went up waveringly in salute.

"How now, fellows," spoke the gold braid and grenadier hat, "did I hear brawling?"

"He attacked us, your Honor," growled Jem, rubbing a tender spot: "I was but doing a little sweethearting, and he——"

The officer turned upon me promptly: "Hey, sirrah?— You Yankee clowns have your own Doll Tearsheets:—let these that favor my men alone."

But here the two women burst out on him: the older in French, the younger in quite intelligible English.

"Is it that I am speaking to a gentleman, sir?" spoke the second.

Now if she had addressed him in our provincial English, perhaps the officer would have dismissed her with a shrug; but the accent and a certain swish and swing of her garments even in that gloom, made him suddenly bend with attention, and she as instantly pursued her advantage.

"If I have the hon-neur to speak to an officer of the twenty-ninth it is for me to say that I am Mademoiselle

Emilie Rivoire of North Square. With my servant I was returning from my friend Madame Johonnot on Brattle Street. I am told the Boston streets are safe for women. From the good folk of Boston I have no fear: I go along Queen Street with Berthe. I meet your men: they speak to me. We answer not, they follow: and then:——"

"Swine!" blew out the officer: "is this true? By gad, you're both almost too drunk to stand! Ho! corporal of the guard——"

Already the noise of the scuffle had penetrated up the street toward the barracks. A squad of soldiers came clattering out with a lantern. In a manner very different from his first greeting the officer turned to me: "And who are you, sir?"

"Roger Gilman, may it please you: I'm from Redford but perhaps you know my uncle, Mr. Eleazer Fifield." It was a lucky shot, claiming kinship with that very prominent Tory. The officer put his hand to his breast and bowed in the lantern light first to Mademoiselle Rivoire and then to me. "Ensign Dunmore—at your service. Forgive my hideous error. The case is very plain. In the name of the twenty-ninth I proffer deep apology.—Here, corporal: lock those two men in the guard house till they sleep off their liquor. God pity them after I've reported to Major Caldwell."

While the guard was securing and bundling off the unsteady prisoners, Dunmore took the lantern, and by his light I could get a better look both at the women whom I had rescued and the ensign himself. Berthe was a short, broad woman of indefinable age, a typical French *bonne* with large motherly features. She was still puffing, panting and repeating spasmodically her *"Mon Dieu! Mon Dieu!"* but her mistress had drawn herself together and thrown the shawl, which the unspeakable Jem had disarranged,

again over her head. I could only see that she was tall but
rather slight, and that her face shone out very pale from
under the shawl like the marble features of the Octavia
which I had once seen in the parlor of the great Frankland
mansion. Her eyes were big and bright, her hair, now in
some confusion, was tumbling in a great auburn mass from
under the shawl. Being only a lad I could merely remark
that her clothes though dark and simple seemed of fine
material and fitted her perfectly.—It is right to add that
I did not feel at all sorry that I had rendered some service
to Mademoiselle Rivoire: though at sixteen I could have
hardly told you why.

The ensign had no shawl about his face. His red uniform was very splendid: but when I saw the features under
his tall cap I was a little startled to recognize an age only
a little superior to mine. He was merely a nice, ruddy
cheeked, slim blond lad—with a clear eye, and something
about him that said, "Be friendly." And I suspect that
among my qualities there was also something that said the
same thing. In any case, by a process never to be understood, but with which all young people of a certain age are
perfectly familiar, before long we were all five—the ensign
and myself with Mademoiselle Rivoire between us, and
Berthe behind, blowing and muttering beside Darius, going
along Cornhill and then Dock Square and Fish Street, talking and asking questions as if we were girl cousins just met
after long parting.

Oh, yes, after a moment I remembered all about
Mademoiselle Rivoire. She was the granddaughter of that
old Monsieur Georges Rivoire, the sugar factor from Martinique, who, Uncle Peleg said, had lately taken a little
house on North Square. And was she not related to Mr.
Paul Revere, the silversmith?—Most certainly. Why then
was not her name Revere too?—Because, she explained

with an audible sniff, the Rivoires were not ashamed of their family name. Cousin Paul's parents could English the form if they desired. They all came of the same Huguenot family, only *grand-père* George had stayed behind in France when Paul's father, Apollos, had come to Boston. It was a long story how the *grand-père* had at last come to Boston himself, she would tell it another time.

Were he and she Protestants? Emphatically they were—thanks be to *le bon Dieu*. (I had shuddered for an instant lest she turn out to be a Catholic)—and the Rivoires had suffered much for *La Religion*: but that again was another story. And how long had she been in Boston? About six months, and was beginning to get well acquainted, especially with the old Huguenot families like the Bowdoins, Mascarenes and the Johonnots—all very respectable. And how did she speak such good English? Because the Rivoires as a family had lived much of their time in Guernsey under the British flag, and because, too, when a little girl her parents (*hélas!* now dead) had passed a year in London.—All of which information increased my satisfaction that I had been of service to this lady of mature fifteen.

By the time we reached North Square I suppose the others knew at least as much about Roger Gilman as he knew about Emilie Rivoire, but Herbert Dunmore, Ensign in H. M. twenty-ninth infantry had answered freely a great many questions too. How long had he been in Boston? Hardly as long as Emilie, having got his commission just before being ordered off with a new draft to the regiment. Was his father an English gentleman? Of course:—he was no one less than Sir Edmund Dunmore, Bart., of Malvers Hall, Wiltshire, and was just now in Parliament, having named himself for the family borough. And was Ensign Dunmore himself to be a baronet some day? Alas, no! (there was a doleful whistle when he said it) being only a fourth son—his eldest brother being now in the Guards, his

second in the navy, his third had just taken orders and the
family living, but had hopes of a canonry—and our humble
servant here present, had to be content with an ensigncy in
a marching regiment, something that cost only three hundred pounds.

By this time we were well to North Square, all inwardly
wondering how short a time it took to traverse Boston. The
little house of the Rivoires was dark, but "Emilie"
("Mademoiselle" had disappeared somehow on the way:
titles of honor seldom endure when you all are in your
"teens") said that the *grand-père* was surely at the Reveres
only a few doors away; so thither we went and found the
front living room quite full of wideawake grown people and
very sleepy babies.

Here was Mrs. Sarah Revere, an ample-beamed, matronly
vessel, full of good humor, and evidently much relieved to
learn that her connection's rescuers had been "so very
respectable": here too was Mr. Paul Revere, silversmith,
engraver, founder and archtinker of Boston, a man some
five-and-thirty, hale, stalwart and rosy, with his own hair
flowing freely over his neckband, and a face not wanting
insight and energy, but which bore more easily a smile than
a frown. He was hardly ranked as yet in Boston circles as
"very respectable," but Uncle Peleg had had many good
words for his intelligent zeal for the patriot cause, and I
knew it was wholly proper to accept any advances. However the one who impressed me most was Monsieur Georges
Rivoire. I saw a very tall, venerable man, with long hair
like snow, and a face white and pink as a girl's, yet lined
with the experience of age. His features were large, his
gray eyes sharp as a sword, and when he talked—in excellent English but with a marked French timbre, you forgot
everything else and looked straight at him.

As for Emilie, of course, she threw off her shawl, then
with one deft motion of pins caught back her unruly hair.

Now I could see that there was plenty of good color in her cheeks, and as she moved about in the candle-light there was a cut and fall to her garments, and a way that she wore them that made Dunmore and myself keep guard lest we seem to be staring rudely. Was it because she was really as pretty and good as one of mother's tall roses, or merely because French girls were different from Boston girls?— Everybody talked too fast for any deep thinking.

You could see all the Reveres making queer eyes at the ensign's red coat, and matters for a minute were awkward when Paul (after hearing of the insult to Emilie) having begun a violent attack against the "abomination of having those beasts called soldiers turned loose in our peaceful streets," suddenly cut short and looked apologetically at Dunmore. But the latter merely blushed in a most disarming fashion, and remarked that if he were a Bostonian he'd feel just the same way: "For my father, sir, is one of Lord Chatham's friends: and when I put on the King's uniform it was to fight Spaniards and Frenchmen (with a perfectly polite bow to Monsieur Georges) and not patrol the towns of *New Englishmen,* who seem quite capable of managing their own business without any of Lord North's foolery."

After that, cider was produced and there was still more chatter and lively talk. In fact it seemed as if we had fallen among family friends, when "boom, boom," from the tower nearby,—the nine o'clock bell was ringing from Old North, and then was being answered by Old South and New South across Boston. I suddenly remembered that Darius ought to have been long in bed and that now Uncle Peleg would be home and Aunt Mercy getting anxious: while Dunmore said he was due back at the barracks. So everybody shook hands, the ensign and I vowed we'd wait on the Rivoires at their own house before long, and I walked off with Darius and Dunmore.

Uncle Peleg's house was at some distance, being at the foot of Charter Street near the graveyard. The Englishman insisted on walking thither with us and on the way he unbosomed his heart. No doubt Herbert Dunmore, Esquire, of Malvers Hall would have thought twice before talking intimately on two hours' acquaintance with the son of a Non-conformist preacher: but Ensign Dunmore was then three thousand miles from Wiltshire and his splendid coat covered a very lonely youthful breast. And so in a few minutes it all came out—what he had been too proud to tell before Emilie: that he hadn't wanted to go into the army but to Oxford, having finished Harrow with credit, but that his eldest brother's "debts of honor" had half ruined the family and even a younger son's scant portion had been involved, when an uncle, the Lord Bishop of Alderford, had solved his future by advancing the price of an ensigncy—and here in Boston the poor fellow was, afar from home, afar from mother, afar from everything he liked and loved, thrust among uncongenial companions, patronized by the upper officers, disgusted at the endless brandy-and-water of the mess-room, and garrisoning a town where the social doors were slammed upon all British officers, except by a very few rich Tories who would never look at an ensign.

"And oh! Roger (we were "Roger" and "Herbert" already) when I went into that little Revere parlor and good women thanked me and talked as good women always talk to young men who try to live clean and honest—I think I could have wept."

Then he made his full confession. Yes, of course there was a girl, more pretty, far more pretty than this Emilie Rivoire. But she was only a poor vicar's daughter: good old family and all that, but no money. Promotion would be awfully slow in the twenty-ninth, and Peggy would starve on an ensign's pay—What hope? None, except the unholy one that my Lord Bishop would die:—he was childless, and gouty, and Herbert believed himself a favorite nephew. But could Peggy hang on waiting for such a chance?

As we approached Uncle Peleg's house, I in my innocence adventured a rash suggestion. Could not Harry sell out his commission, borrow some more money, engage in business, grow rich, marry Peggy, etc., etc. Instantly the ensign had clapped his hand to his sword. "Sir:" he began in a changed, startled voice: "Sir, the Dunmores are gentlemen; *they can have no business!*" Then he broke out into his irresistible laugh: "Oh, how I forget myself.—but I can't explain: Wiltshire isn't Boston—How I envy you Colonials!"

Late as it was we stood a long time in the cold at the gate, leaving Darius to go inside. And the ensign told me now that he and the more decent officers were distressed about the idleness and indiscipline of their men, hated their long sojourn in Boston, feared some serious outbreak and longed to be ordered away: "But the Lieutenant Governor and the two colonels won't have it. They say the honor of the King's Government is at stake and we must stay." While I (without betraying names) gave him some idea of perils of the situation as I had just learned it, and adjured him to keep his men within bounds. Thus we parted after a clasp of the hand and a clap on the shoulder, agreeing to meet at Wharton and Bowes' bookstore the next evening and have great times together.

I went into the house very happy. Somehow it did not trouble me at all that Herbert thought Peggy a comelier girl than Emilie Rivoire; and if you can win the firm, warm friendship of a clean, straight young Englishman of gentle birth, you're a fortunate man,—so bless God for it.

CHAPTER III

THE next morning my adventures seemed over and the stern reality of Latin was upon me. It was still pretty cold and though I may have been "unwilling" I certainly did not "creep like snail" that Monday when I went to school. Uncle Peleg's house was a long way from Master Lovell's abode of learning, but my elders said it did me no harm to stretch my legs twice per day, and I usually allowed enough time to study all the shop windows and take in all the business confusion of what passed as the most stirring town in America. You did not need to loiter that morning to know that something was in the air. The shop shutters were open, but few people seemed passing inside to trade. Little knots of men, usually in shabby homespun, stood about with their hands in their pockets, puffing into the frosty atmosphere and grumbling. Once I saw an officer pass, and one group flung a gross epithet after him, which of course he was too proud to turn and resent. Presently also I noticed a crowd elbowing up to a paper nailed upon the big elm at the corner of Cross and Middle Streets, must needs thrust up in my turn, and at last could read the placard, scrawled in a large, illiterate fist:

> *"Boston: March ye* 5. 1770:
> "This is to Inform ye Rebellious People in Boston that ye soldjers in ye 14th. and 29th. Regiments are determined to joine together and defend themselves against all who shall oppose them."
> (Signed) "Ye Soldjers of ye 14th and 29th Regts."

"They're sore over the Grey's affair:" the hulking ship-wright at my side was announcing. "Well:—let 'em just come to our water-front and have it out. *We've* as good cudgels as the ropemakers."

"They daresn't, the greasy slobs—" rejoined a cooper's prentice, "debtors, paupers and jailbirds all of 'em before they took the King's penny: we'll see nothing but their backs."

"Where they're trained to get their floggings:" roared a third congenial spirit: and I walked away quite convinced that while passive resistance to tyranny was a holy virtue, that form of virtue would never abound in Boston.

At last I reached the Latin School and tried dutifully to put my nose down to my Cheever's *Accidence*. Sometimes I wonder what pedagogues of another age will say about requiring a boy to study through a grammar three mortal times (and sometimes more) learning it word for word by rote, before suffering him to pass on to so much as parsing. I was beyond that first state (praises be!), but Master Lovell never believed in suffering even his oldest pupils to get far beyond "Line upon line, precept upon precept." Praise him or blame him, usually we lads who escaped from the Latin School somehow turned out to be *men*—and men not the most flabby in thinking or puny in application and courage.

Boston schools kept eight hours per day, but that day especially the hours crept on leaden feet. Never did Cæsar fight Vercingetorix more sluggishly. I was not more stupid or wandering than the others. Hopestill Palfrey on my left, although he was a great boy and nearly ready for college, underwent the penalty of the whispering stick, a wooden gag tied in the mouth something like horses' bits, for persistent communication under the usher's very eye.

From the room for the lesser boys the order "Down with your small clothes," and the whistle of the birch had never risen more frequently. During the noon hour when we ate our cold lunch around the big fire in the main hall, Elihu Jeffries (that Jeffries I mean who later went to Congress) told how his father had said that Captain Birtwick had told him that he couldn't vouch for his men if the Boston crowds kept calling them "Lobsterbacks!" because of the military punishment of flogging. Everybody around me kept saying "Something is going to happen:" and I imagine all Boston was saying that very thing from Charlestown Ferry to Roxbury Neck.

Just before nooning was over, little Mat Brimley whose father was on the council, and who had run out into Marlborough Street, raced back to tell us that his father said the Lieutenant Governor had in set form laid before the bigwigs the complaint of Colonel Carr against the attitude of the Boston people. Upon which there was straight talk to his Excellency that the way to stop brawls and tumults was to send the troops to the Castle: whereupon Mr. Hutchinson had suddenly dropped the subject and taken up the smallpox problem in Ipswich; and he would not even put the question whether the troops ought not to be confined to their barracks.

Morning had been long. Afternoon promised to be still longer. Cocker's *Arithmetic* lay before me, yet I could not more get my mind on the problems of "Tare and Trett" than I could name the wives of the Emperor of China. However, Master Lovell (a keen old despot, but who perhaps found it as hard to stick to his texts that day as any of his pupils) suddenly thundered a welcome order from the high desk. *"Deponite libros,"* whereat our books went into the cupboards with one resounding clatter: and the whole school dissolved around King's Chapel and the foot of Beacon Street with the noise of a hundred escaping galley slaves.

A little snow had fallen during the day and it had been just warm enough to change this into a cold Boston sludge —the very thing for snowballs. Parties of men and boys were strolling about Tremont Street and toward the Common, sometimes throwing a few balls at random, sometimes joining in hoots and catcalls. Ten or twelve soldiers presently appeared from their barracks on Brattle Street: they carried heavy clubs and marched in a platoon headed by a tall sergeant. When they reached the Old Burial Ground at the foot of the Mall all manner of the foulest Boston compliments were flung at them, and they inevitably paid back in the richest Billingsgate. More soldiers came in sight, always in little squads and always carrying cudgels. I knew that they found it stupid enough in the gloomy barracks, yet wondered whether their officers realized that the snow seemed almost to be turning into so much gunpowder.

The crowds were cursing the soldiers as "Cowards who daresn't fight!" "Jailbirds shipped from home!" and above all "Lobsterbacks!" and bidding them pull off their shirts and show their floggings. Some of the soldiers had hired long sleds and were driving down toward the Neck, standing up and flourishing sheathed cutlasses and sticks, and bidding the "dirty Provincials" "to come and try the teeth of British bulldogs." Meekness was never a Massachusetts nor an English virtue, and never was it to be more wanting than on that night of sin.

Presently I heard the "Liberty Song" roaring from a crowd down Winter Street, and then the opposing bellow of "Britons strike home" and "Rule Britannia" from the soldiers. In front of an apothecary shop I ran on Dr. Warren who beckoned to me and very gravely asked if I had seen my

Uncle Eleazer? I had not:—"Too bad: he's not at his
house. If I could find him he might at least go to Colonel
Carr and get the troops into their barracks. But *you* had
better go home."

Go home? The last place on earth I intended to seek
just then was peaceful Charter Street. It was beginning to
be dark when another band of soldiers passed along Milk
Street, whither I had drifted. They had been frequenting
the taverns, and were swinging their heavy canes and clubs
in a manner which sent peaceful spectators up into the doorways to let them get past. I suddenly realized that not a
woman was in sight—a strange thing on the streets of Boston. Just as I was taking in this fact, suddenly a hand
plucked at my elbow, and turning I saw the august figure
of Monsieur Georges Rivoire. He had a blue cloak tightly
around him, and a black cap pressed very hard upon his
long white curls.

"Meester Roger," said he: "do you see these men? The
flash in their eyes: the devil in their hearts? What do
you think will happen?"

"Something dreadful," I replied a little scared and much
wondering.

"Meester Roger: I will tell you. I am not afraid to
be *le prophète*. To-night King George takes away his hold
upon his colonies with one of his hands. God knows when
he will have to withdraw the other."

"I don't understand you, sir: things look queer but——"

"These soldiers, Meester Roger, are no more to blame for
what they may do than the grains of powder for taking the
spark. Who sent them hither to take the spark?—There
is the blame!—Ah! It will be a bad, bad night for King
George."

Before I could answer him he had mysteriously vanished
into the crowds, and I stood bewildered:—first Mr. Adams

had bidden "Remember," and now, these strange words of Monsieur Rivoire. I simply could not understand.

I remembered, nevertheless, that it was now time to find Herbert, and Cornhill being fairly peaceful I walked thither to the bookstores clustered around the Town House. Many shopkeepers were closing already and double battening their shutters, but Wharton and Bowes was open and lighted, and there behind a counter I discovered not Herbert, but Henry Knox. Everybody knew and liked Henry, a huge, gentle giant of a Yankee-born Scotchman. His big nose, florid complexion, dark hair and genial features made him one of the most impressive young clerks in Boston. The store was nearly deserted, and Henry stood behind a great pile of new duodecimos just unpacked from London, with his bulky frame bending over a volume on "Artillery Tactics."

"Good heavens, Henry:" cried I, "what will you not read next? I know you've made your bookstore as good as a college; but 'artillery'?—When you've barely learned how to shoulder a firelock?"

Knox put down the volume with a laugh, "Knowledge is like money in a strong box, Roger: never can you tell when you must unlock and spend it! But we've not taken in ten shillings all day. Mr. Bowes is gone and I'd better close and go home."

"Not till I've found Ensign Dunmore," I began, and then a red uniform swung into the shop, and I felt again quite happy until I saw the keen anxiety on Herbert's face:

"Carr and Dalrymple, his senior colonel, are mad. We subalterns can do nothing. Why have the men been granted 'liberty'? Why has a fool like Captain Preston been named officer of the day?"

Of course I could not answer him: but he had a friendly word for Henry, for the bookstore had been one of Dun-

more's few congenial places since coming to Boston. Knox
fastened the shutters and we all went into the street. The
moon was shining brightly: there was plenty of light and
every uneasy spirit in Boston in red coats or homespun
seemed abroad—seven hundred idle, angry soldiers loose in
a very unfriendly town. Looking back on it, only Providence fended off far worse things than actually did befall.

Just as we reached the street the bell in Old First began
rumbling and tumbling. Some lawless mechanics had
lifted a boy into a window and he had found the bell rope.
Almost immediately other bells north and south were
answering. Windows opened, men yelled, "Where's the
fire?" and householders (as law and custom required) began
throwing their buckets into the street that passers-by might
run with them to the conflagration. Presently too we
heard the rush of feet and clatter of a fire engine in a vain
chase up from the wharves. I could not see everything
that happened, but I heard the yelling near Boylston Alley,
and a white-faced fellow soon came running up, saying that
soldiers with drawn sabers now were chasing the people
on King Street. Louder and louder too was rising the
ominous yell, "Town-born, turn out!" matching the answering thunders, "Have at the damned cowards! Have at the
Liberty boys!"

Bedlam seemed raging. Men and boys ran this way and
that, shouting, whooping, waving clubs, firing snowballs.
I heard the crash of glass somewhere in the neighborhood.
Before the bookstore there was a little oasis of quiet, but we
knew it could not endure.

"This is intolerable," groaned Herbert in disgust. "If we
can't clear the streets of your bullies, I'll try to get in some
of our men." And we started past the Town House into
King Street.

Here the lights were still stronger, pouring from scores

of illumined windows. The Main Guard room was on the southern side, directly opposite the Town House: on the northern side, a little further down, the Custom House stood just beyond Exchange Lane. Before each building a sentinel was pacing. Their posts were not enviable. Confronting both soldiers there was now a hooting pack of youths and boys screaming ribaldry and sometimes flinging snowballs. The sentinel by the Main Guard, confident that his comrades were at hand, kept his post quietly, but his fellow by the Custom House and far more isolated, looked pale and jumpy.

Just as we came down King Street a Captain Goldfinch strode out of the Exchange Tavern very near the Custom House, and immediately a barber's prentice who had been hooting the sentry, doubled his yell—"There goes a mean fellow, who wouldn't pay for having his hair dressed t'other night." The sentry swinging his musket sprang from his post with a curse: "Show your face, rascal!" "I'm not afraid to show my face to any man!" retorted the prentice, whereupon the sentry, a private named White, gave him a sweeping stroke on the head with the gun barrel which sent him reeling, and the lad then picked himself up and slunk away blubbering into the dark.

White went back to his post, and for a moment it seemed as if his troubles were ended. The knot of boys dispersed, scared at their comrade's fate. There came even a lull in the yells and confusion that had been rising from Dock Square around Faneuil Hall. "The tempest has blown itself out—thank God:" Henry Knox was saying fervently, when we heard a new shouting and clattering of feet: "Town-born turn out! To the Main Guard! To the Main Guard! That's the nest!" And a pack of the maddest spirits in Boston came scampering out of the darkness of Exchange Lane and ranged themselves before the Custom

House. At their head was a powerful mulatto, Crispus Attucks, who had been particularly noisy all the evening, and who was flourishing a heavy cordwood stick. Heaven later suffered me to live through many scenes of violence far beyond this, but never will I forget the sensation of seeing the dark, huge figure of the half-negro, leaping and flourishing in the dim light, with a dozen companions flinging up their arms beside him, while their yells were worthy of an Iroquois war-dance. At once it came over me that now was the real crisis of the night: nothing earlier had gone beyond noise and fury; but the sight of the raging mulatto confronting that unsteady sentinel set all my nerves to tingling.

"Does the sentry have to keep his post?" I queried of Dunmore.

"Until ordered elsewhere. But he's guarding nothing. I don't suppose they'd sack the Custom House. I'll act if this continues."

There was no break in the tumult this time. Soon behind Attucks and his myrmidons were a perfect swarm of boys, blowing through their fingers, screeching every vile thing that came into Boston imaginations, and now and then flinging more snowballs. White, who had already set his bayonet, now with great ostentation opened his cartridge box, loaded and primed, knocking his breach on the stone steps to settle the charge. If he thought thus to intimidate his tormentors he was grievously disappointed. Soon the yells went louder than ever: "Fire and be damned!" "The lobster dare not fire!" And a sailor pulled out a boatswain's whistle and blew piercingly.

The sentinel motioned furiously with his bayonet, bawling through the din: "If you come near me I'll shoot your brains out." Then in answer to the general hoot which greeted him he gave a great shout: "Turn out the main guard! Help!"

"This is intolerable," groaned Dunmore through his
teeth. "He's in no real danger. They can't murder him
just with noise." And he strode bravely into the
street.

A gallant figure he made walking coolly between scores
of hostile glances: but he was allowed to reach the sentry's
side, for Attucks himself motioned his companions back:
"It's Ensign Dunmore: he's the real quality: not like the
others."

"Private White," ordered Herbert, "go to the guard
room. The Custom House is no danger."

The sentry with a grunt of relief was shouldering his
firelock, when the door of the Main Guard opposite
opened and forth came a short fussy captain, who hurried
across to the Custom House. "Who ordered you from the
post?" he demanded of the private: whereupon (amid a
renewal of yells) Dunmore saluted respectfully and reported
that he had taken upon himself to dismiss the sentinel.
Captain Preston (it was the officer of the day in person)
whipped out a trooper's oath and waved back the demoralized White: "I'm commander here. How dared you withdraw the sentry in the face of this rabble?"

"He was serving no purpose:" answered Herbert, pale
but firm: "I pray you not to risk some fearful event solely
for military etiquette."

"Keep aside, Ensign Dunmore. You presume above
your rank. Give no more orders, damn you."

Herbert saluted again and walked across to where Knox
and I stood silent by Peck's watchmaker's shop nearly opposite the Custom House. He was biting his lip and made
a despairing gesture indicating, "I've done all I can."
Attucks and his gang were redoubling their taunts and
howls, but elsewhere the uproar seemed subsiding. The
soldiers were being recalled from the streets, and the unruly

townspeople restrained by lawabiding citizens, or else they were tired with mere noise and were going home. For an instant I imagined the worst was over.

But now from between the two field-pieces before the Main Guard marched a corporal and squad of men. They had their bayonets fixed, and they cursed, shouted and lunged with their musket butts at the group of more peaceable bystanders who were watching from under the shadow of the Town House. "Damn you, stand out of the way!" I heard the corporal ordering. Preston darted across to his men, drew his sword and led them toward the sentry post where they formed a platoon of eight in a semicircle around the distracted White.

The case was now serious enough to sober all but the maddest spirits in the crowd. The noise partly subsided; several responsible citizens I saw pushing back the turbulent, pleading and warning, at the same time bidding the soldiers to "stand quiet and there would be no harm." But Preston, physically and mentally a small man, and completely swept off his feet, could now be heard in the lull loudly giving the order, "Load and prime!"

Instantly the din was redoubled. Two wretched boys with large sticks kept clattering them together, while Attucks whooped like a drunken sachem, "Cowards!" "Bloody backs!" "Lobster scoundrels!" "You daresn't fire!" These were the gentlest of the things tossed in the faces of the platoon. Henry Knox, who with ferocious energy had been pulling back some of the most reckless of the boys, now strode over to Preston (he had visited the bookshop) and plucked him by the coat: "For God's sake:" he entreated, "get away your men and let the thing pass. Your life must answer if they fire without consent of a magistrate."

"I know what I'm about!" roared Preston: but I doubt

much if he did.—His sword was shaking in his hands and his voice was very unsteady.

When Henry ran back to us I knew instinctively that all would be over in a moment. There were some sixty men and boys out in King Street: partly turbulent, partly harmless if not prudent bystanders. A good many were, like ourselves, standing in doorways or at the heads of Exchange and Quaker Lanes. The moonbeams and the lights from scores of open windows fell amply across the snow, but made long shadows that confused the vision. Up at the head of the street reared the massive Town House. I could see the glint of the royal arms upon the balcony whence they read the King's proclamations. All this I noticed amid the whoops, clatter and cursing, and suddenly for the first time the thought shot over me that Charter Street was a safe and pleasant place. Before, however, I could think this twice, I beheld an unkempt fellow throw a stick at a soldier who, he cried, "had been beaten up at the rope yard," while Attuck's crew swirled in nearer. The stick glanced off the gun barrel, but instantly Preston trumpeted, "Present arms!" And I saw eight bayonets and gun barrels leveled straight into that crowd.

With unloaded muskets one bloodless push with the bayonets would have scattered the whole screeching pack: but Dunmore (who had watched the whole tempest with helpless fascination) suddenly seized me by the collar: "Down! For your life, down!" And he forced me almost prostrate while a voice (whose voice evidence never proved —perhaps not Preston's, perhaps the corporal's) bawled out, "Fire!" There was a single shot; then as the noise still echoed among the houses, again the voice, louder yet, "Damn your blood, fire!" and eight more muskets crackled point blank into that whooping, howling crowd.

A ball sang over me and smashed into the doorpost.

For a long minute sight and hearing almost left me: I was merely conscious of a prolonged and horrible silence. If I saw anything it was a peaceful little bedroom on Charter Street: then I took it in that on the snow directly before me Crispus Attucks was sprawling motionless with something red flowing out about his breast, that Samuel Gray who had been trying to turn back the boys lay face upward with a strange dark hole on his forehead, that there were other figures prone upon the snow, some motionless, some writhing in a manner that made me feel limp and sick. Barring Attucks, not one of the stricken had been actually harassing and insulting the soldiers. "Reload!" I heard the corporal commanding, and other soldiers came running now from the Main Guard, while there was a tramp of feet from Green's barracks where the fourteenth was quartered. "This is what we want!" "Now's the time!" "I'd kill a thousand of 'em," many soldiers were calling. But Preston, by the mercy of God, had pulled himself together. "Shoulder arms!" he had the intelligence to command; "March! to the Main Guard!"

I sprang to my feet and ran to Attucks, but nobody needed to tell me that he was quite dead. Three persons had been killed outright, two wounded mortally and six more within recovery:—all in one flash of gunpowder. And then while Knox and I were carrying Attucks into the Amory House hard by, with a surge of excited people around us, and while I was in a stupor at my first acquaintance with that strange thing called "death," suddenly (it seemed directly above our heads) came the booming of Old First's bell, tumbling like mad around its wheel as if it would leap from the belfry, while from Dock Square to far over toward the dark Common rose one yell tossed from hundreds to hundreds —"*Town-born—turn out!*"

In my daze I remember laying Attucks upon a sofa, and

hearing some one say, "Where's Dr. Warren?" then stepped out into King Street. As I did this a second time that night I felt a pull at my elbow. It was Monsieur Rivoire. His eyes shone with an intense and haunting fire: "I was right, Meester Roger:" he spoke, bending his tall form toward my ear, "King George has taken away one of his hands from the Colonies to-night. I give you joy, *mon enfant:* you have great things to live for."

CHAPTER IV

THE "SAM ADAMS" REGIMENTS

NEVER before since Trimountain had changed to Boston, through one hundred and forty years, had the citadel of the Puritans seen such a night. All the bells were loosed in the nineteen steeples: from high street and alley drums were answering to drums. For Boston was no helpless burgherly town to be trampled upon by a dragooning soldiery. Every man of fighting age had his militia company. In two thousand homes there was a furbishing of two thousand muskets. Meantime other drums had sounded from the barracks. I had missed Dunmore the moment after the volley rang: he had rushed to his duty. Right speedily in serried array—a hedge of flashing bayonets under the moonlight, came company after company of the twenty-ninth swinging out before the Main Guard at the northeast end of the Town House. The troops formed in three solid divisions, and the front ranks began dropping on their knees for "street firing" so that the rear ranks could aim over their heads.

I was sick of soul and terrified, and would gladly have slipped homeward, but progress toward the North End was forbidden by the trampling throngs pushing constantly down toward King Street. I kept fast by Henry Knox, his powerful form towering like a protecting bulwark, and Heaven (as so often to the youthful rash) was kind to me: —otherwise I would have paid dearly enough for that night

47

of skylarking. As it was, broad King Street and all its affluents were becoming a surging mass of people, not wharf rats and tavern idlers now but the solid folk of Boston, and I could hear the hoarse murmur, "The militia are forming in Dock Square;" when, through a house whence he had come by a private passage to avoid the tumult, stepped a personage in a gold-laced hat, before whom men moved back with a little buzz ordering, "Way, way for his Excellency." For here was Thomas Hutchinson, Lieutenant Governor and Acting Governor of Massachusetts Province.

Fiercely as I may storm at Hutchinson, be it said that he played the magistrate of dignity that night. I was near enough to hear him when he went up to the Main Guard, where the soldiers respectfully saluted. "Are you the commanding officer?" he spoke sternly to the white and unsteady Preston. "Yes, sir." "Do you not know that you have no power to fire on any collection of people except you have a civil magistrate with you to give you notice?" "I was obliged," came the faltering answer, "to save the sentry."

Before Hutchinson could say more, a pandemonium of voices came down Cornhill: "To the Town House! To the Town House! Muskets! Muskets!" The surge of the crowd carried the governor with it into the building, while the throngs in King Street ever packed tighter. The people were walking straight up to the points of the bayonets. No threats nor curses now, but a passionate, growling determination. I noticed pistols, fowling pieces and blunderbusses. If there were more volleys the bloodshed would not be all on one side. I could see the officers looking anxiously at one another as they moved behind their platoons. Herbert, to my great relief, appeared nowhere, and later I learned he had duty at the barracks—but the situation was one to go off at the drop of a hat. Then a moment of silence, when forth upon the balcony of the

Town House, looking down on the snow where the blood was scarce frozen, Thomas Hutchinson came before the multitude. At his side stood many members of the council.

In a dead hush (it was approaching midnight and overhead all the stars now blinked clearly) he spoke over the sea of upturned faces. Solemnly he told the people that the "unhappy event" should be searchingly investigated. "The law should have its course: he would live and die by the law." But when he promised to order an inquiry in the morning, and besought the citizens to retire to their homes, there was a deep, fierce murmur of dissent. "Send the troops to the barracks! Send them to the barracks!" came passionately from twenty voices.

"It is not in my power. The command is with Colonel Dalrymple, not with me," spoke the governor. But here there stepped upon the balcony Dalrymple, the senior colonel himself. I think he had caught the meaning of the bells and saw now the glint of many gun barrels coming resolutely down King Street—not borne by his troops but by the Boston Companies. I saw him nodding to Hutchinson, and then rang the order which lifted a load from my heart—"Shoulder arms!" At which the troops broke from firing formation, fell into platoons and tramped away to their barracks. . . .

. . . I shook Henry's hand and scurried away toward the North End, the streets still crowded with people, now mostly distracted or even agonizing women. Uncle Peleg's house was ablaze with candles; but he and Aunt Mercy were too delighted to see me safe to have a word of scolding. It was one o'clock when I tumbled under the feather bed, my head buzzing with the most horrid thoughts which Providence had yet given me power to conceive.

. . . .

After restless hours I rose, threw on my clothes, hurried

down a little fire-cake and went out into the streets. It never occurred to me to go to school: something clear as Gabriel's trumpet told me that Master Lovell himself—being very human—would be anywhere save at the school-house. The first thing I noted was the crowd of strangers coming along the streets; and running to the Charlestown ferry slip I saw all the boats rowing in, one after another, loaded with solid, substantial citizens from Cambridge, Malden, Melrose and even a few whom I recognized as coming clear from Metonomy not far from Redford. Their faces were set and solemn: they were talking earnestly: many carried guns and still more had belted on pistols.

Following again the crowds (very different throngs now from those of yesterday) I let myself wander along to Marlborough Street. All the stores were closed and there was no dangerous patronage at the taverns: but here still another set of firm-jawed, silent men in homespun were coming in sleighs and pungs from Roxbury, Brookline, Dorchester and the towns beyond. They also had guns and pistols. But there were very few young men in sight, and when at his lodgings I inquired for Henry Knox they told me that his militia company was under arms and he of course was at the place of muster.

The regulars had vanished from public gaze: even before the Main Guard there paced no sentry. Everything seemed quiet and orderly—more like the Sabbath than any other day:—except for the great crowds upon the streets and the constant sight of weapons. I picked up a couple of school-fellows and by using our ears and eyes, and by a few bold inquiries of gentlemen we knew, the case became plain to us.

The Lieutenant Governor had sat with the two colonels till three in the morning, when Preston and all the men of the firing platoon had been ordered to prison to face trial for murder. But immediately after dawn the selectmen and justices of the peace had walked boldly before Hutchinson and told him in the name of Boston that the troops must go, and that "nothing else would satisfy the people." To which fiat his Excellency (an extremely smooth man at times) had repeated that Dalrymple, not he, controlled the troops, but that he would summon the colonels, convene the council and discuss the matter thoroughly. Whereupon "the Honorable the Selectmen" had bowed and retired, after saying they would reappear later: their departure from the Town House being hastened by the potent tidings that the freeholders of Boston were convening in informal town meeting at Faneuil Hall, Mr. Thomas Cushing, Speaker of the House of Representatives, acting as moderator.

By the time we reached Faneuil Hall, Dock Square over which it shadowed, was a mass of standing humanity—orderly, conversing in low murmurs, and waiting patiently to get the gist of the discussions inside. We heard that the meeting would not come to order until Dr. Cooper of the Brattle Street Church could be summoned from his parsonage to offer prayer, and that then the closely packed assembly had listened to the careful testimony of responsible citizens as to just what had happened. After that the word was passed out that Mr. Samuel Adams was speaking to the motion that a Committee of Fifteen be sent to his Excellency to inform him that it was the unanimous opinion of the meeting that "the inhabitants and the soldiery could no longer dwell together in safety" and that for the prevention of carnage and blood there must be an immediate removal of the troops. Next we heard that the motion was carried, the committee named, that it would go to the governor at noon, and that the meeting had adjourned until three o'clock, when it would reconvene under more formal warrant from the selectment to receive his Excellency's answer.—It was all as quiet, as deliberate, you might have said as stupid, as a special town meeting to talk about repairing the spiling under Long Wharf.

We hung about the streets until the committee went to the Town House and conferred briefly with the governor. Nothing was given out, but the rumor soon spread that the reply was unsatisfactory. Ever greater swarms of people were pushing in from the towns around—the news must have sped through the night far into Middlesex, Essex and Norfolk. Still no disorder: the weather was now mild and the strangers tramped and retramped the slushy streets, or visited homes of their friends in Boston. But everywhere went the consciousness that a cord was being drawn very tight—when would it snap? Passing one open door I saw a quiet group of men taking a lead kettle from a fire—they were running bullets.

After a visit home for a very hasty luncheon I was out again. Uncle Peleg had gone to see a friend on the council. Aunt Mercy was glad to see me depart if only to quiet her hunger for "more news." But the town meeting was not until three o'clock, and vagrant impulse sent me toward North Square. Merely of course to pick up what tidings I could (I aver that I had no other motive!) my steps took me to the Rivoire house.

It was a small dwelling wedged in between two greater, but a knock on the door brought Emilie (she had been at the threshold or out on the Square all day), and she had me into the little parlor. The sanded floor, the Quimper plates above the fireplace, the pictured lace of the curtained windows, the very carving of the tall black chairs, a score of other touches all bespoke comfort and good housekeeping —but not that of New England. Emilie herself wore a lace cap which I knew Hope Fifield might have begged her father to mortgage his Charlestown warehouse to get for her. The greetings were frank and friendly: a little more ceremonious perhaps than from a Boston girl—but I did not dislike that. Emilie's grandfather too came forward and bowed with elaborate courtesy.

"I also have been on the streets, Meester Roger," he said, "but you are a strange people. I thought the town would explode—*pouf!* last night. Now—where is your anger?"

Emilie gave her shapely shoulders an eloquent shrug. "In France after an *émeute* like this, before dawn the soldiers would have been plucked in pieces or the town would have been sacked. I also cannot understand—all that I hear of is talk, talk, talk."

"You do not understand New England:" I made bold to reply. "Rashness is not our way."

"But your courage is freezing. The troops laugh in their barracks. To-morrow they will be on the streets again, red-coated brigands."

"To-morrow they will be on their way to the Castle, or Boston will be in shambles."

"What do you mean, my friend?"

"Mean," I answered a little proudly: "That I am old enough, if not to know Frenchmen, at least to know Yankees. You have hot rage, our rage is cold. I have been listening all the morning on the streets. Either the troops are ordered away by to-night, or to-night ten thousand men with weapons drive them out."

Her look was incredulous. "King George's regulars? At white heat you might have courage against them. Not after a day of prudent talk. Impossible! We shall see."

"Yet, Meester Roger may not err:" spoke her grandfather gravely: "I also have listened on the streets. You are a strange people."

Whether Emilie was right or wrong I was itching now to be nearer Dock Square. By the time I reached it the whole area around Faneuil Hall was one mass of humanity, and just as I came on the verge of the crowd I heard the mutter going round: "Adjourning to the Old South—it's bigger." Being luckily on the very edge of the throng, it was easy enough to be carried along ahead of it, and although I had rather less business in the great meeting house than the farmers from Melrose, excited conscience troubled me not when I found myself swept into a box pew right under the shadow of the tall pulpit and its canopied sounding board.

Nobody was sitting. The nigger-heaven galleries far above were creaking with the close packed, standing multitude. Well that the fathers had built Old South so strong! —Hardly were we shuffled into place than everybody began calling, "Way, way for the committee!"—And in they came, looking neither to right nor left, but marching straight up to the foot of the pulpit.

A *most respectable fifteen*, with the venerable moderator, Mr. Cushing, at the head, but next to him advanced the chairman of the committee. I knew that the tall, dignified, youngish figure in gold- and point-lace was Mr. John Hancock, the richest merchant in Boston: and you could count off on your fingers the solid fortunes and honored names that walked in behind him. But it was not Mr. Hancock, but the even better-known figure in the shabby-genteel red coat under the flowing gray hair, that mounted beside the moderator, and read the written answer of his Excellency.

The Lieutenant Governor, the paper read, regretted that unhappy differences had arisen, but it was not in his power to withdraw the troops; they were under the command of Colonel Dalrymple who took his orders from General Gage of New York. However, the colonel as a courtesy to the town would withdraw the twenty-ninth regiment (the chief offender) to the Castle. The fourteenth would have to stay until General Gage could issue his commands. Mr. Adams mildly added that Mr. Hutchinson had cautioned the committee that an attack on the King's troops was treason, with forfeiture of lives and estates for all concerned.

When Adams ceased there was a dead silence in that huge hall, so that you heard the confused buzzing of the thousands outside. Then in a few measured sentences the spokesman gave the opinion of the committee:—"That the response of the Lieutenant Governor was insufficient:" and the moderator put the question, "Should the reply be accepted?" A single quavering "Aye!" broke from a Tory hidden in the back recesses of a gallery: the "No" that followed made the old rafters quake.—Still no disorder. A new and smaller committee was promptly chosen to wait on the chief magistrate—Mr. John Hancock of course was again chairman, and there was a Phillips, a Molineaux, a Pemberton, and a couple more of the Very Respectables: but not by chance was it that Dr. Joseph Warren went also, and that Mr. Samuel Adams again was spokesman.

As the seven waited for the crowded aisles to make a lane for them, they brushed directly past me, and Dr. Warren's elbow jostled mine. Was it because he saw the yearning in my face: was it because he knew of my father's great power across wide Middlesex; or merely because the bag which he bore was heavy? Certain it is, he thrust the portfolio into my hands: "We need an attendant. You can carry these papers for us. Come with me."—And down that lane under thousands of eyes I passed as if treading on air.—Then as we went, scores began shouting after us as at a kind of signal, "Both regiments or none! Both regiments or none!" Thus we defiled along Cornhill past Water Street toward the Town House: and behind the densely packed street head I saw that which made my blood tingle yet more. The shoulders of Henry Knox rising above his comrades as they stood resting upon their muskets in their militia company.—In an hour would Henry Knox and Herbert Dunmore be killing each other?

The lane along the cobbles opened for us clear to the Town House. We filed quietly in upon the covered walk, the "Exchange" of Boston, past the public clerks' offices, then up the carven staircase—and we were in the Council Room before the Lieutenant Governor and the Honorable Council.

A fine stately room, large enough for an impressive gathering, not too large for men to look steadily into one another's eyes. Upon the walls hung two huge pictures in gilt frames, of King Charles II and of the evil James II, his brother. They seemed frowning down into our very faces from their robes of royal ermine and from the piled curls of their uncouth, seventeenth century periwigs. In obscure corners, as if abashed to be compared with majesty, hung small awkward portraits of Endicott, Winthrop, Bradstreet and Belcher—honored governors of the old Bay Colony. Right before us, as the committee filed into the room, stretched a very long table: with many gold-laced hats resting among the pens, inkstands and papers scattered on the solid mahogany. At the center of this table sat a man of slight stature and smallish features, not unhandsome or unpleasing—but nearly buried under a very large, judicial, fuzzed wig. It was his Excellency the Acting Governor. At his right in full regimentals, well-bred and smooth, sat Lieutenant Colonel Dalrymple and his junior, Carr, commander of the offending twenty-ninth. At Thomas Hutchinson's left was the blue uniform of a frigate captain: then ranging nearly across the length of the room were the eight-and-twenty of the council, all their heads powdered and white, they mostly, like the governor, wearing English

scarlet-cloth coats or gowns. It was becoming dark: a
dozen candles were burning. The whole impression in the
Council Room was one of whiteness, redness and of a subdued murmur from behind the long table.

As the committee filed in most of the powdered heads
bowed slightly: the governor gave a nod of very formal
courtesy to the nominal chairman, Mr. Hancock: but the
latter with a wave of the fine gloves in his hand turned to
Mr. Adams—and the old red coat stood out again before
their Honors of the Council.

Now all that was said in the deepening gloom of that
hour neither I nor any other man present ever took down
word for word: but the chief things that Adams said and
Hutchinson answered were graven in the memories of all
of us, to be forgotten when old hearts ceased to beat.

Mr. Adams spoke, the first time calmly: he stated in a
few words that the answers of his Excellency had failed to
content the Boston Town Meeting. The troops must go.
Their presence in Boston, quartered upon the inhabitants in
time of peace and without consent of the legislature, was
illegal. They rendered no public service and now had provoked infinite harm. It would be new misery for the town
if they were suffered to remain, therefore the vote of the
people must be complied with.

When he had done the governor rose, bowed not to
Adams but to Hancock, and gave his answer in a quiet, even
voice. He differed from the committee: the troops were
present by royal authority wholly lawful. Hutchinson himself did not command them, but Colonel Dalrymple. That
officer had said only a few hours earlier, "It was impossible
for him to go any further in this matter. The information
given of the intended rebellion was sufficient reason against
the removal of his Majesty's troops."—That, added his
Excellency was the final answer. The twenty-ninth should

go to the Castle, but the fourteenth must remain. He could not say otherwise to the committee.

And so Thomas Hutchinson bowed again to John Hancock and seated himself, and Hancock looked toward Samuel Adams, and Samuel Adams moved from the standing group of committeemen, took two steps toward the long table, then spoke straight in the governor's face. This time his voice soon rang like a trumpet through the wide chamber, and carried far out into the eager press in the corridors and upon the creaking stairs. And as he spoke I saw all the powdered heads stirring behind the long table,— while as his emotions deepened, Adams' arm, of wont at rest during his speeches, shook, pointing toward his Excellency, and his tones vibrated with the mighty passion behind:

"It is well known that, acting as governor of this province, you are by its charter, the commander-in-chief of the military forces within it, and as such the troops now in its capital are subject to your orders. If you or Colonel Dalrymple under you have power to remove one regiment, you have power to remove both: and nothing short of their total removal will satisfy the people, or preserve the peace of the province. A multitude, highly incensed, now wait the result of their application. The voice of ten thousand freemen demands that *both* regiments be forthwith removed. Their voice must be respected,—their demand obeyed. *Fail, then at your peril to comply with this requisition!* On you alone rests the responsibility of the decision, and if the first expectations of the people are disappointed you must be answerable to God and your country for the fatal consequence that must ensue. The committee have discharged their duty, and it is for you to discharge yours. They await your final determination."

As he spoke all looked upon the governor and as Adams

himself wrote later, glorying in his words, "I observed his knees to tremble: I saw his face grow pale: and I enjoyed the sight."

Silence then for a moment, perchance briefer than it seemed, and next we saw Dalrymple himself blenching, bending toward Hutchinson, while two or three of the council rose and walked hastily toward the governor's chair. We could not hear their conversation, but I caught the colonel's mutter, "I am at your orders:" and some one else was saying, "No seven hundred regulars can ever hold down this town." Whereupon others of the council called for the rest of the committee to speak their minds, at which one and all—from Hancock unto Pemeberton—avowed that the people would most certainly drive out the troops; and that this was the firm resolve, not of a mob, but of the "generality of the principal inhabitants:" adding that the blood would be charged to the governor alone, seeing that Dalrymple had consented to obey Hutchinson's orders. Then at length one of the gravest of the council, Mr. Tyler I think, took his post by the governor's chair: we could all hear him. "Look from the windows, your Excellency. Who are outside pressing these demands? They are no mob that pulls down houses. No: they are men of the best character: men of estates: *praying men*. They have formed their plan for forcing the troops from the town: it is impossible that these should remain there. For God's sake take the way of peace."

Hutchinson rose to his feet with some difficulty. His own voice trembled under the huge judicial wig. "Gentlemen of the Committee be pleased to retire while we deliberate. I hope we can content you."

Silently we waited by the head of the staircase, but not for long, and when we reëntered the governor, in tones still unsteady, read from a paper: "Colonel Dalrymple promises that he will begin preparation of the troops in the morning, and there shall be no unnecessary delay until the whole of the two regiments are removed to the Castle."

. . . I can recall Adams' words and Hutchinson's, but no pen of mine can record the thunders of the cheering which shook Old South when the committee made report to the tense and straining meeting. The "Sam Adams" regiments (so Lord North soon called them in Parliament) had become a part of eternal history. . . .

The next day, after I had slept the sleep of exhausted youth, I saw both Herbert and Emilie. The former was rejoicing at a deliverance from a struggle "in which you had either to slaughter honest men or be slaughtered by them." He must of course depart down harbor to Castle William but hoped to get frequent leave to see me in Boston. We tried to plan how we could spend his furlough together.

Emilie's satisfaction was even less contained. With feminine logic she seemed to assume that since I had borne Dr. Warren's portfolio, I must have supplied some of Mr. Adams' eloquence: "Ah! it is just as you said, Roger, my friend. Your cold rage is better than our hot rage.—I love —oh! I *love* you Boston people!"

And though a Boston girl would never have expressed it thus, I was not in the least offended with Emilie.

. . . Years afterward Samuel Adams' redoubtable kinsman, the great John Adams himself wrote thus of the Boston Massacre and the things that came after: "On that night the foundation of American Independence was laid." And the more I think thereon, the more I think that he was right when he also said that for the making of America the surrenders of Burgoyne and of Cornwallis almost counted for less than "The Battle of King Street."

CHAPTER V

AFTER a storm comes a calm. After the Massacre and the
departure of the troops Boston seemed to lapse into
the humdrum bustle of a peaceful trading town. Parliament had repealed most of the obnoxious duties, and there
were plenty of avenues for smuggling in Holland tea!—The
ministers pounded away again in the churches upon "Divine
Grace" and "Sovereignty," and ceasede to debate "The
Things which are Cæsar's." The Tories were sad and
quiescent; the Whigs quietly jubilant, but just a little
inclined to blame Samuel Adams as slightly overdoing matters because he still kept firing letter after letter into the
Boston Gazette, denouncing "ministerial tyranny." In
short, people were tired of "factions," and very glad to con-
fine their worries to trading, shipbuilding, and the price
of codfish.

During these halcyon days I completed my preparation
for Harvard. How at length I fared at Cambridge will be
told in due place, but since I am not scratching away at
fancy memoirs, but only at a plain narrative of certain
happenings, I must perforce tell of many things whereof I
could be no personal witness, however excellent my information. I state this to avoid many tedious "he saids" and
"she saids," or "this honest fellow reported" or "that hardened rogue confessed." What I put down may give a little
better idea of "the times which tried men's souls"—and
that's the full purpose of my story.

Let therefore a certain letter, which came to my hand

years afterward creased and yellow with age, be plucked
from its secrecy. The writer, I confess, was none other than
Mlle. Emilie Rivoire. The language was supposedly
French, but with such an admixture of expressions in good
Bostonese, that it is wisely turned entirely into the proper
tongue of America.

Boston, Massachusetts Province.
August 23d, 1771.

To my dear, dear companion who thinks I have forgotten
her, Mlle. Valerie Denard, once of Guernsey and now of
Rouen: prayers for forgiveness and vows that she is still
near to my heart.

Your letter to Martinique pursued me hither. With
right you complain of my silence—but as of old I have my
good excuse: no ship has been leaving for France with a
captain my grandfather could trust, and as for risking the
common mails you have but to see the packets which come
to us from Europe, and note how clumsily their seals have
been repasted to know what has happened. They say that
even King George and our own King Louis spend much of
their time reading their subjects' letters. A royal amusement perhaps! But now to my news budget.

You have heard how my grandfather persuaded my parents to sail with me from St. Nazaire to Martinique, and
how when we had barely landed the yellow fever smote
both my parents and left that little thing called "Emilie"
alone with grandfather in this big world. The good God's
appointments are not to be discussed. Enough that after
the first sorrow passed, grandfather vowed he would never
risk my life by remaining in that beautiful, pestilential
island. He was considering a return to France when to
him there came a summons from M. le Governeur.

Learn now why no English ship were best entrusted with
this letter. You know, or rather you do not know, that a
full six years ago M. le Duc de Choiseul dispatched a
French officer, M. Pontleroy, to traverse British America
and send him word of the discontents there developing
against King George's government. Four years later he
sent Baron Kalb on the very same errand. M. le Baron

went out and returned saying that the colonists were not yet in a mood for any revolt against their rulers. But our wise Paris diplomats could not drive certain ideas from their heads. So they resolved to send a discreet man to Boston; an honest man, an observer and not a spy; a Huguenot to make the Americans open their hearts; and the head of a little business to assist his mission. In short my grandfather was the man for public purposes.—*Voilà!* He has been here for some two years; a sugar merchant, not apparently rich, yet not very poor; making friends, asking timely questions—and sometimes writing long, long letters to Versailles.—In short that is why, while my English tongue improves, perhaps you'll find I speak it with a Boston accent.

Pleasant enough it has been to claim kinship with the Reveres. Of course our family nigh a hundred years ago was split in twain; there was the Guernsey branch (Cousin Paul's people) and our own, which usually stayed in France despite the persecution, though sometimes visiting Guernsey as did my father. Perhaps you know that M. Jean Rivoire, master of customs in Guernsey, still passes letters with Cousin Paul; therefore after we reached Boston it was an easy matter to retighten old family ties.

Not indeed that Cousin Paul has much of the Frenchman now about him. Born in Boston himself, he speaks French only in the sorriest manner. But he was very proud of his Huguenot blood and instantly opened his home to us. His great acquaintance in the town likewise made many other doors fly wide. Thanks to him finally we have taken a neat little house on North Square near his own: his numerous babies (I can never count them) seem always scrambling over Berthe's nicely sanded floor, while Mrs. Sarah Revere is always sending over so many pies (the New England staff-of-life) that grandfather vows I will never learn to be a good cook myself.

Mr. Paul has a prosperous little shop where he carries on his silversmith and engraver's trade, and which brings in many very proper people to weigh his tankards, caudle-cups and punch-bowls. Here grandfather loves to sit and enjoy the gossip. A viewpoint of another kind we get by sitting in the Revere pew at the "New Brick" Meeting House.

But enough of family matters: I pass to things more interesting to a friend in France.

First and foremost, here in Boston you feel that life is
starting all afresh. Grandfather avows that it sets his old
blood atingling to think that four, six, eight weeks of
stormy voyaging sunders him now from the Old World and
all its pomp and glitter, all its sham and rottenness. Here
we are (he keeps saying) in a new land, a little fringe of
civilization stretched along the edge of a vast, unspoiled
continent. The air that comes to our spirits (he would also
say) is like the wind that blows over a wide pine forest: it
is charged with a health-giving tang and sweetness. Old
hampering laws have fallen away: laws of foolish kings,
laws still worse of foolish social custom. There are plenty
of "Thou shalt nots" in Boston, but they seem very different
"Thou shalt nots" from those of Europe, and they do not
leave you so bound and resentful.

But I will not scare you with philosophy. Here is a bit
of news: your faithful but humble friend suddenly finds
herself almost a fine lady. Such a marvelous thing all
began in this way. Last year, as I wrote you, I had just
made the acquaintance of an extremely young and callow
gentleman, a Mr. Roger Gilman. Well, after a little, up at
our door drew a fine chariot with a negro on the box, and
soon Mr. Gilman was handing out a small, dumpy-figured
girl with a face which made her safe among brigands. "Miss
Hope Fifield, my cousin." said he, "wishes to pay her
respects."

Now I fear me that Miss Fifield came primarily because
her cousin may have reported that upon my table lay certain large, flat books undoubtedly of fashion-plates from
Paris: but after we had complimented a little there was
something about the girl which made you forget that her
stays were laced abominably and that her nose went up
like a lap-dog's. Perhaps too there was something about
my modest self which commended me beyond my possession
of sketches of the hairdressings at the dauphine's ball.
When at last she went away we were kissing one another
like cousins, with Hope avowing, "I'll have you round to
drink tea, my dear!" And the very next day the chariot
and negro whisked me off to a splendid house on Sudbury

Street, for Hope's father is one of the richest men in Boston.

There I met another girl of whom I have seen almost as much as of Miss Fifield—the great Miss Lucy Flucker. "Great" I say, both because her father is an "honorable," one of the high magistrates of the province and wealthy to boot, and also because she herself is an extraordinarily large, strapping girl, tall, rosy and strong enough to lift her friend Hope like a kitten. Lucy and I took to one another as the Bible says that David made love to Jonathan. And after that—but I can hardly explain how—I had many other friends. Berthe complains now that I do not help sufficiently around the kitchen, and grandfather that he must eat so many meals alone or go over to Cousin Paul's. But they dare not cry out too loudly, for my Boston acquaintance is so very, very "respectable."

Is this merely because I am French? There is a prejudice surely against our "wicked novels." Yet I think the vague hope that I may have a little of the devil about me, makes me none the less welcome. Is it because I can teach my friends gratis the polite arts which the papers here advertise are taught in the fashionable boarding schools, "working in cat-gut, satin stitch, quince stitch, cross stitch, open work, tambour, embroidering curtains, and how to make wax flowers, fruits and pin baskets?" Certain it is there will be several "Crown and Diamonds" and "Girl's Love" coverlets put away in well-filled hope chests, which may be the more admired because of your friend's assistance. Is it because I found in our boxes a whole portfolio of spinnet music that once had tinkled in Paris? Perhaps again—but yet your Emilie is vain enough to believe that it is still another magnet which draws all the *men* now so often to North Square.

Let me tell something wonderful. You know we French girls look forward to marriage as our emancipation, after which we enter (if the novels can be believed) into a marvelous realm of flirtations and freedom. Here in Boston we are free already!

Scandals? Grandfather says there are fewer thereof in Boston than in Rouen. Nevertheless I shall not long forget the first day that I drank tea at the Fluckers. Mrs. Flucker was out, no other older woman was present, and I felt a perfect crawling in my back when young Mr. Charles Saltonstall walked in, made his bow, took off his gloves and sat down upon the sofa. I looked at Lucy expecting her to cough, say something about "My mother is away," and that then Mr. Saltonstall would bow himself out. Nothing of the kind. Lucy and he conversed, and she quizzed and he complimented like Monsieur and Madame in a fine salon at St. Nazaire, and I sat dumb and gazing.

Presently he was gone and I could hold in no more: "But at least you and this gentleman are betrothed?"

"Betrothed?—I to that Charles Saltonstall? I know *him* too well!" Then I thought Lucy would fall out of her chair with laughing, when she found what was on my conscience.

That was a year ago, my Valerie: and dare I even write for your proper eyes what since has befallen?—Not once but many times have I walked the Mall with young gentlemen *alone*. I have heard proper maidens order their parents out of the parlor because young men were expected. Nay more, "tell it not in Gath, publish it not in the streets of Askelon" (Boston is the last place wherein to forget our Huguenot Bible) last winter on a sunny afternoon I found myself in a sleigh with a good horse and Dorchester Heights ahead of me and a young bachelor beside me—and not another friend in sight!—And nothing happened, my friend, upon my pious word nothing happened!—No romance, no impropriety, no knitting of eyebrows even by silly old women. Just the comradeship one might accept from a friendly cousin.—Do you wonder that I am charmed with America?

What does grandfather say?—Berthe at first was in anguish, but grandfather is a philosopher. "In France scandalous—" he would remark, "but Massachusetts is not Normandy. I can trust *ma vie* to remember she is as proper as these fine demoiselles of Boston."—So I have had twelve very pleasant months, my dear.

Do I like New England?—Come hither resolved to find a second France, and then you had better seek the swiftest ship homeward. Come hither saying, as grandfather says I should say, "A new land with new ways and a future belonging to God"—how marvelously is everything

changed! True, we must speak English, but not the English
of London, and Ensign Dunmore (often our caller) tells
me slyly, that "My American improves," that "I learn to
talk through my nose exquisitely," and picks me up
triumphantly upon every "I guess."

Crudities yes, and barbarisms which bring tears of
laughter to grandfather's eyes. But he will always add:
"Be the philosopher. This strange America is a tall, weedy
boy, not yet filling up his clothes and very droll—but
remember this: all mighty men were sprung from weedy
boys, and better it is by far to vow 'When I become of age,'
than at last to sigh 'The bowl of life is drained.' "—You
know me well enough, dear Valerie, to know I could never
be happy as an English woman, but *America is not England.*
English ancestry? Yes. Traditions? Yes. But one hundred and fifty years of life overseas has done more than
make rich colonies for Britain. It has put the breath of
great bays, vast forests, lofty mountains and mighty rivers
into this people. They talk of "British rights" (again says
grandfather) but see those rights all through eyes of their
own. They love King George most when he plays king
over them least, and very soon—but I have quoted grandfather too much already. Let me return to the affairs of
your faithful Emilie.

Eh, bien! Worse things can be than alighting in a fine
new country where nobody need to starve, and where the
child of a despised Huguenot bourgeois can meet the best
of the land in her own small parlor!

How does our gay little world amuse itself? Theaters
are sternly forbidden in all Massachusetts colony, although
I'm told they permit such "abominations" in New York.
Sunday, or rather Saturday eve to Sunday eve is kept with
a severity to delight a Jewish prophet. I've even heard of
a deacon who will make no cider on Saturday lest it may
"work" upon the Sabbath. But think not that we young
people "of genteel families" (as the gazettes say) can have
no outlet week days but reading books of divinity or
attending Thursday lecture in the churches.—We can
dance. "Drums," "routs," "assemblies" come trooping on
one another's heels. "Polite stewards" manage them, and
the five-and-twenty couples which average at most of

them are enough for very stately minuets and contra-
dances, not to mention our hornpipes and jigs. Doubtless
a Parisian dancing master would shudder at some of our
figures. What matter if one goes home with heart aglow
after an evening of innocent diversion?

In daytime we drink tea. Everybody drinks tea. Tories
(like the Fluckers) tea that has religiously paid the King's
duty: everybody else tea that everybody knows is smuggled in from Holland. Even Berthe grumbles and serves
hyson when the chaises and chariots draw up to our humble
door. Grandfather makes no show of wealth, but I am
never ashamed to show our little service of plate, nor the
new Sèvres cups nor the wall pieces after Watteau.

When we are not calling from house to house or dancing,
we drive out to dinners or picnics. There are less merry
things than to drive with twenty in a long sleigh on a mild
evening to the George Tavern on the Neck, and enjoy a
"turtle frolic." Equally pleasant it can be to be taken
down harbor in fine weather on a trial trip of one of Mr.
John Hancock's new ships, and sample the lobsters of
Nantasket or Nahant. And for lesser diversion there is
always the walk in the Mall, a fine green common lined
with noble elms, and with a pleasant enough view over
the river to the verdant fields of Charlestown and of Cambridge.

But here, my friend, I hear you asking one thing: to
whom of the fine young gentlemen who offer me their arms
and who put their curricles at my august service, am I sur-
rendering my heart?

How can I make my amazing answer cross to France?
To none.—One of the first things a girl must learn as she
bursts into her New England freedom, is that a tall young
man can proffer a dozen civilities, can say two dozen gallant things—and have them mean no more than if coming
from one's brother. Knowing this saves many an aching
heart. Besides, though there are in Boston a few decayed
old maids of worse than thirty—one does not marry quite
so soon in New England as in France. A young man must
"have his business," as they say; and a girl should be in
no hurry, for once married all her flirtations have an end.
The worst thing they have against us French is the way

our ladies of quality are said to dabble in romance after marriage. So you see why I write little about my men friends—although good and gallant friends they are.

However, I have a few acquaintances so droll that I must name them.—Ensign Dunmore (that fine young officer now at the fort) of course is not droll. I like him greatly, and all the more because he keeps asking me to admire the miniature of "his Peggy." And I will not reckon Mr. Henry Knox, a big pleasant young bookseller who is often at our house; but I know *that* is because he is laying siege to Lucy Flucker.—Her people do not approve, yet here he will be pretty sure of meeting her. He comes, to be sure, of a poor Scotch family not quite among the "very respectable," but I think that Lucy likes him and "he who lives will see."

At three others, however, you would surely laugh, and laugh still more to hear that if my piety were only sufficient I might be already presiding over either an Independent or a Church of England parsonage, according to my wish. For two gentlemen of the cloth are waiting upon your poor Emilie. True, both the Reverend Elnathan Hirst and the Reverend Oswald Fernwood alike *profess* to call on my grandfather to inquire concerning the present state of Protestantism in France: but grandfather winks at me slyly. Well he knows the magnet which is drawing toward North Square.

Mr. Hirst (who assists Dr. Byles) is a widower, but custom frowns on a minister who reverts overlong to single blessedness. He is a Tory (unlike most Congregationalists), but atones for this deviation by an unflinching hostility to the Church of England and all prelacy. Mr. Fernwood is chaplain at the Castle, but reads prayers at King's Chapel when Dr. Caner has rheumatism. He is as chubby and plump as Mr. Hirst is pale and cadaverous, but they alike give proof of their valid ordination by being tremendous eaters. When, however, they call simultaneously it is needless for me to say a word. I merely keep filling their tea-cups whilst they are joined like fighting cocks.

"I repeat to you, sir:" began Mr. Fernwood the other day: "that much as I commend the virtues of your yeomanry and peasantry here in New England, your failure to acknowledge the lawful Church of England is a sorrow-ful mistake. I must wholly agree with that eminent Vir-ginia divine who said, 'I am sure no *gentleman* will choose to go to Heaven otherwise than by way of the Established Church!'"

"Agreed," returned Mr. Hirst solemnly stirring his tea, "in New England *we* are the Established Church. All others are Dissenters."

"The Church of England dissent?" cried Mr. Fernwood, rising as if from a pin in his chair.

"Certainly, Brother Fernwood. Theologically according to the clear meaning of the Gospel: temporally according to the lawful statutes of these colonies."

"I would tell you, sir," puffed Mr. Fernwood turning red, "that I'm told that His Majesty's Ministers, after present taxation troubles are solved, intend to introduce into Massa-chusetts the present happy condition of the Southern Col-onies whereby non-episcopal bodies exist only on tolerance. After a wise system of bishops has been set up in America, our English practice will be brought in, whereby no man can hold public office save as he partake of the sacrament in our Churches—in a less solemn form, to be sure, to suit secular rather than religious purposes."

"And I would tell you, sir," returned Hirst, color at last in his cheeks, "that this hateful spirit of sedition which otherwise I abhor, is fanned and strengthened by the dia-bolical proposal to introduce bishops in this country."

"Indeed?" persisted Fernwood: "Come then to King's Chapel next Sunday. I will read the best of my twenty ser-mons, the one proving that your non-Conformist preachers are without valid ordination."

"And I," cast back Hirst, "next Sunday in Hollis Street pulpit will warn the people against the great Whore of Babylon and the sin of tolerating Episcopacy!"

But here grandfather saved the peace by uncorking some very choice eau-de-vie and inviting both our guests to par-take. Then they departed; Mr. Fernwood with languishing glances, Mr. Hirst speaking of "his solitary chamber, but that the Lord might not leave him desolate forever."

Oh! yes—our third droll visitor. That young Mr. Gil-man. He comes from time to time. After all he is a mere lad, barely ready for Harvard College. His clothes hang poorly: his nose is a mass of freckles: he sits looking dumbly at me, although ready enough to chatter with Hope or Lucy. Still grandfather says, "I like him: he speaks when he has something to say." But in any case he goes to no routs and assemblies, his father being a poor minister. "No prospects," they would tell me in France.

And now, Valerie, best of friends, I have written more than you will care to read; and yet how I have failed to picture Boston and America! Embrace your father and mother for me: and so, till the next ship to Bordeaux, I remain ever fondly your

EMILIE RIVOIRE.

CHAPTER VI

REMEMBER WATCHHORN

HITHERTO, it must be granted, my recital has had mainly to do with persons described in the Boston papers as "elegant and genteel," or as "honored members of the most prominent families," but now far more plebeian characters must intrude. I did not witness the affair next described, being just at the end of my first year at Harvard; but to understand things to come, this incident must not be omitted, my details reaching me from unassailable witnesses.

. . . .

On a fine warm day early in July, 1772, Boston Common was the scene of no common thronging and excitement. The cows which were of wont allowed to graze almost *ad libitum* over the green acres had been prudently confined, and it must be added that the gateways to the grounds of the fine mansions facing or abutting upon the Common had been closed and double locked against vulgar intrusions. This did not prevent, however, the commanding windows of the Bromfield, Bowdoin, Hancock, Faneuil and other great houses from being full of the heads, one hopes for the good taste of the aristocratic proprietors, only of those of the under servants and their intimates.

Be that as it may, the crowds upon the Common were dense. Wagons loaded with heavy-featured farmers and equally solid women had lumbered up from beyond the Neck, and Charlestown Ferry had done an excellent business. A juggler had just descended from his barrel to pass the hat after displaying a dozen commonplace tricks. A boy was hawking dippers of vinegar water and rum—the favorite summer drink, switchel. Two negroes of the lowest sort had cleared a ring and were now on all fours "bunting" each other, dashing their heads together like rams and each boasting violently that he could knock over and break the skull of his rival. Close by in another foul-mouthed roaring circle, a calker and a carpenter's prentice had joined in what they were pleased to call a wrestling bout, but which strangely resembled a brutal, lawless fight, each striving with his thumbs to gouge out the eyes of the other.

The cause for this unselect gathering was not hard to seek. In plain sight across the green mall, at the foot of the little rising close by the frog pond and the town powder house, rose the gaunt and awful timbers of a structure which could have only one purpose. From its upper cross-beam depended a rope, with a noose dangling directly between the two uprights. Boston, it was manifest, was about to be favored with a public execution.

There was a permanent gallows near the fortifications at the Neck, but the good old custom of hanging on the Common had been by no means abandoned. "It was so convenient for spectators," although some said the Charlestown Ferry was still better, such numbers of persons could watch proceedings from the boats. A very old man was regaling his hearers with the story of the hanging of Fly the Pirate and his two underlings, when people came by thousands from all eastern Massachusetts and Cotton Mather himself uttered the long prayer.

The present concourse was perhaps smaller, partly because the case was less famous, partly because very many considered the condemned much more an object for pity than for denunciation.

"Disobedience ain't piracy, and nobody this time was

killed," a one-legged sailor with earrings was saying when the story of Fly ended.

"Well cap'n:" observed a younger and more intact mariner, "you'll allow that discipline is discipline: and when a common sailor on a man o' war can knock his commander down after getting a proper order, and then take nothing to match it, there's a new tot of grog coming on his Majesty's ships."

"I sailed with that Mem Watchhorn," returned the one-legged tar, "on the old *Sea Horse* out of Marblehead three voyages to Jamaica and handy sailor he was, decent and quietish, also mighty pious and psalm-singing, though quick o' temper. Then years later I hearn he was pressed on the *Comet* while he was sailing into Bristol. Strike me if they have the right to press Massachusetts men in time of peace!"

"They tried, but give it up powerful quick, as Commodore Knowles learned long ago to his cost. But Watchhorn, poor scoundrel, was pressed over in Bristol Channel. No doubt Prothero, his captain, was a hell-roaring devil to his men, and Watchhorn had his grievance, but he must have been mad when he knocked down Prothero upon his own quarterdeck."

"Mad's the word. But if hanged he must be, why not neat and seamanlike on the *Comet's* yardarm, instead of all this fury ashore in Boston?"

"Because, messmate, Admiral Montagu, whose ships now cram the harbor, swears that with so plain a case there was never a better chance to teach us province folk what it means to defy the King's officers. So after the court martial, off they took Watchhorn double ironed to Queen Street jail, and now they'll have him out for the dance on nothing."

"The Whigs don't like it," muttered the first mariner.

"The Whigs can do damned little about it," informed his friend. "They can't halt a court martial. But they made enough fuss to get one little matter granted 'em to ease their pride. The actual hanging's to be done by the sheriff's men, as concession to 'the civil power of the Province' as I hearn the bigwigs called it."

This wisdom was halted by a ruffle of drums coming down Tremont and Common Streets, and a small procession came in sight: first a squad of militiamen with awkwardly shouldered muskets, then a more formidable file of tall-hatted marines from the *Comet*, then a two-wheeled car wherein jostled the heavily fettered prisoner, and directly behind which walked two clergymen in severest black, and finally there strode several naval officers. Eager fingers pointed out the resplendent blue uniform of Prothero, commander of the brig, who had suffered the insult, and who now most assuredly was about to reap a competent revenge.

As the cart neared the gallows a dull roar went up from the wide concourse of spectators, whether from brutal excitement, decent pity or active wrath, it were hard to say; but the gallows themselves stood empty with only a single ill-favored fellow sitting upon the base as if he were a kind of guardian.

The procession stopped. The militiamen rested arms: the marines closed about the prisoner, and after a dubious pause Captain Prothero himself stepped forward. "How now? Where are the sheriffs? Where the hangman?"

"Please yer Honor," explained the loiterer, twirling a dirty cap, "the sheriffs knew there would be a deal of praying and preaching before it was time to turn off. They are at the Cromwell's Head and will hustle right over after the Amen!" And he jerked with his thumb pointing towards the tavern on School Street.

"The fiends burn up your toping Provincials," growled

Prothero frowning helplessly (his real oath I dare not write). "Well, good gentlemen of the cloth, speed your piosity. I'm to dine with the admiral on the *Romney*."

But the opportunity for a grand moral spectacle and for warning words before an audience that seldom darkened church doors was one which Messrs. Fernwood and Hirst were the last of their calling to throw away. The first was present in his gown and bands because lawful decorum required that an ordinary of the English Church should officiate at a naval execution: the second because policy, if not humanity, dictated that Watchhorn should be attended at the gallows by a minister of his own New England creed. The marines therefore formed in a circle about the death cart while the Reverend Oswald Fernwood mounted and stood beside the prisoner. This proceeding diverted attention from the fact that, immediately outside the party guarding the condemned, there was a perceptible nudging and jostling. A considerable number of heavy-handed, lantern-jawed fellows whose dress and aspect proclaimed them sailors had pushed up as close as possible; and several of the displaced bystanders fell back muttering, "The wretch's old shipmates must have come to see him off!"

The prisoner himself seemed a model of resignation. He was a man perhaps approaching forty, of moderate stature but of such powerful physique that by very wise precaution he had been double-ironed. He wore a dirty and tattered naval uniform significantly bare at the neck, but held his head resolutely down so as to conceal his swarthy features. Whether he was in prayer or a sullen stupor few could tell, but the knowing remarked that he had doubtless fortified himself for the last ordeal by a double swig of rum.

The Reverend Oswald Fernwood read the appropriate collects with a firm voice. Particularly he dwelt upon that most awful service in the Prayer Book, the *"Service for Persons under Sentence of Death,"* and he recited with fervor its fearful admonitions:

"Remember Watchhorn, dearly beloved, it hath pleased Almighty God, in His justice, to bring you under the sentence and condemnation of the law. You are shortly to suffer death in such a manner that others, warned by your example, may be the more afraid to offend. Your sins have laid fast hold upon you," and so to the final exhortation to the prisoner to *"submit yourself with Christian resignation to the just judgment which your crimes have brought upon you."*

To all of which warnings the condemned appeared most atheistically indifferent: nevertheless the chaplain persisted gallantly, and when he dismounted from the cart it was with the shrug of a man saying, "I've discharged my Christian duty."

As he ceased Captain Prothero motioned impatiently toward the gallows, but the Reverend Elnathan Hirst, in black coat and white ruffles, very deliberately ascended the cart. The officer cast uneasy glances toward the tavern across the Common, pulled out a fine watch, and sent a midshipman running to "Rouse up those damned sheriffs' officers or tell 'em we'll hang him ourselves."

The little flutter caused by the exit of the midshipman and the ascension of Hirst, prevented all save a very few spectators from remarking that a slovenly dressed countryman had ridden down from Frog Lane. He was mounted upon an unusually fine and spirited bay horse, from which he now dismounted and stood idly holding the reins on the fringe of spectators nearest the southwesterly side of the Common. As the second clergyman began his exhortation the prisoner suddenly lifted his head and darted a single glance of hawklike acuteness, not upon the gallows

but around the crowding ring of spectators, and as he did
so, a very few later recalled that the dismounted rider made
a slight flourish with his whip.

The Reverend Mr. Hirst was manifestly determined to
prove the superiority of the untrammelled clerical imagina-
tion to all printed admonitions and collects. Addressing the
onlookers more than the prisoner, he announced he would
speak upon the text *"It is a fearful thing to fall into the
hands of the living God."* He dwelt unsparingly upon the
godly parentage of the condemned, Remember Watchhorn,
his father a deacon of the Church of Marblehead, his
grandfather long pastor in Wenham, and now how their
degenerate offspring, laid fast in that crime of rebellion
which is less pardonable than parricide, was about to be
cut short in his sins. From the Mathers and Jonathan
Edwards the speaker drew a lurid picture of the imminent
plight of the victim, impenitent now despite a youthful
affectation of piety, resisting the consolations of religion, and
about to suffer death in this world, and then as *"A bond-
slave of Satan to be justly subject to most grievous tor-
ments both in soul and body in hell-fire forever."*

During this not short exhortation Prothero repeatedly
consulted his watch and the midshipman returned to report,
"The sheriffs say that they'll be over when Mr. Hirst's
done preaching and praying." The prisoner sat on the edge
of the cart as sodden and imperturbable as the beams of
the gallows themselves. At last, however, the clergyman
completed his fiery epilogue, delivered a few sentences
addressed avowedly to the Deity and not to the condemned, and which therefore constituted a prayer, uttered
a loud "Amen!" (reëchoed by many around) and descended
in turn from the death-cart.

As he did this, seven or eight men, in the shabby blue
coats proper for constables, were seen advancing across the

Common. They carried halberds with whitened staves, and their leader, a squat, shrewd-visaged man who wore his own hair in a prodigiously long pigtail encased in an eelskin, boasted some faded gold lace upon his hat and waistcoat.

"You take your time, Mr. Sheriff," spoke Prothero none too good-humoredly. "His Majesty's service is brought into contempt by your delay. I beg you—dispatch."

"Here we are, yer Honor," replied the leader twirling off his greasy cap, "just as soon as the reverend clergy have got the poor fellow fixed up for t'other world. I take it yer Honor has the proper warrant?"

"A most proper warrant signed by both the admiral and the governor. But are you, sir, the high sheriff of Suffolk County?"

"The high sheriff has gone to Brookline to serve a writ: but by his order Deputy Sheriff Shrimpton (servant, sir!) and these here constables are at your lawful service." All this followed by a creaking bow.

"Trust your high sheriff to slip out of nasty work," growled Prothero: "Damme if I don't begin to feel for this poor scoundrel, kept waiting now a good hour after he expected to be snugly berthed in hell. Here's your warrant, sir. Do your office, or my marines will do it for you."

"Servant, sir: servant:" rejoined Shrimpton good-humoredly, moving with his constables beside the cart. He took the paper in his hand, eyed the signatures and seals, grunted approval, then gestured toward the prisoner.

"Then I understand, yer Honor, the Royal Navy formally surrenders the body of this here man, Remember Watchhorn, into the custody of the sheriff of Suffolk County for lawful execution?"

"Assuredly I do, Mr. Shrimpton, and again—dispatch you."

"Aside then, marines," ordered the deputy; "constables secure the prisoner. Knock off his fetters."

"Knock off his irons?" demanded Prothero in amaze.

"Sairtainly, yer Honor, the irons belong to his Majesty's navy; and he being now in civil custody province custom requires that all hangings be conducted with the condemned pinioned and roped."

The captain spat another oath: "This thing shakes my nerves. Watchhorn, poor dog, I nigh forgive you. Here corporal; unlock those irons,—but one at a time; while the ropes are put on him. He's a desperate man."

The marines had fallen back idly from the cart, which was now driven ominously under the very foot of the gallows. As the fetters were struck from Watchhorn's wrists and ankles they were apparently replaced in turn by stout hemp firmly knotted. The condemned had not uttered one word nor made the slightest motion.

"Hangman, do your duty," enjoined Prothero once again seemingly more high strung than the actual victim.

"Room then, yer Honor:" directed Shrimpton, beckoning the officers and marines to a distance. "Now prisoner, have yer any last things to say?"

As he spoke he mounted the cart directly behind the condemned, whose back was now concealed by its closeness to the gallows. Apparently the executioner was busy with the last fearful adjustments of the noose prior to the final catastrophe. Possibly at some muttered command of Shrimpton, however, the prisoner bent himself forward, and leaned his huge body to conceal these horrid manipulations from the unflinching eyes of Prothero. A low growl and tremor of excitement was proceeding through the crowd. Hardened seamen were averting their faces, and hardly one onlooker beheld Shrimpton when he gave a sudden tug at his belt, caught the glint of a knife running across

the new ropes, or heard the muttered "Now, Mem!"
But a thousand witnessed how in a twinkling the form
of Watchhorn seemed to spring up a foot in stature,
as from a great throat he bellowed, *"Parsons be damned!"*
then flung himself like a catapult shot from the cart
directly toward the spot where the knot of seafarers had
stood gazing, while the stupid constables receded from him
as from a leper, and the thronging spectators rendered it
impossible for the more distant militia and marines to fire
a shot.

The instant pushing of a score of mighty hands opened
a lane through which he tore across the greensward. Prothero was the first to recover wits: "The horse! The
horse!" rang his shout, and with drawn sword he dashed
after the fugitive, when the white stave of one of the constables most unaccountably clattered in his way and sent
him sprawling. The multitude saw Watchhorn dart to the
horse and fling himself into the saddle, while a resounding,
"Go it, Mem! They can't get you!" followed as he vanished down Frog Lane amid a blinding cloud of dust.

Above the tumult which ensued, Prothero could be heard
trumpeting to his marines to "Seize that Shrimpton!" But
in the jostling, scurrying and excitement, the "Deputy
Sheriff" and all his constables had vanished in thin air.
Prothero's oaths did not grow milder when he was told that
the runaway had no doubt a prime Narragansett pacer
under him, and that once across Roxbury Neck (where he
probably was already) all King George's fleet was helpless
to reclaim him.

Naval eloquence was further awakened when tidings
came in from the Cromwell's Head that the veritable sheriffs
and constables had been mysteriously locked and detained
in a private room where they had been emptying a punch
bowl "Just before they had intended to start for the Com-

mon." "Undoubtedly," the captain's Tory informant vowed, "they were well paid for the collusion—but where was the jury evidence?"

The next day their Honors of the Council published a reward of £100 sterling for the apprehension of the notorious outlaw Remember Watchhorn, or any promoter of his escape, but the money remained peacefully in the provincial treasury.

CHAPTER VII

REDFORD AND ITS AUTOCRAT

THE Watchhorn affair made a great noise but nothing came of it. Everybody said that powerful Whigs, anxious to teach a lesson about pressing New England seamen, were behind the escape. Somebody told somebody that Mr. John Hancock looked wise and jingled his guineas when the matter was discussed. Prothero and Admiral Montagu (famous for his powers of swearing) made the governor's office sulphurous, but the more serious business of the destruction of the revenue cutter *Gaspee* down in Rhode Island soon engrossed all official energies. If the crime of burning a King's ship could not be punished, the release of a condemned prisoner sunk to the merest peccadillo.

During this 1771-72 I completed the ordeal of the freshman year at Harvard. I learned much in the hard school of experience: for the manner in which the newcomers were made the butts and drudges of the sophomores and upper-class "sophisters" reminded me of all that Dunmore had told about English schools and their brutal fagging. But at last this era of "profitable chastening" was over. On a hot summer day I tied up my bundle, and scorning extravagance trudged back the twelve odd miles to Redford. I had won fair credit with my Tully and Greek Testament, and knew I would have warm welcome. Indeed among all the lesser joys about which in after years a man can love to close his eyes and dream, not many are preferable to that of the final return from a year at college; when the gate clicks, and the great dog bounds joyously upon the gravel, and father is pushing back his Calvin and rising in his study.

These pages must carry many brisk or bitter scenes even to "feats of broil and battle;" bear with me then if for once I linger tenderly, and recall our Redford of the good old days, when the King's healths still went down loyally in sharp, hard cider, when the wind moved lazily amid the august elms, and life seemed moving simply and placidly in tempo with the breeze. Not that we dwelt in Eden. The serpents coiled behind every apple-tree in many a far-spread orchard. But for all that, what with all our boasted "modern changes," our steamboats and even the talk of making steam coaches fly along rails, and our proud federal government, and the settling of the great prairies almost to the Mississippi, I believe that old Redford had certain things which if they vanish forever from our lives will leave us the poorer. We may boast our new possessions, but woe to us if once those fine chattels themselves come to possess us, not we to possess them!

I say "old" Redford. People are still repeating, "America is a very young country." Yet even in 1772 one hundred and forty years had sped since the axemen cleared the forests by Concord River, laid out the farms, and grubbed from the soil the stones for those walls which stand as mute memorials of the unwearying toil which from the naked wilderness had fashioned the first Bay Colony. Venerable moss clung to full many of the shingles. The paths were well beaten. The trees planted by the first settlers had been mostly succeeded by their glorious children, the God-made cathedral elms, which said to the bare, gaunt meeting house, "Well do you shun all pompous ornament. Never in summer can you be arrayed as are we."

Over the little rivers ran solid little bridges, or you found

neatly placed stepping-stones. Along the one great street
you could wander onward, farm succeeding farm, the houses
at leisurely intervals, each with barns, wood-piles, high
pasture, plowed land, far pasture and wood-lot stretching in a solid principality behind, and so with a certain
spreading of farms at the township's rim afar from the
meeting house, general store, tavern and whipping post,
you were next in Lexington, or Concord, or Billerica; and
old Redford was behind you.

Over this town reigned a benevolent despot. Town meetings, self-important selectmen, officious constables and
tithing men and their like there were, but everybody knew
that my father decreed the destinies of Redford almost as
truly as Pharaoh decreed doom for old Egypt. Father had
been pastor these many years almost since quitting Harvard. After his first famous election sermon before the
legislature, a sermon duly published and pilfered, from
across New England, first Salem and then Boston had
proffered him a mighty pulpit. Always the visiting committees had turned away defeated. "Since Redford was
hewn out of the wilderness (he told them) has its ordained
minister died in his parish. One does not put away one's
wife for a comelier woman. Why should I go from this
town which is part of my life?" At the parsonage therefore he remained on a salary of £66 13s. 4d., cash in good
years, and "country pay" (beef, pork, rye and Indian corn)
in years less favorable, plus the use of the glebe and forty
loads of wood per winter.

Inevitably he was very learned: a fellow minister once
praised him from the pulpit, "Here is a man who can
whistle in Greek." Of course his library (acquired with
infinite sacrifice) was his joy—those great shelves where
Augustine frowned across to massive Hooker, and where
Sydenham scowled back at Fuller. To save paper his ser-

mons were first sketched out upon wrappers, and then copied into a sermon-book in a hand so minute as to make later generations marvel at his eyesight; the letters crabbed as New England winter, but clear and legible as the penman's life. And of course he governed Redford with a black kid glove which in sudden need could wield the rod of iron.

How many unwise marriages he had headed off; how many happy marriages he had promoted; how many faltering husbands he had sent back to forgiving wives; how many creditors had been taught mercy; how many half-drunkards had been scared away from the tavern; how many giddy girls had been steadied into Mothers in Israel; all by a timely irresistible word, the recording angel can number but not I. Nobody ran for pound-master or hog-reeve without at least the passive approval of the minister. Nobody proposed any community change without making sure the embryo measure would not be slaughtered unborn by a few indirect but unmistakable words of doom from the great box pulpit.

Father had been blessed with less than the average clerical family. His first born, my eldest brother, Ephraim, reigned acceptably in a small Berkshire pastorate. His second, Tobias, had perished in very early infancy, having been baptized in the meeting house upon an extraordinarily cold day. My two elder sisters were comfortably married, one in Connecticut, the other in New Hampshire, but around the parsonage still scampered my best comrade Tabitha, one year my junior, and of course Darius was now spindling up with the long legs of youth.

We all worked around the glebe. Father could plow, split, drive oxen with the best, hammering out many a sermon in his mind as in homespun shirt he swung flail or beetle. He could mow the upper pasture with broader,

cleaner swaths than all the help, setting the pace with
crackling good humor; then an hour later down the high
street you might see him moving in state with full wig,
cocked hat and gold-headed cane; perhaps to pray with
majestic words at the side of the dying, and to leave with
the bereaved, if not a perfect comfort, at least the conviction that a Great Power ruled in the heavens, bestow-
ing upon us mortals things better than we could ask or
think. I can hear him thundering from behind the great
Bible words of fiery warning for all swerving by one tittle
from the ways mandated to God's elect, and I can see
him the most gentle, pitiful of men when some poor sinner
came with a tale of personal agony.

The parsonage stood on the high street, straight and
firm as the meeting house, with two arrogant beeches
guardains of its main portal. It was a gambrel-roofed
house, with a huge battery of windows set with very small
panes of glass. A sea captain turned farmer had built the
dwelling in the days of old Governor Bellomont, and the
timbers were as massive and well-tenoned as a vessel's.

Unlike many of its neighbors in Redford which were
painted red or grew blacker unpainted with every winter,
it stood forth in an austere white. Up the paths where
mother's fox-gloves and ladies' delights, bouncing-bets and
marigolds sprang up in season between the lines of southern-
wood and box, you came to that front door, seldom opened
save to the august visitors worthy of the chilly sofa in the
unfrequented parlor. But for all the rest of us there were
the little paths whereof one wound to the common entrance
by the kitchen, and another to a certain little door, concealed by an enormous lilac, where you could steal up a
very twisting stair to father's study. By this he could
reach his sanctum unvexed by the uproars of the ell, and
by this he had been known to flee abruptly toward the

crow-barn when worldly policy forbade him to meet unwelcome visitors.

In the rest of the house ruled Ishmael (legally a slave, actually a potentate whom no coercion could have driven from his dominions), a wiry, affable negro of uncertain years, and his unquestioned suzerain, Yetmercy Tudd.

All the town said that Dr. Gilman ran Redford, Mrs. Gilman ran Dr. Gilman, but that Yetmercy ran Mrs. Gilman, and homage was paid accordingly. Yetmercy was surely a power behind the throne. Once I asked her age: she boxed my ears, vowing "she'd long since forgotten it;" but tradition affirmed she was over forty, having come to my parents soon after their marriage, as a young "took girl" (which interpreted was an orphan, half-servant, half humble member-of-the-family). She had never taken a spouse, "knowing too much," she declared when Phineas Greene became attentive, "to make her dinner on green apples." Every year she seemed a little more dried, her hair a little more dull and carroty, her muscles firmer, her zeal for work more intense. We knew she would cheerfully die for any member of the family; and she knew that we knew it and traded upon her advantage. My mother, I am sure, would have shone as a public ambassador, she had such a genius for smoothing the moods of Yetmercy.

And now I come to the Holy of Holies. What can I say of you, oh! my mother, as I see you across the years? Can I write that in girlhood you must have been incomparably beautiful, or quote the old wives' chatter, "You should have seen her when she came as a bride to the parsonage?" Seven children, six growing to tall estate, a meager income despite donation parties, funeral gloves and timely gifts from her Boston brothers, a social position to maintain as first lady of Redford, constant hospitality demanded, and all the conferences and other gustatory

doings of the clergy, a husband to council and correct in
all things from his wristbands at weddings up to "Don't
say that, Jonathan" touching a ticklish passage in an
important sermon: all these were turning her brown hair to
a silver and had given a soft patina to her cheeks. But
if any man thinks a woman's beauty cannot grow across
the years, as she conquers her burdens lovingly, God pity
him—he knows nothing of noble women.

What did she do?—what did she *not* do about the great
house? To boil soap, dip candles, make dyestuffs, hatchel
and card flax, to card wool and spin it, to weave and then
make up all but the Sunday and gala garments of the
entire family—that was part of the endless process of her
life. From the long hours standing before her loom she
had gained that gracious poise and dignity of carriage
which never left her till the last warp was forever done.
And I think there is still something wrong about a farmhouse door standing open upon a summer's day, unless
from within it I hear, like the echo of the wind in the
maples, the hum! hum! of the spinning wheel, something
normal, homely, domestic, telling without words that inside
dwell thrift and honest peace.

How mother found time for all these things as well as
to rule her kitchen and dairy, I know no more than I
understand the kingdoms on the moon. Nor how she found
time to deal with all us children, so that each flattered
himself he was her first in love, and never dreamed of
keeping a secret from her. But find it she did, and long
after I went to village school she was my best teacher,
laughing at her own ignorance and lamenting that she had
never studied Latin, but somehow wiser (even in many
matters of book learning) than scowling Master Hankins;
and during the long evenings, when to save candles we
all sat by the cavernous kitchen fireplace with the red

light from the logs setting aglow the pewters on the shelf, then in sweet clear voice she would read *Robinson Crusoe* or *Pilgrim's Progress,* or that other Bunyan, (to the carnally minded even more fascinating) *The Holy War.*

Or laying the book aside when the fire dwindled she would tell us the stories of the founding of New England, drawn from that great repertory of wonders, Mather's *Magnalia,* or legends passed on by word of mouth of the forest life of the first colony, of Indian fights and massacres, of adventures, captivities and escapes; of King Philip's War and struggles more recent, Lovewell's heroic battle with the Norridgewocks and all the slaughter, adventure and sacrifice of the frontier warfare with France. All this she had planted in our hearts, and always with the lesson (far better enforced than even by father from the pulpit) that we children of New England were the heirs to a great inheritance, that what we possessed had been wrested from the naked wilderness by toil and suffering unspeakable that we might dwell in a land pleasing beyond others in God's sight, and that we would be contemptible before men and abhorred before Heaven if proven unworthy of our heritage.

What shall I more say? What did the first woman poet of New England, Anne Bradstreet, write of her own mother, in lines quaint and halting indeed, but not too halting to conceal the swelling heart?

> "A worthy matron of unspotted life,
> A loving mother and obedient wife,
> A friendly neighbor, pitiful to poor,
> Whom oft she fed and clothed from her store,
> To servants wisely awful but yet kind
> And as they did so they reward did find,
> The public meetings she did oft frequent,
> And in her closet constant hours she spent.—
> Of all her children, children lived to see,
> Then dying lived a blessed memory!"

"God bless thee, mother!"—even now up among the saints in light, I say "God bless thee!" I write this even if fools on reading cry out, "Popery!"

. . . And that was our home at Redford, where we children rendered implicit obedience, because never for an instant did we enjoy anything but compassion and love. Not that we had avoided the Apostolic operation of the timely "laying on of hands" when the Old Adam incarnate in all normal boys and girls—rose strong within us. But my father was none of those flogging, bullying parents, and like Cotton Mather (who if he was a cruel fool in some things was a merciful Solomon in others) regarded the constant scourging of children a "judgment of God upon the world," and knew how to produce with a frown and a word what Deacon Parker never could effect with his horse lash.

Now concerning our meeting house with its galaxy of uncurtained windows there is less need to tell you. It was like all its compeers in New England, with its tall pulpit mounted by a steep and twisting staircase, its box pews with their hinged seats which shut with resounding bang when the worshippers sat down after standing through the long prayers, its icy cold in winter when the only heat which the parish permitted was "red-hot preaching," its dusty beams overhead whence in hot summer the spiders swung down on the wigs and bonnets of the congregation, its "sabbath-day house" close by, where families from a distance warmed themselves, ate lunch and talked carnalities between the morning and evening service, its notices of auctions, foreclosures and town meetings posted upon the doors. Everybody expected father to preach two-hour sermons and deliver one-hour prayers—he seldom disappointed.

As for the other features of Redford I think the important things will unfold themselves in due place. Nobody was toploftily rich and nobody was starvingly poor.

Inevitably there was the tavern kept by Jeremiah Fitch where loafers lifted their heels all summer upon the piazza railing, and where the post office was in the bar-room and the post rider came from Boston at least twice per week. As unavoidably there was a general store kept also by Fitch where about everything not made upon the farms, from sugar to calico and nails, could be bought for cash or kind. There was a blacksmith shop, and a town tinker who could mend your spinning wheels, reels, looms, clocks and guns. And quite naturally there was a solid set of stocks and a whipping post directly in front of the meeting house, for the lewd fellows of the baser sort who fell under Justice Kingsbury's tender mercies. We boasted no doctor:—in emergencies one could get over from Concord if the snow was not too deep. We enjoyed of course a school which kept a good six months of the year, but for sufficient Latin to enter Harvard we had to be sent to Boston. Redford, in short, was a strictly farming community wherein the main talk was about wheat and hay if it did not drift to town taxes, or Dr. Gilman's last sermon on "Eternal Punishment," or whether it was right for Governor Hutchinson to accept a salary direct from the King.

Narrow and sluggish enough do you say? Entirely right. But narrow and sluggish waters can flow deep. It was still only 1772.

CHAPTER VIII

AFTER the first glad greetings, after I had talked with
proper condescension to my old mate Dick Crummell pren-
ticed to the wheelwright, had heard all about the burning
of Squire Tuttle's barn, had fished for horn-pout in Concord River, had patronized several girls for their quilts
and worsted work, and had mentioned "Harvard" many,
many times, I began to find Redford slightly stupid. I
did my best at the haying, being proud to keep abreast of
father and Ishmael, but on rainy days I found that father's
library was much stronger in *"Divine   rath"* and *"Fore-
ordination Justified"* than in certain secular works I had
tasted in Cambridge. Father shook his head when I asked
for the latter: "Clearly you were wise not to become a
minister, Roger," spoke he, "but I hope they've not let
you read infidel books!" Then just when vacation seemed
a trifle disappointing, my good angel Tabitha came marvelously to the rescue.

Something I knew was in the air, when I brought home
a letter upon pink paper, delicately scented, and addressed
in Cousin Hope's clear writing: *"Mistress Tabitha Gilman in Redford: These in haste. On your life! On your
life!"* Injunctions which the post rider had obeyed by
making an unwontedly slow trip while delivering packages
in Woburn.

After that I heard Yetmercy groaning, "O Lord
o' massy!" and mother mollifying, "Well, we can manage it."
Upon which there was a great furbishing of the spare

chambers and an inordinate manufacturing of pies. I knew then that Hope Fifield was coming out with a guest; this gave satisfaction for I had called Hope publicly my "second best friend," Tabby of course being the honored first.

However, despite knowing smiles by Yetmercy and Tabby, I was hardly prepared when the gorgeously painted chariot of the Eleazer Fifields rattled up to the gate, and Nero bowed double in his blue livery and swung open the door not merely for Hope and for the stalwart form of Lucy Flucker, but, wonder of wonders, for Mlle. Emilie Rivoire!

Doubtless I helped Nero bundle upstairs an outrageous number of bandboxes, but I first really returned to consciousness when in my little back chamber I was slapping a vast quantity of powder upon my hair, and cursing my luck at leaving behind in Cambridge my one good broadcloth suit "which one never needs in Redford." And Tabby never forgot the brotherly reproof for "letting me get caught there at the gate in my haying shirt!"

Tabby of course had visited Hope in the winter. In Boston she had met Lucy Flucker, and also (what I hardly took in at the time) had met Emilie. Most naturally "such dear friends" should be invited out to Redford. But it was surely a dash of sheer deviltry that kept Tabby from telling me precisely *who* were coming out with my cousin!

Well, after our fine new birds had preened their feathers, they fluttered about the parsonage. We unfolded the grating portals of "the best room." Its chilly stillness could not vie with the splendors of Sudbury Street, still the tall brass andirons and the big mahogany tea-table stared at our guests with dignity. The visitors praised my sister's hook work, and then the girls found themselves so hungry that as Yetmercy said, "They ate like ministers." We all sat down on the kitchen benches and put away an enormous hotchpot—a dish incidentally fit for the King of France.

Nothing will put proper young people at ease better than successful eating; and by the time I cleaned my plate I was becoming quite aware that Redford was now the most interesting place in the world.

. . . Three days after the girls arrived whom should I meet in the general store but Henry Knox. "Book business was slack just then," he explained (he had lately opened his own shop on Cornhill) and he had stolen off to try to sell a small farm which his mother had owned in Redford. But what a marvelous coincidence that he had appeared in town immediately after the advent of Lucy Flucker! He slept at old Mrs. Gidding's, but regularly made "one more" over the hasty pudding and flannel cakes of our breakfasts, as well as at the noon and evening parsonage refections. His contagious laugh, his generous smile, his enormous strength and skill when he set an axe to a tree, soon made him a village favorite. Somehow Hope and Tabby always promenaded side by side, and next Henry and Lucy (her not small body only reaching to his ear), and then Emilie would have had to walk alone—if I had not walked by her.

In those days I won a great victory over myself; I made myself talk before Emilie. Boastful and boyish no doubt; but at least under the Redford elms I was blessed with a revealing fluency that had been dried up at North Square. And Emilie had talked too. I learned the story of the Rivoires. Their ancestors had always been staunch Huguenots, but more fortunate than many coreligionists had kept most of their property without having to deny their faith. Grand-père George preferred to live most simply, but he was by no means a poor man. Emilie's mother had been a Guernsey lady and a British subject. She had insisted that her daughter be given an education far more liberal and extensive than customary among most of the strait-laced French Calvinists, and had inculcated in her a taste for polite literature.

Oui! Emilie had even read in the terrible Voltaire, and kept faith in the good God for all that!—Her grandfather, mellowed and experienced, had taught her that "though Heaven formed only one sheepfold there might be several gates," and it were best to be charitable even in dealing with Catholics.

Never in all my forensics at Harvard had I been more pressed in my logic, than when she asked very artlessly, "Why we Massachusetts Congregationalists felt it so very sinful to keep Christmas? Or why, if John Milton, most Puritan of poets, had written an excellent Bible tragedy about Samson, our law made it a crime to play it in a theater?"— After a walk with her my head would buzz as if I had drunk her native champagne.

But talk and questions were not all on the side of Emilie. Why did her eyes so shine when I rehearsed our household legends? When I told of that first Gilman who forsook a rich fellowship at Old Cambridge rather than take the oaths before Laud? Or the tale of that awful winter battle at South Kingston which saved all New England from the Indians? Or of that glorious uprising against the tyrant Andros, when the Puritan towns dared greatly and flung down the Stuart minion? At such tales she clapped her hands: "Oh, this is like hearing the tale of Charlemagne's paladins with one of their grandsons telling it!" And even when I spoke of Louisburg and how the lads of Massachusetts did what the King's regulars could not; then blushed and halted, "Oh! I forgot you were French," I had a quick answer, "What matter! The deed was brave, and the *grand-père* says France and the colonies will join war again."

If I were only a poet, how could I not put in verse the picture of us two, going down those broad leafy streets, with the bright thoughts of a youth and a maid twinkling in the sunshine around us; and behind Old France and young, yet also old, New England—and ahead all the glamour and dream of that for which we barely yet could find a name—America!

Years later (when I was not too vain) they told me that scarcely less than Emilie I made a heartening sight, as I walked along in the pride of my heritage, with my thoughts glowing through a fresh young face. And the walks were always too short, and the picnics by the river always ended too soon, and every day I pondered more deeply whether Homer and Virgil had not limned their pagan goddesses only after companying with Emilie Rivoire.

. . . Nevertheless our golden days together soon had a most unwelcome hiatus. Exactly one week after Henry Knox appeared in Redford what should we see along the road but an elegant two-horse gilded curricle, and at the reins no less a personage than the Honorable Thomas Flucker himself, royal treasurer of the province, as well as a great merchant of Summer Street. Mr. Flucker halted at the tavern, we were told, for refreshment and information: then he sought Mrs. Gidding's house and learning that Henry was (as always) over at the parsonage, drove hither in state. It was just before supper, I was helping Ishmael water the stock, so I do not know how the parleys began, but when I came to the front door Mr. Flucker and Henry Knox were standing face to face, both very red, and Lucy was almost between them, her cheeks not without tears, while mother and the other girls were anxious listeners in the background.

Mr. Flucker was a well-groomed, portly man. The brass buttons gleamed on his pea-green waistcoat, and the silver buckles seemed fairly flashing anger from his knees. Henry stood like a solid boulder, good-humoredly taking the buffets of the tempest, but calmly refusing to yield an inch.

"I tell you, sir," Flucker was saying with ever rising voice, "your business here is a subterfuge. You could have sold that farm through Mr. Brinley."

"I can judge best, please your Honor," returned Knox thrusting his great hands in his pockets, as if to say: "I'm firmly resolved not to strangle you."

"Bandy no words, sir," cried the treasurer. "You'll not deny you came to Redford to wait on my daughter."

"Father!" sobbed Lucy; yet in that tone betrayed nevertheless a possible calculation, "Will a faint or a passion serve me the best?"

"Surely I have the right to call upon Dr. and Mrs. Gilman," replied Henry still courteously, "and if Miss Flucker happened——"

"Miss Flucker happened?" snorted her parent; then he flourished a finger in the bookseller's face, "I'll say it once for all, Henry Knox, to save words later. Your family is fair to middling but nothing extra. No Flucker is going to marry the son of a poor Scotch-Irish. Some of your brothers have run away to sea as ne'er-do-wells. We don't know what's become of them; your mother was a worthy woman but——"

"My mother died last year, sir," spoke Henry, taking his hands from his pockets. "So long as she lived they say I was good to her. Pray mention her no more."

"Agreed," cast back Mr. Treasurer. "My meaning's plain. Now, Mrs. Gilman," he gave my mother a formal bow: "I acquit you of having invited this bookseller's clerk to Redford; but things are as they are, and Lucy's best again in Boston. Henry Knox *then* will find time to sell his farm."

"Mr. Flucker," spoke mother, her little body swelling till she seemed as tall as Lucy herself, "I'm a Fifield who married a Gilman, but as for Henry Knox, if Tabitha, my child, cared for him I'd think twice before——"

"Miss Tabitha can have the honor, madam," darted the gentleman with a sweep of his hat, "if she desires to marry a no-account Whig. *My* daughter is going to marry no Whig, even though that Whig *were* a Gilman and a Fifield."

"Go get your things, Lucy," ordered mother, anxious to have the scene well over, "we are all very sorry Mr. Flucker feels this way."

So amid feminine weepings, protests and uproar Lucy departed in anguish at her father's side, the treasurer making another low, ironical bow as he climbed into the curricle. Hardly, however, had the rattle of wheels died away before mother seemed changing from tears to almost hysterical laughter: "Oh! what fools men be!— Yesterday I *thought* Lucy might care for Henry! Now I *know* it— She'll put in a lovely winter filling up her hope-chest."

Poor Henry, nevertheless, was perforce disconsolate, sold off the land the next day and got a cart-ride home to Boston. However, for two more blessed weeks Hope remained and Emilie with her, and never were two weeks that sped so fast. Never once could I command my cowardly tongue to gallantry and compliment such as I knew our guest received from her fine bachelors in Boston. There were never between us two words which I would have blushed to have repeated before mother. Yet somehow I knew that Emilie was not offended because I had no flowery speech, and treated her like a third sister—along with Hope and Tabby. But oh! why on the last Sunday, when we all

stood up in the minister's pew in the very center of the
meetinghouse, conscious too much that all the women
were cocking their eyes upon "That French Girl," and
when I had to hold the great psalter for Emilie herself, why,
I say, did father leaning down from the pulpit, instead of
a Song of David ordain a chanting from the Song of Solomon? Did I think of "the mystical union of Christ and
His Church" when I saw a gentle hand turning the leaves
as we tried to sing together?—

> "Let him with kisses of his mouth
>   Be pleasèd me to kiss,
> Because much better than the wine
>   Thy loving kindness is.
> To troops of horse in Pharaoh's coach
>   My love I compare;
> Thy neck with chains and jewels new,
>   Thy cheeks full comely are.
> Borders of gold with silver studs
>   For thee make up we will,
> While that the king at's table sits
>   My spikenard yields her smell.
> My love is as Engedi's vines
>   Like campfire bunch to me,
> So fair my love so fair thou art,
>   Thine eyes as doves' eyes be!"

I warrant this was not the first time the jagged old *Bay
Psalm Book* had proved an unholy comfort to youthful
sinners!

The next day as I furbished in my room, I heard the
three girls chattering directly under my window. Most
naturally considering age and sex, two at least were dis-
cussing desirable types of husbands.

"I," said Hope positively, "would like to get a lawyer,
one like Mr. John Adams who has more briefs than he
knows what to do with; that is—" she added with perfect candor and good humor, "if anybody could dream of
taking me."

"And I," said Tabitha with the gravity becoming her pious choice, "would like to have a fine young minister, who could preach as well as father. Of course we would be very poor, but we would have," perhaps with a blush but she went on courageously, "a very large family; ministers always do. And we would be very happy."

"And you, Emilie?" spoke Hope again. But Emilie, of wont the merriest and least reserved of the three, spoke never a word, and as I most unchivalrously peered downward through the shutter, seemed turning away her head.

Three mornings after this Nero and the chariot were again at the gate, and Hope and Emilie were gone. Not one flash of coquetry had the daughter of France given me; not one syllable of encouragement, but as the back wheels vanished in the dust down the Lexington high road, I strode back into the house with the first great decision of my life irrevocably taken;—I must win the hand of Emilie Rivoire.

That afternoon I took a fowling piece and went on a solitary walk by Concord River. There were no birds worth shooting, but in an old punt I paddled out for water-lilies to bring mother and Tabby. The oar-work helped hard thinking. What had I to offer my destiny? Wealth? My uncles were paying for my college. The Gilman name? An honor perhaps for a Middlesex girl, but meaningless to one who had known London and Paris. Something else? Whereupon as the boat shot over the lily-pads and among the cattails, it came to me that there at least was one great thing I could proffer which lay wholly within my own competence and keeping—myself. Unless I could come to Emilie clean of body and alert of mind I had no right to come at all. And then, like many a son of New England, I took Jonathan Edwards' great vow in his youth, *"To live with all my might while I do live."*

A cool fragrant pail of waterlilies I brought to mother that supper-time. About my thoughts and resolution I had been silent as the grave, but there seemed additional tenderness in her eyes when I kissed her good-night after father had of wont bestowed his blessing: "You are a good boy, Roger," said she, "a good boy despite all your faults, and some day you will make some good girl very happy."

CHAPTER IX

THIS chapter I shall tell in my own person, although a few of the details reached me only long afterward.

When I returned to college in the fall of 1772 the days of respite following the departure of the troops were threatening to end. Advices from England were again ominous. People again praised Samuel Adams for warning his countrymen in the *Boston Gazette*, for example, against the "influx of standing armies, ships of war, episcopates, pensioners, placemen, and other jobbers of an abandoned ministry" that seemed impending. Nor was oil poured upon troubled waters when wide circulation was given Lord North's speech, denouncing Boston as a town where "The drunken ragamuffins of a vociferous mob are exalted to equal importance with men of judgment, morals and property. I can never acquiesce in the absurd opinion that all men are equal." Opinions which, incidentally, go far to explain why Britain and America parted.

Boston was not so far from Cambridge as to make it hard for me to trudge frequently over to Charlestown Ferry and visit my uncles. Things were getting tense between Whig and Tory families, but old friends could still talk politics without getting into a passion, and my uncles strove hard to preserve correct relations. Eleazer was a widower, and his home was dominated by the self-sufficient Hope. Peleg had no children, and he and Aunt Mercy were only too happy to have me stop over a night. So I was always welcome in Boston.

Did I revisit North Square? Did I steal hours from my lexicon for the important question, "How soon is it safe to call on the Rivoires again?"—But alas and alack! it was a luck afternoon now when I could have the fair Emilie somewhat to myself. No more walks under the trees, and no more turning of psalm books. Mademoiselle seemed in a fair way to become a dread and mighty princess, "The Toast of the Town."

Presently I heard that at the Bunch of Grapes her name had been drunk standing by a dozen young bucks every one of whose fathers were or had been on his Excellency's council. Dunmore also told me with gusto of how an army captain and a naval lieutenant had had high words at the British Coffee House, as to whether a Miss Van Sturtyvant of New York had a shapelier ankle than Mlle. Rivoire— and of how a duel had barely been averted. Every time I turned into the Square it was to groan inwardly at the fine chair, or chaise or curricle standing about, and I was lucky if there were not two or three; while Hope and Lucy complained openly, "We hardly see Emilie at all now —the men are so tight after her."

Nevertheless I pocketed my pride, toughened my feelings, and called as often as decency would permit. And one great comfort I had through it all: if Mademoiselle had only the same elegant courtesy and friendly word for me she had for Peter Scarlett, she had just the same for Christopher Belcher, and for Lieutenant Perkins. You could defy gods and men to discover her favorite. And if she climbed out of Mr. Addington's calash one day she climbed out of Mr. Sigourney's on the next. She had to perfection the gift (perhaps because she was French, perhaps merely because the Lord put it in her) of making a dozen men

happy through the most trifling favors, completely contented to flutter about her despite conduct that was discretion itself. I gained no encouragement but I was never
reduced to despair.

Naturally I had many wretched hours. I had very little
pocket money. I danced miserably, Redford opinion frowning on much dancing by the minister's family. Such routs
as I attended in Boston were spent mostly in standing up
with Hope or with other unromantic girls who could draw
no better partners, and in seeing Emilie opposite velvet
doublets, silk hose and golden buckles, or else his Majesty's uniform itself. And then came a colloquy that sent
me back toward Harvard in a mood to leap off the ferry
boat—only the water looked too cold.

Paul Revere probably was only intending to be very
friendly. It was a bleak November day. I had called at
the Rivoires—Berthe said Mademoiselle was out—probably driving with Mr. Whittingham. As I walked discon-
solately away, Paul came out of his own door and headed
toward his shop. He mildly rallied me on my vain errand,
then taking a little upon himself said that he knew French
customs better than did I; Miss Emilie would have her
fling with all the proper young men, but would never dream
of accepting one without the consent of her grandfather;
and as for old Georges, he was a solid man of business and
the gentleman who walked off with his granddaughter must
have not merely good blood but a pretty pile of money;
"a good marriage settlement to match the *dot*" such as they
had in France would be very much in order. And there
would be fewer fingers burned if some of those Boston
sparks so understood it.

At that particular moment I had seven shillings in my
pocket, and a bad Rhode Island bill. Uncle Peleg had
talked vaguely about "taking me into his office" if I gradu-

ated with credit. If I could have wrung Paul's neck as means to canceling his words I would have been far happier. . . .

. . . Then presently as that winter of 1772-73 advanced there was one figure whom I always kept stumbling upon at North Square—the gallant Captain Prothero. The commander of H. M. brig *Comet,* 18 guns, may have been an austere father to his men, but he cut a very different figure in a parlor than on his quarterdeck. The reputation he enjoyed for being a two-bottle man in the wardroom, and for having seen Admiral Montagu frequently under the table, somehow did not harm him much with the ladies. They told great stories about his daredevil courage as a midshipman in the old French War, although Dunmore professed that it was an open secret that he had won his latest promotion by extraordinary toadying to the notorious Earl of Sandwich, now head of the Admiralty, and by the constancy of his elder brother at Westminster in always voting with the King's Friends.

Be that as it may, Bernard Prothero knew how to proclaim importance and breeding in every gesture and ruffle. He was the second son of a good Yorkshire family; he was handsome, well-knit, wore his blue uniform as if it had been molded to his skin, and had a salt-water way with him which seemed to justify his boasts that "he loved to play the devil among the women." The stories of a couple of *affaires du cœur* in the West Indies, where he had been stationed, were not vastly to his credit, but for all that he seemed a favorite with Montagu and often spread his feet under Mr. Hutchinson's mahogany.

All this was known about him when he began to make extremely frequent visits to North Square; and he received at least sufficient encouragement to make him a steady caller. Georges Rivoire never concealed a certain good-natured partiality for the Whigs, but reasons which can be guessed led him to show Tory visitors and royal officers every courtesy; and this fact made his home an additional loadstone for Prothero, who (in company with all the army and navy officers) shared the ostracism decreed against them by nearly every Whig family.

Prothero, let one add, was a visitor worth having. I have myself sat for hours, fascinated, if almost stung to desperation, listening to his sea-yarns which he told extremely well, possessing gifts of narration which would have made him a capital romancer had he exchanged the cutlass for the goosequill. And as for Mademoiselle, however traveled and sophisticated she seemed in *my* eyes, I suspect it made no small impression upon a girl in her teens to hear the talk of a man who could speak jauntily of "My uncle Major General," who had been attached to the British Embassy at Paris and seen all the glory of Versailles, who had danced with the Queen of Naples when his frigate was in the Mediterranean, and who claimed, at least, to have rescued the daughter of a Spanish grandee from capture by an Algerian corsair.—In short, a good many people beside myself began remarking, "That Prothero spends a devilish amount of time around the 'Mamselle'," and darting venomed looks at him.

There was no other naval or army gentleman who commended himself so manifestly to her graces, and as for our provincial bucks, Prothero soon betrayed that they did not even deserve the compliment of avowed contempt. "Mohairs" was the term he jauntily applied to all the young Bostonians whom he met sampling the Rivoire bohea; and he took great pains to "Mister" old Major Atterbridge, because that veteran who took a limp away from Ticonderoga, had borne a provincial and not a royal commission. In short he displayed for us all that "tranquil

superiority" which has wrought the British nation more
harm than all the cannon of all its adversaries.

But if two or three Boston sparks of respectable family
felt their skins growing warm under their neckbands, and
talked about "calling the rascal out" nothing checked the
ardor of his visits to North Square and certain naval
dignitaries stood committed to the opinion: "Prothero, gay
dog, has been fairly caught at last. She's leading him on.
Probably they've heard from England that his brother's
childless and consumptive. It'll be a pretty property."—
And then the captain abruptly ceased calling at the Rivoires
after a dramatic incident.

Thus it came to pass. My outraged eyes had told me
that Prothero had visited Paul's shop, purchased a silver
nutmeg holder (a suitable and usual trifle to give to a
favored lady) and then had bestowed it upon the great
Mademoiselle. The gift had been received with a civil
amount of thanks: and I—driven desperate, wrote a lying
letter home. Would mother and Tabby send down a large
parcel of bayberry candles and fine hard bayberry soap,
such as Yetmercy made to perfection and wherein, during
her visit, I knew that Emilie had greatly delighted? Only I
said nothing about Emilie. "Aunt Mercy (ran the letter)
deserved a suitable gift." The packet came: Aunt Mercy
received a minor fraction thereof, and the remainder, done
up in the best gilt paper from Henry's shop, I carried in
state to North Square.

It was a very mild winter afternoon. I had gone early,
hoping to anticipate all visitors, and was successful. As I
came to the door, one of the windows was partly open
and inside I could see Emilie, dressed in something white
and blue, seated at her little table, and performing that
task which no true lady of the day willingly left to servants—the cutting of a great coned sugarloaf into little

cubes proper for the tea cup. Her long fingers were plying
the silver cutting-tongs with the skill of a loving craftsman;
and as she wrought she too, as might a child of the Puritans, was singing not madrigals, but a Psalm. Only never
flowed any of our rugged native psalmody so exquisitely
sweet and canorous:

> "Les cieux en chaque lieu
> La puissance de Dieu
> Recourent aux humains:
> Ce grand entours espars
> Public en toutes parts
> L'ouvrage des ses mains.
> Jour apres jour coulant
> Du Seigneur va parlant
> Par longue experience.
> La nuit suivant la nuit
> Nous presche et nous instruicst
> De grand sapience."

But here, out of the corner of her eyes, she saw me standing half sheepish, half spellbound at the door. Marot's
grand poetry died, and in an instant Emilie was having
me in, giving me her hand and saying with her most unaffected smile: "Oh! Roger, I am so glad. So many people
besetting poor little me, and no time left to show that I
am still friend to good friends. And how are your parents,
and how is Tabby, and have you heard whether Yetmercy
kept her promise to me not to drown the kittens?"

Then I presented my packet with a bow which I had tried
to learn from watching the officers. Emilie opened the bundle. The clean pure odor of the bayberry penetrated the
room. It was really a fit gift for a countess. Emilie was
clearly delighted and was saying the most gracious things
—which might mean so much or so little: then bang! went
the knocker and my vision from the Delectable Mountains
vanished as Berthe ushered into the parlor none other than
Captain Prothero.

The naval officer gave me one sidelong frown when he

saluted Emilie with more than his wonted ceremoniousness,
and next (the ordinary compliments at an end) stated the
reason for his early call. "He was on his way to the
Province House, but desired the honor of Mademoiselle's
company to the great 'drum' at the Sewell house on Saturday night."

Emilie with a very serene smile informed him that Mr.
Addington had already received the pledge of her company;
and Ezra Addington became my friend from that hour,
although I had always considered him a light-headed cox-
comb. Then next with perfect composure she invited the
captain to admire the new gift: "Which I am sure they
could never match in France, and I doubt if they can in
England."

The officer smelled of the cakes of bayberry with a polite
although slightly bored attention: "Some of your peasant
products here are really interesting. And who was the taste-
ful donor—Mr. Addington, I fancy?"

"Mr. Gilman has just brought this."

Prothero condescended to favor me with a patronizing
smile: "A very suitable attention from a very young gentleman from the villages." And then he addressed me a
look that said as clearly as spoken words: "Betake yourself
off: I would talk with Mlle. Rivoire alone." But, as Yetmercy would have put it, I was determined "to hump up
my back and spit." I knew that Prothero would be compelled to leave speedily. I wilfully determined to stay him
out—and that I did, to Emilie's manifest amusement, and
to his own barely dissembled anger. The captain was less
interesting in his anecdotes; the lady had to do nearly all
the talking. Then Charley Sigourney appeared taking off
his gloves at the door, and Prothero and I went out together,
both knowing there would be no private tête-à-tête for
either of us *that* afternoon.

We had reached the street and had walked a few steps apart, when he suddenly called me back:

"A word, my fine lad!"

To a sophomore at Harvard this was not a promising beginning, but I turned with: "What do you wish, sir?"

"My good fellow:" he pursued with his most magnanimous smile: "I realize that although your provincial yeomanry are an excellent stock, with many farmerly virtues, they cannot pretend to that breeding which should teach them to know when their rustic civilities are not wanted."

"Speak plainly sir, I beg," I answered, getting warm and cold by turns, but not yet catching his full drift.

"Can you not see, sir, that Mademoiselle Rivoire is entitled to the company of friends of her own station? Do not presume because you did her a trifling service a long time since, to dawdle in her parlor as if you were their equals."

"Mademoiselle Rivoire," I returned, my face becoming one hot coal, "makes me welcome. I'll take dismissal from her lips or her grandfather's—not from you, sir."

"Our French friends are too generous in their courtesy. I see you cannot take a friendly hint. Let me be plain then. Do not come between a King's officer and his affairs of gallantry, or 'twill be the worse for you."

I know that I was turning white then, not red; my tongue was cleaving in my mouth, yet my speech came out. "No uniform can cover threats like that. He who denies my right to wait on Emilie Rivoire shall eat his words or answer to me as a man."

"You do well, yokel," spoke Prothero, with an oath, but smiling no longer, "to insult the royal uniform. It takes no courage. You know that I cannot fight you."

"What mean you by that?"

"Because a King's officer would degrade himself by call-

ing out any but a *gentleman*. You are five years too young
and only the son of a Dissenting preacher—understand."

He touched his hilt; probably merely to show that the
blade was firmly in the scabbard, but it was the last straw.
I had most of my tall strength now. With a roar rather
than a curse I was on him; and a more powerful man than
he would have tumbled at the onset. One shock, one grap-
ple and the commander of the *Comet* measured his length
in the melting snow of the gutter. When he arose you
might have imagined him damning a crew of mutineers.
His sword started from the sheath. A moment more and
at best a "deplorable affray" would have spread itself in
the Boston papers: and then like an apparition between
me and my adversary there stood the white locks and
gaunt figure of Georges Rivoire, his eyes striking dumb and
rigid the raging Prothero.

"I have seen and heard everything, Monsieur, as I
approached the house," he said to my foe, with icy calmness. "A gentleman and an officer does not taunt and brawl
like a *gros grenadier*. Captain Prothero will not wait on
my granddaughter again or the story of this affair goes to
his discredit through Boston."

Then without waiting the sailor's reply he put his arm
within my own: "Come back to my own room, *mon fils:*
I will talk to you. Because a fool accosts, you do not
become a fool yourself."

Half an hour later, having given me much excellent
advice but neither raised nor lowered my hopes concerning
Emilie, he let me depart. My mistress and Mr. Sigourney
had driven away, and North Street was peaceful and vacant.

. . . .

Prothero, I learned presently, appeared late at the Province House and begged the admiral to give the *Comet* more
active service than at the atrociously dull Boston station.

His wish was promptly granted. Enormous quantities of tea were being smuggled along the Maine districts. The actual promoter might be that High Son of Liberty, Peleg Fifield, or even the mighty John Hancock, but government spies said the actual leader of the smugglers was none other than one Remember Watchhorn, not unknown to Captain Prothero. The latter was to take the *Comet* and several smaller vessels, cruise from Cape Ann northward, and at all hazards break up the traffic and lay the desperadoes by the heels.

CHAPTER X

IN WHICH I AM RUSTICATED

THE doldrums of my freshman period being past I enjoyed a tolerably prosperous sophomore year at Harvard. I had a room in the top story of old Stoughton Hall; that ramshackly building that had to be pulled down a few years later and presently replaced by a better structure of the same name. My apartment was garret-like enough; and the winds often whistled through the crannies so briskly that I was fain to eke out my fire with a cannon ball, heated red hot at the college buttery, and conveyed up three weary flights in a pail of ashes. But it was no colder in Cambridge than in Redford, and we all had become accustomed to find the ink frozen in the morning.

It was my good fortune to come to Harvard just after two blessed changes. The listing of students by paternal rank had just been abandoned. The governor's or chief justice's son no longer headed the class rolls, and a poor widow's son—the best construer in the class—no longer floundered permanently at the bottom. I was not vexed, therefore, by the nice question whether my father's child deserved a position higher or lower than did the offspring of a justice of the peace.

Also I had the luck to enter just after the abolition of the bad old system of having each class taught by a single tutor in all subjects through the entire four years; instead we were wisely favored with having separate tutors in each subject studied. I did only indifferently in mathematics, but logic and rhetoric came better, and I was guilty

114

of some Latin alcaics which were read before the class
by Mr. Tutor Willard for considerable praise.

Furthermore, I learned, of course, many more important
things; for example, how often one could make freshmen
run errands across "to the village," *i.e.*, to what is now Harvard Square, without uncollegiate oppression; how often
it was safe to say *"Non valui"* ("I was sick") when I had
not cared to attend morning prayers, or *"Non paravi"* ("Not
prepared") after a very late return from Boston. I became
a fairly active member of the "Speaking Club," a newly
founded organization with a silly little secret ritual, but
which nevertheless really gave us good experience in debate
and elocution, and which, as the "Institute of 1770," sur-
vives even to this day.

Like all my friends I affected to rail against the college
commons, even harder than Samuel Adams manhandled the
British ministry; and in truth the dining room in the new
Harvard Hall was the scene of plenty of scanty dinners
and godless complaining. We sat in "messes" of eight, with
eight pounds of meat between us. Mondays and Thurs-
days were "boiling days"; the other days were "roasting days"; besides our meat (often gristle and bone) we
rejoiced in pudding, cabbage and greens in season, plus a
"size" of bread, and two unpeeled potatoes. But in any
case we had unlimited quantities of cider—two pewter quart
cans being assigned to each mess, and these being refilled
by the student waiters as fast as they became empty.
Breakfast and supper were not much more than bowls of
bread and milk and cups of chocolate or coffee handed out
amid much confusion to the long lines waiting at the "buttery hatch." Yet although I spent too many pennies at
the Cambridge bun-shops, and although Uncle Peleg's dinners were doubly welcome whenever I saw Boston, I do not
believe my brainwork suffered because of very plain living

and of long evenings spent in nothing more luxurious than a hard, straight chair.

There were about one hundred and sixty of us students. Everybody knew everybody else, and if there were incessant roughness, horseplay and class battles, there was an equal amount of true comradeship and brotherly helpfulness. The son of an "honorable" soon learned where he belonged—often in a very humble corner. The waiters at the commons were among the recognized leaders in their classes; a matter which greatly astonished Dunmore when he came out to visit me from the fort—and told about the abject state of the Oxford "servitors." I suppose future generations will pull queer faces at a curriculum wherein students, even at desire, were not suffered to take French—all I can say is our four classes somehow made their splash in the world, and I think that Greek, Latin and mathematics had not a little to do about it.

In this way I went through the sophomore year, with only the adventure with Captain Prothero, and my miserable uncertainty touching Emilie to plague me. Dunmore had disappeared; to my great regret he had been ordered to New York to join the staff of General Gates: but some of my Whig friends were a trifle relieved lest he might be corrupting the principles of a True Son of Liberty. In addition I had the bad chance of earning the apparent dislike of Tutor Smith, the least popular of the teaching staff, a nosing, prying instructor, who delighted in catch questions and in "screwing" (pressing and quizzing unfairly) on all possible occasions.[1]

Smith was the cause of my receiving a "private," in other words, an informal admonition by President Locke for going skating in study time, and for being fined 2s. 6d. for an

[1] The good colonel probably speaks of Tutor Isaac Smith who was ostracized and obliged to flee to England for giving directions to Lord Percy, April 19, 1775. (Editor.)

unauthorized visit to Boston. But these trifles would never have jolted my college career had I not become chambermate with Sir Jack Prindle.

"Sir" Prindle had never felt the King's sword upon his shoulders. He had acquired his title thanks to the custom of styling all bachelors who had taken their lower degree and who were staying on for a master's, as *Dominus*, anglice "Sir," the exalted honor of "Mister" being reserved for the actual masters and the tutors. Sir Prindle was the son of a wealthy farmer in one of the "Fields" in the Connecticut Valley. He had a moderate liking for books, but Heaven had never intended him for anything but a successful farmer or perhaps a tavern keeper. Family pride had sent him to Harvard, and parental piosity had determined, after he graduated amid desperate hazards, that he ought to become a minister, possessing, as undeniably he did, the gift of the gab.

Poor Jack had never mustered up the grace and gumption to disappoint a very devout mother, and confess to limitations whereof he was very conscious. So at Harvard he had remained another year; keeping for a while out of reckless scrapes more through good luck than good management, although Professor Sewell said he could never read five words of Hebrew, and Tutor Eliot grew sad over his Greek. Prindle had a remarkable way of ingratiating himself with younger students. He had won my heart while I was a freshman by rescuing me from a bullying sophomore. And now when for various reasons both he and I had to shift chambermates, I was more than contented when he proposed that we should room together. My guileless mother was pleased when she learned the arrangement: "It would be a fine thing for Roger to associate with an older scholar who was studying for the ministry."

Every normal youth has at some time made a friend

who for a few months blazed like a comet across his life, lighting and coloring everything in it, and then as suddenly vanished into the everywhere—leaving behind only a sense of profound darkness. Such a friendship now was mine. Jack Prindle became my particular father confessor and commanding general at a moment when I felt particularly disconsolate because of the departure of Herbert Dunmore and a growing conviction that I had no right to push my claims to Emilie.

Jack had a good allowance, was generous to a fault, could talk in a manner absolutely captivating to his juniors, and had an irresistible manner which made me sure he enjoyed a dash of Irish in him. Nevertheless when we became chambermates I had a vague misgiving that I was more likely to be taught to improve my loo and ombre rather than my Xenophon and Natural Philosophy: although Prindle did indeed make fitful efforts at his divinity. He liked to walk about with Shepherd's *Sincere Convert* conspicuous under his arm; and at intervals would scrooch over his table, working desperately upon his Master's disputation, "Whether the Trinitarian Nature of the Deity was revealed in the Old Testament."

Poor Sir Jack—he was his own worst enemy; shunned the grosser vices, was never consciously hypocritical, was ever ready to help a friend, was the life of every gathering. After he quitted Harvard I never saw him again. When the war began I heard that he became a lieutenant and was knocked on the head, fighting very gallantly, at the Battle of Long Island.

So we came toward the end of the college year. Commencement was set for July 21st in 1773, but a week ahead of that time Cambridge began to be in the greatest uproar permissible for a peaceful village. Already by custom a small tribe of very shiftless Indians from Natick had appeared, taken station around Christ Church by the Common and slept in the cellar of that Episcopal stronghold when the weather was rainy. The women set out booths for the sale of baskets and moccasins; the boys tried to inveigle the students into putting up pennies to be shot at with bows and arrows; the men strolled about shiftlessly and spent their squaws' earnings upon tobacco and rum. Negro fiddlers had wandered up from Newport; tables were being made ready for the sale of comfits, cold drinks and hard liquor; the influx had begun of organgrinders, performing bears and monkeys, jugglers, sword swallowers and blind beggars led by dogs.

In fact the great day itself was at hand,—when the Boston shops would close, and when "young men and maidens, old men and children" would flock out to Cambridge, not indeed to "praise the name of the Lord" but to join in a most carnal revel (the one sinful celebration lawfully permitted in our good Bay Province): a festival all the more astonishing because it was in full progress at the very moment the President and Fellows of the College were solemnly escorting his Excellency and the council into the Meeting House for the conferring of degrees. Despite the troubled state of public affairs, everything still promised that this "Harvard Commencement" would live up to its fame, and deserve all the accustomed anathemas of the godly.

"Rioting and drunkenness, chambering and wantonness," to cite the apostle, were therefore in the air. Academic work had almost ceased; and yet nothing had ruined Prindle's ministerial program or my own collegiate prospects. In our room most of our movables had been packed away for the summer. Prindle was coming back. "He felt that he needed to strengthen himself on Total Depravity and the Visions of Daniel before taking his final degree" so he had written his father. As for me, I had abandoned a rash project for inviting Mademoiselle Rivoire out to the exercises—I was two years away from graduating and perhaps Tabby could get her again to Redford.

Very soon Stoughton, Hollis and Massachusetts—our three stolid brick dormitories, would have lapsed into the peaceful care of the "scarecrow," the summer custodian, and all for us would have been well. Then the devil arranged that a glorious new sign should be hung upon the Blue Anchor Tavern.

Every old Harvard man remembers the Blue Anchor Tavern on Wood Street going down to the Great Bridge over Charles River. Many were the punch bowls emptied there by the academical, theological, mercantile or political. Mr. Eben Bradish, the genial host, prided himself on the amount of Latin used by many of his guests—especially after the second cork had popped. We students bestowed our august patronage, and were ordinarily welcome. But right over Wood Street, a flaunting invitation to break the eighth commandment, had dangled the blue anchor sign in bright paint and gilt, and by the working of a natural law far more imperative in college towns than that of gravitation, this sign one night unaccountably disappeared.

After its exit and suitable but vain search, a new sign presently swung and creaked in its stead; but simultaneously President Locke had read in chapel a solemn ordinance of the corporation that any collegiate person caught tampering with tradesmen's or tavern signs should be forthwith expelled from the institution, with no ignominy wanting. There was a peaceful calm in chapel when this law of the Medes and Persians was promulgated, yet I saw a sinful glitter in Jack Prindle's eyes. That afternoon he went to Mr. Bradish; ordered a pot of metheglin, drank it deliberately and eyed the signboard with tender love.

Be it said that Sir Prindle's fifth year at Harvard had
not been without suspicions by the higher powers. One
morning the pigs kept in their family pens behind the buttery in Harvard Hall had been discovered actively grubbing
up the turf by the meeting house. On another fine May
morning the white cow belonging to Professor Wigglesworth,
of the chair of Divinity, and usually watered by her learned
owner at the pump by Massachusetts Hall, was discovered
by admiring cohorts tethered to said pump, peacefully
ruminating, but striped with black paint, and with a placard about her neck "two-horned zebra." Certain unlucky
freshmen had been seized and cross-examined, but they
established alibis. Then guarded inquiries were made about
Sir Prindle's doings upon those nights. No proof devel-
oped, but I repeat that Jack had cause for circumspec-
tion.

It was the morning before Commencement, a rather chilly,
foggy morning, and I was glad to be burning up rubbish in
the fireplace. Next door in Stoughton two seniors were
preparing their room for a graduation "blow" to the limits
of the college statute controlling punch parties. I was just
throwing on the embers some extraordinary verses beginning:

> "The lilies of France
> Set our hearts all a-dance,"

which, thank heaven! had never before quitted my writing
desk; when Ben Forsyth, a fellow sophomore thrust in his
head.

"Hey, Gilman: heard the news?—Just been to Farring-
ton's Stationery—the Blue Anchor sign is prigged."

"There'll be the devil to pay," I replied accurately but
complacently, and then I heard Jack's step upon the stair.
He was carrying something large and flat wrapped under

his coat, and his face wore a tom-cat smile. Silently he beckoned Forsyth inside, closed the door, shot the bolt, and flung back the covering, proclaiming, "You lads can hold your tongues, and besides we all go home to-morrow. Simply *had* to take back to the old town at least one trophy of the chase."

I fear that instead of questioning this unwonted practice for a divinity student, we both fell to asking ways and means in terms implying admiration; and Jack, with artless pride, explained how he had crept along Spring Lane at grayest dawn, whisked around the corner to the inn, yanked the sign with one Homeric leap from its moorings, hidden it in the manure pile behind Professor Winthrop's house opposite the tavern; and now quite neatly had retrieved it, wrapped it up and walked thither: "For nobody will suspect a full fledged baccalarius in broad daylight." We were beginning to admire his knightly courage again, when a perfect bedlam began in the college yard below. Students were leaning from the windows of Hollis and Massachusetts and clattering upon their water ewers with sticks. An indescribable yelling was also arising from the rallying spot around the college pump.

"What's the matter?" bawled Forsyth from our window.

"The tutors are searching Stoughton room by room for Bradish's sign!" came back through the tumult below.

Jack for once began turning white around the gills; he bounded over and bolted the door in a twinkling, and crammed his handkerchief into the keyhole: "I must have been spotted as I slid from behind Winthrop's," he groaned, then glanced toward the hearth. "Thank the Lord, Gilman, you had a fire. There's still a chance."

In a trice he smashed the offending sign over his knee and plunged it into the ashes, but at the same instant an

ominous tramp was heard on the stairway, and I heard
the voice of Tutor Willard saying at the next door: "Open,
Hamphill, we must visit your room."

"Can't we keep 'em out!" implored Forsyth, an innocent victim, whom even in my predicament I pitied.

"Tutors have the right to go through all dormitory chambers at all times:" faltered Prindle: "it's a statute as old
as the college. Ply the bellows, Gilman; for God's sake
make the sparks catch!"

We could hear Hamphill grumbling and protesting his
guiltlessness, and his visitors tumbling up his mattress and
going through his closet. The fire, although not out, burned
very dully. The noise outside in the yard was frightful.
Somebody was flinging thunder mugs from the upper windows of Hollis. I could see a crowd standing directly below
our chamber and pointing excitedly upward. Then came a
beat on our own door: "Tutors Willard and Eliot on visita-
tion, unlock immediately."

"Please, sir," I made answer, "Sir Prindle is putting on
his small clothes, be patient for a little."

"*Ratio non sufficit*," came back the standard reply for
denying an excuse; "unlock instantly."

But here Jack, who had been standing like a man dis-
traught watching desperate efforts at the hearth, suddenly
beamed with inspiration. "Praise the Lord, there *is* one
loophole in the statute," he whispered hoarsely. "A student
is not bound to unlock to a tutor if he is at prayer. Work
the bellows, boy, and all the devils aid you."

"Please, sir," I spoke through the door again. "Sir
Prindle is now at his devotions. We'll open as soon as he
is finished." And immediately in a loud voice, that went
easily through the barrier and into the now swarming,
shuffling passage and stairway, Jack began a most eloquent

petition for the gifts of grace and piety upon the President of the College, the several Professors and more particularly upon the individual tutors. He called them all by name; he failed not to recite to Heaven their well-known personal failings as he besought for them forgiveness, and the fruits meet for repentance.

Standing before the fireplace where by Forsyth's and my own joint efforts a healthy flame at last was blazing, Prindle prayed with a fervor becoming the long prayer at the meeting house. "Too much, O Lord, too much, we fear that it is with the Harvard faculty even as with the backsliding Jews of old, 'an evil and adulterous generation seeketh after a sign, *and there shall no sign be given it*, but the sign of the prophet Jonas!'"

But the offending boards were of stout oak, and had become a trifle dampish. They kindled very slowly despite every coaxing. Prindle, nothing daunted, continued to pray, one eye on his watch, the other on the fireplace. "'Tis good practice for the ministry," he muttered in a pause, "this will pass for a funeral."

We knew by the murmuring outside that Messrs. Eliot and Willard were ready with some implement to force the door the instant the petition ceased, but Jack warmed to his task. After remembering certain students he hated, he passed to the Governor, the Council and the Lower House of the Legislature. Prominent Tories he consigned to the abyss; upon Samuel Adams and Joseph Warren he invoked the heavenly blessing. The fire at last gained headway. The sign was already well scorched. A few moments more and it would have been charred beyond identification. Jack with a smile of relief was just passing on to a final burst in behalf of the Selectmen of Cambridge, when a thunderous roar from the yard told us that something was happening outside, and before we could take the

slightest measure, with a clatter from the roof, down the
leaden eaves-spout and into our window swung my particular adversary, Tutor Smith.

He made one dart toward the fireplace ere his victims
could put forth a gesture, and dragged some of the glowing
boards out upon the oak floor. Black and sooty, indeed,
were they, but part of the paint and a "Blue A——" were
still intact. A moment more and the door had flown open
and we were the center of a howling, gesticulating throng,
in the midst of which Mr. Willard was saying with Labra-
dor calmness; "Young gentlemen, you must accompany us
instantly to President Locke."

. . . Only the proximity to Commencement saved us
from being the center of a great auto-da-fé, one of the most
spectacular in the history of Harvard. Before our terrified
eyes floated those awful ceremonies of over thirty years
back when Professor Greenwood "for the crime of intem-
perance" had been removed from his chair of mathematics,
or when Tutor Price had been publicly cast into outer darkness for like offenses. The status of Prindle, only a little
lower than the faculty; the fearfulness of this lapse of a
divinity student into the crime of larceny followed by an
aggravated form of blasphemy; his own calloused impeni-
tence when first taxed with the deed, all left him open to
"expulsion from the hall," with the president publicly
reciting and bewailing his sins and commanding the students to take long warning from the reward of depravity.

But the long tables were being set out for the Corporation in Harvard Commons; the Latin addresses were being
polished; his Excellency's troop of horse was already furbishing its uniforms; the professors' best wigs were being
dressed; and President Locke, the most ineffectual magnate
who ever inhabited Wadsworth House, was anxious not to
add one more to his distractions and troubles. Poor Prindle

took every blame upon himself, confessed unfeignedly, and did his uttermost to clear Forsyth and me. Of course his own case was hopeless. He left Cambridge that night, broken-hearted at last over the letter dispatched to his parents, and only saved from the Long Lane jail and a thievery charge by the good nature of Bradish.

As for Forsyth and myself we convinced all of our judges but the implacable Smith, that we had had no part in the direct roguery and were at worst accomplices after the act. Nevertheless the case was open and notorious. We had connived at a fearful act of impiety. To condone such an offense was impossible. Forsyth, however, was the son of a lawyer in good standing in Worcester, and my own father was a man not lightly to be humiliated by undue severity upon his offspring. We therefore escaped the catastrophe of Prindle, but with mingled sorrow and thankfulness received a lighter doom. We were not to go home for vacation. We were to be rusticated—Forsyth to review his Greek for the rest of the summer with a minister in Attleboro, while I was conducted to Boston in the custody of Tutor Eliot to take the stage-chaise running to Salem— there to study in like manner under the admonitions of the Reverend Mr. Truswell.

I got a letter from Prindle written just as he started homeward, pouring forth his abject regret at involving me in his disaster, and addressing me in the best Harvard manner among friends, *"Vir honoratissimus and tiptoptissimus"*; but it did me little good as, dazed and stunned, I trundled through Saugus and Lynn. What would my uncles think, what father, what mother? And above all else what, oh! what would think Emilie Rivoire?

CHAPTER XI

THE Reverend Obediah Truswell was an elderly minister
of weak lungs who sometimes substituted at the Tabernacle
Church of Salem in the absence of the pastor, and who
eked out a small income by receiving for tutoring rusticated
or backward students from Harvard. I believe that Professor Wigglesworth had been so kind as to write that my
offense was more technical than deliberate. In any case
the Truswells received me kindly. I put in an hour daily
with the good man over Homer and the *Cyropaedia,* but
the rest of my time in Salem was very much my own.

That time, except for longings for Redford, passed not
unpleasantly. Wedgèd among Bellamy's *True Religion*
and like tomes, I found in the family library Rollin's
Ancient History and Hume's *History of England;* and I can
never think of the campaigns of Alexander or the wars of
the third Edward without also thinking of Truswell's little
garden upon the Salem waterfront, where I often sat snif-
fing the aroma of kelp and eel-grass with the salt waves
almost plashing at the foot of the grand old trees, while I
could hear the "knock, knock" from a ship yard, or the
creak of block and tackle of a snow or schooner casting off
and making sail.

After expected interval came the much dreaded letters.
Father was sure this "awful Providence" would keep me
from even worse things; but mother (beloved soul) said she
would not add to the sorrow she knew I must feel, and sent
down a supply of newly darned stockings, a big parcel of

seed-cakes and two bright guineas—filched, I fear from her own slow savings to rebuild the milk house. Hope wrote that Uncle Eleazer swore he would cast me off as a reprobate after another such escapade, but that Uncle Peleg had laughed at the affair outrageously and had vowed that "he was glad the boy wasn't all pious Gilman but had some good old, rascally Fifield blood in him!" As for Emilie, Hope hadn't seen her lately. At their last meeting she had said something about going to visit some old Huguenot connections whom M. Rivoire had discovered settled in Falmouth. This was comforting to me; anything to keep her away from those fine Boston blades and sparks!

Salem commerce was not what it became later, but the second town of Massachusetts was already a thriving port. The great Derby family had given its name to the bustling water-street over which it lorded. Essex Street was full of dark sea-captains and supercargoes. Broadcloth gold lace and bag wigs you could meet in all the shops and counting-rooms, or entering those stately dwellings around the lovely common which rose as solid witnesses to the rewarding thrift of this stronghold of the Endicotts and the Higginsons.

In Salem I came to a clearer realization of the increasing bitterness of the debate with Britain. Day by day, in tap-room or along the West India sugar wharves, in the ship yards at the nooning, in the chandlery shops amid the bales of oakum—always the same arguments. Had Parliament any right to tax us? To pass laws cutting off our trade with the French islands? To harass our coasts with King's cutters? To make our governor and judges salaried placemen of Britain? And finally, had our fathers' fathers crossed the seas, helped only by a scolding frown from behind, merely to create provinces which after they became rich and strong were to be denied "the common rights of Englishmen"?

Every one of these incessant arguments would end with an unflinching "No!" Then perhaps silence, after which some fish trader or brigantine's mate would demand, "What then?" Whereupon everybody would give a solemn whistle and the conclave would dissolve.

In Boston and Cambridge there had been so many Tories among the Very Respectables that one seldom uttered harsh opinions unless first sure of one's company. Redford also had been only mildly interested in politics, but at Salem I was astonished at the vigor and unanimity with which men were Whigs. The Liberty Song seemed veritably in the air. I speedily changed one of mother's guineas for a Locke's *Treatise on Government*, burned out a big candle reading about a subject which had suddenly become more fascinating than the adventures of *Perigrine Pickle*, and the next day I astonished mild Mr. Truswell with a remarkably cogent argument in favor of the sovereignty of the people. I was even preparing a letter on "Ministerial Usurpations," to be signed "Valerius Publicola" and inflicted upon the *Essex Gazette*, when my sojourn in Salem terminated under circumstances now to be rehearsed.

I had been wandering along Derby Street, somewhere near the lane to the old many-gabled Turner house, when I espied a red coat ahead of me. King's uniforms were scarce in Salem, and not always properly welcomed, but I thought I recognized the fit of that belt and gaiters. My pace quickened; I knew I was right, and next it was "Hullo there, Herbert," and lo! I was gripping the hand of the dear fellow himself. Dunmore had arrived the day before and had lodged at the Sun Tavern. He was a lieutenant now, he proudly informed me, high in the graces of General Gage at New York, and had come up by water to Salem to confer about certain victualing contracts with famous "King" Hooper—the Tory magnate of Danvers.

My own explanation of my presence in Salem was less satisfactory, but Herbert wept with laughter when I told of poor Prindle's collegiate demise, and as for me he comforted, "Don't groan over flea-bites; hear now how *my* brother was sent up from Trinity." So we had a very happy day together, wandering out upon the willow-clothed Point, with its sea views toward Cape Ann, Great and Little Misery Islands and the rocky headlands of Marblehead, and talking on one congenial thing after another as long parted comrades will. Dunmore had just had a letter from Peggy, "a very nice letter indeed"; and he was trying to persuade himself that somehow they could manage to be married before long. I was trying to encourage him, when suddenly a tall vessel that had been standing into the harbor yawed a little, showing the tier of guns of a brig of war. Herbert shrugged his shoulders, "The *Comet* and your dear Captain Prothero, I'll be bound! I knew she was on these coasts."

"Her cruise has been down Isle of Shoals and Cape Elizabeth way, I've heard," I answered him, "and the coasters all curse at his officious hailings and searchings. But I think this is some other King's ship."

"I know the *Comet*," he replied confidently, "she didn't ride within biscuit toss of Boston Castle while I was there, that I should miss the swing of every yard of her."

As I gazed at that smart ship coming in past the little battery, with her spars jauntily squared, the white foam at her bow and the bosun whistles sending the men aloft to furl, instinctively I knew that her coming brought us no good. I was not so much troubled for myself as for Herbert, and I took measures on the spot: "You are staying at the Sun," I began; "I'll find you lodgings, Mrs. Truswell will help me."

"The Sun's a very clean tavern," he replied wonderingly, "why should I change?"

"Because Prothero is sure to go to the Sun, all naval men do. I feel it in my bones that my friends better not meet him."

Dunmore slapped his lieutenant's coat proudly and leaned his head ever, gazing at his epaulet, "Dear fellow," he cried; "do you conceive I can hold a commission and fear to meet that bullying rotter in a coffee room? *I* did not fling him into the gutter. Since he refuses to fight with you and you have thrashed him, there's an end on't."

Thus we parted under promise to meet before noon the next day. I saw the *Comet* anchor in the inner harbor and a couple of boats come off, but I did not meet the trig figure of Prothero leaping upon the wharf, therefore I dismissed the matter and sat up late pummeling away on my letter to prove that "a judiciary paid by the King and removable at the royal pleasure would become the corner-stone to the House of Tyranny." The next morning I was down in the Truswell garden sprawled out on the bench and deep in the Wars of Hannibal, when the gate clicked and there was Herbert. My exclamation of delight was cut short when I saw the pallor of his face.

"For heaven's sake!" cried I, "what has happened?"

"You were right," he commenced, with a sorry attempt to smile, "I should not have been at the Sun. I met Prothero. We quarreled. Now I am in a bitter scrape, and I fear much lest I have pulled you in after me."

He thrust a paper in my hand: *"Captain Prothero's compliments to Lieutenant Dunmore, and will he have the goodness to name his second to confer with the bearer, Lieutenant McVitie, in order to arrange for a mutual meeting according to the practice of both services?"*

"There was nobody else I knew in Salem," lamented Herbert, "stranger here, no garrison—and so I have named you. McVitie will meet you at the Ship Tavern at two o'clock to arrange details as per custom."

If the ground had flown up and struck me I would have been less astonished. Nevertheless I pulled myself together, demanded causes and details, and then my heart burned.

Prothero with a junior officer had stumbled on Dunmore in the tap-room. There had been no Salem gentlemen present, otherwise the dialogue might have been somewhat different. Prothero had begun by hoping that Dunmore along with his promotion had shed some of his d—— partiality for mohair company and Sam Adams' principles. Herbert had intimated that he did not conceive that wearing the royal uniform obliged him to applaud all the mad policies of Lord North, Earl Sackville and Lord Germain. The captain had rejoined that all intelligent men knew that somebody much more exalted than those three noblemen was actually directing the treatment of colonies, and that loyal officers had better choose their language. Herbert had begged the captain not to let his gracious Majesty intrude into their discussion. Prothero had thereupon informed the lieutenant that he had assuredly formed his notions and his arguments by consorting with "that Gilman mountebank" (my humble self) and he marveled that a British gentleman should degrade himself to the point of an intimacy with the son of a Yankee ranter. After that Dunmore's account became confused. He did not quite remember his own words or actions. The one sure thing was that Prothero had parted thundering, "You shall hear from this!"— And so poor Herbert had.

The next six hours passed in a manner of lurid dream. If only Herbert had been involved in any quarrel not of my own innocent making! Whatever may have been lax New

York and hot Virginian usage, duels were not common in Massachusetts and a drastic statute of the province punished them. I knew of course what was the practice in the royal army and navy; nevertheless I used every conceivable argument to convince Dunmore that he was not obligated to take up Prothero's challenge, but always came back against the answer, "If I do not fight, I must throw up my commission and slink home to England branded as a poltroon." And as for declining to act as his second, I knew that he was not personally acquainted with another soul in Salem, and that my refusal, considering the cause of the incident, would have shattered our friendship. Even my Puritan conscience could not demand a price like that.

So with my heart rising in my throat I went to the Ship, as a kind of neutral ground near the waterfront, and met Lieutenant McVitie. He was a lank, raw-boned Scotchman in naval uniform, Prothero's second on the brig. He bowed very low when we met in the tap-room, strode over to the bar, ordered two half-pints of sack, lighted his pipe deliberately with the pipe tongs dangling near the smouldering fireplace, then motioned me to be seated at one of the little tables. It was all as calm and businesslike as if Uncle Peleg had invited a customer to discuss a cargo of shingles.

"A-weel, Mister Gilman," he began candidly, "we'll nae talk politics, otherwise ye may find me echoing Dr. Johnson's words that the Colonials are 'a race of convicts that ought to be thankful for anything we allow them short of hanging.' But since Lieutenant Dunmore has had the astonishing taste to think otherwise we'll drop a' that.—You have na experience in affairs of honor, sir?"

I confessed that this was the case, "Then, sir, leave all in my hands. Andrew McVitie's a gintleman, sir, a gintleman, and your principal can be shot as doucely and discreetly by my arranging as if he were my own friend. It will be pistols of course? I have a very good case left me by my third cousin by marriage, a McDugall who went out in the Forty-five."

After that we conversed with reasonable amiability, I becoming convinced that the sailor, after his lights, was honestly determined to afford fair play. He deplored the "unfortunate prejudice" in our colony against "little affairs with small arms," but I convinced him that if a duel was unavoidable, a certain abandoned ship yard going down to the Point was a very proper place. The neighborhood was so accustomed to the shooting of plover and sand-peeps, that the noise of firearms would not prove alarming, and otherwise we need not fear molestation. I went back to the Sun, found Herbert and gave him the tidings. He was to fight at six o'clock: "A vera nice pistol fight indeed," the North Briton had asserted.

Proffering some miserable excuse for absence at the Truswells' I dined with my friend at the Sun. He was very white and could not talk steadily. After all he was hardly yet a man except in his fine inches, and if neither he nor I expressed what was in our minds it was because we both thought the same thing—that Prothero had a reputation as to trigger-skill through the squadron and was said lately to have "killed his man" while on the Florida station. Dunmore had barely a modest experience with pistols—so it was crowns to farthings that the duel could have only one ending.

The whole iniquity of the thing took hold of me. I knew that my plain duty as a son of my father and a freeman of Massachusetts was to walk straight over to the Town House, denounce the whole proceeding to the selectmen, and have both of the would-be duelists put under heavy bonds to keep the peace. Why didn't I? Why have thousands of finer young men than I acquiesced in that which they knew to be horridly wrong?—Because some "good friend" required them?

As the hours wore on Herbert shut himself in his room, but presently emerged with two carefully wafered letters; one to "Lady Mary Dunmore," and one to a "Miss Margaret Whitehead." He put them in my hand, saying with a sorry attempt at nonchalance, "You will give these back to me to-night—unless something, something goes amiss."

That accursed afternoon faded at last. Herbert was paler than ever, but he had summoned up that strength which clean lads have within them, and his hand was steady and his eye had a cool look that gave me a little comfort. I knew Prothero would not deal with a helpless victim. We went out of the tavern and tried to wander casually past the spacious doorways of Essex Street, as if a King's officer and a colonial friend were out for a leisurely stroll on a perfect evening. As we got away from the houses Dunmore began to hum a song. I knew the lines were composed by Wolfe as he waited for his desperate chance before Quebec!

> "Why soldier, why
> Should we be melancholy boys?
> Why, soldier, why
> Whose business is to die!"

We pressed on; I striving desperately to talk about Prindle's humorous college scrapes, and at the old ship yard, pacing the soft carpeting of the sawdust, and with the healthful odor of the chips all around, we saw McVitie, with Prothero near by leaning against an abandoned piece of keelson. The Scotchman was in his best blue uniform, although Prothero had already stripped to his shirt. As we approached the captain gave me one ugly look, ripped off an oath and muttered: "You're meat for the cat o' nine tails, not for seconding a duel among gentlemen."

His comrade, however, patted him on the back, ordering.

"Na, na, captain! Steady your hand. You're almost groatable. You Southrons can nae carry too mickle usquebaugh." And I saw that Prothero, unlike his opponent, had been drinking more than heavily.

"My principal is ready," I announced, with all the dignity I could command. "Let us conclude our business."

McVitie delightedly took charge. I helped Herbert off with his shirt, and in his behalf inspected the loads of the pistols.

"Ought you not to have brought the surgeon of the brig?" I suggested.

The Scotchman gave a shrug, "The captain would nae have it. He swore that *he* would never need him!"

Then in a kind of daze I knew that McVitie was pacing off the distance between some old ship-frames and saying, "Gintlemen, to your places!" I was handing Herbert one of the pistols, after a last frantic click of the pan to make sure of the priming. He and Prothero were next face to face at fifteen yards, the sailor very red, the soldier very white; both of them holding their long barrels upright. Overhead light summer clouds were sailing, and there was a gentle wind just waving the red birches beyond the timbers. I was giving Herbert my hand and deep "God bless you!" and getting the grip of his left in return. Then McVitie, dangling a fine white handkerchief, was standing out halfway betwixt the combatants but a little to Herbert's right. "Back, Mister Gilman. Now gintlemen? Ready? Yes—Ha!"—Down fluttered the little mass of white: and the crack of two pistols blended together. I heard a ball sing past Herbert, and saw the white splinters leap from a knee piece. Herbert was standing with a smoking pistol and gazing down at it in a kind of dumb wonder. Instantly I was at his side, crying in ecstasy, "Missed you completely! Thank heaven he was so foxed!"

But Dunmore had stiffened up, and stared straight ahead of him, "My God! Look at the captain!"

Prothero had in fact tumbled upon the deep bed of sawdust, and McVitie had run to him. The captain barely stirred, and his shirt was turning red under the left shoulder. The Scotchman bent over him while we waited dumbly through a very tense minute. Then the second looked up with a knowing shake of the head.

"I ken it's the lung. He'll gae out in a few hours. Our boat is at the wharf below, I'll ha' up its crew and take him to the brig. But as for you, sirs: since the unco' laws of this province touch affairs of honor, you'd best look to your safety."

CHAPTER XII

THE "COMET"

FROM the instant I had learned of the challenge at the Sun Tavern to the moment after the two shots had cracked, only one picture had been dancing before my distracted fancy—Herbert lying upon the ground and Prothero grinning over an empty pistol; and now the Ruler of the Universe had ordained otherwise. My first sentiment despite McVitie's horrifying words had been one of complete relief.

This blessed moment, however, endured only a twinkling. I had not helped Dunmore on with his coat before the whole blackness of the new situation dawned. Herbert himself was shaking and trembling as he had not been before the shots sounded. "God pity me!" he was moaning, "I've killed him. Forgive me, Prothero. I never meant that." The fallen officer gave only some gasping unintelligible reply, and McVitie deliberately snapped the pistols back into the case. "Make off!" he commanded. "Ye'll need all your free cable. I'll ha' the boat's crew directly. Perhaps this will na' leak too soon, if I can get the brig out to sea."

Herbert and I hurried thence with fearful glimpses over our shoulders, as if sheriff and constables already were tracking their quarry. Once clear of that accursed ship yard we both paused for breath, then Dunmore protested passionately, "I'll never be happy again. To think that I had to do it! But it was in fair fight, and a meeting such as the army and navy suffer in every garrison and squadron."

"I know that," I groaned, "but we are on Massachusetts

138

soil and under province law. There's but one thing for both of us——"

The lieutenant shook his head vehemently; "You are blameless before heaven and man. Oh! for my confounded temper. I must fly, but you can get out easily. No one has seen us. Come what may, McVitie and I will never name you. Leave me and go quietly to the Truswells."

Herbert's injunction did me good. I left off shaking and simply blazed up with anger. "Now in God's name," I vowed, "do not insult our friendship by dreaming that I quit you 'til this thing is through. Come woe, come gallows, we'll face this out together."

"Then we must fly," said Dunmore at length calmly.

"We must fly," I echoed desperately, "and to-night. Thank heaven Salem's a seaport."

After we had cooled sufficiently to talk with purpose, we saw a man-of-war boat gliding off from an obscure wharf toward the *Comet*. It was reasonable to hope that McVitie for his own ends would give none of his seamen liberty ashore and would weigh anchor as soon as possible. But the death of a naval commander from a bullet wound, even if upon his own ship at sea, was not likely to be long covered up. Clearly our one chance was to seize the respite, decamp from Salem, seek some tolerable hiding place and wait to learn if our storm could possibly blow over. We could not muster up our courage to go boldly along Essex Street, but stole back into the town by devious lanes hardly daring to look in the eye the few children and spooning swains and damsels whom we met—though they seemed blissfully unconcerned about our goings.

Fortunately that morning I had been along the wharves and had some notion of conditions in the harbor. If there had been a West India trader ready I might have here to record a voyage to Belize and Nicaragua, but at least I knew that a coaster to the Penobscot would probably slip down with the favorable evening tide, and she was our best chance. Herbert was still in his uniform, but I whisked him in through the Truswells' garden gate, and thanked Providence that Keturah, the pious family's only "help," had gone to a church lecture along with her master and mistress. Dunmore had providentially paid his reckoning at the Sun that noon, and I left him in my chamber to dress in some of my homespun, and boldly went myself after his mails, the abandonment of which would have put tongues too quickly wagging.

When I returned he was tolerably if not perfectly disguised to pass as a young farmer, and of course I could look that part with little difficulty. Time there barely was for scratching a brief sorrow-laden note to my parents; conjuring them by all that was holy not to believe that I had willingly admixed in anything wrong, and that I would return to Massachusetts as soon as was possible without disgracing them. The paper was thrust in a volume of Rollin—the Truswells would find it sooner or later. Then with two very light bundles we made for the harbor—the rush of events mercifully shielding us from too many agonizing thoughts concerning the "why" and the "whither."

It was still tolerably light along the wharves, and, just as I imagined, the good sloop *Teal* was almost ready to cast off her moorings near the Becket yards. Her master, a deep throated Captain Nowell, was a little nonplussed when I said we wanted passage for the new lumbering port of Bangor. The look of neither of us was that of a timberman, but Dunmore (who luckily was reasonably in funds) clinked his wallet and the bargain was soon made: we could bunk in the forward cuddy along with the three hands, and content ourselves with the crew's rations. The last of

the sloop's cargo—tierces and crates of West India goods,
cloths and hardwares, the outfit of a general store, had
been slung aboard; then just as the sunset dimmed out
behind the town, the blocks of the halyards began their
steady creaking; the mainsail went up the mast, the jib
followed; the hawser plashed into the glassy water and
the *Teal* began silently slipping down toward the bar.
Directly ahead of our bow, a score of hands shaking out
her upper canvas, the black bull of the *Comet* was also
gliding toward Naugus Head. Herbert gripped my hand
hard and I returned his grasp—we both would have given
everything we could hope to possess to know then what was
the connection of soul with body for the captain now in
the brig's cabin.

I saw the lights toward Naugus Head and Marblehead
coming out one by one as if in answer to the multiplying
stars. The great, steel gray abyss of the evening ocean was
widening before us. It was a delicious summer night,
balmy and clear, with just enough breeze to carry the sloop
onward when the impulse of the tide forsook her. The
small crew paid us little enough attention. Nowell had
gone below, and the lad at the tiller was irresponsibly
attempting a song:

> "I, John Turner,
> Am master and owner,
> Of a high-decked schooner,
> That's bound for Carlina,
> Tara, tara, tara." . . .

Then finally, when I saw behind me the receding lanterns
of Salem gleaming, longer, longer over the darkening waters,
and with one surge it was borne to me that only three
weeks since I had been an honored student at a noble college, a credit to friends and with honest hopes before me,
there is no shame in saying that my cheeks were wet with

tears. And I think that Dunmore, overwhelmed by like
thoughts, proved himself no better stoic.

Our night was wretched enough. As the *Teal* got past
the Misery Isles and fairly took the Atlantic swells although
no storm arose both Herbert and I became somewhat seasick. The cuddy of the sloop was dirty and stifling, in no
respect improved by the fetid smell of bilge water; the two
bunks assigned us were seemingly fashioned of granite and
nails. As I lay thus tossing, my thoughts were not lightened by the keenly remembered story of the famous Woodbridge and Phillips duel which had outraged Boston some
forty years back. How these two scions of great and godly
families had brawled in a tavern; how they had fought with
swords on Boston Common; how Woodbridge had been run
through the body and how Phillips had barely escaped on
board a man-of-war and got to sea, thanks to the efforts of
his mighty kinsmen, the Faneuils—all made a very horrid
story. Also how later the stern province law against the
ling had been enacted; the slayer to perish as a murderer;
the slain to be denied Christian burial and interred near the
site of the gallows; the participants in non-mortal duels,
each to sit one hour on the gallows with a rope about his
neck and then to be imprisoned one year without bail. My
legal lore did not extend to the fate of "seconds," but sur-
mises were gloomy. Far back in Governor Phipp's day there
had been a remote Fifield who had been hanged. The family
still spoke of the event with a shuddering whisper.

As morning broke the wind had stiffened. The *Teal* we
knew was running northeasterly upon a fairly steady keel,
and probably was working well out beyond Cape Ann; we
were just preparing to rise and test the offerings of the
smoking little galley, when a ship's gun sounded suddenly
and I heard Nowell, then standing aft, give out a curse:

"A thousand fathoms of damnation to that *Agile*. Can't that blind buzzard see I'm a lawful coaster? Hold your course, boy."

But after an instant a second gun went booming, and Nowell's lips spat out a louder oath. "There goes the shot across our bows. Can't be helped—fiends strike him! Up into the wind, fellow, and let him search us as he will."

The second gun had naturally hastened Dunmore and myself upon the deck. For a moment we actually dreaded lest the province sloop with a sheriff's party had been chasing us, but a glance was reassuring. A smart schooner with four light guns threatening through her starboard bulwarks was almost aboard us; and at her main peak whipped the cross of St. George. Nowell openly shook his fist toward the knot of seamen busy around the falls of a quarter-boat.

"Tyrannous lubber, that Crag. Almost the scoundrel that's his chief Prothero. Overhauling every harmless sloop upon the coast! Can't he tell a cock-boat from a whaler?"

"Is this schooner under Captain Prothero's orders?" Dunmore asked.

"She is—blast her. Prothero and the *Comet* are high admiral and three-decker of the revenue craft in these waters; Crag of the *Agile* is his chief bully. We've got to let 'em aboard, the dog-faces. I've neither tea nor madeira —that's what they smell for. But I'll lose half a day to Cape Elizabeth if I miss this breeze."

The schooner went up into the wind gracefully, with her booms creaking and her sails flapping. The boat rattled down from the davits and in a trice an officer followed by four armed seamen went swinging up the side to the narrow deck of the sloop. Crag manifestly was a square-shouldered, rum-and-water seadog, who had risen from the forecastle to the command of the smallest class of King's ship. Every second word was garnished with unprintable oaths.

Nowell's display of papers, and his protest that he had cleared the Salem custom house only the night before, might as wisely have been addressed to the capstan. In a moment the *Teal* was in confusion, boxes and crates were ripped open, parcels of groceries strewn upon the deck, heavy tierces dragged up from the hold. The search, however, produced nothing but blasphemy and discomfiture. The officer might have returned to his boat with a surly, "You can go—this time," had he not detected a premature grin upon the weatherbeaten countenance of Nowell. Crag shot his eyes ominously toward the three hands of the sloop. "No contraband in sight, master," he announced, "tho' my dooty *should* be to search those bottom hogsheads. But I'll trouble you for two of your crew."

Nowell matched oath with oath. "What y'er saying? This big sloop can't make the Penobscot with only one hand, and even *you* know it."

"Captain Prothero's orders," leered Crag. "Two of his foremast men deserted from the *Comet* when she lay at Portsmouth last week, and I'm to pick up two likely lads in the high seas to replace 'em."

Here followed another broadside of nautical profanity; Nowell furiously threatening the man-of-war's man with every temporal and infernal penalty if he deprived him of the crew necessary for completion of his voyage, and citing with ferocious emphasis the promise given by the naval authorities a few years earlier after the affair of the *Romney*, "no one shall be pressed belonging to the province, or employed in the coastwise trade of the Colonies." Crag was countering with a picturesque villification of "sea lawyers," when his eye lit on Herbert and myself standing silently by the cabin. "Nine pounders and trunions, what-'ave we got here? Are these hulking lads part of your crew, master?"

Nowell shrugged his shoulders. "They came aboard just before we cast off. Said they were bound for lumbering."

"Not of your crew? Then *they* won't disable your slimy hooker if they're called to serve the King. Well—my tall lubbers, you'll hardly make Penobscot. Get your dunnage bags and follow." Herbert glanced at me, and I did the talking—putting forth my best Yankee drawl. I had heard plenty about naval press gangs, and the affairs off the coast had been common talk in Boston. Sufficient therefore was then said, if not done, for the honor of Massachusetts and the legal rights of her citizens, but when I saw Crag's big hands twitching dangerously, and that Nowell would never push the tiller to save two unknown passengers so long as his own crew was left intact, I requested the right for a word with my companion: "What shall we do? They are five to two besides help from the schooner. We are to serve not on the *Agile* but the *Comet*."

Herbert puffed through his teeth: "If truly the *Comet*, the exchange can at worst be an even one. McVitie commands her now. He's at bottom a gentleman, if raw Scotch. For his own comfort he'll treat us fairly.—So we'd better take the chance with what grace we may."

"You have the force with you, sir," spoke I to Crag with mingled respect and bravado. "You and Captain Prothero, your chief, will find in proper time what it is to impress Reuben Ashton and his cousin Jehu Somers, law-abiding farmers of Newbury. I call you as legal witness Captain Nowell, that we are unlawfully and contrary to the admiral's express promise kidnapped within sight of the coast."

"Hold your jaw and be damned to you," roared Crag. "Step lively or taste a rope's end."—And so with what dignity Dunmore and I could command, we found ourselves going down the side into that bobbing quarter-boat.

. . . Our treatment on the *Agile* if rough was not brutal. We were stowed in the small forecastle in such filthy bunks that I was reminded of how one of my father's clerical friends had expounded the saying of St. Paul, "I have fought with beasts at Ephesus" as meaning that the good apostle had perforce to pass the night at a very foul tavern. Our food averaged not much better, but we were both young and healthy and suffered only in spirit. Since our stay on the *Agile* was to be short no attempt was made to give us naval clothing or put us to any duties.

The *Comet*, however, was nowhere on the horizon; for several days we continued on the schooner, gradually acquiring our sea-legs, and becoming not too seasick as she beat to and fro between Cape Ann and Cape Elizabeth, usually with the land just visible upon the horizon, chasing and overhauling one coaster after another. A brief witnessing of the process taught Dunmore as well as myself the oppressive folly of that clause in the Navigation Act which gave officers of the class of Crag power "to stop, examine, and if suspicious, seize" any merchantman along the shores of the colony possibly smuggling tea, wines or other "enumerated articles," with the perilous incentive of a great reward to the captor for every condemned cargo.

At the end of four days of zealous effort Crag had gained nothing but the anathemas of twenty skippers, trumpeted over their taffrails, as he pulled away after breaking up and half ruining their cargoes. He had, however, gained certain information—the patrol on the nearer coasts was becoming so very hot that the tea smuggling was being driven more and more to eastward. Indeed it was rumored to be centering near the mouth of the Kennebec, and the notorious Remember Watchhorn, reputed leader of the lawless, was alleged to have boasted in a Wiscasset tavern,

"They'll drink only Holland tea next year from Falmouth to New Haven."

On the sixth day after the duel, at length the *Comet* hove in sight. She was a fine spectacle with her heavy yards, her shining black hull, yellow port lids, vivid red upper works, and the protruding battery of twelve pounders. The two vessels signaled, hove to at easy distance and we saw Crag respectfully rowing aboard his chief, then being received by a midshipman at the gangway. Presently also we beheld McVitie pacing the brig's quarterdeck, and next the boat came back with orders for "Ashton and Somers to come on board the *Comet* and report." With our hearts à-thumping we went in the boat; were marshaled past a few curious tars and marines, were ordered up the gangway to the quarterdeck and came face to face with three officers, Crag, McVitie—and, pale and limp, yet clothed in unmistakable flesh and blood, Bernard Prothero!

The captain's face was ghastly and he was supporting himself by leaning on a gun carriage, but he was well able to cast an appraising glance upon the two "pressed landsmen" whom the grinning Crag was turning over for his complement. The whole thing was so unforewarned that Dunmore and I stood blinking like two dumb fools. Crag, however, having already finished his business and received his orders, promptly saluted (a little nonplussed perhaps that he was not asked down for a glass in the cabin) and descended toward his boat, with only the very perfunctory farewells of his superior officers. The instant he was beyond hearing, McVitie, first to recover wits, exploded with "The devil!—'Ashton and Somers!' Of all daft daffins!"

Herbert by this time drew himself together with his proudest military salute: "I thank God, Captain Prothero, to see you alive and recovering. A load has quitted my mind. Of course our quarrel was not mortal. We have exchanged shots like gentlemen, and so the affair is ended."

Prothero pulled a very wry face: "And I have been well paid out for touching a bottle when I had such business in hand. The surgeon says you missed my lung by a hair's breadth. This is my first day on deck."

"I sairly regret I over-alarmed you gintlemen," spoke McVitie. "The captain was bowled over quite as much by the usquebaugh as by the bullet. But a's weel that ends weel. Now just keep this little matter to our four selves, and no thrapples will be wrang for ony of us. I ken now how the wind blew on the *Agile*.—Of course you'll have to enjoy our wardroom hospitality for a bit until we make some bonny haven."

Prothero spat over the side: "Lieutenant Dunmore is welcome to our port and sherry. Of course that large-boned provincial who calls himself 'Ashton' must sling his hammock forward, report to the master's mate for duty, and be paid off when the crew is released."

Only my best angel saved me from felling Prothero that instant on the quarterdeck and perhaps winning the penalty from which Watchhorn was so barely delivered, but I had no need of knotted fists or words; Herbert's eyes became terrible and McVitie flushed to the roots of his sandy hair.

"This is a monstrous jest, unworthy of your service, Captain Prothero," blazed Dunmore, "my friend is here because you challenged me to a duel. His powerful family you know. Imbecile as I conceive the policy of ministers to be, I understand well enough that they do not wish to goad the Colonials to fury by countenancing an act like this."

"It would be a sair act, Captain," remonstrated McVitie. "Being myself the other second I feel my own honor touched. The callant showed muckle delicacy in a' the affair. You dinna mean it."

"He can go forward," returned Prothero with a hard expression.

But Herbert took two steps nearer. "Mr. McVitie is my witness, sir. Crag's act in these waters was lawless, whether we were two Massachusetts farmers or a bearer of the royal commission and his gentleman associate escaping from an affair of honor. I have not seen the performance of the *Agile* under your orders for nothing. You will give the same treatment to me as to my friend, or as the sky is now above us I swear this—my father Sir Edmund will rise in full Parliament and demand of Lord North a full answer as to your conduct on this coast, and as to your conduct touching Mr. Gilman in particular."

If Prothero had not been too weak, he would have leaped at the unflinching soldier. As it was he merely gripped a halyard and cursed unspeakably. McVitie seized his arm: "Dinna be a fool, captain," he enjoined, and his superior at length drew himself up with a smile and a sneer.

"Spare your heroics, Lieutenant Dunmore. I'll call it a jest if so 'twill please you. But no hulking fellow like this Gilman can clutter up my cabin. While he's on the *Comet* he can stay below in the midshipmen's cockpit and not come on deck. Those are your quarters if you prefer *his* company to those of gentlemen, and I counsel you to stow yourselves comfortably. You'll go ashore when we make Newburyport or Falmouth—and since we're cruising now for the Kennebec that won't be right away."

CHAPTER XIII

THE FALMOUTH PACKET

ONCE again to tell my story as it was seen first through another's eyes.

The summer of 1773 had been outwardly a happy one for Emilie. Mr. Ezra Addington had pushed his advances to considerable length, but receiving no decisive encourage-ment, he called less frequently at North Square and talked gloomily of a voyage to San Domingo. He had, however, plenty of successors. "That French puss was a sly minx," genteel wiseacres had it, "and was making up her mind carefully." Therefore Messrs. Hirst and Fernwood still came around to enjoy their weekly hyson and to smile their hopeful smiles.

Mr. Hirst once in fact drew the talk around to how Mlle. Rivoire in Boston like the Prophet Samuel in Bethlehem had been sent by the Lord to review the sons of Jesse and select some one of them for the royal honor. Whereat, to his open confusion, the young lady retorted that in that case a voice had told her of every gentleman in Boston, "The Lord hath not chosen this one"—but perhaps there was still one left elsewhere "who was the youngest and keeping the sheep."

In due time came the horrifying tale of my downfall at Harvard; but be it recorded in history that Mademoiselle so far from professing a sense of pious outrage, went off into such gales of laughter, French, English and Colonial, that Mr. Hirst (that day present) later told old Dr. Byles that "he was even led to doubt whether despite her elegant

150

person and pious ancestry she was completely summoned to
share the burdens of a minister of the Gospel."

Roger Gilman, in any event, was in banishment at Salem,
and Tabitha sent no new invitation to Redford. A great
ministerial conference, wrote she, had exhausted the energy
and the provision stock of her mother and Yetmercy.
Hope's father had become feeble and crochetty; she hated
to leave him. Emilie therefore was very open to a different
invitation. The Huguenot families had seldom lost trace of
one another in their wide dispersion. During the winter
M. Georges had learned that a remote kinsman, Mr. Henry
Dubois, had drifted to the northern harbor-town of Falmouth,* and become a prosperous merchant. A letter had
been followed by a hospitable invitation. The Duboises
knew the Reveres; Mrs. Dubois (herself a good Yankee)
"could never understand it if the Rivoires did not come."

Partly therefore to silence importunity, partly to clasp
the hands of even distant kin, Georges Rivoire consented to
the visit. He and his granddaughter could go up by land
on the new stages running to Portsmouth, and thence hire a
chaise on to Falmouth. Preparations had been nearly finished, when in came a letter from St. Kitts that a large
cargo of molasses had just been consigned to M. Rivoire.
He must await it. The expedition to Falmouth seemed
knocked into a cocked hat.

But could not Mlle. Emilie go alone? A Mrs. Dorcas
Kenniston rose above the horizon. She had met Emilie
through the Peleg Fifields. Her husband was a man of
substance in Falmouth. She had been visiting in Boston.
"The Duboises were going to be *so* disappointed!" What
was easier than for Emilie to be convoyed to Falmouth
under Mrs. Kenniston's matronly protection? Her grandfather could join her later.

* Renamed "Portland" immediately after the Revolution.

To this suggestion Mademoiselle Rivoire said a ready "Amen!" Perhaps she was growing a bit weary of drums and routs and picnics and turtle suppers and tea drinking. Boston after all was not the whole of that "America," which filled so great a place in her letters. Besides, the journey would require barely a night. The Kennistons were heavily interested in the Falmouth packet, a solid ketch, making the trip weekly. It would be safer and swifter than the coaches. The thing was settled; the *grand-père* had consented; Berthe had duly wept but had promised to keep the house on North Square while her mignonne had a few weeks' pleasure. The packet was to sail on an afternoon, and in the morning Emilie was fain to revisit Cornhill, avowedly to plunder Henry Knox's shop of some such volume as *The Renowned History of Goody Two Shoes* to bear to the young Duboises, but also, I am told, to drop in at the post office upon that high street and ask Mr. Hubbard, the postmaster, for letters—"from France or the West Indies?—Or was there possibly one from no further than Salem?"

The post office rewarded her with nothing, but just as Henry Knox was praising the educational virtues of *Mrs. Winslow's Collection of Moral Tales,* he stared to see Mademoiselle quit him abruptly, and dart under a cart horse's nose directly across the street. Through the open door Emilie had seen the compact, sinewy figure of Yetmercy Tudd.

Was Yetmercy glad to set eyes on Emilie? Her countenance beamed with effulgence.—What had brought her to Boston? The marriage of a cousin who would not take 'no' for an answer.—How were all the dear people at Redford? Yetmercy ceased her beaming; "Oh! Lord o' massy, Miss Emilie! And haven't you heard the news? Dr. Gilman and Mrs. Sabra are all broke up over Roger. You know he's gone from Salem. Clean disappeared. And there's a most awful story working round; and then they've found a note that he left his mother——"

By this time Yetmercy was being marshaled into the little office of the bookstore and Henry Knox, forsaking all customers, was looking almost as distracted as was Mademoiselle.—The good woman at length peddled out all the news or rather the rumors that had been sent by Mr. Truswell to Redford. Roger was missing. A young officer, his friend, lodging at the Sun had suddenly disappeared. Roger's conduct the day before he vanished now seemed strange and unaccountable. A hired lad about the tavern tap-room had overheard a very peculiar altercation between an army lieutenant and a naval officer. Two wretched children had seen two naval officers enter an abandoned ship yard, and open a case of pistols: later they had heard two shots very close together. The *Comet* had next left port very suddenly, although her bosun, when he earlier came ashore, had declared that she would remain at Salem for some days. Finally Roger's letter had been discovered.

That was all which Yetmercy could supply, except the vaguest gossip. But it was distressing enough, and when she mentioned the *Comet*, Emilie demanded almost passionately, "Are you sure that was the name of the ship?"

"Certain sure. It's one of the few things there ain't no doubt about."

Mademoiselle's face was so bloodless that Knox made haste to inquire something about "A cup of water? Or just a swallow of Jamaica rather?"

He was waved aside, "No, it was only the heat."——

But Yetmercy looked upon her, marveling, "Why, miss, you're white as a sheet!—The sun don't do that." Then of a sudden she almost crushed the younger woman's hand in her own strong grasp. "Oh, Lordy, where have been

my wits?" Whereupon she put her indescribably homely
face close to Emilie's; next spoke in a whisper Knox could
not hear—"He don't scrub as he ought to Saturday nights,
but he's good and clean inside. *No gal who took up with a
Gilman ever was sorry.*"

By this time, however, Emilie was so red again that Knox
was entirely convinced it was the heat. The young lady
gathered up her ruffles, made many apologies for interrupting him at the counter, and assured herself that Yetmercy
had told her everything. There seemed nothing to be done.
No legal charge had been lodged against Roger at Salem,
he had merely disappeared and his mother of course was
nigh frantic. Emilie could do nothing either to clear up
the mystery or to console. She could simply put Yetmercy
under bonds to convey the first new tidings to Hope Fifield,
and by a hurried call upon that loyal gossip make sure that
a letter was started to Falmouth as soon as there was anything to write. Then there were bandboxes to close, last
counsels to give Berthe, last embraces to give the *grand-père*,
and the hackney coach, already a familiar sight in Boston,
was lumbering over the Ann Street cobbles to Wentworth's
Wharf where lay the Falmouth packet.

The packet, the stout ketch *Annabel Swan*, Silas Hodgdon master, seemed loaded to the gunwales with boxes, barrels, coops of poultry, a sad and distracted cow, and many
people of both sexes and all ages. Two returning traders
from the Androscoggin region were debating a deal in bark
and lumber. Two more from Prout's Neck were wrangling
over a transaction in alewives. There were several women
and all of these, except solid and respectable Mrs. Kenniston
and Emilie, seemed accompanied by a perfect retinue of
children who were clambering over the empty returned her-
ring kegs and chasing the vessel's cat. Being merely on her

weekly trip the formalities at the departure of the packet were brief. The light gun boomed; the ropes splashed in the water; the mainsail and the "jigger" on the smaller mizzenmast crept up their length and filled, and the *Annabel Swan* went down the harbor under a comfortable breeze.

The wind held moderately until the luxurious green islands which made Boston harbor a joy to incoming strangers were fading behind, and the long outer horizon, bounded only by the blue skyline, began to open between Long and Deer Islands. Then the breeze perceptibly stiffened and the whitecaps multiplied. Soon the ketch was laboring and creaking. The bark and lumber traders mysteriously vanished from the scene; the alewives traders followed them. The children no longer scampered on the decks. Emilie and her companion most blessedly were more immune to the motion, but, as the wind increased steadily before they were even off Nahant, Mrs. Kenniston (presuming on the fact her husband was part owner of the vessel) made bold to accost Hodgdon with, "I'm afraid it's going to blow big guns. Hadn't you better scud back and lie behind the islands till morning?"

This advice the skipper received with merely decent politeness, asserting, "It was only a capful of wind:" and muttering to his mate that, "She-males held the tiller enough on land, but they needn't try to steer his craft on salt water."

Nevertheless, an hour later Hodgdon himself was beginning to question whether the worthy woman had not counseled wisely after all. The capful of wind was steadily changing into a clear, hard gale from the land. It was impossible to round Nahant in its teeth and fetch back upon Lynn harbor. An attempt to make Marblehead seemed equally futile as the wind rose to a veritable tempest. The mate privately admonished his captain that, "They'd better try for Gloucester or they'd be in for it:" but Gloucester in another hour was as out of the reckoning as Marblehead. The sun went down in a perfectly cloudless sky, and the stars peeped out with crystalline clearness, with the ocean being whipped even more furiously into a tossing mass of foam, and with the *Annabel Swan* being as steadily driven seaward.

Long before twilight Emilie and her companion, to save themselves from the incessant splash and spray of the decks, had taken refuge in the women's cabin, the hatch whereof was at once tightly battened down by the master's orders. The other women and their children had long since been reduced by inner qualms to that point where they hardly cared whether or not the packet parted her seams and descended to the bottom. Mrs. Kenniston at last became too helpless even to squall aloud when an unusually hearty billow flung them. But Emilie (favored as some delicate landsmen unaccountably can be) remained immune, and therefore fearfully conscious of the mounting of the tempest.

The cabin was of course pitch dark, the uproar indescribable. Overhead Hodgdon and his small crew could be heard racing and hauling like demons. Applying a measure which her grandfather had declared very comforting during stormy voyages, she listened intently to catch whether the seamen were still swearing, and repeatedly took courage from the dauntless manner wherein they defied the wind gods.

These objurgations nevertheless grew less frequent, and about midnight she heard the mate's voice rising during a momentary lull, "I'm only a poor sinner, Lord, but I've a pious wife and four little girls in Biddeford, and for their sakes——"

Here a perfect screech through the rigging intervened.

Amid the blast Hodgdon fairly bellowed, "There goes the jib! Bend on another canvas forrard, or we're——"

For the first time in years Emilie Rivoire veritably knew fear. What if never again she was to see the little parlor at North Square; never the *grand-père,* never—someone else? Were those the voices of her parents calling her above the demoniacal howling in the cordage? Emilie Rivoire was the daughter of a gallant stock and a brave woman; but she was very human. The next hours were passed in that awful cabin amid paroxysms of dread.

The *Annabel Swan* fought nevertheless for her life bravely. The waves flung themselves against her bowsprit with the thunder of artillery, but like the mass of well-wrought oak and iron that she was, she hurled them back. Her crew spurred to a mortal energy put forth the resources of Down East mariners. Twice the ketch was nearly stripped of canvas, and almost went off into the trough of the waves where all would have been over in a twinkling; twice by frantic skill a scanty sail was hoisted and the prow brought back toward the galloping seas. The tempest was carrying them to eastward; there was no fear of a lee shore. At last the first bars of light gleamed out upon the horizon above the flying spoondrift. There were signs that the gale was beginning to blow itself out, although the waves still raced high. Hodgdon looked at his racked masts, his broken main boom, his flying cordage and for the first time stared at his mate, a little more calmly: "If she's lived this long, she ought to live it through.—Good Lord, but that was a night!—Now you'd better sound the well."

The mate staggered forward and came back still in a sorry mood: "Some butts forrard must have started. We've made a foot already—and she was pumped dry just before we cast off."

The next hours passed amid calming seas and falling wind, but with the crew and such male passengers as had recovered strength and intelligence striving desperately at the pumps. The ketch had been nearly stripped of canvas; enough sail was now at last made to give her a slow steerage-way and she was put back upon her course; but, as Hodgdon confessed, she had been blown far out to sea, and two days at best it would need before he could hope to see Peaks Island and the fairway into Casco. Meantime the water was barely kept down in the hold: the one boat carried by the packet had been shattered: the least gain of the leak might doom thirty souls.

So the day passed while the *Annabel Swan* crawled now like a bird with broken wing over the increasingly glassy water. Emilie had recovered her courage. She even offered to take her turn at the pumps—a proffer promptly rejected by Hodgdon with a "Lord save us, we hain't yet come to *that;*" and more effectually she aided Mrs. Kenniston rekindle the fire in the galley and prepare food and drink for the famished company. Then, just as the sun was dropping a second time, all gold and glory, into as calm and beautiful an ocean as ever shimmered near New England shores, a glad shout went up from the broken bowsprit—a black hull was in sight and bearing directly toward them. Hodgdon whipped out his little spyglass, and gave a grunt of relief.

"Never, I'd have sworn yesterday, could I have welcomed the sight of that bloody King's ship, but she's welcome now. Prothero may be a heller, but he'll see us through this. It's the *Comet.*"

Thanks to the fading wind, it was long past dark before the man-of-war could come within hailing distance, but the disabled state of the packet had been seen; and the bulwarks were gleaming with friendly battle lanterns, when

no less a personage than McVitie himself sat in the stern
of the first cutter as that craft pulled alongside the ketch.
The Scotchman was in his element as he moved comfortingly
among the weeping women and squalling children, and
ordered his squad of blue jackets to relieve the wearied
men at the pumps; but when he came face to face with
Emilie (he had once attended his chief to North Square)
his long pigtail literally curled upward with amaze.

"Brig o' Sterling, where are my e'en!" Then he bowed
very low with his cap at his breast, "Ah! your bonny leddy-
ship—this is a braw evening for the honest gintlemen of
the *Comet.*"

The plight of the ketch indeed left only one thing in
humanity possible. After more signals to the brig a heavy
pinnace was lowered and came over to the distressed packet.
Hodgdon readily assented to the proposal that all his passengers should be transferred to the man-of-war, while the
carpenters made certain efforts to stop the leak and after
that with the aid of two or three naval seamen he could
probably bring the packet into Falmouth.

When the proposal was broached to Emilie, Mrs. Kenniston attributed to the nervous shock of the storm her friend's
violent reluctance to go upon the *Comet.* "The lieutenant
swears his captain will put his own cabins at our disposal,"
was her loud assurance. "We will have every comfort.
The ketch still makes water very fast. Tempting Providence not to quit her!"

With what grace she possessed, Emilie therefore suffered
herself to be conducted into the pinnace. She was met at
the side-ladder of the brig by Prothero in person, brave in
his best uniform, and with his junior officers, marine guards
and side-boys saluting in the lantern light as if Admiral
Montagu himself were coming aboard.

CHAPTER XIV

WHAT BEFELL AT CAPE NEWAGEN

PROTHERO had lived up to the bare letter of his promise
to me. I had been taken to the midshipmen's cockpit, and
the sentry at the gangway ordered to forbid me the deck.
Herbert had passionately vowed that any treatment
awarded his friend he must consider his own. This self-
banishment from the wardroom, of course, pleased Prothero
and did not greatly trouble McVitie.

The cockpit made one wonder that any lad would serve
four years as midshipman in order to advance to the glories
of naval lieutenant. We were on the orlop deck below the
tier of guns, where a few very tightly screwed deadlights
and a few rush candles alone made darkness visible. The
four midshipmen, quartered in this den, had slung ham-
mocks; but Herbert and I perforce accommodated ourselves
upon the table, whereon were served our meals, and on
which, we were told, the wounded were stretched for ampu-
tation after a battle.

No perfumes of Arabia could have sweetened the odors
arising from the bilge-water swashing in the hold below,
and from the rancid butter and rotten cheese in the purser's
stores close by. Our food was the same as that of the
midshipmen, food which made the *Comet* a perfect school
for profanity, bread walking with weevils, and salt-beef
hard as stones and hardly ever soaked clear of the brine. I
could well believe the men who vowed that the pieces
neighed or brayed when the cook plunged them in his coppers. Fresh vegetables (although we were near the coast)

were so lacking that it was a marvel the whole company
was not down with scurvy. The one thing abundant was
beer, every man on the brig, whatever his station, drawing
his gallon per day; so that many a morning a good part
of the company was unfitted for duty despite constant
warnings with the cat o' nine tails at the gratings.

The midshipmen were a cubbish lot, but left us largely
alone. The weather being fine we saw in fact little of them.
Being thrown much upon ourselves Herbert had ample time
to tell me much about England. A Briton is seldom boastful concerning his own country and my friend now was in a
peculiarly cynical mood. Whatever my earlier readiness to
denounce the King's ministers, hitherto "England" had
summed up a kind of golden world where, barring an unfortunate leaning toward Episcopacy, lords were truly gentlemen and ladies of quality ladies, where peace and order
reigned and British pride was justified by public and private
morality. Now I learned in detail how that Parliament
which handed down our laws was chosen by an unblushing
corruption at so many thousands per seat. Or that while
we could ride from Boston to Albany with a full purse and
never a dread, London streets were infested with foot-pads,
and that every Yorkshire stage coach often paid its tribute
to knights of the road.

I heard likewise of rabblings and mobs; of deans and
bishops who could drink earls under the table or, leading the
chase, be in at the death with the hounds; of King's
ministers who after naming our governors and deciding our
taxes hurried off to their theater boxes with their kept
mistresses beside them. I heard too of gaming on such a
scale that I imagined Herbert was fabling, of noble ladies
who won or lost fortunes in a single night: while such
resorts of fashion as Ranelagh, Vauxhall or Mrs. Cornely's
became for me as sinks of infamy from that day.

Thus we killed time through tedious days. At length came a heavy storm in which we both were miserably sick, and I gathered that the brig was in some danger. Next a clattering upon the deck told how a coaster had been rescued and her passengers taken aboard. We were glad of this, because we believed that his guests would soon force Prothero to make a convenient haven. But the next day we learned that all the passengers had been put on another inbound coaster—except two women.

"Except two women?" asked Herbert twitching his eyebrows. The youngest of the midshipmen, a merry blackeyed rascal named Siddons, but more commonly styled "Boatplug," gave a cunning laugh, "One of them is plump and old enough for my mother, but the other,—Neptune and little fishes, she's a comfort to sore eyes! I think the captain's known her somewhere. Said the craft on which he put the others was not safe for ladies. Keeps 'em on the *Comet* until we make a proper port. I think he's in no hurry for *that*—ha!"

"Captain Prothero is a credit to his Majesty's service," I returned in a tone which brought back only a sagacious wink and bow.

That afternoon to our great comfort the hatch to the gundeck was wide open. I was not allowed to mount the ladder, but the sunlight and air were very welcome, and I could hear much of the chattering in the waist of the brig. The quarterdeck was out of sight but sometimes voices drifted down from it. We caught Prothero's in particular, and once or twice McVitie's, also that of some strange woman, and once (I almost cried "Liars!" to my own ears) a French accent that marvelously resembled that of Emilie Rivoire.

The thing was so improbable, so inexplicable that I did not even tell Herbert, to spare myself the things which one

young man inevitably remarks to another, when the second
seems to have a certain young lady very much upon the
brain.

Then after one more extremely tedious day we heard the
creaking of the blocks furling sail, and next the great splash
of the anchor and racing of the cable through the hawse
holes. Boat-plug coming down for a cap and great coat, I
inquired whether we had made a suitable haven; in which
event Herbert was prepared to go on the quarterdeck and
make formal demand that we both be set ashore. The midshipman only grinned. "We've made a bad anchorage off
one of your cursed rocky headlands; Newagen I heard the
sailing master call it. Damme, if I know what the captain's up to! They say it's tea smugglers, but guineas to
shillings it's for something else. There's a small island off
the cape. Nice solitary place. Oh! the captain is a fine
devil for gallantry." And he popped up the ladder.

As he did so I heard the bosun's whistle and the order
"Captain's gig away:" then, after a short interval the rattle
of the boatfalls and the pull, pull of four oars. The brig
had swung sufficiently upon her mooring so that through
the deadlight a long green clad shore with a small rocky
island nearer at hand, were clearly visible. The breakers
were crumbling on the island. I could see a few weather-
beaten structures, probably summer fishermen's shelters. As
I gazed, directly across the line of vision and within half a
pistol shot sped the gig, her crew bending to their task. In
the stern-sheets was the blue uniform of Prothero, the figure
of some unknown woman, and another—who was indubitably and unmistakably Emilie Rivoire.

My sudden cry brought Dunmore over beside me. The
boat had sped on but not too far for a clear glance. His
lips, as he turned away were almost quivering as my own.

"Holy Power," he exclaimed, "what means that?"

"Herbert," spoke I, "Prothero, by some chance of the devil, has got Emilie upon the brig. I'll break free to help her, or before heaven I'll turn stark mad."

"Keep calm and think clearly:" he enjoined, advice that was assisted by more whistling on the deck, and the command, "Long boat and pinnace away!" Whereupon almost immediately we saw the two largest boats of the *Comet* pulling off crowded with men rattling their muskets and cutlasses, with McVitie at the tiller of one and Dosworth, the other lieutenant, at that of the second. Manifestly some expedition was abroad and we both looked at each other questioning. "You'll serve me best," I declared at length, "if you break this absurd self-imposed captivity of yours and go on deck; find what's happening and who's in command of the brig."

Herbert nodded and mounted the ladder. The marine on duty, a very young and stupid sea-soldier, looked at him hard, but having been only ordered to stop "That province fellow Gilman," let him pass. My friend might have been gone half an hour, when he returned with a very grim look on his face and a chart in his hand.

"Prothero is ashore on the island with his gig's crew and a few others. McVitie and his second have taken a heavy draft of men and rowed west to the mouth of the Kennebec to lie in wait for smugglers. The brig is stripped of more than half her company, and those left on board are becoming beastly drunk, having been denied 'liberty' promised in Salem and their officers wishing now to content them. The command has passed to Nairs, the sailing master, a dirty fellow with a rope of oaths, who in any case is fast getting himself utterly befuddled."

"And what did you learn," I pressed, "about, about *her?*"

Herbert tried desperately to speak lightly: "Nairs was just groggy enough to be talkative. The women came aboard

from the Falmouth packet which was rescued. With Emilie
was a Mrs. Kenniston, I judge a very proper woman. Prothero was very forward in his attentions, but dared not
carry matters too far before Mrs. Kenniston and McVitie.
Now he has taken the women to this Cape Island whence
he swore he could speedily send them to friends on the
mainland; but Nairs let out his suspicions with a leer: 'It'll
be deuced easy now for the captain to *get Mrs. Kenniston
separated* from that Mam'selle Rivoire.' "

"I must get loose," I cried, starting toward the gangway, "I'll wring that drunken sentry's neck."

"Keep your head:" ordered Dunmore, "the worst probably can't come immediately. The brig is here for some
time. McVitie's men took provisions for four days. We
must plan how to get clear, although," he added with his
habitual whistle, "how we two even if at large could take
Miss Rivoire out of the power of Prothero, I'll be shot if
I know."

"We are off the Maine counties," I returned, "within the
province of Massachusetts. Whatever Prothero may do on
the high seas he is now under province law. His detention
of me here is lawless; his detention of Emilie ashore still
more lawless. Let me reach some town, and if I know little
of their lordships in Britain I know somewhat of my own
folk in New England. I see you have a chart."

"Yes," he admitted, "it was lying on the wardroom table.
Fair plunder, I thought you might care to see it."

I was no navigator, but Uncle Peleg's office had been
cumbered with coastwise charts, and I had talked with
many Down East skippers. A brief search put my finger
on Cape Newagen with the little Cape Island beside it.
Five miles to northward along the coves and headlands a
crude tracing indicated a village, Townsend, in the Boothbay township. Townsend I had no more visited than I had

Liverpool, but it could be taken for granted its denizens spoke Yankee English and did not love the King's Revenue.

"I must see that village:" I announced briefly.

"And what then?"

"Trust in the Lord Jehovah and the wits of my countrymen."

Herbert laughed wryly: "A nice affair for an army lieutenant! And after all Nairs may have lied. McVitie would hardly enjoy too dirty an act by his chief."

"McVitie, as he himself would say, is a canny Scot. His honor in the affair of a duel is one thing; coming between his captain and a woman is another. I must get loose."

"It could cost me my commission:" hesitated Dunmore, but then his hand tightened upon my arm. "What's that trifle beside the call of a friend and the need of a lady!—Be patient. It's nearing evening.—I'll reconnoiter again."

.   .   .   .

I have spent many leaden hours; none, however, heavier than those in that stifling cockpit while Herbert pretended to take his ease on the decks above. On war service the *Comet* needed a full hundred men, but on her revenue cruises some seventy sufficed, and of these nearly fifty were either in the boats to the Kennebec or with Prothero upon the islet. The remaining twenty were in that state of indiscipline into which sailors can fall when the bands of authority are relaxed and their competent officers absent. All the midshipmen had joyously obeyed the summons to go with the lieutenants, while Nairs, I was presently told by Dunmore, was lying prostrate on one of the wardroom benches with a bottle beside him.

The nominal command of the brig thus passed to his mate Stevens, who swaggered about the quarterdeck for a little while enjoying his brief honors and bawling ill-obeyed orders, then sat down upon a grating and began casting expectant eyes toward the galley whence came the odors of plum duff. As the darkness increased, Herbert continued upon the deck, carefully observing the lay of the shore and the condition of the brig's boats. The long boat, pinnace and captain's gig were gone; but a quarter-boat and a light dinghy swung from a boom projecting from the gangway. The only other craft, the second quarter-boat, was tightly stowed aboard on her regular davits.

I had given not the slightest trouble during the voyage, never showing my head above the cockpit, and most of the ship's company had probably forgotten my presence. The marine sentry at the gangway had repeatedly quitted his beat to fetch a pannikin of rum and water, and by the time that darkness had fairly settled he was (so far as he had wits left for anything) casting frequent glances toward the forecastle for his relief. We were nautical enough to know that the tide was favoring a boat trying to make shore. It was now or never. Any instant might bring Prothero back on board, therefore Herbert at length went up the ladder boldly.

"Fine night but stupid duty, my man."

"Yes, your Honor:" answered the marine with tipsy gravity.

"Your relief will come immediately. I hate to see a stout lad moping about. There's better drink to be had of the purser. Take this and go forward. I want this bit of the deck to myself."

The marine was almost in a state to see two moons, but he could still see well enough by the rush lantern to know that Herbert was proffering a guinea. That an army lieutenant had not the slightest right to give orders upon a man-of-war was entirely beyond the sentinel's existing state of comprehension.

"You've a soul to be saved," mumbled the rascal with

his best sea compliment. His hand went out, his musket was awkwardly stood against the bulwark, and away he shuffled into the gloom toward the forecastle. The instant he had disappeared, I, who had been waiting upon the second rung of the ladder, shot up noiselessly.

We had both taken off our shoes, and I had pillaged the midshipmen's lockers to the extent of prigging a good knife and a pair of pistols. There were lanterns on the forecastle, and others on the quarterdeck and in the stern cabins, but at first we found ourselves in the black reaches of the brig's waist, stumbling upon the gun carriages and with the dim tracery of the spars and rigging just showing on high against the stars. It took us an instant to get our bearings; however, we found soon the gangway to the boats. A second marine I knew was properly stationed there, and we were prepared for desperate recourses, but the post was luckily vacant. If no seamen, we were at least well-muscled and active, and handed ourselves out along the boom until first I and then Herbert dropped into the dinghy. So far not a sound had betrayed us; the afterpart of the brig was silent as the grave, from the forecastle came the wailing of something like a bag-pipe, while as a counter blast to this profane music somebody in a state of maudlin piety was singing or rather roaring:

> "Ye monsters of the bubbling deep
>   Your Master's praises spout:
> Up from the sands ye codlings leap,
>   And quirk your tails about!"

Right here, however, one of us must needs upset an oar, which fell with a reverberating "bang" loud enough for a blunderbuss. Instantly we heard a "What's that?" followed by "Ho there! What's that noise from the boats?"

Never did I envy the cats who can see in the dark more than I did that instant. The painter of the dinghy it seemed as if we could never find, but at last my knife was through it. Dunmore was just giving us a push when, by an inspiration I felt my hand also on the painter of the big quarter-boat and its last strands had been severed and both craft pushed out beyond the length of a boat-hook before figures came sliding out along the boom.

The tide was running strongly landward. We saw the hull and spars of the *Comet* sliding by above our heads just as one lantern after another went racing toward the stern, while Stevens' voice came thickly. "Stop there or we fire!" But we had slipped fairly clear of the brig and had a saving patch of black water between us, before three musket shots in angry succession spat out from the quarterdeck and sent their balls singing into the low waves. We released the quarter-boat to be carried far upon the tide, and bent ourselves to the oars of the dinghy.

We were not trained rowers but mortal dread is a potent teacher. The water fairly sang around our prow as we sent that dinghy out into the night. On board the receding *Comet* there was an infernal cursing and swearing, a great running to and fro, and a perfect broadside of blasphemy when the quarter-boat was discovered missing as well as the smaller craft. Nairs had evidently recovered his legs. At least we could hear him pouring out a pirate's prayer to Stevens. If he had ordered the second quarter-boat to be cleared away immediately, by a bare chance we might have been overhauled. As it was, the climax of the uproar came with the casting loose of one of the light swivels, and a ball went screeching off at random, the discharge of the gun illuminating the spars of the brig with one lurid flash.

At last, after a precious delay, we heard a fumbling which told that the last boat was being made ready; but by this time we were fairly under the shadow of the land where a heavy boat would ground much sooner than the dinghy. Nairs must have known this; we were not chased.

After the heat and excitement were over Herbert and I rested on our oars, recovered breath and stared at each other in the starlight. We were in a small open boat upon a perfectly strange shore. It was a magnificent summer night with the ocean giving one deep breath after another. We could hear the small waves gently crumbling down the white line of the beach barely visible, and behind this rose a black silhouette of woods. Behind us the lanterns of the *Comet* were still sufficiently near for compelling prudence. At last Herbert dipped his oar again with, "You are admiral here. Where are we headed?"

"Blest if I know!" I rejoined candidly, but then hastened, "See! A light!"

Down the dark coastline at an uncertain distance undoubtedly a light as of some house or camp was flickering with a dim shimmer across the steely water. A bare chance of course existed that here was a landing party from the *Comet*, but this seemed improbable. For some time we pulled in silence, my own thoughts very full of Emilie, until we worked near enough to make out that there were three lights and not one close to the pebbles which apparently gleamed from fires rather than from lanterns. At times they died to mere sparks, then blazed up brightly as if replenished by persons around them. After another quarter hour we were fairly up to the shore; and being now quite accustomed to the darkness could make out the lengths of skiffs drawn up upon the pebbles. Our own oars, however, must have betrayed us, for quite suddenly we heard a voice trumpeting in melodious nasal Yankee, "Douse the fires, you fools!" And instantly the gleams disappeared under dashes from pails of water, while the same voice now went out toward us; "Boat ahoy! What do you here at this hour?"

"Friends," replied I, stopping paddling.

"Friends of whom? If you're from the King's ship learn now that ten muskets cover you."

"We're from the man-of-war," I answered, "but we fear no muskets. We've made off ourselves, and if you are province men——"

"Deserters from the brig, Shrimp," put in another voice; "that boat's too small for a strong party. That explains the gun. Have 'em ashore."

"Come in then, if you ain't afeared to be questioned," pursued the first speaker; and a moment later Dunmore and I having made a very awkward landing on a barely visible sandspit, clambered up the bank, tripping over sumach and blue-berry bushes, and found ourselves (the fires now crackling up again with fresh pine boughs) in the presence of some half score swart-featured, roughly habited men who clustered about us with watchful curiosity. All that I said to them need not be recalled; but later Herbert liked to assert that then I proved forever my right to be a good jury lawyer if not a convicting preacher. When I had finished there was a great clattering of boat-hooks and drawing of sheath-knives, and Shrimpton, the prime speaker, led the way to his own whaleboat, with the vow, "As God Almighty looks from Heaven, this ere's a case for Mem Watchhorn."

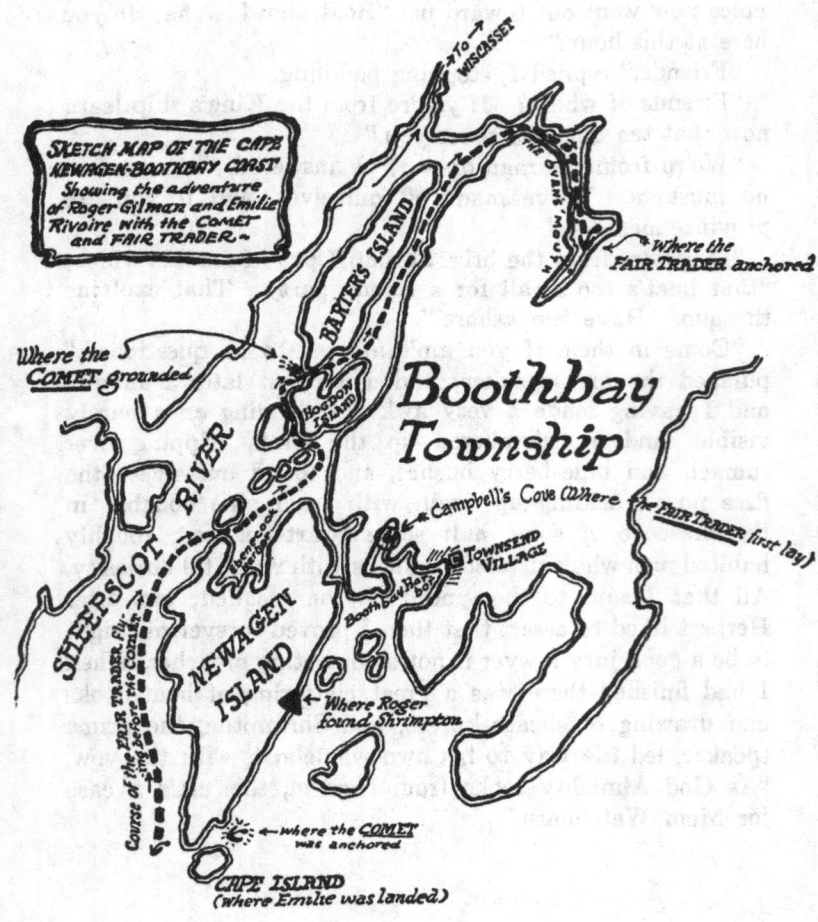

SKETCH MAP OF THE CAPE
NEWAGEN-BOOTHBAY COAST
Showing the adventure
of Roger Gilman and Emilie
Rivoire with the COMET
and FAIR TRADER~

To WISCASSET

THE SHEEPS MOUTH

Where the
FAIR TRADER anchored

Where the
COMET grounded

BAXTER'S ISLAND

Hodgdon Island

Boothbay
Township

SHEEPSCOT RIVER

Campbell's Cove (Where the FAIR TRADER first lay)

TOWNSEND VILLAGE

Jeremisquam

Boothbay Bar

Course of the FAIR TRADER flying before the COMET

NEWAGEN
ISLAND

Where Roger
found Shrimpton

where the COMET
was anchored

CAPE ISLAND
(where Emilie was landed)

CHAPTER XV

REMEMBER Watchhorn, once of Marblehead, may have
been an abject and desperate creature enough when he stood
in the cart beneath Boston gallows; but it was as a gallant
captain of his fate that I met him, after Shrimpton's whaleboat had darted at red dawn into an extraordinarily
sequestered cove, and alongside of a rakish and undoubtedly
speedy small schooner.

The master of the *Fair Trader* was of modest height,
but one glance at those shoulders and the knots of his muscles told how their owner could fell an ox. He was dark
enough for a Spaniard, his great breast was open and hairy,
and his long arms were adorned with elaborate tattooing.
The week's growth of black beard which adorned his chin
was all the more startling because of a rusty brownish red
wig, assumed, so he averred with perfect gravity (after we
became better acquainted), "because all his own hair had
been blown out by the roots during an extra violent gale
off Hatteras." His features were rough as a gull's, his steel
blue eye went straight through you; as for his dress it was
a marvelous combination of tinsel and sordidness. A heavy
ring adorned one finger, and a second ring gleamed from his
left ear. I did not envy Prothero with such an enemy.

Introduced by Shrimpton I told my story with what
power I might, appealing to him "as a New Englander and
a Christian" to help me to the uttermost. In reply he put
me not a few shrewd and searching questions, betraying a
remarkably close knowledge of the Very Respectables,
questions which he excused as needful to protect himself

against "white mice" and "fancy men," otherwise spies and informers. But when I finally claimed Peleg Fifield for my uncle, he smote his great thigh:

"By Jasus born in Ireland (an accustomed stretch toward profanity) we'll run no tea to-night! That Kennebec yarn was sent out to draw the King's boats thither while we raced in the Holland chests from the old cache at Monhegan.—The bohea'll have to keep.—I know that Cape Island and its cabins. Oh! to get that prinked-up devil there under these two hands (the hands clinched decisively), and to think that the Lord should proffer me this chance!"

"Will you set me on to the village, sir," I requested, "and bring me before some magistrate so that I can swear out a warrant?"

Watchhorn almost shook the bulwarks with his laughter. "Warrant, lad? D'ye imagine that blackguard Prothero with his men at hand would give one of our provincial warrants anything but a dose of the cat for the constable? Toll him ashore to the village, why that's another matter, but——"

"The case is urgent—Miss Rivoire——"

"Is your gal, young feller; so don't tack up and down but toss it out. And we must get her off—But you can kill a pole-cat without making the varmint bunk with you. You say the woman with her seemed to be called Kenniston?"

"So we've gathered."

"If she's Dorcas Kenniston, your young lady's with a woman whose eyes can see through a gimlet hole and whose brain can outwit the Old Boy. Husband owns half of Falmouth and her brothers, the Gamages, half of these parts. Them two women won't be pried apart in no hurry. Does Prothero know that you know they two were aboard?"

"I believe not," interposed Dunmore, "I questioned only Nairs about them, and he was too far gone to remember what he said."

"Then," reasoned the smuggler, "when the captain hears you're flown, he'll only think it a nateral escape. His schemes won't alter. Nairs'll be cussed out and threatened, and Stevens very likely'll lose his mate-ship. But for us there's nought to do but to lie quiet till to-night—and then if you can say prayers for success, why say 'em!"

. . . If, however, Watchhorn, his schooner and my very impatient self had to lie quiet all that live-long day, there was a considerable coming and going across the landlocked cove in skiffs and dories. We saw twos and threes of lean, strong-boned coast dwellers come piling over the bulwarks of the *Fair Trader*, some with harpoons, others with fowling-pieces. Meantime Shrimpton and his whaleboat had disappeared, but late in the afternoon he was returning to the Cove, and I heard his report to his chief.

He had skirted the long shore of great Newagen Island until near its southern cape, slipped on the land, beached his boat in charge of her crew and stolen down to the Cape itself. After that it had been a simple matter to find an old skiff hidden under the pines and birches, pull boldly over to the smaller Cape Island, which made a natural breakwater beyond the main promontory, and there trudge about with basket and rake as if for clams. The fishermen's huts had been opened, the *Comet's* cabin steward had placed in them certain furniture from the wardroom of the brig, a fire had been lighted in one of them and to judge by odors a fine meal was cooking.

Under guise of asking "if the gentlemen wanted lobsters" Shrimpton had actually sauntered up to the encampment itself and satisfied himself that Captain Prothero was present with two women, one young, one older. The boat's crew of five for the gig, plus a few other seamen, had come over from the *Comet*, and were loitering about the islet or attempting a game of bowls along the beach. When Shrimpton approached the steward with his offer of lobsters the fellow had at first seemed affable, but at the sound of a strange voice the captain had come running and ordered the intruder in the fiend's name to pack off. Shrimpton had promptly obeyed, but not before he had had a good look at the women; one was undoubtedly Mrs. Kenniston, "and if ever a young gal looked worried, the other leddy there was that gal."

"I always knew Prothero was a rotter," commented Herbert savagely. "I did not think him equal to this. He is close to Townsend. He knows assuredly that Mrs. Kenniston is near to friends. Every law of honor would make him send both women up to the haven. He takes them to this islet guarded only by his own crew. To get Mrs. Kenniston over to the larger island upon some pretext——"

But in mercy he stopped, for he saw the workings of my face.

"Son," said Watchhorn, laying a great hand on my shoulder, "I know what you're thinking. I've been in that rattlesnake's coils myself. But no harm's done yet. If the good Lord can pluck me put of the shadows of Boston gallows, He can give wit and gumption enough to get that young female safe and sound off of Cape Island. Now trust the Almighty, trust the *Fair Trader* and trust Mem!" And he smote the mighty chest of the third member of his Trinity.

As the sun went down the sails crept up the tapering masts of the schooner, and presently there was a clank, clank of the bars around her small capstan. Watchhorn had perhaps twenty men aboard, who had stowed themselves into the crevices and cabin of the *Fair Trader*. Any craft hailing her, would have concluded she carried only her skipper and a very small crew. In absolute silence the tea smuggler slipped out of the landlocked basin which the natives styled Campbell's Cove, around a juniper crowned promontory and then headed, not southward along the far stretching wooded coast of Newagen Island,* but at first into a narrow, twisting waterway where the channel some-times ran so close to the rocks and pines that one might almost have leaped ashore from the gliding deck. Dis-tracted as I was, I could but admire the easy skill with which Watchhorn and Shrimpton, controlling tiller and sails, sent the smuggler along past craggy headland after head-land, where every moment I expected to hear the ledges grinding against the keel.

It was now perfectly dark. By the time this Gut had been threaded the shores were sinking into a black mass of pines barely outlined against the dim horizon. There was a cold opalescent glint from the water around the prow. Presently we knew that the shores were no longer pressing so closely. Like a ghost the *Fair Trader* was sliding beside small islands; next the helm was swung abruptly, and again we were greeted by the clear breath of the open sea. We were now, informed Watchhorn, in the lowest reaches of the Sheepscot, and were seeking by the outside western chan-nel the outermost tip of Newagen.

The men crept up on deck but continued very silent. Once or twice a pipe was lighted but was instantly extin-guished by a word hurled by the watchful skipper. Once an uneasy fisherman was overheard asking his mate to "slip him that flask of kill-devil," a peculiarly atrocious form of rum; which brought on him a sudden blow from Watchhorn that nearly shattered his jaw, and the warning

* The maps of a later age name this island "Southport." (Editor.)

"the first man whose breath gives a whiff is battened in the hold 'til morning."

In this way, the air being extremely light and our topsails being lowered after we had got into open water, we crawled along until approaching midnight when a very small inlet was abeam, and the schooner was cautiously hove-to and allowed to drift in the tide while Shrimpton gave a deep but guarded "loon's call" twice. After a little, a skiff was seen gliding off from the islet, and in almost pitchy blackness some scout came aboard us.

"You've the lay o' the land, Si Greenleaf?" queried Watchhorn, leaning in the dark against his main boom.

"Aye, skipper, and a very rum lay it is too."

"How's that?"

"Somebody's split or that Scot lieutenant's got too wise. The long boat and pinnace are back from the Kennebec. The brig has most of her people aboard and seems ready to trip anchor."

"I swan," avowed Watchhorn, with a start, "—not in my reckoning. But the women?"

"They were there ashore this evening. But d'ye know, Cap'n, I slipped on Cape Island myself. It was dark, but I knew every bush like my mother's kitchen. Got up close to the cabins; a great howdy do was in progress; two women talking angrily and very fast; one of them—I think Mrs. Kenniston—was just exploding, 'You vowed you'd send us to Townsend to-day, Captain Prothero; where are your promises?' Then a man's voice seemed saying something smooth and mollifying. I couldn't get his answer. Presently this man went out of the cabin and down to the sand-spit where lay one or two of the brig's boats. I had sneaked off my shoes and stole along readily. Here he called another officer—'Lieutenant Dosworth' he named him —ordered him to get a cutter ready; then I got it clearly:

'I'll bring the two women to the shore. You hand that blowy
Mrs. Kenniston aboard and have all ready. Then when I
whistle pull away like mad—leave *me* to talk with the
other.' 'And what am I to do with Mrs. K., Captain?' asks
the lieutenant. 'Do? Drop her to feed the dog-fish for
aught I care; but you better dump her on the beach a
couple of miles further up the shore. She'll find some farmhouse before noon to-morrow.' 'This is coarse work, Captain Prothero,' says Dosworth, 'McVitie washes his hands
of it, and if known by Admiral Montagu'—'Damme, Lieutenant,' says the captain, 'don't get a queasy stomach!
Here's my word my whole aim's honorable; I'll merely compass it so that to-morrow morning a certain lady'll be proud
and happy to get the chance to change her name to Mrs.
Prothero. It's a very genteel affair.' After hearing which
I snaked back to my skiff, and so presently to you."

"The damned business's plain," vowed Shrimpton; "but
with the brig full of lively men what's to be done? The
plan cannot be risked."

Watchhorn's oath almost trembled the mast-head, "The
plan must be risked—or I'm double-baked in hell."

"It's for you to say, skipper," assented his loyal adjutant,
and my own heart which had been sinking to the fish on
the bottom gave a great bound. For some moments thereafter the *Fair Trader* drifted, while as silently as possible
her people lowered her topmasts that they might not be
seen moving above the trees against the skyline. Then
heavy sweeps—long oars plied by two men, were thrust
out and muffled with canvas in their rowlocks. The
schooner thus began working in toward the shore, as close
as her practiced navigator's eye made it wise for safety.

In this manner we crawled along until suddenly the belt
of dark forest to starboard opened. We could distinguish
the great wide void of the sea, stretching away to the east,

and two blinking lights, one nearer, one slightly more remote. They both seemed much alike to me, but Watchhorn had no trouble in saying, "The nigh one is from the cabins on the islet; the further is the brig. Pray the Lord now that the party back from the Kennebec has all been given double tots of black strap to slow 'em up.—Whist! What's that?"

"That" was the sound of a steady man-of-war stroke of a boat bearing apparently from the islet and pulling toward Newagen. It was coming directly toward us, and only the altercation raging on board must have made her helmsman oblivious to the *Fair Trader* until the schooner was almost upon him. A woman's voice, shrill and angry, was going out into the night, "Where is she? She's not aboard? Put back, Mr. Dosworth. If you are a man and had a decent mother put back."

"You gain nothing by this uproar, madam," a masculine voice was saying.

"Hard on the starboard sweeps," thundered Watchhorn, in answer to which summons a united tug made the *Fair Trader* quiver to her keel. She spun about so suddenly that before the boat's company could back water or even cry out a pair of long boat-hooks had seized them, and their smaller craft had been hauled alongside. Then followed a mad, scrambling struggle in the darkness; oars, harpoons, belaying pins, and knives and fists all making a pandemonium together.

Somebody in the boat fired two pistols at random toward the mainsail, but the affair was all over in a twinkling. The schooner's people were next dragging aboard four very demoralized sailors, and some one, apparently an officer, who was raging like a bull and volleying curses. More gently the victors were assisting to the *Fair Trader* a large woman, puffing and moaning, who, however, the instant she touched the deck of the schooner leaped upon Shrimpton and hugged him like a motherly bear:

"Thank God for your good twanging voices! I'm Dorcas Kenniston; Dorcas Gamage that was. Don't lose a minute. There's the whitest little girl in the blackest danger. Oh, the smooth devil, how he lied! If you're Down East men save her."

"That's what we're come for, Dorcas," interposed Watchhorn calmly. "But those two pistol shots don't help much. It's getting after midnight; some light in three hours. We'd better be stirring. Throw those fellows down the hold and their lieutenant after 'em. Gag 'em if they won't keep still."

"Dare you imprison a King's officer?" bawled Dosworth.

"Wait 'til you see Wiscasset jail, young man," returned the skipper calmly. "I'd lock up King George himself if he played light with a woman—Now Dorcas, tell quick. Is Prothero on the islet, and the mam'sel? Yes?—And how many others? His steward and perhaps three or four? —It'll be touch and go if the brig's waked up, but nothing venture nothing have.—To the sweeps, men."

And towing the captured cutter behind, the schooner began again crawling over the water so close to the shore that only the second sight of the helmsman could have avoided the ledges. As we moved onward the contour of Cape Island stood out even clearer against the stars, and beyond it was manifestly the hull and tracery of the brig with lights at several portholes. Over our side now were noiselessly lowered three dories, into one of which by arrangement Herbert and I slid with Shrimpton. The schooner lay under the outermost promontory, barely hidden from the brig and the islet, but no skill could conceal our three boats as they shot out from the bulwarks and across the open stretch of two hundred fathoms of water.

"There are times to trust the good Lord," Watchhorn had announced coolly. "This 'ere is one of the times."

I did my share at my oar and Herbert likewise but I never knew that a dory could maintain such a snail's pace. Watchhorn in the first boat steered straight inside a tiny natural breakwater, and there was just light enough to discern a pebbly beach where we all glided up upon a gentle landing. The island was silent as the grave; a single light burning in one of the cabins. But even as we touched the shore the three boats must have been discovered by the lookout on the brig. A sudden flare burst out from the forecastle followed an instant later by a musket shot—then another.

Dunmore and I plunged after the others through a path or rather a trail amid tree trunks and bushes. Once I fell, rose instantly and never knew till the next day that I had bruised myself painfully. Watchhorn, sure as a homing pigeon, plunged through the thickets toward the cabins. Under the starlight I could make out three rude buildings with a dying fire gleaming before one of them. In the central cabin a ship's lantern was shining through the window. I had one glimpse of the interior, a crude, unfinished room, garnished with several sofas taken from the *Comet* and a table on which were the remnants of a meal and several bottles. In the midst of the room, her face torn with terror and agony indescribable was Emilie Rivoire, confronting firmly Prothero himself. The latter was very red from his potations, and was not standing over steadily. He had his arms outstretched in a kind of maudlin supplication. I could just hear, "All's right. No harm meant.— Married in Boston.—Word of honor——"

His cups and his passion no doubt saved his life, for evidently he had not heard the muskets and made not the slightest resistance as we rushed into the cabin. His pistols

were in his belt; had he reached for one Watchhorn's har-
poon would have transfixed him instantly. As it was, he
merely gaped dazedly while the skipper sprang upon him,
swung him up in his arms as he might a firkin and flung
him bodily through the window with a rending crash.
Emilie stared at us as in a catalepsy then uttered a dis-
traught moan and fell across the table.

I was beside her instantly, but Watchhorn swept her out
of my arms with a great snort. "You've a good heart, boy,
but I've the shoulders,—come!"

It was time. Shrimpton and the others had indeed
knocked down and pinioned the steward and two or three
fellows who crawled sleepily out of the other cabins; but
there had been unavoidable scuffling and uproar, and now
an ominous noise of activity was proceeding from the
brig. McVitie could be heard across the water, "Buoy off
the cable and shake out the foresail!" Next the call of one
of the midshipmen, "Long boat's crew for duty away."
Then the shrill bosun's whistles and the brawl of voices.

Watchhorn again led us all, despite his burden, back to
the dories. To twirl them again into the water was like
tossing corks. I had at least the comfort of having Emilie
now in our own boat, but the poor child lay like a dead log
at my feet as with all the strength that was in me I wrought
upon that oar. The *Fair Trader* had crept down to the
uttermost verge of safety. A dozen hands dragged us over
the low bulwarks, and when we passed up Emilie I heard
a deep "Thank the 'Tarnal," from more than one leathern
throat at my side.

Herbert and I had her down the ladder into the small
cabin, and there by a dim tallow dip, Mrs. Kenniston fluttered over her like a great matronly hen reviving a chicken
just plucked from the hawk. I was distracted enough to
linger while she rubbed something on the girl's forehead and

pressed something else to her lips. Then when Emilie opened her wonderful eyes, the good woman burst out with "They haven't harmed you Lady-bird, you are safe, quite safe."—But here the reverberations along the shore from a heavy gun, sent me back up the ladder. The *Fair Trader* could summon all her speed.

CHAPTER XVI

KING GEORGE'S SHOTS FLY WIDE

ALREADY when I regained the deck there was the first flush of light in the east, a little lifting of the night and fading of the stars. The sweeps were all working furiously, but directly along the shore we could hear the pulling of a heavy boat, while looming up to an ominous grandeur were the spars of the brig, now whitening with her sails against the lingering darkness.

"Blast those men-o'-war crews," Shrimpton was bewailing, "there go their top-gallants already. She be down on us directly, and the big boat is coming up along the shore like the Day of Judgment."

"Shut your jaw and mind your tiller, Shrimp," ordered his unflinching skipper; then to others of his crew, "Get our top-masts up instanter, if you don't want the feel of double-irons!"

Dunmore and I flung our best strength now into one of the sweeps, but for so large a craft as the *Fair Trader* they would at best have only prolonged the chase had not skill and speed sent the top-masts again up to the fids. An instant later a wide spread of canvas began to send the schooner gliding ahead through the water, and away from the nearing long boat. But this operation set us steadily away from the shore, and now as the yellow bars in the east steadily strengthened, we saw the *Comet* under full canvas bearing up menacingly.

185

It was also light enough for Watchhorn to profess to see (although I could not) one of the cutters bringing away from the islet persons who were undoubtedly the painfully sobered Prothero and his unfortunate boat crew. The skipper shook a knotted fist toward the brig: "God showed me mercy when I fell in your hands and you've your life now—but may I be keel-hauled by the devil forever, if another time I spare you!"

This was no moment, however, for long-range anathemas. Better now than in the darkness earlier, I understood the peril involved in our adventure upon the islet at a time when the *Comet* could get promptly under way. A light, steady breeze was coming in with the morning from the open sea, and the man-of-war, with her towering spars now covered with far-flung top-gallants, royals and scudding sails, was taking a wind which the lower canvas of the *Fair Trader* as yet failed to receive. The distance between the brig and the schooner was narrowing dangerously. The dawn had now advanced far enough to make the long boat plainly visible pulling along by the land with a formidable swivel grinning from her prow. The escape on land to the Newagen shore (which I had imagined easy if the schooner were abandoned) was thus cut off completely. The duel was unavoidably between the warship and the smuggler.

For a few moments the two vessels continued thus, running diagonally away from the land and across that broad arm of the sea which makes the lower Sheepscot. The desire of the *Fair Trader* was obvious; to slip out to southward into the open water, when the whole deeply indented Maine coast would have become hers in which to play hide and seek, but McVitie, who I could not doubt was controlling the *Comet*, cautiously avoided pressing his quarry so directly that she could make a sharp turn around some of those ledges in the estuary, upon which the mild waves were crumbling, and then by superior power of tacking win complete advantage.

For some minutes as the breeze improved and the sweeps were abandoned as useless, the *Fair Trader's* people stood or sat silent on her decks watching the pursuer. The sun had at last burst above the horizon, and sent a flying glory out of sea, rocks, and heavens. The *Comet* herself, looming to a fearsome size beside the frail smuggler, stood out like an enormous white plumaged bird with a dark belly skimming the sparkling water. Her decks were alive with men throwing out every possible stitch of canvas and "the white bone in her teeth," the water about her prow, rose almost momentarily higher.

The warship's gain therefore was steady, and I was casting desperate eyes upon one of the dories and muttering to Dunmore, "If worst comes to worst we can put *her* into that, and take our chance with the long boat," when Watchhorn's long finger went out toward the sea behind the warship; "Salvation of sinners—just in time, the wind!"—And we saw a long blue ripple running along the surface of the waves and leaving them all dancing and crisping. It struck the *Comet,* and her whole panoply of canvas first made a graceful bend, then seemed to give a long leap toward us. But the breeze raced past the brig, and in a twinkling our upper spars gave a perilous creak, while the *Fair Trader* listed heavily as she fairly tore through the water.

In a very few moments our speed was doubled. Some of the more reckless of the smuggler's people pulled off their caps and cheered, but were sobered again by the noise brought down by the wind from the brig. The drum of the *Comet* was sending forth a peculiar beat, short, broken, shuffling, which every man with knowledge of a King's ship understood. "He's going to his guns," remarked Watchhorn quietly; "now to look out for hail-stones."

Through the spyglass which the skipper passed me, it
was easy to see the people of the *Comet* taking the tompions
from the guns, and running them in for the powderladles
and rammers. After an interval during which her officers
must have discovered that the *Fair Trader* was now more
than holding her own, there was a great puff and a thunder
from the port chaser, and the twelve pound ball went skimming over the water, leaping from wave to wave like a lad's
pebble skipping across a pool, until at last it plunged from
sight in a flurry of foam. The shot had been so wide that
many of our people hooted but their skipper only gave a
surly, "He'll wedge his quoin higher next time," and swung
the helm so as to send the schooner directly northward up
the Sheepscot, thus presenting her stern, the smallest possible target, toward the man-of-war.

The second shot came near enough almost to send a spad
of water upon our decks. The third was a trifle wider, but
by this time the rising wind was carrying the *Fair Trader*
up the river mouth at a speed which was perceptibly widening the distance between her and the brig. Under the potent
warning of the cannonade Watchhorn's crew now flung overboard everything which could lighten the vessel. Spare
spars were cast adrift, and two of the three dories piled
with small movables were turned loose after them, on the
chance of being brought ashore by the tide and later recovered. The brig presently resumed firing, but the range now
had become such that with her style of artillery and the
probable quality of Prothero's gunners a hit upon our hull
or spars was wholly a matter of chance.

The schooner nevertheless seemed to be flying up the
Sheepscot on a course which could have but one ending.
Fifteen miles of narrowing estuary would bring her to the
head of navigation by Wiscasset where she must inevitably
surrender or ground. It would then be a desperate adven-

ture for her people to escape on shore before the man-of-war could seize her. In expectation of just this chance could be seen the two boats swung out on the davits of the *Comet,* ready to drop in the water the instant the tea-smuggler gave up the struggle.

Some minutes thus passed with only a trifling shift of rope or helm needful to hold our course. The *Fair Trader's* people, a weather-beaten, blue-shirted lot were now gathered in her stern to lift our bow and assist the speed. They spoke only in undertones and never took an eye from the brig. Only Watchhorn, now at the tiller, seemed in his element. Often have I wished that a West or a Copley might have caught him then. He had flung aside cap and wig and stood with the intense light of morning beating upon his closely cropped skull, his deeply lined face, and his enormous arms leather brown save for the blue tattooing. From time to time he would draw an enormous plug of tobacco from a pocket, bite off a portion, and chew with solemn emphasis. After the brig had fired yet a fifth time and barely missed our main boom, he began to sing in a perfectly cheerful manner but in a voice like a quavering foghorn, one of Watts' most melancholy hymns.

> "Conceived in sin, O wretched state!
>   Before we first draw breath,
> The first young pulse begins to beat
>   Iniquity and death.
>
> "How strong in our degenerate blood
>   The old corruption reigns!
> And mingling with the crooked flood
>   Wanders through all our veins."

He had hardly commenced before first Shrimpton, then others joined their deep bass to his with all the abandon of a catch or rondel, and a good part of the crew came in on the third stanza:

"To all that's good averse and blind
    And prone to all that's ill;
What dreadful darkness veils our mind!
    How obstinate our will!"

To what pitch of enjoyment in total depravity our people might presently have wrought themselves, who dares to say? For just as Watchhorn was sending forth a fourth stanza with a peculiarly nasal quaver:

"What mortal power from things unclean
    Can pure productions bring?"

a bustle and a rustle came from the cabin ladder, and up to the deck climbed none other than Mrs. Kenniston followed by Emilie Rivoire.

It was a sight for a Hogarth's pencil now, or for a greater than he: Mrs. Kenniston, fat, wholesome and matronly, the group of uncouth Down Easterners, as raw a group of honest fellows as ever stood together, and amid them this being of snow and pink who might have played shepherdess at the fêtes of the Trianon. Emilie had caught up her unruly hair and ordered her dress. She was still unwontedly pale, and her great eyes were dilated with excitement; but the mortal fear had passed out of her. I motioned her to a coil of rope, but she insisted on standing unflinchingly, shading her eyes with her hands as she gazed upon the still towering brig. "That of course is the *Comet?*" she asked.

"As you say, marm," responded Watchhorn, staring upon her with the honest tribute of unaffected admiration, as in fact were doing all of his men.

"Those were her guns? We are still in danger?"

In answer another smoke wreath flew from the chaser and the ball sang past the schooner within a yard of our port bulwarks, cutting an unimportant rope. The crew had involuntarily ducked, as without shame did Dunmore and

I; Mrs. Kenniston uttered a loud squall and almost fell
over.   Only Emilie stood, stirred hardly more than the
unmoving helmsmen.   Then her face was clouded with a
new agony: *"O gracieux ciel!* You are all running this
peril for my sake. What worth is a poor girl like me for
brave men to do all this?"

"Partly for your sweet face," answered Watchhorn with
perfect honesty; "but still more for what every honest
coastwise man should do for every honest woman.   And
on my own account, just a leetle more readily because that
sarpent Prothero's at t'other end of the devil's work.—
Now, Hi McKown, lay along forrard and sing out if you
see water between Green Island and Dog Fish Head."

"You won't try Ebenecook Harbor, skipper?" cautioned
another of the crew. "We're trapped there and driven
ashore."

"I haven't hauled cod since I was seven not to know
that, you fool," rejoined his unflinching commander. "Now
if the Lord will only fuddle the aim of them twelve
pounders.——"

Another ball this time tore completely through the main
topsail, splitting the canvas almost in twain. A distant
cheer came up on the wind from the brig. The *Fair Trader*
continued flying on her course, but with the gap betwixt her
and the *Comet* no longer lessening. The crew became tense
and silent, while somehow by a process never to be explained,
I found myself standing beside Emilie and her hand within
mine, and somehow after a manner I felt happy, although
the *Comet* fired again, this shot however safely clearing our
taffrail.

"Whatever happens, Roger," she was saying close to my
ear, "I shall never forget what you have done for me. You
are my *preux chevalier*. My grandfather——"

"Look to booms and sheets; she'll jibe," trumpeted

Watchhorn, swinging the helm so violently that the
schooner gave an abrupt lurch nearly hurling us to the
deck. Instantly along the pine clothed line of Newagen we
saw opening a new waterway to the northeastward. The
Fair Trader went toward it with a leap. The movement
was instantly noted upon the brig and we could see the sail
passers tugging at the tackles to swing the long yards and
put their vessel upon the other tack. The *Comet* went
about smartly, but no square-rigger could make such an
evolution without losing many fathoms to a flying schooner.
Immediately we were flying into more completely landlocked waters; little bays, islands and headlands were about
us, but the tea-smuggler continued speeding onward, seemingly directly into the unbroken land.

"Watchhorn's purpose is clear," whispered Dunmore, long
silent at my elbow. "He will cast his craft away in some
cove where escape ashore will be possible. The brig can
pound us to pieces in ten minutes once we are aground."

"I think not," spoke Emilie who let nothing escape her.
"Some bolder purpose. You can see it in his eyes."

The arch-smuggler was now indeed a spectacle, standing
as he did at the tiller with every muscle alert, taking advantage of the least possible flaws in the wind, and with his
gaze glued upon the barrier of rocks and pines now rising
steadily beyond the bowsprit. His men were at length
motionless. Every possible sail had been hauled taut. On
the *Comet* they had momentarily ceased firing; seamen
were standing at the braces to tack instantly the moment
that shoal water appeared ahead and others were already
entering the boats, ready to secure the prize whenever the
chase was driven aground.

Yet Dunmore, Emilie and myself joined all in the breathless, "Ha!"—Again in the approaching shores appeared a
waterway, down which like a dove skimming before the

eagle the *Fair Trader* went flying. Soon we were threading
between islands along a rippling channel where the jagged
maws of the rocks thrust at perilous intervals above the
surface. On the shores the black pines seemed reaching out,
beckoning, encouraging us. On little sandspits tall gray
herons could be seen blinking solemnly at this intrusion
on their philosophies, while for long intervals there came no
sound but the rushing of the water about our prow and
the creaking of the blocks before the steady gale.

The *Comet* held on doggedly. McVitie or whoever
directed her helm kept her safely in our wake, missing no
turn and with his people trimming the yards with seamanly
precision. Then as we doubled a peculiarly craggy head-
land all the *Fair Trader's* people suddenly leaped from their
apathy, crowded their bulwarks and roared defiance
toward the pursuer. Watchhorn, again with a fierce swing
to the tiller, shook his fist in triumph toward the brig:

"Now dirty King's lugger, you're where I want you. You
can torment the coast but you'll not sweep the Oven's
Mouth.—The fools! I thought they'd do it.—One last
squall now, and it's done for!"

Before us two points of rock reached out, approaching so
close that my heart stood still as I saw the *Fair Trader*
headed between them. Momentarily I thought the rocks
would tear against the keel, but all my gaze was called
back upon the brig. Conscious at last that his quarry was
fairly escaping, her commander had sent her about suddenly,
bringing her full broadside to bear upon the chase.
Instantly the hull of the *Comet* was shrouded in a dense
cloud of smoke as her nine guns all thundered together.
The water about us was tossed high in foam; a great bowl-
der ashore flew in splinters; one ball tore whistling through
the mainsail, and another cut through the gaff of the foresail as though it had been snipped by shears. But the

Providence which had befriended earlier befriended still. The hull was untouched, and scathed but uncrippled the schooner raced along the narrow salt river.

Nor was this Watchhorn's final triumph. For in the confusion of disappointment the *Comet's* people had failed to allow for the narrowness of the channel, and the set of the tide against unseen ledges. The brig had emerged from her smoke cloud, and seemed tacking again into the fairway when suddenly her progress stopped. A moment more all her sails were aback, shivering with noise like musketry while scores of sailors went streaming from the gun-deck up the ratlines with frantic haste to furl canvas before shrouds and masts gave way.

The skipper released our helm to the ready Shrimpton, sprang into the ropes halfway to his own mast-head, and sent out a voice almost to match the cannon: "Full tide! Turning to ebb! Hard aground betwixt Hodgdon Island and Barters. Thanked be the Almighty for sending me this day!"

For the next four miles or more we continued to pursue a waterway so narrow, so tortuous that no boat from the *Comet* could have had the temerity to follow. For the first time since quitting the Cove in the evening the little galley of the *Fair Trader* began to smoke, and presently solid wooden trenches of equally solid ship's fare began to be passed about the deck. Dunmore and I had not slept for eight-and-forty hours, and I at least had almost forgotten such things as meat and drink existed. We sat upon the cabin roof of the schooner, too dazed and hungry and happy to take it in that since gray dawn we had been under the batteries of a man-of-war. Emilie sat beside me. The color again was in her cheeks; the gleam of the summer waters matched not the brightness of her eyes. What matter if still I was far from home? If a thousand things were yet to be explained at Salem, at Harvard, at Redford? That my fortune was the change left from two guineas?— Something was singing all around me, and it was no longer the purling of the water. Dunmore had eaten his fill, and was now gazing upon the gliding shores, stupidly, drowsily. He had played a man's part, dear fellow, but this was not his hour of gold.

As for me slumber seemed the last thing in the world, while Emilie leaned close to my ear (the brush of her flying hair against my cheek tingling all through me like strong wine) and whispered, "What a tale we'll have to tell in Boston, won't WE *mon* Roger?"

At length we dropped anchor in an utterly secluded basin, with green trees reflected on the rocky bottom, and the shores gently sloping away and dotted with cool white farmsteads. The channel by which we had entered was so completely hidden from view that we might well have floated upon an inland lake, save for the seagrass bared by the falling tide, and the aroma of drying seaweed.

Remember Watchhorn turned from stowing the mainsail, looked on the two women, then went through the motion of pulling off his cap: "Well, leddys," he remarked unaffectedly, "I guess we may say that Mem's brought you safe through the Oven's Mouth."

Mrs. Kenniston was clearing her throat for elaborate thanks, but Emilie with one arch look, had darted forward and instantly flung her arms about his swarthy neck:

"Oh! you strange men—so brave, so cold—I must do it— there!—" and twice she kissed the leathery cheeks of the dumbfounded Mem before all his gaping crew; then in a voice which went through us all, "You men of America who have done so much for me, God suffer me at last to do some noble thing for *my* America!"

CHAPTER XVII

IN WHICH WE AGAIN SEE BOSTON

It was evening, and only after a hard jolting in a spring-less cart over nigh impassable roads, when we found ourselves borne across country to that village then known familiarly as Townsend, but since become more recognized as Boothbay Harbor.

Long before our arrival I discovered that although my spirit continued gallantly willing, my flesh was becoming extraordinarily weak. Emilie disappeared somewhere into a great hospitable farmhouse of interminable length, belonging to some relative of Mrs. Kenniston, and we were both too limp and sleepy for more than a very perfunctory farewell. Herbert and I at last were set down at a hostelry kept by a Mr. Pinkham, and whatever its unpretention, the chamber to which that friendly host showed us seemed a restful elysium beside the quarters upon the *Agile* and the *Comet*. Dunmore and I hardly loosed our shoes before casting ourselves upon the feather-beds; and after that I was dead to the world until the sun was high in the heavens.

When Dunmore and I went into the twisting streets of the little town, already crowds of lean wiry men in checked or blue shirts were standing in knots before the general stores and ship chandleries. The horseshoe shaped harbor was alive with boats. A sloop was scudding in from Pemaquid. Many eyes followed us curiously and not without approval, for every tongue from the Sheepscot to the Dam-

196

ariscotta had been wagging half the night about our exploits. The guns of the *Comet* had startled the haymakers beyond Head Tide. The whole country was in a blaze.

Where was the brig? Hard and fast upon the ledge by Barter's Island. She had torn off her false keel and sheathing and would have to lighter out her guns before she could be floated. Meantime the tea cached at Monhegan "would of course stay just where they'd hidden it"—so we were informed with an arid chuckle!

The odor of the cod and hake drying upon acres of racks in the sun gave the entire village an odor which Herbert vowed he would continue to smell when he lay on his bed in Wiltshire; he also inquired in his most serious manner of our host "if the Boothbay people were of the Church of England." And being informed that "there wan't no 'Piscopals this side of the Kennebec," he told Mr. Pinkham that he was surprised "because the town contained so many *curates*, not indeed engaged (he confessed) in the cure of souls but in the cure of fish." Which remark being instantly caught up as a capital jest, quite established his reputation for being a wit as well as a very courageous fellow.

About noon there appeared at the tavern a solid, important looking gentleman clad in dark broadcloth not too rusty, an archaic two-pigtailed wig a little over-plastered with powder, and a three-cornered hat with faded gold lace. "Mr. Justice Ichabod Gamage," he was introduced to us, the brother of Mrs. Kenniston, and after an exchange of compliments he put both Herbert and myself through an exceedingly shrewd, albeit kindly, interrogatory as to our entire adventure, and how we chanced to be on the *Comet*. On this point, inasmuch as the duel had ended without tragedy, we had already agreed that veracity would be the best policy, especially at a spot so remote from Salem. We therefore told our story accurately, I, however, making a special point to bring out that Dunmore had jeopardized his life in defending us Colonials from foul aspersion, and that Prothero had been in all senses the aggressor.

Our statements were so far satisfactory that the justice invited us to join a small party around a hearty sea-food dinner, which was not the less sociable because it was washed down by much good Madeira which had doubtless forgotten to pay tribute to the King. We were just rising in the dining room, and I was wondering how I could compass an interview with Emilie, when mine host jogged Gamage's elbow: "Boat from the brig at the wharf, squire; and that Captain Prothero has come ashore and asked for you, as I'm a sinful man!"

The glance that went around that table was the glance of a circle of cats suddenly informed that a desired sparrow was about to alight in their center. The justice rose, gravely adjusted his wig, winked equally gravely with his left eye to his neighbor at table, a portly fish-merchant, and went out with his best official stride toward the tap-room.

"I knew Prothero was a blackguard," muttered Dunmore, "I did not know he was so rash a fool. What will happen?"

"Happen?" caught up the fish-merchant. "When Dan'l was chucked in the lions' den, he didn't get chawn. But *then* Dan'l didn't walk in of his own accord, and he was a sanctified man. Which ain't true of that dog-fish in the fine coat, just talking to the squire."

Prothero (as we saw through the door) bore visible marks of the gentle dealings of Watchhorn; his left arm was in a sling, and a great scratch went clear down his forehead; but as always he wore his blue and white uniform magnificently, his hair was handsomely clubbed and powdered, his brass buttons and steel scabbard gleamed. At his elbow was McVitie, quite insignificant, however, beside his chief, in his shabbier uniform, while halted at the tavern door were some six seamen from the brig clattering halfpikes and cutlasses.

Gamage clapped on his hat, pulled it off again and bowed to Prothero affably. The captain gave him a tolerably respectful nod, then stated his business: "He had come in the name of his Majesty's navy to make requisition upon the magistrates of the town for lawful assistance; first of all to secure the instant apprehension of a notorious deserter from the King's service, one Remember Watchhorn, capitally convicted and known to have escaped to these parts."

"Anything else?"

"The services of the sheriff and constables to seize the smuggling schooner, *Fair Trader*, known to be lurking in some cove around Boothbay."

"Anything else?"

"To procure the immediate release of Lieutenant Dosworth of H. M. brig *Comet* and his boat crew, supposed to have been lawlessly kidnapped and held prisoners upon this *Fair Trader*, with of course the punishment of all parties concerned in the crime."

The justice smiled urbanely: "The first two of your requests, Captain, will take time; the third we can perhaps handle with dispatch.—Mr. McVitie, I believe?" (The Scotchman bowed) "Will you and your commander do me the honor to be seated and accept a trifle of our hospitality? If your men will go to Mr. Wylie's tavern down the street refreshment also awaits them. Is it gin, rum or sherry, gentlemen?"

The two naval men sprawled down at a table just as I saw two or three of our companions slipping out at a back door. A moment later out of the tail of my eye I beheld little knots of men gliding up from the wharves. Some bore harpoons or eel spears, but there was a sprinkling of muskets. They seemed quietly arranging themselves around the tavern. Gamage in the meantime threw back his waistcoat, pulled out a bundle of papers, and began pawing them over, puffing, gossiping and at times proffering the officers snuff from a huge silver box which he kept drawing from his coat-tails.

"We waste time, my good man,—" at length fumed Prothero, "worshipful sir, (he corrected himself, with an audible aside to McVitie "Damn those bumpkins that I must title them!") You said that you could procure the liberty of Mr. Dosworth?"

"I said I could *handle* the affair of Mr. Dosworth," rejoined Gamage, suddenly pushing back the papers as a slight whistle sounded outside the door, "Mr. Sheriff, produce your prisoner."

A side door to the tap-room opened suddenly, and a very consequential personage armed with a tall black truncheon abruptly marshalled into the room Lieutenant Dosworth himself. His uniform was awry; his aspect sheepish and on his wrists clinked a pair of clumsy and rusty handcuffs.

"Before God, sir:" exclaimed Prothero bounding from his chair. "My officer in irons? What means this?"

"Very simply, Captain," said Gamage collectedly, "that he has been held in the strong room of the tavern which serves as our jail. A complaint has been duly sworn against him for unlawful assault upon and detention of one Mrs. Dorcas Kenniston at or near Cape Island. He will be taken at once to Wiscasset for proper examination."

Prothero smote the table with his free hand until the glasses danced and jingled: "You provincial Dogberries shall learn your place! Strike off those handcuffs and release my lieutenant immediately."

Not a figure in the group moved; hardly a muscle stirred. With a naval curse the captain turned to McVitie, "Call up the boat-crew and force off those irons. And you yokels, who are answerable for this——"

"Save your dignity, sir," remarked Gamage in unruffled voice, "until you apprehend your true situation. Sheriff Tibbetts, you know your duty."

The functionary with the truncheon laid a firm hand on the officer's shoulder and held before him a document bearing a formidable seal. "Quite in form, sir," announced the sheriff, "warrant to seize the body of one Barnard Prothero on charge of kidnapping and attempted insult to the person of Miss Emilie Rivoire at Cape Island within the jurisdiction of this Lincoln County."

Prothero flung the paper across the room, and reached for his hilt, "Of all jests intolerable! To lay hands on a King's officer. Your town should be knocked about your ears for this. Here, McVitie, where are the men?"

"There's an unco' broiling in the streets, Captain," reported that discreet officer, "and I ken the crew are disarmed. There are fifty loons with weapons about the tavern, and counselling as a friend I'd speak douce and lightly if ye'd see the *Comet* again this even."

His superior drew himself up with a great effort to rein in his fury. "I must capitulate to local custom I perceive, sir," he said addressing the justice, "tell your man that I give an officer's word that I will hold myself at disposal of your magistrates after I have duly reported to Admiral Montagu."

"An officer's word and a farmer's word are alike in an eastern county, Captain Prothero," spoke the imperturbable Gamage. "The charge is for a felony; the complainant appears to be a responsible young woman; there are supporting witnesses. You will give bail through three competent freeholders, or Mr. Tibbetts conducts you with Mr. Dosworth to Wiscasset jail, there to lie until next grand jury."

Prothero flashed out his sword and with "Follow me, McVitie" dashed toward the door, only to be met by the point of a fish spear firmly presented by none other than Remember Watchhorn at the front of a heavy press of men, who now surged into the tap-room.

"Don't run your snout in a trough of hot swill, Cap'n," adjured Shrimpton's nasal voice from the background.

The officer fell back, now white with vexation and rage: "Filthy yokels.—What a plight for a gentleman.—I'll become the butt of every wardroom!"

"Then listen to reason, sir," ordered Gamage sternly, "and do not disgrace your uniform by other follies. We desire not your blood but to purge the coast of your company.—A private room, landlord, and you, Mr. McVitie and you also Mr. Dosworth favor with your presence."

. . . The captain, bent and sobered, followed the justice into the chamber, whither presently two or three local potentates were invited to join them. The conference was long; to the listeners without there escaped the jar of angry voices, but in the end Prothero came out with his face like a ghost's, and half collapsed on the arm of McVitie.

"You may discharge your prisoners, sheriff," ordered the justice, and while the naval men, joined by the released Dosworth, were making hurriedly toward their boat, I at length knew what had happened. Prothero in consideration of withholding the heavy charges against him, had signed and sealed the resignation of his commission, and given bonds for an undertaking to return to England within one month or forfeit three thousand pounds jointly to Mrs. Kenniston and Miss Rivoire. McVitie and Dosworth had in turn put their hands to a document certifying that their

commander's conduct had been unworthy of an officer and
requiring court martial had he remained in the navy.

"And so," concluded the practical Gamage, "the province
is spared the price of his victuals and jail fees; and Britain
and not Massachusetts can some day buy him his halter.
But now, Mr. Gilman—how did I forget it!—I'm to conduct you to my own house, where all the women folk'll
be most happy to see you. And they tell me a certain
young French lady asks for you in particular."

.   .   .   .

The gladdest of glad parties we had at the Gamages that
night. Our fame had spread abroad. We were heroes. We
had compassed the downfall of one of the most hated characters between Boston Light and the Penobscot. I hope
that I bore my honors gracefully, and refrained from letting
too much unaccustomed liquor get to my head. Dunmore
was gayest of the gay. And Emilie?—But when the best
of Young France, the best of Young England, and not the
worst (I dare to say) of Young America sit all together in
happiest mood—there is an evening to be remembered!

Emilie was kind; extremely kind. And I had her very
largely to myself, for Dunmore insisted on doing the honors
to the married ladies of the party, engaging them all with
his gracious ways and delightful English accent. For the
first time since that accursed duel at Salem I felt reasonably
easy in my mind; and the presence of my mistress, the
sound of her voice praising me for an absurd amount of
daring, the knowledge that I had been suffered to render
her a service which none of her Boston gallants could
match, nearly swept me from my bearings. Only that
restraining inner self, which is one of the blessings and
banes of a New England heritage, kept me then from saying or doing things for which my conscience later might
reproach me bitterly.

Dunmore and I walked back to Pinkham's tavern beneath the cooling stars. After a few steps Herbert began his usual whistle preliminary to saying something important. "Peggy is Peggy," he began, "but if it weren't for her I'd begin to get jealous."

"I don't follow," I returned although "following" perfectly.

"You've stormed the French citadel. The garrison is flying white flags from all the battlements. Anybody can see it to-night with half an eye. Hurry now, and accept the surrender."

"Herbert Dunmore," answered I severely, "if you truly believe that because I have aided in rendering Emilie Rivoire a service in which you completely shared, and in which the true hero, is that satyr Mem Watchhorn, I will claim from her that which I would have no right to claim otherwise, you grossly abuse our friendship."

"Heigh-ho!" spoke he, twirling his hat, "I thought you Colonials had left far behind in England that cursed thing called 'pride.' Well—I'm poor enough and yet I've the holy pledge of Peggy."

"You have your commission," I rejoined, "an honorable career despite slow promotion. What have I? Prospects thin as moonbeams!—A Yankee girl could be asked to take her chance on our 'twenty acres and a cow'—Damn those French marriage settlements and dowries!"

"Dear fellow," spoke he with the most comradely nudge, "I'm no theologian, but I know Heaven never intends that Roger Gilman and Emilie Rivoire should both continue miserably unhappy forever."

Then with his wonted kindness he changed the subject, and I turned into the tavern with a certain tempered gladness. It is easy to scale the ramparts of Fortune when

your mind is not yet twenty, and a pretty girl has spoken
to you more with her eyes than with her voice.

.   .   .   .

We could have enjoyed Boothbay hospitality for weeks.
Prothero had slunk on board a coaster for Boston. It soon
came out that McVitie had loathed him, and had barely
held to his duty on the *Comet*. Being now in command of
the brig, the genial Scotchman soon won the good graces of
the native people by his liberal payments for supplies and
his convenient deafness to all tales of smuggling. The
Comet was presently lightered, floated and departed for
New York for overhaul. Weeks later I learned that every
respectable officer along the coast had heaved a sigh of
relief, when with alacrity Admiral Montagu accepted Prothero's resignation, ere the latter sailed for England, "Thus
making," as Herbert wisely remarked, "one less scoundrel
engaged in prying Britain and America assunder."

But for ourselves the moment that fear for personal
safety ended, thought for anxious friends began. The day
after the feast at the Gamages, we took up our journey for
Falmouth under Mrs. Kenniston's frigate-like convoy. Of
coasters all had had enough, but friendly carters rattled
us to Wiscasset whence more commodious chaises took us
to Woolwich, and then by the Kennebec ferry to George-
town * and on to the pretty village of Brunswick. The next
day we saw Falmouth, already the first town in the Maine
counties, and I took in the glories of Casco Bay, in truth
one of the noblest sheets of water in the entire world.

Falmouth, however, could not detain Dunmore and
myself, and as luck would have it could not detain Emilie.
Her visit to the Duboises would have been most awkward.
The smallpox was scattering in the town, and the whole
family had shut itself up to be inoculated, several friends

* Known a little later as Bath.

having been, as per custom, invited in "to join a genteel smallpox party." Unless Emilie wished to share this polite recreation, her only home must be at the Kennistons. Here of course, she might tarry for months, for Mrs. Kenniston was vowing her to be "dearer than a daughter," but M. Rivoire himself, venerable and unspeakably anxious, swung into Falmouth in a hired curricle, and wept and poured forth thanksgivings in mingled French and English when he discovered that the "light of his eyes" was safe and well.

Back therefore to Boston we hasted in joyous company. Our first halting was at the comfortable Earl of Halifax in Portsmouth, and then by one of Mr. Staver's new "Flying State Coaches" we were whisked clear to the Charlestown ferry with only one night on the road spent at Ipswich. It was all done so safely that we felt quite cheated of adventures.

When we passed near Salem Herbert and I shared certain inward qualms, Emilie having passed on to us the floating rumors; but M. Rivoire only listened to our tale with tolerance, muttered something about "young blood," then counselled me not to communicate immediately to any of my family, but to remain very quietly at the Paul Reveres' while he could "bestir himself." Bestir himself he did most effectually. What he said to Admiral Montagu and the commandant at Castle William never came to us, but Herbert soon learned that satisfactory excuses for his conduct were going forward to General Gage. As for myself, the old gentleman secured the intervention of none other than Dr. Joseph Warren. Soon I gathered that an influential Whig in Salem had been informed that inasmuch as the rumored duel "if fought at all, had been occasioned by a magnanimous defense of the rights of the colonists" the matter had better be dropped. As to my Harvard rustication the doctor acted even more decisively. He visited Cambridge in person, talked engagingly to President Locke of "using his interest in behalf of the new lottery" then in process for raising funds for the college and next added his firm opinion that I had been sufficiently punished. My rustication was forthwith revoked, and I was at liberty to spend the remainder of my vacation as I pleased, and to reënter Harvard with full junior standing. After that if the return of the prodigal to Redford lacked the slaying of the fatted calf it was not for want of forgiving raptures not merely on the part of Tabitha and Yetmercy, but of father and mother.

CHAPTER XVIII

THE HOUSE ON PURCHASE STREET

AFTER about a week at Redford and before the delight of another home-coming could quite wear off, I returned one evening from a tramp with my gun along Nutting's Pond in Billerica and found father anxious to have me come to the study. There in the twilight he put a letter in my hand. You can guess how I received it.

"Dr. Warren's compliments to Dr. Gilman. And if Mr. Roger Gilman desires until the college reopens to render important services to the cause of his country, let him report at early convenience to me.

Your obdt. servant, Jos. WARREN."

It was late the next day when I found myself again in Boston and tapping the knocker of the Warren house on Hanover Street. William Eustis, the doctor's pleasant-faced student-assistant, let me into the little private surgery. The place was crammed with presses for ipecacuanha, jalap, Venice treacle, diacordium and other drugs and compounds; long shelves arrayed with many colored phials, a retort for philosophical experiment; two very sour-looking plaster busts labeled "Galen" and "Harvey," and in one corner the inevitable skeleton; in short the usual paraphernalia of a physician of large practice in that day when apothecaries were few and poor. The whole place smelled of pungent chemicals. I noted, however, that half the books upon the shelves had to do with history and political theory and not materia medica nor anatomy, and on the table lay an open copy of Montesquieu, with many passages marked.

The doctor entered almost immediately. He had the same fascinating friendly presence as ever, but a wide band of black was upon his sleeve, his face was lined unmistakably and was less youthful. Only a few months had passed since Elizabeth Warren, his passionately loved wife, the mother of four beautiful children, had been laid to rest after a brief illness before which the ablest physician in New England had stood powerless. After that (said his friends) her husband had been more than ordinarily gentle to his patients, more assiduous than ever in the patriot cause, but his old contagious laugh and smile had never been precisely the same.

In any case, however, Dr. Warren greeted me heartily, inquired concernedly for my father, then unfolded his business. It was now eight years since the passage of the Stamp Act had set variance between the British ministry and the Colonies. There had been lulls in the contest; a partial repeal of certain obnoxious statutes, a temporary flagging in the opposition by the Provincials, but each truce had ended in new aggression, new resentment, new estrangement. It was now the wane of 1773 and every advice from England had it that matters could not thus drift forever. The report indeed was abroad that George III had told his ministers he was resolved *"to try the issue with the Colonies."* "And if that be true," spoke Warren in his most suggestive accent, "it behooves honest men to look for sound lawyers and an impartial jury."

And wherefore was I summoned? Because, said the doctor, the task of handling the great correspondence thrust now upon the patriot committees went beyond the abilities of any small group of busy men. More particularly Mr. Samuel Adams needed a temporary secretary. Mere zeal for the good cause was not sufficient; they could always summon an abundance of that. But a young gentleman who, along with unflinching principles, commanded a good knowledge of the classics, could write in vigorous English and handle at least minor details with discretion—he was less easy to obtain. "And could Mr. Samuel Adams enjoy my present services?"

When next I went down Hanover Street my head felt itself lifted to the tops of the tallest elms. For a whole half hour I actually committed the treason of failing to think of Emilie!—True there might have been a certain policy in the proffer. No shrewder flattery could have been paid to my father and to Uncle Peleg than to have their son and nephew thus initiated among the very highest of the "High Sons of Liberty," but that possibility did not make me one whit the less happy. Within another day I had resumed my old quarters at my uncle's house on Charter Street, although spending nearly all my time at the other end of Boston—in Purchase Street, beyond the South Battery down by the wharves, and almost hourly was holding converse with the "Grand Incendiary."

It is an old saying about not seeing the forest on account of the number of the trees. I have been in great battles wherein I imagined that I witnessed everything, and then learned that the day had been lost or won because of happenings far beyond my sight. If therefore I had been a New York mynheer, or a Pennsylvania Quaker, or if my father had raised tobacco in Virginia or rice in Carolina, I would no doubt have a story of our Revolution to tell, but it would be a story far different from this. Placed as I was, to me until after the contest joined and swords made good the appeals to Freedom, the debate with England meant the cause of Massachusetts, as set before the world by the voice of Samuel Adams.

Others were greater than he when armed deeds perforce became the best state papers. Others knew better than he

how to build for the future, when the decrepit old had
been toppled down. But for those years when good men
groped for light, when the dying allegiance not yet was
dead, when out of the whirlwind, the earthquake and the fire
sounded the still small voice "Go forward!"—for those
years I say, he was the leader without fear, without
reproach, who saw his goal while others walked in darkness, and who thought "America," who dreamed "America,"
who proclaimed "America" with the devotion of the lover for
his bride, of the soldier first to surmount the battlements
of death.

Wondrous days were those in the early 1770s; when common or careless terms leaped into holy meaning; when
"freedom," "liberty," "country," "nation," "America" suddenly became glowing words, summoning those fierce loyal-
ties which make life itself weigh as the small dust in the
balances of God. And if this Republic of ours was worth
the making, close below the Virginia gentleman and Poor
Richard, upon the master builders' roll let there be written
the name of the man in the old red coat in the shabby
house on Purchase Street.

I have heard the Sneerwells throw out that if George
Washington had been honored with a colonelcy in the royal
army things might have been different, and the same if
George III had only tossed a baronetcy and some ribbons
to Benjamin Franklin; and that if the elder James Otis had
only been named chief justice of Massachusetts we would
have heard far less about the iniquities of Writs of Assistance. But never have I heard that Samuel Adams ever
set his face against the power of Britain save from the
sincerity that was in him, and any schoolboy may read the
reply of his relentless foe, Tom Hutchinson, to the query
from England, "Why hath not Mr. Adams been taken off
from his opposition by an office?" "Such is the obstinacy

and inflexible disposition of the man that he never would
be conciliated by any office or gift whatever."—Human he
was, as those who knew him best confessed most freely.
But his were the failings of a Titan, and of a Titan pure
in heart.

. . . Herbert had cleared up his much postponed business
at Salem with tolerable credit and betaken himself to New
York. I saw him go with mixed feelings. Earnestly as he
assented to the claims of the colonial cause, bitterly as
he denounced the fatuous policy which was setting America
by the ears with Britain, his face grew increasingly wistful
as the debate intensified and as men began to show the
stealing dread of that fearful thing which not yet could
they put in words. To have met me day by day, while I
was in the service of Samuel Adams devising evil for the
potentates of England, would not have racked our friendship, but must have tormented Dunmore sorely.

My work was not wholly at Purchase Street. Often I
had to sit in at the conclave which met above Edes and
Gill's printing office on Court Street; where in a small musty
chamber smelling of damp paper and inking balls, and with
the thud, thud of the pressmen pulling the *Boston Gazette*
sounding below us, I listened to the wit and wisdom not
merely of Samuel Adams, and of Warren, but, in his better
intervals, of poor James Otis now lapsing into a mental
cloud, of Josiah Quincy, that fervent young advocate who
would have risen to the seats of the Highest had not the
hectic flush been already upon him, and last but not least
of John Adams, Samuel's kinsman, who if he figures little
in these pages needs no tribute of mine to prove him a
surpassingly great man. Yet most of the time I spent at a
big clumsy desk assigned me by Samuel Adams himself in
his own house. In fact I carried in my pocket the keys to
the front door, to the little study, and to the cupboards for

all the private files, passed in and out at will, and had the proud consciousness of access to the arcanum of state secrets.

Apart indeed from this excitement of learning every day concerning matters whereof his Majesty would probably have poured out guineas to get wind, mine was a most fascinating experience. The Purchase Street mansion was a rambling old dwelling with a cupola commanding a noble view of all the island-studded harbor, the numerous shipping, and Castle William, as well as of the town of Boston rising fair upon its hills. The dwelling needed paint and repairs; so did the rooms, garnished with well-worn furniture. As for the garden its fine fruit trees and elms stood in sad need of pruning.

Nevertheless it was a homey, comfortable house. Ceremony vanished as you clicked over the threshold. Mrs. Betsy Adams, an "eminently respectable" matron, was no toast to upset the young men, but an astoundingly efficient housekeeper who kept the family fed and clothed on a distressingly small income, and who had always a plate of shad and hot flannel cakes for "one more," when her husband (never with the slightest warning) marched home a friend.

As her chief lieutenant there was wholesome black Surrey, technically free but who could have been driven from the Adams service only by bayonets; while round the yard bounded great Que, an extremely intelligent Newfoundland, who was alleged to possess a great appetite for Tories' coat-tails. Often too you met Samuel, Jr., an intelligent young fellow learning medicine in Dr. Warren's office along with Eustis, and last but not least, Mistress Hannah, sixteen, though no beauty, but solid, friendly, full of common sense, and very promptly a cousin to you and never anything else.

Over this family presided the most friendly master in the world. "The last of the Puritans" some fool has called him, as if there will not be Puritans until the last Yankee twang dies in the graveyard. True he hated stage plays, French novels and lax Sabbaths; but there was no canting "Saint" in the man who took intense pleasure in singing what were by no means always psalm tunes, and who delighted to sail down to Nahant with John Adams and scramble on the rocks exploring "caverns"; or to visit Harvard as one of the Legislative Committee and join in one of Bradish's never abstemious dinners.

Never was there public leader with more time to squander on the trivial concerns of the young. Hannah was always interrupting; I was only one of a dozen lank youths in whose affairs he took an intense interest, and to whom he often proffered detailed advice—always with so genial a touch there was no sting in a plain rebuke. Thanks to him I was strengthened in my love for the ancient classics, as an incomparable enrichment of my life. Plutarch and Livy, Herodotus and Tacitus in their originals lay ever on his table, and many is the time I have checked over the well-turned phrases of his papers and noted the Greek or Latin which gave the glowing thoughts that, under a dozen thin pseudonyms, he poured constantly into the Boston papers.

No man was more indifferent than he to personal advantage: he never dreamed of applying his prudent councils to himself. His foes said that he had practically failed in the malting business, had made a boggle as tax collector, had run through a substantial inheritance; and that Mrs. Betsy could never pay the fish-peddler and grocer if her husband lost his pittance as clerk of the legislature. Samuel Adams heeded none of these things, so long as his "infernal ingenuity" drove Hutchinson into sustained blasphemies, and his Majesty to writing angry memoranda to

North. Adams had never journeyed beyond a few miles from Boston, but his correspondence reached to Georgia and Britain. His old red coat grew ever dingier; yet he seemed to hold the greatest town of New England in the hollow of his hand.

Great he was in Faneuil Hall scourging "ministerial aggression"; greater he was in some ship yard, with a knot of heavy-handed mechanics around him, every man of them inwardly remarking "Mr. Adams feels just the way we do." Everybody he could call by first name; he knew exactly whose wife was sick; and he also knew with uncanny expertness how to inculcate the feeling that America and Britain were so diverse in interest that some parting of the ways must come right quickly.

After I became his helper, I learned his methods—how night after night, far into the small hours, the gleam of his study lamp would fall into Purchase Street, while through the great dark house would go the scratching of his quill. "Sam Adams was up punishing the Tories," friends would whisper. Then a few days later his Excellency in his Milton manor house would be writing long, alarmist dispatches to England.

In those weeks, when I had thus the freedom of Purchase Street, I learned more than in any ten times that period at Harvard. I heard discussions, I copied papers charged with ideas commonplace now, but which then came as the revelation of a new heaven and a new earth. I gained insight into those great Committees of Correspondence, the creation of which was the joint masterpiece of the Massachusetts and the Virginia Whigs;—that organization which the Tories soon denounced as "the foulest, subtlest and most venomous serpent ever issued from the egg of sedition," and which waxed and prospered under new shapes, even until that day sixteen years hence, when a New York crowd flung up its hats calling, "God save Washington, President of the United States!"

I learned, too, in those weeks all the issues we had with Britain. My young heart burned as I conned those Parliamentary statutes forbidding the shipment of a single yard of cloth from one colony to another, and prohibiting the erection in any corner thereof of "any rolling, slithing or plating mill, and any manufacture of steel." Nor was my blood cooled when I read Hutchinson's speech to the legislature laying down in coarse nakedness the British doctrine of Parliamentary supremacy;—that our forefathers by coming to America had forfeited the Englishman's right to choose his own rulers, and that "no line could be drawn between the supreme authority of Parliament, and the total independence of the colonies."

Was I the only Massachusetts man who thought, as he thus neared the Valley of Decision, that if such was the case there were worse catastrophes than "Independence"?

So my pen copied and my brain teemed with long thoughts. Like many a friend I stole hours from sleep to read Locke and Leibnitz, Bolingbroke and Berkeley. I was present at that gathering when the sedate John Adams suddenly announced his opinion that "There was no more justice left in Britain than there was in hell, that he wished for war and that the whole Bourbon dynasty was on the back of Britain," then muttered some apology for "rash expressions." I was witness, too, when Hannah Adams, watching her father writing a lengthy petition to the King, remarked in an awesome whisper, "Soon, papa, that paper will be touched by the royal hand." Whereat Samuel Adams smiled most grimly, "Soon, my dear, it will more likely be spurned by the royal foot."

. . . I have no skill to write of these things as could a

historian. Enough if I can make Roger Gilman and his
friends tell a plain, honest story.—The vacation waned.
Soon I would have to return to Harvard. My relations
with the Rivoires I leave till a little later, simply remarking that I soon learned that M. Georges gave Watchhorn
and Shrimpton very adequate reward for services rendered.
But another item can be mentioned here—the final break
between my uncles, with myself the innocent cause.

My presence in Boston of course was known, and my
attendance upon Samuel Adams. One evening therefore I
returned to Charter Street only to find dear Aunt Mercy
in tears:

"It had to come, Roger; it had to come, but I feel awful
about it."

"Awful over what?"

"Over Peleg and Eleazer. Why must King George
besides taxing and threatening us, smash up families! Eleazer was over to-day; said he'd heard why you were in town,
and he'd have none of it. Wouldn't scold if his nephew
followed Peleg's and Jonathan's disloyal opinions in private, but as to having him actively helping Sam Adams, he
put his foot down *there!*"

"And Uncle Peleg?" I inquired in some concern.

"Told Eleazer he'd better keep his Tory compliments
locked up in his own parlor. Then they had it hot and
heavy. When Fifields *do* want to use plain English they
succeed. It ended by Eleazer saying he'd not pay any more
of your term bills unless you quitted Sam Adams' company
instanter; and Peleg's telling him, 'I'm not so poor that I
can't stand for *all* my nephew's college, without bothering
for money made through rum and slavers!' After that
Eleazer went out the door with an up-and-down to his wig
and back buttons that told how he and Peleg would not
even nod when next they met in King Street.—And we're

glad to do it all for you Roger—but, oh! soul and goodness, I wish it hadn't come to this."

There was nought that I could say, except that I was sincerely sorry, but a certain wicked pleasure came the next day when I received the following from Hope:

"Dear Cousin: Papa commands that I must not let you visit here on Sudbury Street any more. But he has not forbidden me to call at the North Square. If you want a good excuse for dropping in there yourself, say that 'You are expecting to find Miss Hope Fifield.'—But if you don't chance to find her, perhaps you'll not feel too mournful!"

Before, however, I could turn to advantage these possibilities, that very afternoon I came on Herbert Dunmore himself headed toward Charter Street. He could hardly contain himself upon seeing me. "Give me joy, dear fellow, give me joy. I'm back to England. The ship called at Boston and how could I quit America without one word to the best friend that a fellow ever had in the world!"

"I'm happy because you're so happy. But what has befallen?"

"How can I mourn the gouty old wheezer as I ought? My uncle the bishop's gone off in an apoplexy. Left me not all his money, but a tidy part of it. Nice little income in the funds. I've got leave from General Gage. I can sell out my commission if I wish. I'm going home—to Peggy."

After that we had as pleasant an evening as Boston could provide for two young men, one of whom was extraordinarily anxious to spend money. Herbert paid his adieux at North Square and I was not at all displeased when Emilie said to him with her sweetest smile, "And tell Miss Whitehead that I know you so well that I am sure you will make her very, very happy."

The next day I accompanied him on his ship out as far

as Nantasket. We talked about the *Comet,* the *Fair Trader*
and our adventures, and speculated on the possible career
of Prothero in England. I made Herbert swear that he
would keep clear of duels and not be drawn into hot dis-
putes about the Colonies. "Defend us gallantly," said I,
"and make your friends know that Americans will put
forth for their liberties all that Englishmen will for theirs—
but remember, no pistol smoke will ever repeal bad taxes."

Herbert gave one of his shrugs. "For Peggy's sake I'll
be as cool as an iceberg.—But after *her* business is settled,
what one honest man can I'll do, to heal up this brawling
mess before those asses around Parliament House have
made it all too late." And then he became more intimate.
"Dear fellow; I feel like a dog sailing thus homeward, and
leaving your happiness still unconquered."

I gave him a downhearted grimace; "Let's not talk about
that. Neither of *my* uncles have died. One of them has
just turned me out. The other stands for my term bills,
but I heard him telling Aunt Mercy 'All my profit goes
on the rocks if the non-intercourse agreements hold.' "

"Damn your pride," cried Herbert in vexation. "You can
see the girl cares for you. Speak out and ask her promise
to wait."

"Tell me she's Yankee or even English and I'll say yes;—
curse those French customs."

"She's not English," smiled Dunmore leaning on the rail
and staring at the black rock of Nix's Mate, "but 'pon my
soul I doubt if she's now French. There's something catching in your western air. I vow she's half American already.
—It's well I'm going home, or in another year I'd have a
nasal drawl with the best of you, and knock off ale for
hard cider."

"Ah! Herbert," spoke I clutching his sleeve, "if only
Peggy and your joy were not so far, so very far away!"

"Oh! I'm coming back——" he vowed confidently.

"God grant it's soon," cried I, "for do you know I feel something in my bones—ere six months pass something will happen here in America that will make the ears of King George to tingle. And after that God send wisdom to those who rule England, or our ways as people part forever!"

"Your bones feel wrong," he laughed. Soon the pilot was casting off. I was over the side and we had parted after bantering words which had none the less of a throb behind them, because we both envied secretly the girls who could kiss and cry and make of farewells such sweet sorrow.

Herbert's tall Bristol ship glided down into the graying eastern horizon, and I went back to Boston and presently to my little room on Charter Street. His departure from America had taken hold on me. It seemed as if something very vital was passing beyond my ken. I lay awake long after the clocks were stroking midnight. All that of late I had heard or read concerning the life of the ruling powers of England was racing before my mental eyes: the wealth and glory of the upper classes, the feasting, the gaming, the bedizened mistresses of Rigby, Earl Sandwich and the Duke of Grafton and other high counsellors of the King. Half sleeping I pictured one of the fashionable halls of chance, with the titled macaronis and pensioned placemen, staking their thousands upon one great hazard, while glibly talking, even as Dr. Franklin wrote us, of *"Our* colonies," *"Our* subjects," *"Our* right to lay taxes."

My thoughts ran to the royal Hanoverian himself—narrow-minded, rigid in his notions of right, taught from youth to "be a King"; chasing the Pitts from his cabinet and replacing them with the pliable Norths and the unspeakable Germains. I thought of that other Britain, whereof came Herbert Dunmore, the Britain of the Chathams, the Burkes and the Barres—and I knew that for the hour they, one and all, were helpless. Then I tried to visualize Windsor and St. James, the great palaces and their pageants of age-long authority and military might. And last of all I saw the run-down house on Purchase Street and a gray-headed man in a shabby jacket, sitting by one faint candle at an old desk, and scratching, scratching with a stubby quill.

To whom belonged the future? A century hence to whom might Boston perhaps be rearing statues of bronze? To George III or to Samuel Adams? I fell asleep musing upon the question.

CHAPTER XIX

UNCLE ELEAZER SETS GOOD WINE

FROM this time onward I felt increasingly like a passenger embarked on a vessel sailing into a vast bank of fog. Others stood on the deck beside me. We all entered the gray void together; but what lay ahead, rocks, stormy billows, watery death or summer wavelets and welcoming havens,—that no man knew. That vessel I came to call "America." We were all aboard her. The one thing certain was the clinging density of the fog.

Soon now I would have to resume at Harvard, and as often as I dared my steps turned toward North Square. M. Rivoire had uttered heartfelt words for my services at Newagen. If he had not proffered material recompense it was out of a perfect delicacy. I was always sure of a friendly greeting and preferred rights in the little parlor. The situation tantalized me almost to madness.

What if Emilie's eyes flashed a welcome surpassing the touch of her hand? What if her grandfather was the personification of venerable graciousness? How could I bring myself to say to either, "I am the penniless son of a country minister. My business hopes are utterly uncertain. Nevertheless, presuming upon a debt of gratitude, I make bold to claim—?" There were times when I wished to heaven that mine had been no part in the rescue. With clear conscience and a head held high I could have made my demand, "We are in America not France and therefore—" Then if I had met refusal, I would at least have tried to

222

take my sorrow like a man. But now?—A hundred times I echoed Herbert's dictum, "Damn that Gilman pride!"

Uncle Eleazer's attitude at least gave me a decent excuse for more frequent visits to North Square than otherwise might have been seemly. Everybody knew my friendship for Hope, and that young mistress was a constant invader at Mlle. Rivoire's, being just then in the process of initiation into all the mysteries of lace-making. The parlor table was always strewn with lace pillows, bobbins and the like, and during long calls the only words I seemed to get were "Fond de Neige," "Point de Tresse," or "Demi-Marguerites."

Lucy Flucker also came almost as frequently as Hope; her zeal for lace-making was far less, but her visits had an amazing way of coinciding with the precise times when Henry Knox found that he was not needed at the bookstore. The two usually found means to sit in some corner, looking into each other's large, adoring eyes, while I tried to follow the lace-making or drew out of M. Georges one anecdote after another of his adventures in the West Indies, and also in India itself where he had served as clerk at Pondicherry while yet a very young man.

In the intervals between the work on the table, Hope would regale us with inimitable recitals of the present siege being laid to her by no less personages than those reverend gentlemen, Hirst and Fernwood, both having at length despaired of victory before the Rivoire intrenchments.

"And if I haven't your pretty face and wonderful ways," she would say in unaffected honesty, with an affectionate pat upon her beautiful friend's cheek, "I suppose they know that papa, like Mr. Flucker, has vowed that his daughter shall marry no Whig—and that young men who are Tories are scarce as hen's teeth around Boston. So they wrangle and jangle in our parlor just as once in yours, and Mr.

Hirst sighs and quotes the text 'It is not good that man should be alone,' and Mr. Fernwood looks at the ceiling and replies, 'A bishop must be blameless, the husband of one wife.' Then they both look hard at me, and after that they both ask father 'Did your black ivory venture get safe at St. Kitts?' Whereupon he chuckles, 'It certainly did,—and only sixteen put over to the sharks out of a good hundred.' And next they look hard at me again, each mentally remarking (you can all but hear 'em) 'I could stand her.' But when I'm upstairs before my tall mirror I make my eyes snap—this way,—and say aloud all to myself: 'Hope Fifield, Hope Fifield, if you aren't good enough for a Whig boy to marry you, at least God wants you to die an old maid!' "

. . . It was, however, upon that very day, as I was going along King Street that I ran squarely into Uncle Eleazer just emerging from the Bunch of Grapes Tavern. He stopped and looked queerly for an instant, then beckoned me to him. I obeyed readily, for we had never had any direct words in anger. To my great surprise he smiled benevolently, shifted his big gold-headed cane to his left hand, put his right through my arm and began conversing in an extraordinarily friendly fashion.

"Well, boy, don't think that because I've called a spade a spade to Peleg, I've anything agin *you.* Children must follow their parents, and you're a Whig just as Hope of course is a loyal dyed-in-the-wool Tory. We mustn't let Parliaments and taxes make our homes too miserable.—And so you're kind o' clerking for Sammy Adams—eh?"

This unexpectedly kindly approach was enough to put a less trustful fellow than myself off his guard. I betrayed no secrets, but admitted that I was frequently at Mr. Adams' house and employed in a confidential capacity. My uncle laughed, remarked that he feared Lord North would grow no gray hairs over *my* state papers, then asked if I

would be at liberty the following evening. At liberty I
was, and we parted with Uncle Eleazer smiling and nodding, and finally telling me not to be late at Sudbury Street
that evening, but to join him for supper.

The whole cordiality of his proceedings was such that I
continued my walk slightly clouded by suspicions, but a
little reflection convinced me that, like many another man,
Eleazer Fifield had repented of his quarrel with his brother
and was seeking a roundabout reconciliation. I had also
great hopes that he would renew his offer of half of my
term bills, for Peleg's shipping business was being heavily
cut into by the non-intercourse agreement against England,
he being one of the few greater merchants who observed it
strictly. I would therefore relieve him in every way possible.

The "supper" at the Sudbury Street house, however, proved
quite an affair. The black butler was in his bravest livery;
the mahogany groaned with the plate, the cut glass, the
napery and the magnificent Lowestoff punch-bowls. The
guests matched the splendor. If they were few, I had at
least the honor of putting my feet under the table along
with an Auchmuty, an Oliver and a Vassal. The feast also
was a triumph of turtle, whipped sillabubs, "fools," floating
islands and every other flummery which a rich merchant
could set before rich friends, not to mention the meat and
poultry. No ladies were present and at first I was fearful
the talk would be disagreeably political, but in this was
happily disappointed. Considering my age I was treated
as a person of some distinction, "A chip of *two* good old
blocks, eh, Fifield," Mr. Vassal was pleased to remark. By
the time the Parmesan cheese, the porter and the burgundy
came on I was entirely at my ease:—and Yetmercy used
often to say that she knew "Roger was a true Gilman—
he liked so to hear himself talk."

Alas! Talk I did, especially after the second glass. Since

that day I have seen much gain and some loss in our good
New England customs, but no greater gain than this—that
it is ceasing now to be necessary for a young man to know
how to "carry" well, as an indispensable part of his education. I had a reasonably solid head, but was still anything but a past master in the gentle arts of the table.
After the third glass of burgundy I knew well enough that
it was time to stop, but my uncle kept motioning for the
butler to do his duty and for me to do mine, and like a
jackanapes I continued. The conversation at length wandered along to the affair at Salem and Newagen: "Deplorable that Dunmore should thus unreservedly have taken the
Whigs' side—but I certainly had acted like a lad of spirit."
"Of course Prothero was an ass and a libertine—a blot upon
the scutcheon of loyalty." Later, indeed, I heard that I
set the whole table to roaring about the final scene at the
Townsend tavern.

The talk at last, however, drifted around to Samuel Adams,
and when I heard Mr. Oliver give out the broad hint that
Mr. Adams could wisely consider himself a "Sunday gentleman"—a bankrupt who ought not to show himself except
on the Sabbath for fear of seizure for debt, the strings of
my tongue were loosened—I know that I poured out such a
passionate defense of my chief and of his principles that
some of those present grew very red and threw back the
taunt, "If you were an older man, sir, then—" My uncle
nevertheless came vigorously to my rescue, "My nephew's
principles may be bad, sir, but at least you'll grant you've
put him on his mettle;" whereupon they all encouraged me
to speak yet more.

By this time my head felt extremely hot. I knew perfectly well that I ought at all hazards to hold my tongue,
yet I could no more have done so with that accursed burgundy inside of me than to have flown to the North Pole.

On and on I went, making boasts about the work of the
Committee of Correspondence, of the encouragement from
our friends in Virginia, of the plans for tightening the non-
importation pact and a dozen other things concerning which
silence had been golden. At last I lost all track of what my
mouth was saying, and my next clear recollection was that
of Nero helping me into the chariot to rumble me back to
Charter Street. I was barely sober enough to thank God
that there was strength left in my legs to take me into the
darkened house and upstairs to bed without assistance.—
And it was a late and shamefaced secretary who came to
Mr. Adams the next day.

But a far worse humiliation than a pricking conscience
was in store late on the afternoon following the dinner. I
had carefully estimated that another call at the North
Square was decorously in order, and thither I betook
myself to find in the parlor not merely Emilie and Hope,
but Paul Revere showing some newly imported clock-works
to M. Georges. Emilie's greetings were entrancingly cor-
dial, but Hope at once sprang at me in a kind of fury, her
black eyes literally starting out of her head.

"Cousin Roger—you are a traitorous fool."

"A fool, certainly, please your ladyship; but why the
'traitorous'?"

"Do you think I didn't overhear everything that passed
in that dining room? Do you suppose those broadcloth-
and-ruffles King's men listened to you just because you
have a slashing way and a deep strong voice? What was
my father fishing after? What was it last you said?"

"Much that was silly," I weakly defended, "nothing that
will do great harm. I'll be wiser next time."

"Next time?" Hope poured an ocean of scorn into her
tones. "Next time? What did you say *this* time?"

"I don't understand," I confessed.

"Well, just before your head went down upon the table you had been boasting that you carried keys to Mr. Samuel Adams' house, his study and writing desk all the time in your pocket; then you jingled them, and boasted that if Governor Hutchinson knew what you knew he'd gladly tell out a thousand guineas."

"Thank God they are safe here," I cried producing the key-ring with a burst of relief. "I was far gone indeed if I did that. If I had lost them——"

"Roger," continued Hope, passionately, "for goodness' sake swear you will not go to dinner at our house again."

"And wherefore?" interposed Paul Revere laying the clock-works carefully upon the table. My own mortification was such that if the cracks in the floor had been a trifle wider I must have gone through them, but everybody was now gathering around Hope and all were too excited even to reproach me.

"Papa would give me the stocks and ducking stool if he knew it," pursued my cousin, "but ears will be ears and chances, chances. I heard everything that passed to-day between him and Mr. Flucker. The Tories are desperate for revenge since Dr. Franklin sent back those copies of Governor Hutchinson's letters which betrayed his full mind about the Colonies. They say the King himself will give ten thousand pounds for the evidence that will put Mr. Adams in England and on the road to Tyburn. And now they think they see a way.—Roger is going to be invited to my father's again."

"Ha!" came from Paul and M. Georges together.

"Of course this time he may leave the keys behind—but probably he won't. And this time if the burgundy's a little stronger——"

"The keys could disappear," remarked M. Georges, "but in the morning our Roger is sad and sober. He seeks his keys. They are missing. In sorrow he tells Mr. Adams. *Voilà!* The keys become useless."

"The keys are not missing," rejoined Hope, "five minutes away from Roger while his head buzzes, then they can jingle again in his pocket; just a matter of a little wax. And I heard Mr. Flucker say 'Jo Wiggam's in town. He's our fellow for this.'"

"Everything's plain," remarked Paul staring hard, while as for me the room seemed whirling; but I straightened myself and confessed boldly, "I've played the fool and make no denial. Hope has saved me from an error that might have blasted my life. Of course I shall never accept another dinner from her father."

"Oh, but *mon* Roger," cried Emilie, her face lit with an inspiration, *"il faut,*—you must!"

"I don't follow," I confessed, being nearly out of my wits.

"But I do," cried Paul springing up with one of his great hearty laughs. "When Mr. Fifield bids you to dinner, go, drink hard,—*and be sure the keys are in your pocket!*"

Whereupon my brain ceased reeling, and for the first time since Hope began her horrid accusation, I began to see a little daylight, while Emilie clapped her hands for joy that the original thought was hers, and also (dear girl) because now the wretched affair might end in a manner not wholly to my discredit.

"Who's Jo Wiggam?" I demanded.

"Cooper on one of your Uncle's Newport slavers as I remember," quoth Paul. "Got in a stabbing affair at Provincetown and had to drop out of the ship's papers. Last I heard was that he was spying ashore for the revenue, just before Duddington came to grief at the burning of the *Gaspée.* Rum fellow to use—but 'all's fair in love, war and controversy' I guess Mr. Flucker would say."

There was very little to be arranged. Paul with a know-

ing wink reënforced by a *"Bien"* from M. Georges, informed
me that "The less you know of the business the better,"
and directed me to do only one thing—if I was invited by
Mr. Eleazer Fifield again to leave timely word with the
Rivoires. Hope thereupon stipulated that whatever befell,
no personal calamity should light upon her father, a condition to which Paul (somewhat reluctantly it seemed) consented. Therefore at last I went away with as remarkable
an adventure before me as ever awaited a brisk collegian.

Four days, however, elapsed with no move by my uncle,
and I was hugging the chance that Hope had been egregi-
ously deceived, when Nero himself accosted me as I came
along Mackerel Lane from the Adams house. With his
full moon smile he presented his master's compliments, and
"inasmuch as I would soon have to return to Harvard could
he again have me for dinner that evening?" I had only
time to hurry back to Peleg's (of course by way of North
Square) in order to make ready.

With many misgivings I was changing the key-ring into
the pocket of my best suit, when a new anxiety seized me.
What if, before I became befuddled enough to rifle, my
tongue became so loosed that I gave the secret away? A
refusal to drink copiously would have provoked instant
suspicion, but my good luck recalled to me the alleged
feats of divers sea-captains when they wished to outsit a
rival. I therefore practiced at their old trick, turning several glasses of water down my shirt bosom. The attempt
of course ruined a shirt, but the results were tolerable. An
amazing amount of liquid could certainly be made to trickle
inconspicuously along my chin and out of harm's way. The
stains from wine, of course, could not be wholly concealed,
but they would not be too great to pass for the spillings
of an inexperienced toper.

All this nice experimenting, however, took time, and I

was hard put to it to slap my head with powder and slip
into my best small-clothes and waistcoat. Even then when
I reached Sudbury Street upon the run all the older guests
had assembled; a right Tory company as might have been
imagined, Mr. Flucker, of course, and one of the younger
Hutchinsons, a member of the Royal Customs Commission-
ers, and several lesser fry, among whom I recognized the
saturnine countenance of Elnathan Hirst.

It required all my self-command to conceal my feelings
when my uncle gave me a very effusive welcome. He spoke
feelingly about "having no son of my own but being blessed
in my nephew," joked about "fear of being taken up for
misprision of treason by rubbing elbows with Sam Adams'
secretary," but then that "politics should stop when we
carve the mutton." Again I was treated as all but the son
of the house, but my ears being now primed, I caught the
whisper of my uncle to Flucker "There's a click from his
left pocket," then the reply "He's to sit by Bovary"; and
beside a Mr. Bovary of the Revenue Bureau I was certainly
planted, an utterly dumb fellow during all the courses,
whose standard utterance after the cloth had been cleared
was "Pass the port."

Many worse ordeals than this dinner have I endured, but
none more curious. Heaven denied me marked gifts as
an actor. At one moment disgust at the whole proceeding
nearly overcame me, and I was fain to allege illness and slip
out of the dining room with the keys still safe and sound
in my pocket, but I was diverted by the discussion over
the means of avenging poor Mrs. Leonard, who, for enter-
taining a British naval officer, had awakened that morning
to find her front doorway outrageously tarred and feath-
ered.

After that the subject circled back to the old straw of
the taxation problem, and Flucker surpassed the rest in

praising Lord North's familiar gospel, "The properest time
to assert our right to taxation is when that right is refused,"
and that "America must fear you before she can love you."
Certain present (possibly not in the state secret) deliberately baited me, and I recall wishing that I had enjoyed
the rights of a Dunmore or a Prothero to call out sycophants who defamed the motives no less than the objects
of my chiefs. Nevertheless somehow that live-long evening
went by. No doubt I was less defiant and talkative than
at the earlier dinner. My shirt managed to cover a considerable amount of good liquor which had miraculously
escaped my gullet. This time I became extremely stupid
and sleepy. I spoke less and less; permitted a coarse sneer
at Dr. Warren to pass unchallenged, and finally appeared
so far gone that I just knew when Flucker was giving a
very perceptible nod to Bovary. Then I felt a hand very
gently sliding into my pocket, while a great weight simultaneously slid from my mind.

Once more when the party broke up the cool night air
wakened me, and I got safely home without disgrace. The
keys of the Adams house were again reposing in my small-
clothes.

CHAPTER XX

AGAIN I must write of what I saw not with my own eyes, albeit my evidence is indubitable.

On a warm September evening in 1773, Thomas Hutchinson stood in one of the inner parlors of Province House. Chief Justice, Judge of Probate, Lieutenant Governor and now actual Governor of the Province of Massachusetts, he had risen to the highest position possible for an American subject of the King. No man in all the thirteen colonies had seemed more to be envied. A just judge, an able financier, a devout church member, a personal lover of righteousness, he would, if Grenville, Townshend, North and their royal master had restrained their itch for meddling with the Colonies, have ended his days as one of the acclaimed worthies of British America.

No family among the Very Respectables was more respectable than his, and few boasted a better fortune. Among his neighbors at Milton he was democratic and popular. His *History of Massachusetts* was the ablest historical work as yet written in the New World. His town mansion on Garden Court Street (repaired now since the sack by the mob in 1765) was one of the most luxurious in Boston; his large library matched the stately mansion. Providence seemed to have marked the owner to be one of the builders of America, if such a nation was written upon the destinies.

But Thomas Hutchinson (a man slight but not insignifi-

cant in stature) was pacing this chamber of his official
residence with bent head and a pursing of the lips. Around
him the coils were tightening. Eight years before, when
first the clouds blew up between Britain and America, he
had made his choice. Was it because he was a royal
official? Because he hated the Adamses and the Otises?
Because he saw gain for his family in the new taxes?
Because he was honestly persuaded by the High Tory argument as to the supreme power of Parliament? Who shall
say?—Where is the mortal who takes an adamantine stand
from an absolutely single motive?

But in 1765 when others were saying "Resist," he
(although he disliked the Stamp Act) had answered "Submit." And after that official position and personal pressure
had swept him into the leadership of the New England
Tories. The King had honored him, but he knew his own
countrymen hated him unspeakably. The affair of the
Boston Massacre had brought to him intense humiliation,
when Sam Adams had put fear in the heart of Thomas
Hutchinson. Now in 1773 the serpent-wise Benjamin
Franklin had sent back to Massachusetts copies of the
governor's private letters. All the province knew that its
first magistrate had written his British friends advising the
drastic coercion of the Colonies, and how for America there
must be "an abridgment of what are called 'British priv-
ileges'." The legislature had formally petitioned the King
for Hutchinson's removal.

What comfort to him that the petition was likely to be
flung back in anger and Franklin to be publicly disgraced
by the ministry? Hutchinson knew that his influence in
Massachusetts had nearly vanished. Around him still clung
only a little coterie of Tories, wealthy, polished, genteel,
but politically helpless. The little finger of Samuel Adams
was thicker than the loins of the royal governor; and

Hutchinson hated Adams now with a perfect hatred and would willingly have seen him to the gallows.

The parlor in Province House was of fitting official dignity.   The paneling was of San Domingo mahogany. Above the elaborately carved mantel was a large painting showing a fleet of battleships defiling before the Rock of Gibraltar. Transparencies of the royal arms were blazoned upon the windows, portraits of the royal family looked down from upper wainscoting. Bronze lamps threw a luxurious glow over the massy furniture, Turkey carpets and pictorial tapestry. Province House in short was the social center of Boston and the official focus for all the public life of Massachusetts.

His Excellency had been alone, but now with suitable scrape and flourish a scarlet-liveried African ushered in three gentlemen, who received greetings due to their importance; Mr. Flucker, the royal secretary, Mr. Eleazer Fifield, and a slightly younger man, Judge Robert Auchmuty of Roxbury, honorably famed as one of the ablest and most reasonable of the Massachusetts Tories. The governor motioned them into chairs, and they soon were in deep council.

"All's ready," announced Eleazer, in confidential tones, "We know Sam has gone on a long journey for him—to Dedham to see some other of his seven devils. Won't be back till late to-morrow."

"There's his family," remarked Hutchinson, thoughtfully adjusting his wig. "We've got over many eggs in that one basket. Fine eggs if they all get hatched; but if the basket falls——"

"All's provided for, Guvnor. The signal to Wiggam will be by starting a fire over at Hill's wharf. A little hay, a big blaze.—Austin'll see to that. Then the bell on New South'll ring. That'll bring the hull house and neighbor-

hood running out into the streets. The alarm should last
long enough for every purpose. We've learned the Adams
women-folk are crazy about fires; they scoot out to every
one of 'em."

The governor gave an uncomfortable cough. "You know
how little I like the matter. I wish it were well ended."
At which opening Auchmuty interposed earnestly, "And I
wish rather it were never begun. I've never dissembled.
This business goes beyond what's allowable for honorable
men."

"Pooh, pooh, Judge!" laughed Flucker, "you'll begin to
sing psalms over at Dr. Cooper's church. Who but a Whig
parson could have pumped you with such scruples! Hasn't
his Majesty himself looked for evidence these seven years
upon Adams?—And now if Fifield's scapegrace nephew's
boast is half correct there's enough rope in that writing
desk to make strong halters for every Son of Liberty in
these parts. By gad, sir, Fifield here was a cute 'un. He'll
get thanks and something better from London."

"As no doubt he shall," assented Hutchinson. "I need
hardly tell you that my last expresses from high personages contained hearty assent to the idea we've so long
urged—that a special peerage should be named for America,
a House of Lords for each province.—The loyal friends of
the Crown will not find they serve an ungrateful master."

"And you will be Baron of Medford from your distillery
there, eh, Fifield," chuckled the secretary, "and Auchmuty
here Viscount of Roxbury,—while Earl of Milton is the
smallest honor in store for his Excellency."

The judge however flushed and frowned, "We divide the
bearskin while the bear is dangerously alive. I will speak
plainly. Samuel Adams I count a dangerous man. If
admissible evidence exists against him, he should be tried
and punished; but we cannot be sure of the convicting
character of those papers; we can only be sure that the

royal cause will be wounded nigh mortally if such a scoundrel as Wiggam is employed to rifle that house and the least truth leak out. My friends affirm that thanks to these keys the house can be entered and Adams' papers mysteriously spirited away without traces of a vulgar robbery sure to kindle suspicion. What are the chances? To prove these papers, they must be traced to their origin. At best Wiggam's part must presently become known; at worst our own part will be discovered and Mr. Fifield's nephew, who I hear is a fine young spark although on the wrong side, will be branded as a spy, and treated as a leper even by the King's friends."

"Roger can take his chance; can take his chance," announced Eleazer doggedly. "I thought to teach Jo Warren a lesson when I knew he'd put the boy in that adder's nest—and by G——that quack doctor will know it and Sammy the serpent too."

"I appreciate your scruples, Judge," said Hutchinson turning politely to Auchmuty. "We have indeed only a choice of evils in this sad business. The project was Mr. Fifield's and Mr. Flucker's, not my own, but I cannot reconcile my duty to his Majesty with repulsing this easy chance to get convictive evidence against the man who has done more to alienate the King's subjects from their lawful allegiance than all the other Whigs in America. Let us to business, gentlemen."

The negro reappeared with decanter and glasses. The governor and his visitors fell into easy attitudes.

"Everything's arranged," spoke Flucker, "everything I mean but just one item on which at the last minute I'm shaky—who's to assure us of Wiggam?"

Auchmuty spat in sheer disgust. "The King is driven to use polite instruments!—But I thought you said the fellow was to be trusted."

"Why so Flucker and I *believe*," complained Fifield, "but

after all, as is oft said of better rascals than he, 'Every man has his price.' Hancock and Cushing and Molineaux if not Sam, have their guineas, and Jo Wiggam of course knows it."

"We floundered in deep mire when we chose this path," confessed Hutchinson, not without signs of sharing Auchmuty's sentiments, "but after the betrayal of my letters in England I feel loosed from over-qualmish hesitancy. The only way now if we are not to turn clear back is straight across. Some one of reliability must go with Wiggam to keep that scoundrel to his duty."

" 'Tis no errand, I grant, for a gentleman," remarked the secretary, "nor for any man who bears royal appointment be he only a tidewater. I have it, Fifield—this is a job for that sniffling parson of yours who groans and thunders at Hollis Street when jolly old Byles 's abed. His long limbs and long nose will keep tight after Wiggam."

"Mr. Hirst, do you mean?" returned Eleazer a little uneasily, inwardly conscious that people had been coupling that minister's name somewhat with his daughter's. "Why, he's a man of most correct politics and straightest orthodoxy, but yet I hoped——"

"If another *must* accompany Wiggam, Hirst is the man," interposed the governor decisively, "slim as an eel and absolutely committed to the honest cause." He touched a bell, another negro entered and soon departed with a hastily written memorandum to bear to Mr. Hirst's widower lodgings on Orange Street. Then for half an hour the four bent over papers touching the latest controversy about the payment of the provincial officials direct by England.

.   .   .   .   .   .

Elnathan Hirst was not a man prone to self-searching in any matters not connected with the precision of his theology, but he had most unpleasant thoughts when he betook himself out of Province House. Four years earlier he had quitted an obscure Connecticut charge, where his parishioners had revolted more at his personality than at his hyper-orthodoxy, and accepted the summons to assist Dr. Byles. Hitherto he had taken little part in the public debates with England, but then it had been necessary, in order to secure the position at Hollis Street, to profess immediate and unflinching adhesion to the royal cause. All the other Congregational churches of Boston had been captured by the Whigs; for that very reason all the Tory influence had been mobilized to assure at least one pulpit where Sunday after Sunday the audience could be warned that "The powers that be are ordained of God."

Hirst had discharged his part of the contract faithfully. As a result he had been ostracized by all his fellow clergy in Boston, who had tolerated the witty, reasonable and aged Byles; and although Elnathan was a very thick-skinned man he knew that even the Tories were giving him merely a contemptuous patronage and using him sometimes for very unchurchly purposes. The task laid upon him this evening was the worst. He had come in his innocency to Province House imagining Hutchinson had some state secret to confide to him—and lo, the state secret was this!

Hirst, be it said, had made a respectable number of protests, "The Lord, he was positive, had not called him to the work;" but the governor had fixed upon him a very cold eye, "We must all sacrifice our feelings in the King's service, Mr. Hirst," and the latter had known that a parish meeting was soon approaching when the problem of his reappointment would be the first business on the calendar. —And here he was walking along the darkened streets from Province House rubbing elbows with Jo Wiggam, as ill-favored and squatty a fellow as ever had shunned hand-cuffs and hemp.

Wiggam was from Rhode Island, the abode of strange men and strange sects. Hirst thanked God that neither Connecticut nor Massachusetts claimed his birthplace. The ex-slaver's walk and conversation were what might have been expected from one whose life had been spent between Middle Passage forecastles and dodging the thief-taker. He had consented to " 'commodate Mr. Flucker" on the distinct understanding that something would be arranged so that he could show himself with greater free-dom around Long Wharf.

One of Hirst's most essential tasks now was to ascertain before the Adams premises were quitted that Wiggam had been literate enough to gather what were genuinely impor-tant papers. The minister also carried in his pocket the ring of carefully filed new keys that were to make entrance safe and easy. It was to be hoped that nothing would be discovered before Adams returned to Boston, and by that time every important document would have been under microscopic scrutiny at Province House. If Mr. Roger Gilman was next accused by the Whigs of succumbing to a loyalist uncle's blandishments, why, doubtless it would be very awkward for the young gentleman, but all was law-ful in so good a cause.

Wiggam, however, was in an unfriendly mood. Why wasn't he trusted? What business had a long-legged gos-peller like Hirst in the affair? True, Hirst was not actually to enter the Adams house. All the technical breach of the law was reserved for the other, but that award of perilous honor did not content the Rhode Islander.

"Yer being well paid, parson?" he queried, when hardly had the iron fence gate of the governor's grounds clicked behind them and they were out in Marlborough Street.

"It is for the love of the King and of God who ordains him, my man," corrected his companion, austerely.

"Love of King and God? Huh!—Love of the 'blunt' as Englishers say, I warrant. Parsons and A. B. hands, they all steer the same course although they call the old port t'other names.—Dash me, though, if I like the soundings. It's not a cable's length round to Mr. Hancock's. He's an open-handed man——"

"Have a care, fellow," warned Hirst; "the old charges are still over you. The Whigs will hardly help you as they did that Watchhorn."

"No, damn my eyes; my hand's given and my oath's sworn, but once out of this, I'll serve the Whigs for a moidoire.—Well, it's good and darkish. We'll be soon down Long Lane and then watch for the blaze on Hill's Wharf. —Roast me to 'Tarnity, if I don't like tapping tills and strong boxes better—but gentlemen must be obliged."

"Peace, man of sin," ordered Hirst with his best clerical dignity.

"Now, do cuss me out with a dozen fathoms of good bilgewater oaths," objected Wiggam, "anything smelling like a prayer turns my innards and spoils my luck." The ill-assorted pair continued to traverse in silence first Milk Street and then the narrower and much darker Long Lane. It was still only the middle of the evening, but quiet Boston citizens turned in early, and they passed almost no one. The new street lamps glittered along King Street and its main arteries, but all the minor ways were plunged in blackness. Elnathan went along with most uneasy pictures of his own snug study at Mrs. Crandall's wandering through his head. A certain resentment against his royalist patrons was flaring within him. What a position for a minister of the Gospel? Were the anti-Whigs' arguments in truth so strong? Had he the least real chance of storm-

ing Miss Hope Fifield and her father's guineas?—
Once, however, he turned his head suddenly at the
founderous corner where Long Lane merged in Cow
Lane and plucked his companion's arm, "Hark! Are we
followed?"

"Only cats chasing," growled his confederate. "Ha!
There goes the blaze. What a flare a little hay makes!—
And there goes the church bell.—Now to whip into this
black alley where we can watch the house, and glue our
eyes on the door. People are running down Summer Street
already, but it may take the engines to fetch out them
Adams."

Wiggam had evidently surveyed the premises. He took
advantage of the noise and racing in the street to produce
flint, steel and a small lantern which he now lighted and
hid under his coat, he also (to Hirst's great discomfort)
loosened a long sheath-knife in his belt and made sure that
it would slip out easily. The tumult toward the wharf
mounted steadily. Figures came running even down quiet
Purchase Street. If the two emissaries were discovered
it would be assumed they were merely on their way to the
fire.

The Adams house had been dark when they approached.
Now candles shone in the windows, and first the honest
black face of Surrey and then Hannah and Mrs. Betsy
were peering forth in excitement. The blaze lit up the
spars of small vessels along the water front. There was a
yell, "The sloop's in danger!" and next followed the
thunderous racket of forty men running with the ropes as
the nearest fire engine came grinding down Summer Street.
The most placid household was never proof against such
temptation. The house door swung open. Que issued forth
leaping and barking wildly; then Surrey, then Hannah,
finally Mrs. Betsy herself, carefully locking and plucking

out the key. They all vanished toward the red glow and
noisy excitement.

"Guess your prayers hit after all, parson," rejoined Wiggam. "Even the dog's gone out. He might ha' made trouble,
that's why the knife. Now them keys. Thank 'ee. What
with such smooth picklocks, everything should travel into
this 'ere bag as quietly and gently as—" He had taken the
ring from Hirst's reluctant fingers, and was whipping in
through the shrubbery by the door.

Elnathan muttered something partaking of an oath. He
had never been in such a predicament in all his forty years.
Verses about the lawfulness of "spoiling the Egyptians"
jangled in his head with the familiar mandate "Thou shalt
not steal." After all, the deed had been devised by Flucker
and Fifield. It was being executed by Wiggam. He
Elnathan, was merely a harmless and necessary intermedi-
ary in the King's, and therefore in Heaven's, service. But
whilst his head buzzed his companion had quitted him. The
clergyman could hear Wiggam give one rattle at the door.
The key apparently fitted to a nicety, everything was again
silent.

Hirst had intended to remain at the head of the black
alley in the street. The law could then surely fasten
nothing upon him; but was the alley really a safe place?
Once or twice a party of tall boys and girls ran shouting
and whooping down Purchase Street almost brushing
against Elnathan. The Adams grounds, spacious, covered
with an ill-tended garden and untrimmed bushes, seemed
to offer better shelter. And although Hirst neither saw nor
heard any person near him, that uncanny sixth sense which
will awaken in moments of danger seemed to tell that he
was somehow watched. It was not too late. He could forsake Wiggam and leave that worthy to finish his work and
make his own report at Province House.

Elnathan was almost in the act of gliding back into the safety of Long Lane when a crushing thought arrested him. The robber had spoken of Mr. Hancock. If Wiggam were left an instant after he had secured the papers, what was to prevent him (perhaps with the aid of a more intelligent crony) from sifting out the documents, selling back all the more condemnatory to the Whigs and turning a mass of worthless writings over to the governor against his fee. This was the very treachery feared at Province House.

There could be no turning back. Hirst pictured the Hollis Street meeting and Eleazer Fifield rising to "move, Mr. Moderator, that we proceed to the question of a new assistant for Dr. Byles."— He swore again under breath and then, following his dread rather than his reason, darted straight through the garden gate and planted himself behind a tall lilac bush by the Adams door.

Outside, toward Hill's Wharf the blaze was beginning to go down. Two men passed along Purchase Street, one remarking loudly, "Not much of a fire—queer how it started." Soon the Adams women-folk would be coming home, accompanied (serious consideration) by the redoubtable Que. Had the dog a keen scent? Had Elnathan put pungent hair oil on his wig just before obeying the summons of the governor? Why in the name of—angels, was Wiggam taking so long? Had he turned traitor already?

At last there was a faint sound from the interior of the house. Wiggam had completed his errand and was descending the staircase. Now he was reopening the door and flinging back his coat to expose the lantern enough to find again the keyhole. His sack dangled from his shoulder; it seemed well filled and heavy. Elnathan's caution forsook him, he edged up to the very elbow of the robber.

"Did you find the study, the desk, the letter books?" he began whispering.

"All here, bag's full, what with these 'ere keys 'twas easy as drowning a puppy in a mill-pond. When the old fool git's back from Dedham he'll think——"

Here Wiggam's voice died in a cough and a gurgle. Some extinguisher seemed being thrown over his head. Elnathan in animal terror let out a cry fit to raise the church-yard. He made one bound toward the garden gate and freedom, tripped over something, fell half-stunned upon the brick walk, and felt a heavy body lighting upon his back. Next force irresistible dragged him to his feet, and a lantern was flashing in his face while a voice sounded:

"All's done very neatly. Now which one has the keys?"

While a second voice replied: "Lord Jehovah, but it's the parson who give me Job's comfort on Boston Common."

The first voice was from Paul Revere, the second from Remember Watchhorn.

CHAPTER XXI

THE NEW USE FOR FEATHER-BEDS

AFTER the departure of their emissaries Hutchinson and his three friends continued deep in business. A fast vessel was about to sail. If the Adams papers met expectations the technical evidence, so long desired, against the Whig leaders would soon be far out to sea on its way to the attorney general. This sanguine circle was presently joined by none other than Chief Justice Peter Oliver, the stiffest, most hated Tory magnate in the province. To him the new prospect was at once revealed, and he joined in applauding "the boldness and courage of Mr. Flucker and Mr. Fifield—but why had they all been so squeamish earlier as to let like chances slip."

"Egad!" fumed Auchmuty at length, "we're not been squeamish now. Hang me for a traitor but I hope these papers will come to nothing. Adams' a clever fox."

"Only a little more evidence," avowed the governor, rubbing his beringed fingers. "The old affidavits were almost enough. Only a few unguarded, reckless phrases. —But what a chance if we can also put lime on Johnny Hancock, or Warren, or even those big Virginians—Sam surely writes to them."

"His Majesty'd all but patent a peerage," remarked Oliver, sampling the steaming punch-bowl now on the table, "for something to send to England against that Patrick Henry, or young Tom Jefferson or that rich planter—what d'ye call him—oh! yes, George Washington."

"Over-estimated man, that Washington," corrected Hutchinson. "Bad opinions certainly, but no originality, no force, so I hear. Good listener merely, lets other fools talk. Got a big fortune through his wife, and though he may flirt with the Whigs, he'll never risk his acres when it comes to a lawing matter."

"My Virginia correspondents rate Colonel Washington otherwise," observed Auchmuty in quiet dissent.

"Well," laughed Flucker, "we'll let your fine planter fellow pass. Only I hope something's found against Ben Franklin in London so he can be moved over from his neat chambers to snugger quarters at Newgate."

"Gentlemen," said Auchmuty, his fine features curling, "we take once again the wrong course against our misguided countrymen. We are here among ourselves. My own loyalty I hope is beyond reproach; but what is the whole story of this unhappy broil betwixt America and Britain save one rope of blunders by ministers? Writs of Assistance, Stamp Act, Townshend's mad taxes, the dispatch of the troops, the harrying of the coasters by that foot Duddington of the *Gaspée* and that libertine Prothero —blunders all!—and why finally (to eke out the India Company's profits) are North, Sandwich, Germain and the rest, who know no more of the state of America than I know of Argylshire, proposing to force this tea issue in a manner sure to set Charles River and mightier streams afire?"

The governor and chief justice alike grew very red, and the former turned on Auchmuty with asperity:

"Remember that you hold office of the King, sir."

"I do, and because I would have his Majesty retain the affectionate allegiance of these colonies, I speak with freedom. For myself I believe that an attempt to seize Sam Adams, noxious though he be, will precipitate the very

thing we dread. I hope that Wiggam will fail. I hope
that the dispatches to-morrow will beseech ministers to
retrace a path that has not quite led to the final disaster
—but which approaches its calamitous goal."

"Auchmuty likes to have his say," growled Flucker,
"well—Fifield and I will get the royal thanks, he needn't."

"Judge Auchmuty is of course as loyal as the rest of us,"
spoke Hutchinson, more affably. "The evening wanes. We
ought to hear from Purchase Street ere long.—Fill your
glasses, gentlemen—the fitting toast, 'The King'." The
glasses clinked, and Flucker and Oliver started the familiar
if unpoetic royalist catch:

> "God save the King!
> Long may he sway,
> East, north and south,
> In fair Americay!"

This being promptly followed by the more jovial,

> "King George, and may he go round, go round!—"

They were halted abruptly by the apparition of the negro
flunkey, his eyes rolling with consternation:

"Please, please, suhs,—there's a great mob of people
coming down Milk Street, and dragging two pussons to the
jail!"

The color crept from Hutchinson's cheeks. "It cannot
be that Wiggam?" he began hoarsely.

"I'd best inquire for your Excellency," proffered Auchmuty going out, while a dull roar as of many voices swept
through the open casement, and the others looked at one
another in startled silence.

Auchmuty returned speedily. "No time for recrimina-
tions, gentlemen," he reported, in a black frown, "I will
chide no one; but I learn that Jo Wiggam and Elnathan
Hirst are now on their way to the prison on Queen Street
surrounded by a growing rabble. The word is going about

that they were seized quitting the Adams house with a bag crammed with papers."

The picture of Hutchinson was pitiful, his lips moved without words. The state of Flucker and Fifield was hardly better, but Oliver kept his poise, possibly because he was less committed.

"They have nothing to connect them with Province House," he observed.

"Nothing," said Auchmuty dryly, "except their own confession which they will surely give soon, seeing the terrors that surround them. After that the common knowledge that they would never have run such risk without enormous motive will do the rest."

"Betrayed! Before God, who was the villain!" groaned Fifield; "Oh! to have his heart's blood."

"It's wiser to save our own hearts' blood first," remarked Oliver, puckering his shrewd lips.

"I can't think clearly," lamented the governor, "Auchmuty, Oliver, good friends, stand by me. Use your wits. My conscience was against this, but Flucker and Fifield over-persuaded. For the honor of the King avert this scandal!"

"What must be done, must be done quickly," declared the younger jurist. "It's stroking ten. The town's rising. Mark that yell now. *Get a rope!*'"

"If they are hanged in the street," cried Flucker in tones of relief, "our danger is over."

"There'll be no hanging—yet," spoke Oliver more sagely, "trust your diabolical Whigs for that. Wiggam and Hirst will have time for a very full confession."

"In heaven's name," urged Hutchinson, "have you no expedient?"

"Only a bitter one," said Auchmuty, "but one to be used immediately.—Judge Oliver, as chief justice of the Prov-

ince, you are entitled to demand that these prisoners be
given an immediate hearing. Send to the jail and command
that out of regard for the peace of the town you will have
the two brought to Province House instantly. Meantime
with his Excellency's permission I will betake myself to
the one personage in Boston who I think can control the
mob, and afford an avenue to safety,"—And he reached for
his hat.

"Where are you going?" demanded Hutchinson.

"To Hanover Street,—to Warren."

The governor wrung his hands, but nodded a gloomy
assent: "If it must be, it must. He's the best of the Whigs,
and will play the game like an honorable enemy.—A thousand pounds if only this night were well over."

One of the constables always on duty about Province
House was sent away with the chief justice's precept to
the head jailor to bring over the two alleged robbers immediately, and for some minutes the group of Tories sat in
a gloomy silence while the candles sputtered in their
sockets. Wiggam and Hirst might have been terrified into
a complete confession already, although this was unlikely
in view of the evident tumult attending their arrest. And
for once in his life Thomas Hutchinson prayed fervently
that Joseph Warren had been that night in his surgery
devising works of treason.—What if sick old Mrs. Belling-
ham had summoned him to her bedside again?

Before this doubt could be resolved, the renewed trampling and many voices coming from the not distant prison
proclaimed that the chief justice's order had been obeyed,
and that the jailor had sent over the prisoners almost before
they had been placed in his custody. The gates in the iron
fencing about Province House had been swept open; a
couple of hundred men and boys, many of them bearing
lanterns, came tramping up the gravel coach paths and

over the fine stretch of lawn before the high flight of stone
steps to the entrance hall.

The governor, Flucker and Fifield not unwisely failed to
show themselves, but Oliver, a man of years, dignity and
reasonable courage, presented himself upon the raised landing before the portal. As the lantern light fell on his long
scarlet cloak and enormous official wig, there was a partial
hush and a falling back of the crowd.—Tory or no Tory
it was a great thing to be chief justice of Massachusetts.

"I am informed," sounded the voice of Oliver from his
post of vantage, "that an arrest for a serious crime has
been made. The noise in the streets indicates imminent
danger of a breach of the peace. Being at Province House
to consult his Excellency I have felt it incumbent upon
me, both in justice to the prisoners and in vindication of
the laws, to have the accused at once brought before me
in order to be satisfied——"

"Better satisfied if we hadn't nabbed 'em,—hey, Jedge?"
bawled a voice from the dark recesses of the rear.

"Silence," ordered the hearty tones of Henry Knox, whose
big frame was conspicuous under the torches. "Everything
in order! Produce the prisoners, Paul. Then tell the
chief justice the circumstances of their arrest."

For sufficient reasons Watchhorn remained inconspicuous,
but Paul Revere, a stalwart associate Lendall Pitts, and
a pair of constables promptly hustled to the foot of the
stairway the two prisoners. They were abject spectacles,
Wiggam had resisted just enough to cause his captors to
maul him thoroughly. Hirst had resisted not at all; but
he was the color of a whitewashed post, and his black
coat and white neckband were tattered and mud-splashed.
Both captives were too terrified for more than reckless
mumblings.

Oliver apparently recoiled with horror as his eye lit

fairly upon Elnathan. "By heaven, gentlemen, do I see the godly Reverend Mr. Hirst?—Some horrid mistake."

"Perhaps he walked in his dreams, please your Honor," asseverated Paul, "but I seized him with my own hands in Mr. Adams' garden while he peered into the sack of plunder brought out by this pretty fellow—whom all the catchpoles have been seeking." And he applied his boot to the crupper of the cowering Wiggam.

The justice put on his best dignity; "These good people must understand that we can only hold proceedings inside, and that only the parties making the arrest and the immediate witnesses can be admitted to Province House. Constables, bring in the prisoners."

The two victims were hustled up the staircase, followed by about twenty of their guards or captors. The candles had been lit around an enormous glass chandelier in one of the banqueting parlors. The coverings were over the elaborate furniture, but the lights shone across the polished parquet floor, the high white wainscoting and an extensive tapestry depicting the campaigns of Marlborough. A full length Copley portrait of former governor Bernard in official regalia stood out in startling contrast to the angrily excited or chalk-white faces which were gazing now upon Oliver.

The atmosphere was that of a Leiden jar. Barring the negro servants and three or four inept and unvalorous constables, Province House was unguarded. Outside, the crowd was multiplying and roaring. A spark could send it off. The chief justice beckoned for silence, adjusted his wig, and seated himself before a heavy table. Only by an extreme effort did he restrain himself from imploring the prisoners then and there, as they loved King, country and their own happiness, to keep silence. As it was, and desperately sparring for time, he obtained a modicum of silence, and asked "under what circumstances the arrest had been made?"

Paul Revere with firm accents recited how he had seized Hirst, and how "a friend" had captured Wiggam. They "had had their reasons" for watching the premises. The two prisoners had been seen gliding down Long Lane and Purchase Street in a stealthy manner, they had lurked by the Adams house until the alarm of fire had sent the inmates toward the blaze, then Wiggam had entered the dwelling using a set of keys that fitted the locks perfectly, while Hirst had entered the grounds and stood close to the entrance, evidently to assist in the felony. When Wiggam came forth his bag was found to contain not the family spoons but "something else."

"Aye, *something else!*" came as a warning mutter from a dozen voices, and their tones sent the courage of despair through Hirst. He bounded forward from his captors, found his tongue and poured out frantic pleadings. "Oh! Your Honor won't let them manhandle me. You know at whose command I went all reluctant. His Excellency said——"

"Silence, prisoner," ordered the justice, one shade less pale than the captive, "you cannot be heard until the charges against you are fully stated." The avowal of Hirst was not however lost on the others. The mutterings rose to a dull roar. They were being echoed by noises from without. Oliver knew that forty men were crowding the staircase, and listening to the voices inside. Most ominous of all were now the scattered shouts, "Where's the gov'nor? Trot out the gov'nor!"—The justice saw before his eyes a more horrid repetition of those Stamp Act riots, when he with all the Tory chiefs in Boston had fled in terror for their lives. Matters were thus at the tensest when to the utter relief of Oliver the crowd was seen parting, and the torchlight revealed many rough fellows pulling off their

hats—"Dr. Warren; way for Dr. Warren, good people."
And the first lieutenant of Samuel Adams was beheld coming up the steps side by side with the flushed and excited
Auchmuty.

The doctor was scrupulously, almost finically dressed.
He had not forgotten his gold-headed cane, nor to shake
out a fine lace handkerchief. In his bearing was neither
insolence, excitement, nor condescension. He pulled off his
hat before Oliver and gave precisely the bow owed by a
high-bred gentleman to an important magistrate. He set
his eyes with a mingled caution and a barely betrayed
twinkle, upon Revere and his company, and calmed them
instantly. He gave Hirst one hard glance, and the wretched
prisoner lapsed into silence.

"A thousand pardons, your Honor," his voice was polite
and even, "I was returning from my attendance upon Mr.
Pendleton (his fever is better, I rejoice to say) when meeting Judge Auchmuty I was told something of the strange
event of this evening. Inasmuch as Mr. Samuel Adams is
out of town, as his intimate friend I take the liberty, his
property being concerned——"

"Your intervention, sir, is very welcome," Oliver had
not addressed a Whig with such cordiality for years. "The
circumstances are so peculiar, unwarranted suspicions so
easy to excite, that I, we, the governor I may say——"

"I apprehend, sir," Warren's tone had the least tinge of
irony, "that political passions will of course color the
thoughts of even the most zealous; but now if the constables
will be responsible for the prisoners and these excellent
people will wait, your Honor and Mr. Hutchinson himself
perhaps will confer with me in an inner room." As the
justice beckoned him toward an inner door, the doctor
contrived to pass close to the captives with the whisper,
"Keep quiet if you would live till daylight." Whereupon
he was shut from view.

Not even to the highest Sons of Liberty was revealed all that Joseph Warren said and heard in that inner parlor; the one thing certain is that when after an interval long enough to make the crowd now in the halls and ante-rooms again restless and muttering, Thomas Hutchinson was seen in the doorway clasping the hand of the doctor; and the governor's voice sounded clearly. "We are honorable foes, Dr. Warren, and our contest shall always be one of principles and not of personalities. Assure Mr. Adams that as long as I am magistrate no measures save those strictly sustained by the law will ever be permitted against him."

Revere, Knox, Pitts and others came crowding about Warren as he stepped out among them. He took forth a silver snuff box, took a pinch deliberately, then said with a voice that carried to a score: "All is satisfactorily explained, gentlemen. The prisoners of course acted from their own criminal motives. They will now be taken to jail."

But even while he spoke Oliver was muttering to the constables: "Yes—take 'em back. But if anything happens on the way—*don't risk your lives defending 'em.*"

The crowd left the grounds of Province House in a tolerably orderly manner. It was afterwards alleged that Wiggam and Hirst were certainly conveyed, unmolested by anything worse than curses and carrots, until near the Old Brick Meeting House. At this point a sudden rush of men down Cornhill swept them in a twinkling out of the custody of the constables. Somebody came tearing up from the Long Wharf clattering a warm tar bucket. Somebody threw open an upper window and flung into the street two enormous featherbeds. Fragments of clothing said to have pertained to Hirst and Wiggam were later passed on as precious relics especially in the families of Henry Knox and Paul Revere. The last competent report of the two unfortunate prisoners had it that they were to be seen (in

Scriptural language) "high and lifted up," each clinging for
dear life to stout poles upon the broad shoulders of ship-
yard workers. They both were marvelously clad and were
being prodded with boat-hooks when they failed to join
heartily in the new militant refrain of the Liberty Song:

> "For Freedom we're born, and like sons of the brave,
>   We'll never surrender,
>   But swear to defend her
> And scorn to survive if unable to save!'

The next day Jo Wiggam and Elnathan Hirst had vanished like a mist from the good town of Boston. Remember
Watchhorn had disappeared likewise. It was remarked,
however, that one of Mr. Peleg Fifield's schooners had just
sailed for Honduras after a cargo of mahogany, and that
her captain must needs pass close to certain unfrequented
islands where the old pirates were wont to maroon unwelcome shipmates.

It is more certain that soon after these events Governor
Hutchinson averred in public that if Dr. Joseph Warren
was mistaken in his politics, for all that he was a magnanimous, true-hearted gentleman, and when Messrs. Flucker
and Eleazer Fifield called next at Province House they
were both informed that his Excellency was too engaged
to see them. Mr. Flucker, however, upon meeting Mr.
Samuel Adams on King Street was greeted by the latter
with an unwontedly ceremonious bow, and the smiling
remark that "he understood that he came near to being
indebted to Mr. Flucker for a voyage at public expense to
England."

As for Mr. Roger Gilman, when next he visited North
Square Mlle. Rivoire gave him one of her most rippling
laughs, and demanded, "How he enjoyed being compelled
to *transpirer* for his country?"

CHAPTER XXII

WHAT THE CANDLE HEARD

THIS episode around the Adams house brought me no small credit among the semi-initiated. Even Mr. Adams himself believed that it was I who had lured the Tories on into a pit which they had digged for others. But for myself it was a matter of intense humilation,—how would my convivial folly have ended except for Hope? As it was, Dr. Warren spoke a kindly but unmistakable word about "This being a lesson," yet then added others about "least said soonest mended," and then bade me copy certain correspondence so confidential that I knew that I had been restored to full graces; a thing I met with sober thankfulness.

. . . We were entering the autumn of 1773. Hitherto in the debate with Britain there had been long periods of sullen quiescence. Now the contest blazed up with unfailing heat. Ever higher the flames and the passions which fed them. Intervals there were none save those of hectic preparation. While deeper and ever deeper went the searchings of the hearts of men.

Often, I imagine, during these years of foreboding, from the Stamp Act to the martial clarions, almost any thoughtful man in America could have written what John Adams would so often jot in his diary "Sunday—at home with my family—*thinking*." Eternally true also is what he was to record in green old age, "The Revolution was affected before the war began. The Revolution was in the minds and hearts of the people."

But now this time for "thinking" was almost over. Even the years of war which were to summon me to stand to my chance of a soldier's death seem less tense, less vivid in my mind, than those twenty months which sped from the first tidings that King and ministers were resolved to throw down the gauntlet to America to that April morning when the gauntlet was taken up.

Enough time has now gone for me to see the things that soon may be coming. To another age we of the Revolution may seem heroes undaunted, spotless of motive, valorous as paladins, enduring as saints. Men will canonize us, will almost deny that our passions and our wisdom were strictly mortal.—And they will be very wrong.

Then in reaction will come other men. They will belittle our motives; will seek behind the invocations to Liberty for the sordid chink of coppers; will gleefully drag to light our human failings; will deny that our grievance against Britain was worthy of great passions; will give us a seat in history only a little higher than for those ministers who blundered into the acts which we saw fit to brand as "deeds of tyranny."—*And they will be still more wrong.*

Let any man read without bias the story of the laws which George III and his Parliaments laid upon the Colonies, read them, I say, with a full knowledge of the British and the colonial inheritance of freedom, and all that it implied, and he will know of surety how that freedom was in jeopardy and demanded vindication even unto blood. While for ourselves, who were permitted to join in warfare, and many of us die, that our children's children might dwell in a free land, growing ever into the light of God's more perfect day—what can I claim?—I can claim in the words of John Adams that we have the right (however in person unworthy) to be "ranked with that mighty line of heroes and confessors and martyrs, who since the beginning of history have done battle for the dignity and happiness of human nature against the leagued assailants of them both."

Likewise the man who, for smoothing present feelings toward England, or perchance because to him all wars seem horrid and warriors undesired heroes, denies the bitterness of our grievance or the necessity of what we did, defaces not the memory of the Men of the Revolution, but the eternal tablet of Truth.

Was it only for pelf, relief from taxes, less hampered trade, that in those years of trial we marched forth into the night? Can there never come to men of limited knowledge, narrow interest, commonplace ambition, gleams from the mountain-tops of a wider and better country? No chords of the Nobler Music? No consciousness of being used for some great end beyond mere finite knowledge?

Was Jonathan Edwards alone, when long before Independence dawned, he affirmed his trust that "God would presently renew the world of mankind; and that there were many things which make it probable that this work will begin in America?"

Was Philip Freneau alone in his thoughts, when, in 1772, he made his Acasto and Leander sing together of how America shall spread,

> "Dominion to the north and south and west,
> Far from the Atlantic to Pacific shores;"

and there bring forth a civilization wherein

> "I see a Homer and a Milton rise
> In all the pomp and majesty of song,"

in a vast land where shall be

> "Fair science's smiling and full truth revealed,
> The world at peace and all her tumults o'er,
> The blissful prelude to Emmanuel's reign."

Was John Adams alone among his fellows when, as an obscure country lawyer, in 1765 he wrote: "I always consider the settlement of America with reverence and wonder, as the opening of a grand scene and design in Providence for the illumination and emancipation of mankind all over the earth"?

At least this is true—I was not the only young man in those years who saw visions, nor was Samuel Adams the only old man who dreamed dreams. A power like the great surges of the sea seemed to be possessing us, carrying us onward, and onward,—sometimes reluctant, sometimes willing, until at last we looked forth with startled eyes upon an altered world. "Old things had passed away and behold all things had become new!"

.   .   .   .

I had to go back to Redford for a few days immediately before Harvard opened for the very humble yet necessary reason that my wardrobe needed replenishing and mother "would not think of laying it all upon Aunt Mercy." For a frantic interval therefore mother and Yetmercy darned and mended, and sewed their fingers almost to the bone. They did not quite accomplish the feat performed in many a New England house, when a son was going to Cambridge—that in a single week the wool that had been running about on a sheep's back was clipped, washed, carded, spun, dyed black, woven and sent out of town in the form of a very presentable suit upon the back of the self-confident junior; but wonders hardly less they performed.

Father was long and late in his study busy with letters to all the many ministers of his acquaintance from Falmouth and Kittery to frontier Pittsfield in the Berkshires, setting forth the need of preparing their flocks for some great ordeal fitted to test manly courage and Christian virtue. For we all knew days fearful and wonderful were

coming. Out from beyond that gray eastern horizon
whence issued the stately ships, at any hour now might
sail in the packet with a mandate handed down from ignorant London three thousand miles away, that would send
New England, and we said confidently now, New York, the
Jerseys, Maryland, Virginia and the Carolinas into fever
heat. The very vagueness of the thing was what appalled
us, as often with impending private calamities there swelled
the passionate desire of those who took life thoughtfully
"to know the worst."

And yet how still and peaceful old Redford was! The
mild wind was creaking the great elms now turning rusty
on the edge of autumn. The shrunken current crept along
in the drying bed of Concord River, the turkeys and geese
squabbled comfortably behind the long placid farmsteads.
Around the tavern there was the usual grumbling about
"the very poor rye and potato crops" (they had been average) and the accustomed assertions, "The squirrels are laying in lots of nuts—we'll have a powerful hard winter."

Among the Redford youths I was now something of a
hero. The story of my Newagen exploit had been greatly
improved by Yetmercy's recitals, and it was known that
of late I had been of intimate service to Messrs. Adams and
Warren. I was deferred to, my words caught up with attention, but I tried to bear these honors modestly—remembering well what might have been my plight if Cousin Hope
had not been my good angel. Although so far as actions
were concerned, the conduct of the Redfordites was harmless enough (the town was blessedly free from Tories); the
hay and harvest being largely in, many men had now much
time on their hands and incidentally much hard cider to
put under their waistcoats. There was a deal of loose
talking, cursing of the governor, cursing of "ministers"
(everybody knew what high percentage that euphemism was

beginning to cover) and announcements of "What we'll do!" "What they've got to do!" and "How *we* ought to talk to *them!*"

On the last afternoon before my return came a petty incident that sent me back to the parsonage silent and thinking hard. The ordinary crowd had gathered before the meeting house, while Selectman Gibbs stood on the horse block and auctioned off the keep of an imbecile pauper. Then we loitered over to the tavern to look on the door and see if certain names had been added to the posted list of common drunkards to whom it was forbidden to sell strong liquor. With his heels on the rail and his filthy reddish wig down over one ear, sat Faithful Hovey, peddler, gossip-monger and professional ne'er-do-good, who by the merest squeak had escaped finding his name among this peerage of honor. Somebody (Bill Sanders, I think, an extremely talkative and light-metaled farm hand) was saying in a loud voice, "Everybody must get together in town meeting and *just tell 'em* over there in England!"——

Whereupon Hovey broke in with deep rasping voice, "Tell 'em what, Bill?"

"Why, that King George must once and for all quit all ideas of taxing us."

Faithful's horse-laugh made the rotten balustrade clatter: "Figger it through, Bill. Figger it through as I've done setting here.—What yer going to do if King George *will* tax ye, for all yer fuss and feathers, town meetings, and booming talk? What'll ye do—take yer whipping lying down?"

"He'll see a hole through a ladder," returned Bill testily.

But we all dispersed a little more silent and sober than when we came, and I strolled home with one huge interrogation point walking straight before me all the way up that quiet road.—"What if King and ministers were just as resolved that their way was right as were Samuel Adams and Patrick Henry? Had we in very truth 'figured it through?'"

In after days I could never believe that it was mere coincidence when, just before supper, Tabitha and I drifted arm in arm into the austere precincts of the best room. There above the chilly mantelpiece hung the black portrait of Great-uncle Waitstill Gilman, captain of Massachusetts Colony, and under it, in the flaking leathern scabbard, that famous sword which he had put through the high-sachem Pogantiauk the Nipmuck, and saved half of Middlesex in old King Philip's War. The sword was securely wired to its place and we children had been taught never to meddle with it any more than non-Levitical Israel with the Ark of the Covenant, but we were older now, and first Tabitha, and then I helping her, took down the scabbard, and next we drew out the weapon itself "to see if it needed cleaning." The scabbard was weakening but tight, the hilt was strong, and the blade was hardly rusted. It gleamed hard and bright, as the last bars of sun shot into the windows. Tabby and I took turns holding out the sword, watching the light play upon its length, testing its edge with timid fingers, and Tabby (who had a most unholy love of the actress about her) waved it above her head like a charging Amazon and made reckless passes toward solemn Uncle Waitstill himself. "I wonder, Roger, I wonder," spoke she, delighting in the flashing of the blade, "if ever this sword will be put to use again?"

"Very quickly," cried I in alarm; "you seem tired of the sight of your brother's ears, but I tell you, mistress, I've still a mind to wear 'em. Look out!"

"No, I mean in a war," returned Tabby swinging less perilously. "I've heard folks say, 'Now that Quebec's lost to the French we'll never have another big war—not in our day!'—But again—I just wonder."

"Children," called mother at the door, "big as you are, put up that sword, or father's still strong enough to dust you both."

The blade slid instantly back into the sheath. The weapon soon resumed its harmless vigil beneath the panel of its owner; but Tabitha drew close to me as we went out to supper: "Roger, I can't get it out of my head, I know I'm silly—yet somehow I think before it's time for you to quit Harvard that sword won't be hanging over that mantelpiece."

"And I know you're silly," came back with brotherly candor. "When the Turks or Spaniards march into Redford, why, take it down—but I don't see them just yet setting fire to the meeting house."

. . . Did mother know what Tabitha had said? Had Yetmercy repeated what I had repeated, of what that fool Hovey said? Was it only because there were stirring in her heart the same thoughts then swelling in half the mothers of New England?—I never knew, but that same night, after father had finished evening prayers and had given me many practical admonitions about matters at Harvard, and after I had tumbled into bed in the rough little room that had been mine since I first went to school, I saw the candle-glow coming down the passage and knew that here was mother. She entered wrapped in the warm-colored Paisley shawl which Peleg had given her. Her long braid fell forward upon her bosom, with the rays playing upon it gently. Under the dim light she seemed to have the face and the form of a young woman. She sat down beside me on the bed and I took hold of her hand. I had often told her that her hands were the most beautiful in all the world, I did not repeat that then, but fell drowsily

to wondering whether even Emilie's hand could be softer
to the touch or dearer.

"You are going back to college to-morrow," she said,
putting down the candle and pushing the hair back from
my brow. "Of course there will be no more Jack Prindles.
I've not come to say that. You were not to blame—but,
Roger, I have come to say just a few things, which somehow
come best with none of the others round."

"Just a few things."—Gentle reader what are the "things"
which probably follow you all your life? Are they not
often the "things" which your mother said after you had
gone to bed, when the candle light was catching the gleam
of her hair, and she talked in a low sweet voice?

At once I was in great anxiety. Was she about to say
something about Emilie?—But mother was far too wise for
that. She knew me much better than I did myself.

"Your father," she went on, "of course shows me his
letters. Peleg has written. I have heard you talk. I suppose there is no doubt that the King and ministers are
determined to wind up the issue with the Colonies—and
in their own way."

"Everything we hear proves this, mother," I said.

"If that is true what will you do?"

"What will you have me do, mother?" I replied begging
the question.

"I'm a fond and foolish woman, Roger, and I'm growing
old; I counted my gray hairs to-night—their number frightened me. Your father's no longer young. I have lived
through all the stress and sorrow of the old French Wars.
Your youngest uncle, Stephen, died at Fort Edward. He
was a fine young man when he marched away.—I think you
look like him.—Every time that I pray I add the words
'Give peace in my time, O Lord!'"

"Do not get frightened, mother," I came back, "I've not

the least mind for taking the King's shilling—and everything's at peace."

"Oh, Roger," spoke she, "let's not beat around the bush. We all know what's in our hearts. How will this hot talk with ministers all end?"

"By Britain at the eleventh hour hearing reason," I spoke as confidently as possible, for I knew the dear soul was sore beset, and I would almost have cut off my right hand to comfort her.

"Oh! Roger, Roger, that's what you all say; but I'm ceasing to believe you. There is something coming which people will write books about until the call of God's great trumpet.—And when it comes, boy, what will you do?"

"Do, mother?" I confessed. "I would to heaven I knew what 'twere right to do. What would you have me do?"

She continued patting my cheeks and hair. "Roger, my son, I have no wisdom from books. No knowledge of laws or courts, or Parliament or kings. I've tried to read the Whig letters in the *Gazette* and the Tory letters in the *News Letter*. They put my poor head in a maze. Then I go back to the kitchen and help Yetmercy with the pies; but this thing I know, and let me tell it once again. One hundred and fifty years ago our ancestors came over seas and wrestled with the savage wilderness, not for glory, not for pelf—but for the better pleasing of God, to make in some wondrous fashion under His Providence a new land where men might live worthier and nobler than anywhere else in the world. And upon you, my son, there has descended a greater heritage than upon any baron or belted earl, for your ancestors who sleep in the churchyard in God's keeping have trusted the future of this New England to their children's children."

"And now—" her voice shook a little but she persisted,

"if Heaven should so order things that once again the gold should be purged from the dross in the fire, if our days of peace should end, if the men of New England and that greater New England we call America should have to endure even to the uttermost, lest this glory be dimmed, this heritage wasted—I know that no son of mine will fail in the good choice, or prove unworthy of the noble blood that is in him."

I did not answer mother. What need was there to answer, except to press her hand?

"You are a good boy, Roger," she continued, "and a brave one. Some day we will talk of other things—more cheerful, and nearer to your heart. Only," she put her face nearer, "I wanted you to understand how if such a summons came—how your mother would want you to decide." Then she kissed me, went out very quietly, and I saw the candle light dimming away as she went down the passage.

Was Sabra Gilman the only mother then who said such things to her children? I never asked, but I have my surmise.

.   .   .   .

The next day I was back in Cambridge and absorbed in the bustle of opening college, a junior sophister now, free from oppression and entitled to lord it over the lower class-men. As released slaves usually make the hardest masters so, I fear, I made myself a stern initiator to many youths two years younger than myself. The condition of the college, however, was already becoming unsettling for academic learning. "Taxation and representation" were intruding like unbidden guests into every Greek translation, every rhetorical exercise. Even the tutors and professors (being, despite their dignity, men of like passions with ourselves) were hard bestead to reconcile their own zeal for

the patriot cause with the duty of maintaining the routine
of fair learning.

The Tory students were in a weak minority, but to do
them justice they had often the courage of their convictions.   I had great respect for the bravery if not the
principles of Tom Lechmere, who, after persistently refusing to wear homespun upon week days, finally strolled the
full length of Hollis in a newly imported suit of blue velvet
with white silk stockings, despite a dozen pitchers that were
emptied upon him. I was one of his friendly enemies who
rescued him just as they thrust his head beneath the college pump, and I helped to prevent his being expelled from
the Speaking Club, although several told me that "Mr.
Adams should hear of my hobnobbing with his adversaries."

Other things, however, weighed on my mind more heavily;
besides the increasingly serious news that was coming from
England, I was becoming doubly tormented as to my honorable duty toward Emilie Rivoire.

CHAPTER XXIII

HIGH among the minor mercies of my life I reckon the fact that I was not judged harshly upon my scholastic performance at Harvard during my last two years. In them to be sure I studied prodigiously—but not for the tutor's classrooms. Nobody else, however, in those particular years learned more from his textbooks than did I. Many a time have I seen grave Professor Wigglesworth running across to the Court House opposite the college, after a deplorably perfunctory lecture on divinity, to demand "Are the Boston expresses in?" and to jostle with a dozen other dignitaries for the papers.—And I was incessantly pouncing upon wonderful books whenever they came back to the hard-worked library—Hooker and Sidney, Hobbes and Grotius, Puffendorf and Vattel, and even that fruit of the tree of perilous knowledge *The Social Contract*. I had to hide the volumes till I finished them lest they be purloined by some of my fellows.

As for Boston, I pinched my small allowance to pay for lifts on the chaises to Charlestown and then the ferry tolls. Fewer white hairs would I possess to-day could I recover that sleep lost in intricate calculations as to "when it would be right to revisit North Square." There I would receive welcomes that would first send my heart bounding with gladness and then sink it down to my boots. For to add to my other troubles the story was passing around that Uncle Peleg had named me his heir. Now Uncle Peleg

was a close-mouthed man, he had other young kinsmen with
just claims upon him, besides, the steady collapse of the
imports was actually bothering him to take up his current
bills.—But how could I tell what folly had got to M.
Georges? Assuredly I could not say to him gratuitously,
"Welcome me not. My Whig uncle will probably leave
me ten guineas and a mourning suit!" And although I
gave what deprecatory hints I could, they were far too
likely to be set down to mere modesty.

Nevertheless it was a tantalizing delight to sit in the
little parlor, and merely listen to the music of Emilie's
voice. She was deliberately learning our Yankee idioms
and accent, "Because" as she said unaffectedly one day,
"I guess I'll always live in America." Her other admirers
still hung on, but I was no longer so jealous save as to my
fortune. I was becoming known in select circles as a young
man of consequence, and could have wasted much time at
routs and drums beauing any one of several most genteel
young ladies. My adventures in Maine, my intimacy with
Warren and Adams made me a social figure, which (I discovered) was wondrously helped out by a little self-assur-
ance and a timely swagger.

M. Rivoire, when he wended home from his little sugar
office by Dock Square, was often magnet enough to bring
me to his parlor, even without his granddaughter. All the
epic story of his oppressed Huguenot people he knew. Long
have I sat in wonderment listening to imprisonments, severance of families, deaths-in-life in the galleys, wanderings
in exile, the heroically mad revolt of the Camisards, and
of the "Church of the Desert" meeting in the waste places
when temples were forbidden. Yet through it all, spoke
the old man simply, a remnant had kept the Faith, and in
France as in Israel the Lord had yet "seven thousand, all
the knees that have not bowed unto Baal." And now

(praise be *le bon Dieu!*) the active persecution had largely ceased, and the government winked at the breaking of the laws of oppression.

"And are you not bitter against France?" once I asked.

"Not so," answered he with a shake of his snowy crown, "we are Frenchmen still as well as Protestants. And when the better day dawns for *la patrie* we Huguenots again will give to France heroes and leaders. Only for me (his eyes lit tenderly on Emilie) all that I have in the world is in this little room. Here in America shall I leave my bones, and if the blood of the Rivoires is to subsist, by another name here in America must it live on."

So one day I trudged down Middle Street whistling to keep my courage up, and in my brain for no earthly reason raced those most contrary lines in the hymn book, buzzing away, I suppose, because after every visit to Emilie I could never think straight:

> "The Lord will come
> And He will not
> Keep silence but
> Speak out."

Amid this wool gathering as I was going along with my hands in my pockets and gaping vacantly in the shop windows, I felt a tap on my shoulder, and there in the inevitable red coat, its buttonholes newly darned, was Mr. Samuel Adams. He beamed at me as affectionately as might have my father.

"Whence and whither my lad, and why are you frowning?"

"Cambridge bound," said I, "and if I'm frowning, its because of that abusive attack upon you yesterday in the *News Letter.*"

"Oh! that Dan'l Leonard. Why, his brick bats and stink pots glide off of me like water from a duck's back. Do you mind a bit more of work for the Committee? I was just going to write you at Cambridge."

Did I mind? For some blessed minutes I forgot all my worries about Emilie.

"Then come along to Hancock House. We're going to have a talk—just the two Johns, Hancock and Cousin Adams, with Warren and me. If you care to listen in, perhaps you'll get a stray idea or two for those letters to the *Spy* for which I'm asking."

Therefore up Tremont Street I went, with the arm of the most powerful personage in Massachusetts hooked into mine, and not a few of the Very Respectables gazing enviously upon the young man whom this king delighted to honor.

"Seen your Uncle Eleazer lately?" asked Adams, nodding affably to right and left.

"No indeed, sir; and you can guess why."

My guardian chuckled: "I vow that I guess why. Hutchinson's as good as slammed the doors of Province House on him, and on Flucker too. They'll have to cool their heels outside until there's another governor. Tom H. won't use *that* kind of a devil's spinning wheel again, even to make a rope for Your Most Obedient. I've heard, however, he said of you t'other day 'That young Gilman's got to take his chance of being swung for treason along with the rest of 'em'."

"I am not afraid, sir," said I straightening.

"Don't go blindfold, Roger, don't go blindfold. 'Taint right. I'd not see a fine young fellow set foot in our boat, till he knew the risks and felt that the voyage was worth the making.—I've got so accustomed to having a hemp collar *almost* fitting me, that 'twouldn't seem natural to have it otherwise. Makes me a better Calvinist every day to realize everything's predestined and in the Lord's hands. Johnny Adams got talking lately 'Brutus and Cassius were slain, Hampden died in battle, Sydney on the scaffold, Harrington in jail—That's cold comfort!'—But he steers right on with the rest of us."

"And so will I," came my youthful boast.

"And so you will, lad. But not rashly. Keep your ears open. To-day I may get started talking and you may learn a thing or two."

So conversing we went straight on to where School Street merged with Tremont and Long Acre, and next Adams led me up the hill behind the old Granary Burying Ground, strolling along Beacon Street which was then not much more than a very pretty lane. There upon the slopes of Beacon Hill itself, with a commanding view over the elms and pastures of the common, rose Hancock House, the proudest citadel of Whiggery.

. . . .

I had met Mr. Hancock several times, but only at the Edes and Gill printing office. Not Province House itself was more imposing than this focus of the greatest fortune in Boston. Hancock House was a massive two-story brick mansion with high tiled dormers. A substantial stone wall cut off the property from Beacon Street. We passed up the brick walk through a flower garden neatly lined with box, other fine gardens stretching up the hill to a genuine park on the summit with a summer house near the public beacon. Liveried Africans ushered us into the stately reception room, garnished with bird's-eye maple furniture upholstered with floriated damask. Through the partly open doors could be seen the magnificent dining room ample for forty guests. One glance at all the mahogany, carving, and glittering sideboards told why John Hancock was almost as little loved by the Tories as was Samuel Adams himself. The very mansion flung back the charge that the Boston

Whigs were impoverished malcontents, seeking public broils merely to shun the debtor's prison.

The master of the house met us with elaborate courtesy. John Hancock was six-and-thirty, his thin, lightly stooping figure rose to a good six feet. His purple velvet coat, richly embroidered, his choice linen, great rings and seal fobs, red morocco slippers, all betrayed the fine gentleman. A hot fire of Nova Scotia coal was on the hearth, and Hancock had replaced his wig with a red velvet cap. His features were regular, his color high, heightened perchance by good living, his lips amiable but not weak, his gray eyes honest and intelligent. Not a great man doubtless, but the Tories made more than their wonted error when they branded this merchant prince as merely "Sam Adams' tool." All America knew that if the colonial cause went down, none could lose so much as this John Hancock.

Warren had come, and with him John Adams, that taciturn, fascinatingly homely young lawyer, whose few words went as cold, bright bullets to their mark, and who might have taught logic to Aristotle. Warren simply was Warren—the most fascinatingly friendly man in the world. They all knew me already, and Hancock graciously thanked the elder Adams for "bringing young Mr. Gilman along that he might know how to work up his articles." Then Marcellus, an unusually stately Ethiop, produced long clay pipes, whereupon we were seated, and as always at such times, Samuel Adams talked the most.

Committee details engrossed the conclave first: "X was zealous, but Y lukewarm, and Z only a talkative fool," etc., but soon the talk went around to the impending tea duty, and Warren spread out a recent letter from Franklin in London, "The ministers have no idea that any people can act from any other principle but that of interest, and they believe that three pence in the pound of tea is sufficient to overcome all the patriotism of an American."

Whereat Warren laughed, Hancock shrugged, John Adams rubbed his chin, and Samuel Adams fished in his coat-tails.

"Seen the last *Gazette* yet, Jo?" he asked grinning at the doctor.

"Not I—Young Middlecott got pitched from his horse. I've been setting his ribs and comforting his mother."

"Well," and Samuel unfolded the smudgy sheet, "I guess you all know who the fellow that writes under 'Z' is. I'll read something he says—much to the point. First of all he declares it's no use trusting any repentence by Parliament and so——"

"Well?"—demanded Hancock fluttering his lace sleeves.

"Why 'Z' is moderate but clear. 'Form an independent state, *an American Commonwealth,* and I can't find any other plan is so likely to answer the great purpose of preserving our liberties.' "

You could have heard the proverbial pin drop upon that table. The reader looked from one to another of the little circle with great seriousness, yet with just a little of the bravado of a schoolboy who has suddenly proposed some daring wickedness to his mates. Then the younger Adams spoke: "Is that 'Z' the same 'Z' who has written before, Samuel?"

"You can ask at the printing office," came the diplomatic answer. "I haven't."

Warren's honest features were clouded with concern. Hancock had turned a little white. "Whoever wrote that letter," he said at length, "has a large fish on his hook. I hope he knows how to land him."

"Peter the Apostle said 'I go a-fishing.' He'd no right to complain when he made a powerful big catch," remarked

Samuel unabashed, then he ran his fingers through his long gray hair and gave a characteristic laugh; "Egad, gentlemen! What have we been doing all these years but fishing, fishing in troubled waters for the Lord knows what?— And now haven't we reached a point when we must either hook up Leviathan or row back home to say like numbskulls, 'We have toiled all these nights and caught nothing'?"

"I hope it hasn't come yet to that," spoke Hancock soberly, and Warren nodded his head.

"Well Jo, and John, and t'other John, not forgetting you, Roger," Samuel Adams' smile was very elder-brotherly, "if you can put your wits to work and find some other way out of this brash, something that'll save us our fathers' liberties, find it.—I can't. And you know all my failings, but dissembling with *you* isn't one of them. Now let's have it squarely—isn't 'Z' right?"

Hancock leaned his elbows on the highly polished table and gazed across at his oldest associate; then spoke:

"Dissembling with us? Never, Samuel; but keeping something back, often.—Since you've said this much, you must say more. When first did you harbor this notion of independence?"

The answer came with a hardly concealed chuckle, "You're almost as thick as Tom Hutchinson, John. I've had this thing in mind day and night, waking and sleeping, in fashion and out of fashion, summer and winter, since that hour the troops first were sent to Boston five years ago.—And you three who pass as fit to head the Sons of Liberty have only just found it out!—" I thought Samuel Adams would thereupon laugh as at a capital joke, but as we all gazed on him in a twinkling his countenance changed. We had been looking upon a genial humorous elder, suddenly we were confronting a possessed prophet.

His eyes shot lightning, and John Adams, who had started to speak, moved his lips, then lapsed into silence.

"My friends," pursued his kinsman, "do you remember what I wrote in that first time of the great testing when the two regiments were camped among us? 'If an army should be sent to reduce us to slavery, we will put our lives in our hands and cry to the Judge of all the earth, 'Help us, O Lord our God, for we rest on Thee, and in Thy name we go against this multitude.' "

Hancock snapped the pipe stem in his fingers as he listened; Warren let his own pipe drop smashing upon the floor, only John Adams smoked stoically, as the speaker swept on—"And now, my brethren of the good cause, let us not deceive ourselves, right soon will we have reason to raise this very prayer."

John Adams stirred in his chair, Hancock held up his hand, but Warren at last found speech; "I'm a believing man, Sam. I know what you imply but I can't yet get myself to the conviction that a righteous Providence will force us to what we've called 'The Last Appeal.' "

"And besides," spoke John Adams, "between taking arms to defend American liberties and sheer independence is a mighty long mile—You are travelling over fast."

"Slow or fast," answered Samuel deliberately, "I know the road and see no turnings all the way to the last horse-block. Don't think I've lost sleep seven nights a week for nothing. Unless at the last moment the Almighty turns our new Pharaoh's hard heart, we'll all be risking the Red Sea waves or something worse ere man or lad of us be many years older."

Hancock emphatically shook his head: "I'm with you to the end, Sam, be that end the gibbet; but you should drink more good madeira and less of your cursed thin cold water —it will hearten you. You think too ill of British obstinacy. There is plenty of blow and bully; but when we put 'em to the test they flinch. Where's the Stamp Act? Gone in thin air. Where's the Townshend revenue acts? Gone too—all but the tea, and we drink our fill of Holland. Where're the Massacre regiments? Idling down harbor at the Castle. Where's the punishment for the *Gaspée?* A big packet of angry letters. Where's the penalty for treason they've been tossing about for us all for years? Here we sit, and Marcellus will soon bring the punch-bowl. Face 'em down with this tea business and they'll grow tired: the King'll call Chatham or Shelburne to the head of the council board. Why, they'll be naming you governor, Sam, in a few more years—if you want it?"

The elder Adams shook his flowing locks over his shoulders. "Governor, perhaps?—It's an honorable ambition. And you before me John; but not over Massachusetts Province. You read what 'Observation' held forth in the *Gazette* two weeks ago; maybe 'Z' and he had nibbed the same quill pen, and he urged that 'A Congress of American *States* be assembled as soon as possible, to draw up a bill of rights and publish it to the world, choose an ambassador to the British court, and act annually for the United Colonies'—Massachusetts Province is dying—as old Greece and Rome once were dying. *Massachusetts State* will stand forth proud as Michael when he trod down the infernal dragon."

"It is a fearful risk," remarked John Adams evenly.

"That's no doubt what they said when they went aboard the *Mayflower*," replied his kinsman.

"King George with all his narrowness and ignorance will at the last moment learn wisdom."

"He will not," came the unflinching answer.

"He will at least recoil from shedding his subjects' blood."

"He will not."

"If not the King, at least even his most headlong ministers will flinch before the deliberate destruction of the British Empire."

"They will not."

"Or at the worst, our English brethren, many of whom actively support our cause, will hold back their government from a crowning folly."

"They cannot."

"What then, Samuel? What must we do?

"*Fight:*" the older man's eyes burned as they held us rigid and scarcely breathing. "Fight, endure hardship, hunger, cold, wounds, prison, death. Fight as your sons, your grandsons and your three times grandsons will fight—for the honor and life of the America that must be."

Hancock's and John Adams' faces were tense and still. Warren, I heard whispering to himself very softly, "If so God wills, Amen!" But Samuel Adams who never let a bow be drawn too tense, gently laid down the newspaper before him, flung back his coat, produced a huge well-worn leathern wallet crammed with letters, and began turning them out upon the table, with one of his half audible chucklings, as if he had stolen a march upon his acquaintance and delivered himself of something long on his mind, but which act he would now have them momentarily forget:

"Well, I've given you a powerful big dose of those tragics and heroics. You'll all go home muttering 'Sam's gone clean off his noddle.' Till the exact news of those new tea acts comes we can't do a thing but mark time, 'hayfoot,' 'strawfoot,' as they do with raw recruits. And now, Roger, will you favor us by taking down these heads of proposals for the better organization of the Committees in Worcester County."——

The autumn day was well advanced when the conference broke up at Hancock House. A large part of the time had been taken up in deciding the membership of the Whig committees, how these committees were to be chosen by the "spontaneous action of their fellow townsmen," and how they were to do precisely what the central committee intended, and how every member was at the outset to be profoundly convinced that all his acts originated strictly with himself. Not without humor I observed that when Samuel Adams had anything important to propose, he so framed the case that Hancock immediately caught up the motion as his own, and supported it very heartily. Warren originated little, but played the wizard adjusting human details. John Adams seldom spoke, but then went to the bed rock of the argument; and twice Samuel paid him the high compliment of saying, "You're right, and I'm wrong, cousin. Your way's the best."

As we went out Samuel tried to get me to walk home and take a bed at Purchase Street and the doctor the same on Hanover Street, but I told them Uncle Peleg was half expecting me, and declined them both. However, when nearly at Charter Street I reflected that I was due at an early exercise at college the next morning, and hated the idea of turning out for the first ferry. It was a cool, clear night and the walking not unpleasant. So I took the evening ferry, and although a carter at the Charlestown slip offered to take me back to Cambridge for tuppence, I stretched my legs, strode out of the village, skirted Breed's Hill and Charlestown burial hill, and then saw the ampler heights of Bunker Hill rising before me white and clear in the mooonlight.

Right ahead stretching off toward the west, ran Milk Row, the road along the causeway to Cambridge. A dead calm had settled upon the hills, the rivers and the marshes. Far away I heard a dog barking in some farm across the arm of the Charles by Lechmere's Point. I was entirely alone but that did not trouble me; the Charlestown and Cambridge roads were then as safe at all hours as a banker's strongbox, and there is no better helper to clear, firm thinking than a brisk, solitary walk on an open way under the moonlight.

As I went down the causeway and saw the Mill Pond on my left, the narrowing shimmer of the Mystic on my right, it seemed as if years had passed over me since I had whisked out of my last classroom that morning. The words of Samuel Adams were ringing in my ears. I saw a mortal struggle before me, a struggle in which I was inextricably mixed, a struggle in which better men than I must perish and out of which a vast new empire could perchance be born. How could I play my part therein? How could I prove myself a true heir to my birthright from the Puritans?

Then my mood changed and drifted. Other thoughts pursued, and just as with slightly slackening strides I swung along the slope of Prospect Hill, and saw the first Cambridge farms standing out white in the moonlight, there came to me as it were a voice, a voice as clear and strong as Samuel Adams'; "If Emilie Rivoire casts in her life with America, as a woman of America she is to be wooed and won," and then again, "If you, Roger Gilman, have not strength of mind enough to conquer your pride and tell her your honest love, you have not strength enough to face King George's firelocks."

I made a vow with myself as I walked that last mile over Butler's Hill into Cambridge. The snow should not melt from another winter before Emilie Rivoire knew all that she was to me.

CHAPTER XXIV

THE BREWING OF THE TEA

THEREAFTER events marched so fast that were I writing a formal history I should have to spoil much good foolscap.

First of all came Herbert's letter; he having made a very lucky passage, and the letter having caught an equally speedy westbound ship.

. . . "Peggy and I are to be married next week. How all the world loves a lover! 'Tis a marvel also, how much more importance I have put on around the Hall from the gamekeepers up, since the bishop had the goodness to die and leave me that legacy. Even my toplofty oldest brother praises the way I wear my small clothes, and swears 'Damme, but you have a pretty leg!' Peggy is terribly busy with 'preparations.' I can never understand the mysteries of a wedding. It is surely a 'chastening experience' (as your Yankee parsons would say) and teaches man his proper station. Peggy seems wholly in the clutches of linen-drapers and their ilk. The only comfort for a bridegroom is that he resembles some inner wheel of a watch, wholly unnoticed, yet without him the whole mechanism promptly stops!

"Ah! Roger, if I only had you to stand with me at the head of the parish aisle. If I could only teach Peggy to know and to love her tall New England brother!—And when will some great news come from Boston, linking your name with North Square?

. . . "But to pass to other matters. By this time the

full blundering of the tea business will reach you. I keep from moralizing. Great people, so I'm told, were quite willing to let the sleeping dogs in America lie, but what counts *that* beside the waning profits of the Honorable East India Company?—Therefore if sore trouble comes, let the first curses light on that foul management which let the Company import to England seventeen million pounds of tea more than it could market—to the anguish of the lordly stockholders. Before this of course you know how the Company is to sell tea in America direct through its own agents, and how by juggling conditions in the trade the stuff can now be sold to you cheaper than it is in England, and cheaper than even your smuggled Holland tea, and yet pay threepence per pound to the King. Lord Chatham snarled at the project, 'Government has dressed taxation, that father of American sedition, in the robes of an East Indian director.' That's the very case!

"I'm told that weighty people advised Lord North that the duty had better be dropped outright; the old impost had barely paid the ruinous expenses of the coast cutters. But a Certain Exalted Personage (I daren't name him) frowned like the British lion, and wrote to the Prime Minister 'I am clear that there always must be one tax to keep up the right to tax America, and as such *I approve the tea duty.*'—And so the tax stayed!

"Of course your non-importation agreements, such as your Uncle Peleg observed, can now help you little. The Company will sell direct to your small shopkeepers. Your wholesale merchants will be helpless."

"What Americans may find it expedient to do, who am I to tell you? But, in all candor, I fear that you can reckon little on the aid of our British Whigs. While Peggy has been battling with the seamstresses I have been in London pushing my captaincy—the legacy makes the case prosper.

My father, whose outward affection remarkably increased the moment he found I no longer needed an allowance, has taken me to meet many gentlemen of the first importance. Private talks with noble lords I will not report; but this I can say, that my Lords Chatham, Shelburne, Rockingham and their friends feel miserably hopeless as to driving ministers to better courses, and some of them are almost minded to abandon the fight. Lord Shelburne, I'm told, has been heard to say that if the King's power is actually asserted in America, as sycophants and placemen pretend that he now desires, the liberties of England herself will not keep long from ruin—we will have to fight 1689 all over again.

"As for the Commons to-day, the majority eat from North's hand. Mr. Burke can hardly get a respectable number to follow him into the Whig lobby when he divides against the Government. I have just seen Mr. S.—— whose estates are near my father's. He says openly he has just paid £5000 for his Cornish borough sold him by the Marquis of D.—— and that 'He'll be damned if he'll see the value of his seat lessened by having the right of Parliament to tax the colonies disputed.' Sir Edward J.——, I hear, was favorable to America, and promised to vote with Mr. Burke, but ministers gave him a sinecure Wardenship with a thousand a year—and now he trots out behind the "King's Friends." Lord C.—— also used to vow over his punch bowl that 'You were devilishly in the right and Sam Adams a deuced clever man':—but at the last awards his Majesty was graciously pleased to pass him a piece of ribbon,—and now Lord C.—— sits dumb as an oyster, or never quits Brookes' club when there's a Parliamentary division.

"As for the run of our honest English folk they know as much about your affairs as you about ours. We swallow what is told us and join in 'God save the King.' What, however, country gentlemen, yeoman and tradespeople *do* know is that taxes here since the French War are crushing, and that it will be a godsend if America can be forced to pay something to abate them. If our people were honest they'd probably say what a blunt old gentleman did to me the other day when we were thrown together for dinner at an inn: 'The Stamp Act was outrageous—very true, and all that—but money *must* be had. Everything here is strained to the uttermost, and since all the world are slaves anyway, North America shouldn't hope to be an exception and to be free.' " *

At the end of all this Job's comfort, Herbert pathetically and illogically closed with a fervent exhortation not to let ourselves be goaded into acts of folly which would alienate our friends and give joy to our enemies. But I warrant you his postscript did little to temper the warmth of those letters which a certain "Vindex" sent off the next few days to the *Spy*, the younger comrade to the *Gazette*, and circulating even more than that organ among the farmer and mechanic classes.

. . . From that fall of 1773 began the subtle but unmistakable alteration in all language concerning "him." *"He"* of course was his Majesty King George. Hitherto, judging from every public utterance, we ought to have been happy under "the best of Kings," although mistreated by "his evil ministers." All this now was changed. Two years and more could pass before the official demise of all loyalty to "our natural sovereign," but for practical purposes the solemn force of blessing the monarch while cursing the ministers was ended.

"The King" disappeared from our toasts. "God save the King!" was sung only by defiant Tories. We knew that George III hated us for our defense of our liberties; that no desire of his kept our chiefs from the scaffold;

* These sentiments are remarkably like those also expressed to Josiah Quincy when he visited England at this time.   (Editor.)

that he had chased our British friends from his councils; that he was flogging on his reluctant ministers and mustering all the enormous social strength of the Crown against us.—Yet that same moment out of the dying loyalty to the King, phoenixlike the nobler loyalty, loyalty to *the Country* was being born.—Those were great days for us all, from the Penobscot to the Altamaha.

. . . .

One afternoon at Harvard an instructor beckoned me as I was leaving Stoughton Hall, and passed me a paper with, "Lucky fellow, Gilman; of course you can go." Thus I read:

"Dr. Warren's compliments to President Locke; and he begs that Mr. Roger Gilman, junior sophister, may be excused for the present from classes in order to render essential service to the Massachusetts Committee of Correspondence."

A classmate who boasted a riding horse was proud to lend the beast, and I could not pound fast enough across Brighton Bridge and Roxbury over the land road to Boston. Henceforth for many nights I slept at Charter Street, but my very hectic days were all at Purchase Street or the Edes printing office.

At first my task was copying for local circulation John Dickinson, the Philadelphian's, denunciation of the East India Company as a pack of avaricious Nabobs who by "unparalleled barbarities, extortions and monopolies had reduced whole provinces to ruin." Also I was very busy writing to New York, Philadelphia, Williamsburg, and Charleston. And it came home to me then, as not before, how farflung a thing had become "America"; how infinitely the new love and devotion must outrun the narrow confines of New England.

Yet although encouragement came in from every hand;

though Yorkman and Jerseyman, Pennsylvanian and Cavalier seemed rising as sworn brethren to reject that weed which now was denounced as the source of "spasms, vapors, hypochondrias, apoplexies, palsies and consumptions," yet upon Boston was falling the main burden of good fight; and the knowledge that if we (who had led the debate so long) should falter now, resistance everywhere would crumble.

As for Boston, never among all the British follies was there a greater than that when the East India Company named as its local agents, two of Hutchinson's sons, his nephew Clark, and two other merchants who knew the back doors into Province House. Every man in Massachusetts believed he could hear the clinking of the shillings of his Excellency's interest in pushing the sale of the tea. "Bowing down before the golden calf!" so a score of pulpits openly reminded us. And indeed without some such fell motive he could scarcely have displayed an obstinacy as great and almost as ruinous as his royal master's.

After the details of the London plot came in, after the company consignees had been named, after the handbills had reached us from Philadelphia urging "by uniting we stand, by dividing we fall," what a going to and fro there was among our own Sons of Liberty! At any daylight hour you could have seen the old red coat and flowing locks of Hutchinson's "chief of the faction" walking about, buttonholing, talking confidentially, now to the Very Respectables, now to "substantial mechanics" and now to smaller fry at length made so much of as "worthy fellow citizens."

I cannot recall all the conclaves which I attended as secretary. Sometimes they were at the Edes office, sometimes Hancock House, but above all just then at the Salutation Inn on North Street. Here the North End Caucus (nominally of mechanics, actually frequented by

an abundance of ruffles and broadcloth) met and debated
and debated; until came finally that crowded if secret meeting which put down formally the members' decision "to
oppose with their lives and their fortunes the vending of
tea" sent in by the accursed East India Company.

This the preliminary; but how can I list all the things
that came after? The huge mass meetings in "Liberty
Hall" the area beneath Liberty Tree, that majestic elm
which spread at the corner of Orange Street and Frog Lane?
The formal summons posted upon November third for the
consignees of the tea to resign their office? The committee
of the Very Respectables which waited on these consignees
at Clark's warehouse, made their demands in the name of
"The Whole People"—and met with a stiff refusal to resign?
Then more meetings, strictly formal town meetings now in
Faneuil Hall, with Mr. Hancock in the chair and Mr.
Samuel Adams and Dr. Warren on the floor speaking very
calmly, and silencing the hot heads who bawled "to arms"
when the consignees still proved obdurate.

Very calmly Boston went about its business. The ham-
mers in the ship yards continued their peaceful knock, knock.
Henry Knox in his bookshop smiled pleasantly at Lucy
Flucker, who "had merely dropped in to buy an Addison."
Paul Revere grumbled over the set of ivory false teeth he
was carving for old Mrs. Boutineau. The Committee tilted
back the chairs in the Edes and Gill Office and talked—it
seemed aimlessly. But Samuel Adams was sealing off a
letter to Arthur Lee in England; "One cannot foresee events,
but, from all the observations I am able to make, my next
letter will not be on a trifling subject."

. . . .

Thus passed ten days, during which my hand grew
cramped and numb and I wore out a score of goose quills,
multiplying letters at that tall battered desk on Purchase

Street. Days during which the Tory *Post Boy*, an organ
of Province House, announced in semi-official tone: "We
learn that his Majesty has declared his intention of supporting the supreme authority and right of the British
Parliament to make laws binding on the colonies." Days
also during which tea, lawful or unlawful, miraculously
disappeared from every table in the polite world of Boston;
every table, that is, whereof the owner was not ready to
brave the chance of seeing tar and feathers plastering his
front door or having a bucket of filthy slops hurled in at
his parlor windows. My Uncle Peleg tried hard to maintain
his wontedly jolly face. "The trade in Holland is gone,
my lad," he admitted to me over the supper table. "If the
East India tea comes at all, they can sell it cheaper than
Watchhorn can run it in. It's their tea or none. I've two
hundred chests of Holland good and snug in a barn in
Malden; better two good bales of hay! Nobody'll buy it;
nobody ought to buy.—Well, maybe Eleazer'll be bidding in
this house soon at sheriff's sale; and Mercy and I'll be clut-
tering up your back attic at Redford.—But tell Sammy for
me—*screw the ban tighter!*"

Then on the seventeenth came in a fast brig straight from
London.—She had passed three tea ships in the Channel
with their bowsprits all pointing toward Cape Cod. And
we knew what was being said by Thomas Mifflin, the great
Pennsylvanian, then in Boston, "Will you engage that the
tea shall not be landed? *If so* I will answer for Philadelphia." Whereupon there was apparently only another town
meeting and a new demand on the consignees, and an ironically courteous reply signed by them all: "Our friends in
England have entered into general engagements in our
behalf merely of a commercial nature, which puts it out
of our power to comply with the request of the town." At
which the meeting once more adjourned with astonishing

abruptness, and no less a person than Hutchinson himself was compelled to write, "This sudden dissolution struck more terror into the consignees than most minatory resolves."

After this we could only live from day to day. It seemed simply a question of wind. The November gales were sweeping the Atlantic, and the ships, said the wiseacres, were being kept back. The consignees, sick and sorry, were now vainly endeavoring a compromise which would appease the town and save their own dignity. But no comfort came to them from selectmen or the unflinching committee, and to escape from the coming earthquake we heard they were retiring to their country seats, while his Excellency, their leader, meditated taking refuge in the Castle that he might in personal safety (as he put it) "more freely give his sense of the criminality of the proceedings."

We kept Thanksgiving day with peculiar solemnity that year. Never were the tables more laden with good things, did more turkeys perish, more pies garnish the linen, more hard cider heighten patriot courage. Many a householder told his wife, "Spread out the best of it—only the good Lord knows what next year we'll have to be thankful for." But from every pulpit in Massachusetts, save those few where Tory ministers lamented over dwindling flocks, the thankfulness poured out was of a sublime nature: "Thankfulness for the courage that was in us, and for the determination to keep unspoiled the gift transmitted by our fathers."

Then after the leftover dishes passed, and we were back again to the everyday leeks and onions, on Saturday the twenty-seventh there was a special conclave at the printing office. The Adamses of course were there, and Hancock, Warren and a few more, such as that other brave physician, Dr. Young, who many a time stayed up the hands of his more famous colleague, and again I nibbed my pen and played the secretary. The business was the approval of the circular prepared by Samuel Adams to the towns about Boston bidding them join us in facing "this black design upon their liberties," because "we are reduced to this dilemma, either to sit down quiet as good-natured slaves, or rise and resist this and every plan laid our destruction as becomes wise freemen."

After the text had been approved there came another of those moments when everybody smoked in very grave silence, whereupon John Adams deliberately struck the ashes from his bowl, and uttered one word, "Well?"——

"Well?" spoke his kinsman genially blowing a cloud of smoke. "We are jogging along the road and soon'll have to rattle over a pretty long bridge. I know what you're thinking, John. Time to see if we've the needed horseflesh and provender before we decide to drive ahead?"

"One can't help thinking it, Samuel," said the younger Adams.

"Of course not, John, of course not. Still time to turn back. Much's to be said for it!" and the older man likewise knocked out his ashes.

"We must exhaust every peaceful means," said Hancock, once more a little tensely.

"We'll exhaust them," rejoined Samuel.

"When committed we're committed," said Warren in a voice lower than usual.

"We're committed, Joseph."

"We'll be blamed by many warm friends as answering illegality with violence:" remarked John Adams slowly refilling.

"We'll be blamed, John."

"If the King and ministers use the opening given them wisely, the whole patriot cause may be undone," spoke Hancock, nervously.

But here Samuel Adams sat upright in his chair, "John Hancock, if Heaven decides against us in this matter the patriot cause is indeed undone; but next to my confidence in Almighty God *I put perfect trust in the folly of our enemies!*"

"Let the Committee direct the secretary," sounded the firm tones of Warren, "to enter in his private minutes that the policy agreed upon in event the tea is forced upon us *stands*." He looked around the circle. One by one each man was nodding silently; then he spoke to me. "Make the entry, Roger; and put it *nemine contradicente*—Now the matter's with the Lord, Samuel."

The next day I rose very early, having papers to deliver to the local committee at Cohasset, being charged to bring back an immediate reply. It was Sunday, the twenty-eighth, and as often enough in late November there had come a fine balmy day, the last of the Indian summer. I was glad to avail myself of a Sabbath-breaking sloop that was running down the harbor to bring back a load of mackerel for Monday market, thus saving myself many miles of dreary roads. The wind was excellent; the seas around Hull not squeamishly choppy. I did my business, got my answer and put back just before noon.

As we came with a fine wash around Point Allerton, we swung up to a handsome ship just heading in for the main channel by Georges Island. A staunch and gallant vessel, but from her mended rigging, scarred paint and a big 'fish' upon her repaired foresail manifestly she was ending a long hard voyage. The skipper of the sloop veered close beside her, as she walked past us, four feet to our three, and he sung out a friendly question. One of the mates upon the quarterdeck trumpeted through his hands the reply "Ship *Dartmouth*, Hall master—London to Boston; eight weeks out—" Then he called in a kind of laughing bravado after us, "and we've got *one hundred and fourteen chests of tea* in the hold!"——

Since the day when the *Mayflower* lifted the sand dunes of Cape Cod, has other vessel sighted the shores of America laden with more fateful cargo?

CHAPTER XXV

THE SERVING OF THE TEA

Across those weeks I saw little enough of the North Square. Truth to tell, however, my zeal for the good cause did not abate because the rumor had leaked out that I was now arch-scrivener and messenger-about-town for the all powerful Committee. All the girls came to look on me with a kind of awe, and Emilie knew this entirely. The few times when I could call on her, any young sparks in the parlor would sit silent and gawky, letting me do the talking, although I competed with Faneuils and Cushings.

Emilie, dear girl, like every other of her sex in Boston, was experimenting upon the awful problems of steeping raspberry leaves, loosestrife, golden rod, sage or any of a dozen other dubious herbs and pretending that they made good tea. I had to push back a cup she proffered me, and avow, "There's no substitute for good bohea and hyson. So let's enjoy our full martyrdom."

Next she would try to tease me as to what went on at Edes or the Salutation, or that other trysting place, the Green Dragon Inn. At which I would gravely affirm that Dr. Warren had persuaded the others that the fight was hopeless and we all had better sue out our pardons from the King. At which she would jump up with a *"Ma foi, what a mensonge!"* whisk over to her spinet, and begin tinkling off some Rameau opera just come in M. Georges' mails from Lorient.

Such episodes helped much to take my youthful brains

from public matters which made them spin daily. Besides, my committee work made me forget my day of sentence, when in accordance with that accursed vow I must face the cannon's mouth and learn my fate. Many times I regretted that pledge to myself sworn upon the moonlit road to Charlestown, but sworn it was, "before the end of the winter." I staved off thinking of my ordeal as much as possible.

The rival gallants around my mistress in any case had plenty of chances. From November twenty-ninth to that eternally memorable December sixteenth, if any man in Boston was idle that man was not Roger Gilman. The *Dartmouth* had quietly dropped anchor at the Castle, but the young secretary of the Committee of Correspondence had knocked at Warren's door before Captain Hall could greet Quaker Rotch, his owner, upon Long Wharf; and that Monday morning Boston had been splotched with placards from North Battery to the Neck.

"FRIENDS! BRETHREN! COUNTRYMEN! The worst of plagues, the detested *tea,* is now arrived in this harbor. The hour of destruction or manly opposition to the machinations of tyranny now stare you in the face."

Therefore let the friends of freedom rally that morning at Faneuil Hall.—Fiercely emphatic words? Yes—and penned around midnight for the eager printers, by men who knew that multitudes can never be stirred by the mincing terms which please philosophers.

Again therefore a crowded hall and swarms standing in the streets. Samuel Adams again talking his homely Bostonese. Adjournment again to the ampler Old South. A close packed meeting house. Samuel Adams speaking to the motion, *"It is the firm resolve of this body that the tea shall not only be sent back, but that no duty shall be paid thereon."*

A reverberating "aye" that might have shaken the carven mantels in Province House.

Kings, lords and commons were ordaining at Westminster. Town meeting was ordaining at Boston—Was the recording angel as he leaned from his heavenly casement, bidding some assistant cherub to take down a new blank folio?

.   .   .   .

More parleying. A well-meant attempt by Copley (a mild and well-liked Tory) to negotiate with the consignees. A tactless refusal by the latter to do more than store the tea pending new orders from Britain. Then a deed that stiffened every jaw; for into a packed meeting in Old South, as John Hancock sat with his ruffled sleeves in the moderator's chair, advanced Greenleaf, high sheriff of Suffolk County, the tool of the Hutchinsons, who formally read the governor's proclamation that town meetings were being held for the "violating, defying and setting at naught the good and wholesome laws of the Province"; and that therefore the governor "warned, exhorted and required you, thus unlawfully assembled, forthwith to disperse and surcease all further proceedings at your uttermost peril. God save the King!" Whereat, as Greenleaf's voice died away, in answer as from the assembled serpents in Milton's Pandemonium, one "loud and very general hiss" rose from the entire meeting house, and pursued the blinking, quavering sheriff as he edged hastily through the door.

"Is there a motion that this meeting adjourn?" sounded from the pulpit. "No!" came the roar which shook the steeple.

Still the consignees skulked in the Castle, refusing to resign, but resolve after resolve had been thunderously voted that the teaships be guarded, that the Committee be vigilant, that help should be summoned from the country if needful, and last but not least, that the folk of Boston would execute these resolves "at the risk of their lives and property!" Soon the expresses were pricking out to every colony, even to the far Carolinas bearing the words of John Hancock, "I am willing to spend my fortune, and life itself in the support of so good a cause."

Two more tea ships were next to glide up the fairway and tie near the *Dartmouth;* but the chests rested firmly in their holds, for on the wharves patrolled five and twenty well-thewed men with Henry Knox as their lieutenant and long French-war muskets upon their shoulders. Day and night their "All's well!" told that the tea had not been landed, while Boston tried to go about its common tasks; though the eyes of all America were upon us, and Philadelphia wrote our Committee, pledging the aid of the Quaker City and of New York to keep out the tea, yet adding the caution, "All we fear is that you will shrink in Boston. May God give you virtue enough to save the liberties of your country."

Those were the weeks when the wife of one American president and the mother of another, Abigail Adams, wrote: "The flame is kindled, and like lightning it catches from soul to soul," and when love or money could not purchase a pair of pistols in all the shops of Boston.

We knew that December sixteenth would end the armistice. Then by law the tea must be landed to avoid confiscation by the custom house, while in mid-channel swung the men-of-war *Active* and *Kingfisher* to sink the teaships should they put back without his Excellency's permit. Daily the common question was in ship yard or warehouse, "Have *they* resigned?" And the answer was always, "No." The consignees were still behind the ramparts of the Castle, playing piquet with the idle officers. But who were the consignees but pawns now for Hutchinson, who, sure of the letter of the law, was holding himself studiously aloof? In secluded splendor at Milton he was letting Boston boil and bubble while writing to ministers that at last he saw his foes the Whigs "involved in invincible difficulties."

Consignees and governor, however, had left an innocent victim, poor harmless Rotch, the owner of the *Dartmouth.* I saw him often, a fussy frightened little man in his long Quaker gray and ill-fitting bag-wig. The tea had been to him merely profitable freight, until behold! he was haled before the terrible Committee, and found trade, good name, everything but bare life itself at stake unless those chests sailed back to London. Between the devil and the deep sea; the wharf guards and the warships; the unlucky Rotch began saying "Yes" to everybody; then discovered himself being forced to say "No," with ugly charges of double dealing to boot. The sixteenth was nigh; if the seventeenth dawned with the tea in the ship's holds, the custom house, under strict orders from Milton, could lawfully put the chests ashore and guard them with the admiral's marines. We were at the crisis.

Boston waxed hot; but not Boston alone. Post after post brought in the resolves of the crowded town meetings from all the hill towns of the province. Meetings where broadcloth and dignity "moved and seconded" the red hot resolutions to which their fellow townsmen bellowed their unanimous "aye!" Malden was proffering "its blood and its treasure." Lexington (with prophetic vision) was ready to sacrifice "yea, life itself." All Worcester County exhorted us to keep the faith. The fishers of Marblehead were prepared "with their lives to assist their brethren."

Day by day I silently listened to the debates in the great Boston Committee, and day by day on Warren's orders, I made one prudent entry, "No business transacted, matter of record." Then on Wednesday the fifteenth, Rotch made

formal request of the collector to clear his ship for England without having discharged the tea. "No" came back
unflinchingly. Nevertheless Hutchinson himself had power
to issue a harbor pass which would be honored by the warships. The whole issue therefore rested with Samuel Adams'
dearest enemy, and we knew the highest Tories themselves,
the Grays and the Royalls, the Ervings and the Fayerweathers would all heave one sigh of relief if his Excellency
decided to give way—to throw back the problem upon its
originators, My Lords in London.

From the hill of Milton came nevertheless no sound, and
with the crisis before us we awoke to that day of days,
Thursday the sixteenth.

A rainy morning. I had sat up till the small hours copying letters to fly forth over Essex and Middlesex. The
ship yards and rope-walks were silent as on the Sabbath.
Men of substance were crowding the ferry and the road
from Roxbury Neck. When I walked with the heavy-eyed
Committee from Edeson Court Street to the Old South it
was between two dense ranks of long coats and full-bottomed wigs. No loud talking. Little noise. It was as
when friends gather for some family crisis.

No other town meeting in all New England had ever
been like unto this. Seven thousand were standing outside
about the meeting house. Inside the standing room was
packed, yet there was no scuffling nor elbowing to force
admission. Winter though it was, the windows had been
flung wide, and snatches of the oratory were passed from
mouth to mouth to the edges of the crowd; and the shout
rippled out to the snowy Common when the question was
stated "whether it be the determination of this body to abide
by its former resolution with regard to not suffering the
tea to be landed?"

Who can recall most of that spontaneous eloquence, cau-

tioning or exhilarating, which wrought more perchance for
the world than many stately apostrophes by Greek or
Roman? But never could I, nor any other, forget the solemn
warning of young Josiah Quincy when the thoughtless too
soon began clamoring "A vote! A vote!"

Forth he stood, slim and gallant, with that hectic flush
kindling his cheeks which told that never would he be suffered to do battle for the America he loved, and often did
I recall his words when the conflict thickened and the
heavens rained blood:

"Shouts and hosannas will not terminate the trials of
this day, nor popular resolves, harangues and acclamations
vanquish our foes. Let us consider the issues before we
advance to those measures which must bring on the most
trying and terrible struggle this country ever saw."

So the hot heads were stilled, but Dr. Young, Samuel
Adams and others spoke gravely to the half-Tory profferers
of faint counsels; "Now the hand is at the plough there
must be no looking back."

Half past four. The short winter day was ending. A
keen wind whistling down the alleys was turning the slush
to ice, when the chairman rose to put the question, "Shall
the tea be landed?" Then like a broadside echoing along
vast crags, from the church, from all the standing thousands
without came back the "NO!" Next followed shouts
"Adjourn!" but adjourn we did not. Our Rubicon was not
yet crossed.

Poor Rotch, fearful for his ship and his skin had driven
to Milton to lay one last plea before Hutchinson for that
pass which might avert the crisis. He would be back at
six, and till six we waited, dinnerless and almost in the
dark—and Boston waited with us.

It is written that Hutchinson took his stand with none
of his great royalist friends around him: no Auchmuty, no

Flucker, no Admiral Montagu. The most loyal of them
would have urged him to yield, and give London its last
chance for deliberation. Wise, learned and devout was
counted Thomas Hutchinson but by that blunder upon that
December afternoon he struck his name from among the
reconcilers of the English race, and graved it among the
non-worthies of America.

It was six when the noise outside the meeting-house told
that a chaise, driven furiously, was coming down Marlborough Street. The crowds were calling "Room for the
owner!" and at a nod from Warren I went with Paul Revere
and escorted Rotch through the jammed aisles and up to
the foot of the pulpit.

The luckless merchant's stock and wig were all awry. In
the light of the few candles which had been set near the
pulpit he peered forth, scared and cold, at the dim sea
of faces gazing upon him from out the great gloomy body
of the building. Never there was a less impressive orator,
nor one less anxious to blurt out his message. But deliver
it he presently did, others taking his halting words and
flinging them far and wide.

Rotch had offered to send back the tea if Hutchinson
would give him a pass to clear the guns of the Castle and
the warships. His Excellency had coughed and palavered,
then at last doggedly repeated his refusal; "To grant a pass
to a vessel which I knew had not been cleared at the custom
house would be a direct countenancing of the violation of
the acts of trade"—So closed the interview.

When Rotch and his interveners had finished, a long low
roar came out of the darkness; then reckless voices were
raised "A mob! a mob!" Yet in a great quietness the final
question was formally put to him, "Whether he, Rotch,
would send back his vessel with the tea in her, under the
present circumstances." The man's hesitation was pitiful,

but at last he got out his answer; "He could not possibly comply, as he apprehended a compliance would prove his ruin," and if lawfully summoned he must perforce land the tea for his own safety.

The church, I repeat, was nearly in darkness. Only around the great pulpit was a little circle of candlelight. There were dim gray panels where once had been the windows. Suddenly now into that candlelight emerged the form of Samuel Adams; under the dim tapers his face shone deathly pale, but there was the wonted ring to his tones as he shook back his long hair, then flung his voice out into the darkness; *"This meeting can do nothing more to save the country!"*

From the back galleries and windows, high above the muttering and growling of the crowd there pealed a yell, piercing to spine and marrow like the howl of the Iroquois; at which summons I charged for a friendly window and leaped forth into the night.

. . . It was in a carpenter's shop near the church, where we smeared our faces with paint, stuck tall feathers in our hair and bundled ourselves with blankets. I remember how a tall, gawky boy, Jo Lovering, held the candles while we put on our thin disguise, then brought to each one of us a dependable hatchet.

It had been agreed in the Committee that the names of those asked to join should not be told even to their comrades. It might well be a hanging matter,—everybody knew it. Each man approached had been told to count the cost. Under those blankets there was many a laced and ruffled coat, but many, too, only of solid linsey and fustian, for a hard bit of stevedoring lay ahead, and the work could not fail through lack of Yankee muscle. Revere, I soon recognized, grinning behind paint worthy of a medicine man, but the leader was the tested and iron-handed Lendall Pitts.

relied upon to hold down the boisterous and see that all things were done decently and in order.

There were only about a score of us when we stepped forth in our blankets into the dark street. The lamps had been lit at the crossways, and a few lanterns escorted us over the dirty ice and snow. It was becoming a keen, crisp night. The streets were still full of people, and as we passed along, a short silent column, one heard the word running on ahead of us, "Here come the Mohawks! Here come the Mohawks!" As we advanced others began falling in behind, usually very poorly disguised. Some were mere lads ready for a lark, but more were square-shouldered determined men who knew their business. We marched quietly in a loose military formation, down Water Street and then cut past Battery March and along the water front. The spars of the shipping and the tall black wharf-houses loomed up like spectres out of the darkness. As we passed dwellings there was a flinging up of windows, and against the candle-lit rooms we saw the figures of leaning, wondering girls. But there was no wild shouting, no tumult. By Fort Hill indeed some enthusiast in the attendant crowd struck up an impromptu song:

> "Rally, Mohawks, bring out your axes,
> And tell King George we'll pay no taxes
>   On his foreign tea.
> His threats are vain, and vain to think
> To force our girls and wives to drink
>   His vile Bohea!"

No one, however, in that grim, set column caught up the refrain. Stolidly we tramped along the water front, with a great scuffling of feet behind us.

Out at their anchorages we could see the rows of lights from the men-of-war, but not a sound drifted from them. Montagu was snug ashore drinking wine with a rich Tory; he had given no orders. His Excellency was warming his slippers in Milton. We came down upon Griffin's Wharf; and as we approached a line of men with muskets stood before us, then Pitts near the head of our column muttered some password and the armed files opened like magic. It was the militia guard over the teaships, its chilly vigil ended. I thought I caught Henry Knox's tall form in the darkness, but said nothing. The wharf was almost deserted; the crews had been paid off, and only the ship's keepers and the officers were aboard. It was low tide and the three Indiamen, with a few lights from the windows in their high stern cabins, were resting aground in absolute quiet, with their spars dimly canted to one side.

There they were, the *Dartmouth*, the *Eleanor*, and the brig *Beaver*. We tramped out onto the wharf, our heavy feet making the old timbers rattle like musketry, but that was the only noise. During the march the word had been passed quietly down the line how the band was to divide. I followed Lendall Pitts' party, and after we crossed the gangplank of the *Dartmouth* and trampled her deck, rioters and worse now before the law, we drew together and in relief from our long silence gave once again our piercing warwhoop, bringing a frightened second mate instantly out of the stern cabin. "Keys to the hatches, candles, matches —and be quick!" Pitts was ordering, giving the fellow no chance to parley, and in a minute we had the keys and the lights. The *Eleanor* and the *Beaver* we knew were likewise in good hands.

It was awkward work for some of us, but there were at least a few in our band who displayed a marvelous knowledge of where the tea was stowed and how to get it out. We took turns at the block and tackle hoisting the heavy chests from the hold. Once on the deck our axes smashed the boxwood, and the noise of the chopping must have gone far along the water front. When sufficiently shattered the chests were deliberately flung over the bulwarks. If some struck upon the bare flats a hundred excited boys, sternly restrained from entering the ships, were proud to speed the good cause by floundering into the cold mud and completing the destruction.

After our single warwhoop there was no shouting, and the throngs of people who piled out upon Wheelwright's, Gray's and other wharfs, or scrambled upon roofs or even the masts or rigging of near-by shipping, kept also a marvelous silence. It was stiff, hard work, never giving us a minute for moralizing. Once we hoisted and almost demolished a case of innocent goods—it cost us some trouble to put it back. Once we detected a fellow (a late volunteer) cramming some tea into his pockets. Everybody knows how we dropped him incontinently into shallow water. He hit on his side, had all his wind knocked out of him, and only by a mercy got safe to the spiling.

The moon came out at last, and the wind blew very chill, but we were warm from the work. It had seemed a trifling task when we talked of it; but never had I imagined it could take so long to break out all that quantity of tea. "Enough," vowed the man beside me, "to steep all Cape Cod Bay!" At last after three hours of unremitting hoisting and chopping the pulleys rattled for the last time. "All out!" shouted Pitts. "All over!" shouted back a companion spirit, probably Revere. And the men at the other two vessels had likewise completed their tasks.

Without another order we walked back across the gangplank, and ten minutes later the *Dartmouth* was as silent as we had found her, not a spar, not a rope the worse, only perchance some splintered case boards and Indian sacking and a certain scattered blackness upon her decks to tell that the good ship belonged henceforth to history.

We reached the head of the wharf and again formed in

a little column. The men-of-war had stirred not; no alarm gun had boomed from the Castle. Hours later we knew that all the royalists about Boston were only too glad to have the fearful tension end without recourse to bloodshed. The next move was London's, and London was three thousand miles away. "All things," John Adams could write the next morning, "were conducted with great order, decency and with perfect submission to government."—To which government?

The strain being over, and we all being very human, some of the younger of us began now to yell again and to flourish our axes. It was growing late, but not too late *that* night for the lights still to be burning in every Boston window. Somebody produced a fife and began to shrill the Liberty Song. Our hundreds of loyal attendants caught it up, as we trailed back through the town toward the Green Dragon where it was agreed that our cohorts should disband. Of course what befell when we passed the Coffin house has become an old story; for Admiral Montagu himself leaned from the rich old Tory's window, and called down on us as we passed, "Well, boys, you've had a fine evening for your Indian caper. But mind, you've got to pay the fiddler."

"Never mind, squire," roared Pitts, now in a daredevil mood, "just come out and we'll settle the bill in two minutes!"

The window closed with a bang. Our column swept on to King Street and right up that still crowded thoroughfare to the doors of the Green Dragon. Then we Mohawks all, for an instant, stood close together upon the snow under the torch light, and with a solemn thought behind our loud bravado, thundered the new refrain to the Liberty Song, every man clasping a hand with the man beside him:

"In Freedom we're born and like sons of the brave,
    We'll never surrender,
    But swear to defend her;
And scorn to survive if unable to save!"

At the last note Pitts gave the good old Scriptural command for dispersal, the wonted formula for the Sons of Liberty, "Each man to his own tent!"—And our brotherhood for an evening dissolved forever.

With some slight improvements in costume and countenance at length I made my way to North Square. It was nearly eleven but the Rivoire house and the Revere house were alike ablaze with candles. Lucy Flucker and Hope, evidently spending the night, came rushing to the door with Emilie, when I appeared "simply to give the news." "Will you have *tea*, this late?" cried the three girls together, flushed with excitement. "No," I replied with my most important air, "I detest tea. Give me a cup of good Yankee cider." Whereat they all burst out into screams of laughter, as the black dust came shaking out of my clothes, stockings and even shoes. Only M. Rivoire looked at me, white and solemn. "To-night, *mon* Roger," spoke he, "King George has taken away the other hand by which he held America. Now he only holds on by his teeth."

CHAPTER XXVI

WHAT EMILIE SAID

AFTER that night of the Tea Party in a vague way we all imagined that something startling would instantly follow. Nothing did. In fact there was a momentary lapse of public interest with lassitude and reaction.

Kind Providence attended to a fourth tea ship, casting it away on Cape Cod long before it could see Boston. Of course excited messengers carried the tidings of the Mohawks far and wide to every white settlement in British America. John Adams wrote off to his friend in Plymouth, "The die is cast! The people have passed the rivers and cut away the bridge!" Paul Revere also went tearing away on a good horse toward Philadelphia to bear the great news to the Whigs, and to be saluted with clangorous bells and public jubilation. Nevertheless around Boston there settled the steadying calm of a cold, hard winter.

After the tidings spread, there presently came back, to be sure, very many resolutions of sympathy and support, and also guarded suggestions from cautious Whigs that we had been precipitate and might have held back forcing the issue a little longer. But forced it was now. No man could doubt the tenor of those long dispatches which Thomas Hutchinson was sealing off to Lord Dartmouth, his colonial secretary; or that after they reached London something more than tea would be brewing. It was still harsh weather, however. Passages to England took six to ten weeks.—In

Boston for quite a time the chief public question seemed
to be, "Is dried dittany better than hardtack or goldenrod
for a substitute for tea?"

Paul Revere presently returned from Philadelphia, cheerful and consequential, and settled down to enjoy his renewed
domestic happiness. I write "renewed" advisedly, because
during 1773 Mrs. Sarah Revere had died suddenly, leaving
a perplexed as well as a very bereaved husband confronting
a large family. But five months after the death of Mrs.
Sarah, a Miss Rachel Walker "an excellent and charming
woman" (as her husband soon wrote of her) felt summoned
to become Mrs. Revere and took charge of a household "in
sore need of a mother's care." The genial engraver's new
matrimonial adventure had indeed taken place in October
during the very dawn of the tea crisis, and the excitement
among the women near North Square had seemed to be
quite as much over the social event at the Revere house
as over the newest fiat from England.

As for me, I perforce returned to Cambridge, as was
quite needful, if with any self-respect I was to pursue my
diploma. There was a let-up in the frantic secretarial work
for the Committee of Correspondence; a couple of other
trustworthy young men were helping to copy the letters.
The tutors made things as easy for me as possible, but until
the January vacation I had to put my nose to the grind-
stone, however reluctantly, and by a desperate exertion
recover the lessons of the past weeks. There are times when
classical studies seem unassailably precious and significant;
there are others when they seem the dreariest, most hack-
neyed pursuits in the world, and that winter the second
mood was surely upon me. Many was the moment I sat
before my fire strongly tempted to fling the lexicon upon
the red logs, and send the *Agricola* after it; while I could
see nothing with my mind's eye but the shadowy decks of

the *Dartmouth*, hear nothing but the rattle of the pulleys dragging up those everlasting tea chests.

The weeks of my reprieve furthermore were creeping by; every red morning brought nearer that fearful moment when I must speak my heart out to Emilie. The demands of my studies gave a proper excuse for being seen now seldom in Boston, but when I did show myself at North Square my manner was probably so constrained and reserved as to perplex my good hosts sadly. Once I caught two young bucks talking behind my back as we took leave together from M. Georges: "Gilman's head's turned since Sammy gave him his arm and let him wear war-paint." "His head may be turned, but his fortune'll be his Uncle Peleg's debts if what my father says of counting house gossip is true."— If I could have picked a quarrel then and there, Boston might have discussed another duel, law and conscience to the contrary. I could only jam my hands in my pockets and march away with the swaggering whistle of "The World Turned Upside Down," in order to cover a very angry heart.

It was that same day that I found Henry Knox in his shop opening a large case of books, and I stared at the titles,—Sim's *Military Guide*, Bland's *Exercises* and a whole battery of other treatises upon the gentle art of killing men by thousands. Henry assured me that the demand for such books was excellent and steadily increasing. "In fact," he added with a laugh, "they go over the counter so fast that I have hardly time to read them myself!"

Even as he spoke there entered a big-framed, Quakerly dressed man of just past thirty, who turned on us a singularly peaceful, open and intelligent face. Henry introduced him as Mr. Nathaniel Greene, up from Warwick, Rhode Island, one of his best customers, whenever he visited Boston.

"And shall it be more translations from the classics and more political science, Mr. Greene?" spoke Knox moving toward certain shelves, whereupon the visitor with an unrestrained laugh began picking up the military books one after another. "Not to-day," he directed, "make up the bill for these."

Probably I dissembled my astonishment very poorly, for Greene looked at me with plain amusement, and I could not restrain, "Egad! Mr. Greene, you make a very strange choice for a Quaker."

The Rhode Islander's laugh became louder and heartier than ever. "Why I *do* look queer to thee, friend Gilman to be sure. But as I told the elders of our meeting when I joined the militia company, there are some parts of the discipline I can never take to. Aren't we plainly warned 'Be not overcome of evil, but overcome evil with good'? And the Boston brethren have so fixed it that there's like to be only one way left for *this* kind of overcoming—So I'll take all of these books, friend Henry."

"A farmer and blacksmith who can talk learnedly with your Harvard bigwigs," remarked Knox as Greene trudged away with a heavy bundle. "There's more than one way of going to college."

"As somebody else has found out," I rejoined, as he slid a work on "Ballistics" into his private bag lest some would-be customer should light on it.

In this manner I finished the term with sufficient credit to quiet the tutors' consciences, my case being greatly lightened by the uproar caused by the sudden and mysterious resignation of President Locke, which event put the college into a state of inefficiency and confusion until the election of his successor, Dr. Langdon. It was a very bleak winter day when I started home for Redford. The night before I had tried to persuade myself to go straight to Boston, visit

North Square, beard the lion and know the worst; but I could not whip myself sufficiently to do it. Therefore I walked straight home, being blessed with the company of classmates as far as the Monroe Tavern, where we all had a bowl of not too befuddling flip, and then I did the last five miles to Redford alone under a bleak sky, stumbling over icy ruts so deep that my small bundle became a burden.

All this fatigue soon passed into happy memory when I sat in the dear old kitchen and father and mother and Tabby and Darius, and Yetmercy and Ishmael, and the big dog and the four cats all listened open-eyed and breathless when I gave my version of December the sixteenth. They had heard it all before, but then "Roger's story was different." I did not say outright that I had been one of the Mohawks whose deeds I described with remarkable detail, but I can still hear Tabby's wild scream when I passed her a very small paper packet "Something from Boston, not to drink but keep it carefully!" and she opened, then almost dropped it, crying "Tea!"

Father was a trifle more than ordinarily kind, and gave thanks at family prayers "That it was permitted to one of this house to serve under those who serve well their country." Mother asked with great particularity about all her Boston friends and relatives, and then in a most incidental, casual manner added, "And have you happened to see anything of that Rivoire girl?" At which I believe I did not turn red while answering, "I've been too busy to see her more than very rarely." But Tabitha said nothing about Emilie at all, although talking instantly of Hope and Lucy Flucker, and I was a little grieved; for I feared that something had come betwixt the girls (women are far more fickle in friendships than men—I have always observed it), and although probably it would not at all matter, still

it would be too bad—*should* things turn out as I prayed, if
my sister and Mademoiselle Rivoire had any quarrel to
compound between them. I was sure the fault was Tabby's,
and studied how best I could reprove and chasten her.

There was little enough of excitement in Redford then
and I was grateful for it. I was weary in spirit though
not in body. It did me good to go out with an axe to aid
the parishioners as they dutifully were cutting and bringing
in "the minister's wood," none of your crooked sticks and
snapping worthless chestnut, but good straight shag-bark
hickory, or solid oak or beech or maple. There was then
a great coming and going of sleds, and later after each big
snowstorm I tramped away with Ishmael and our oxen to
make up the twenty yoke that in one great snorting, steaming, lowing mass broke out the roads and kept our village
from becoming a little island in the midst of a sea of whiteness.

It had been arranged that in the second half of the vacation I was to go back to Boston and assist the Committee.
By that time we could begin to hear from England about
our Tea Party, and, as Samuel Adams himself put it, "Letters are likely to prove worth reading." That time also I
had selected for taking my life in my hands and learning
my destiny. But my guardian spirits were arranging otherwise. I never could learn just how it really was managed,
but one afternoon as I came back from the tavern with my
nose in the *Gazette*, despite the fact that it was squeaking,
crunching cold, I started out of my "Interesting Intelligence" sufficiently to know from the ruts that a heavy sleigh
had driven into the yard and discharged passengers. This
meant nothing, for father was expecting three extraordinarily hungry ministers to spend the night and discuss a
case of discipline, and Yetmercy had spent the whole morning frying an enormous bowl of doughnuts. Nevertheless

I had given one step into the little back hallway to the kitchen when I heard a voice that made my heart turn over:—and there straight under my mortal eyes, all bundled in wonderful capes, shawls and furs was Emilie Rivoire.

Her hair was flying out in red-gold from under the blue of her hood, her cheeks (she abhorred wearing silly travel-masks) were like the new snow and the first soft pink of the dawning. How I envied mother, how black jealousy rose against Tabitha when I saw them kissing and fondling Emilie, asking how she had made the journey, and saying over and over again (woman fashion) "how glad they were to see her!" After a while they abated gurgling sufficiently to let me come forward, and with my best Harvard manner express to Mademoiselle Rivoire "my intense gratification at seeing her again under our roof," but voicing also my profound regrets that for a second time she had visited us here, yet I had been left unaware of the honor impending.

It was a very fine speech I am sure, and one impossible in that summer not twenty months earlier; but since then Mr. Roger Gilman had learned much. Before, however, my lady could reply, Tabitha charged in, avowing that "Emilie's visit was so uncertain" that she had said nothing lest somehow I might be "inconvenienced."—Though why she said "inconvenienced" I never could understand.

No matter, we had a glorious time that night; with the cold making the twigs crack outside; with the ministerial guests and father whetting their theological knives upon a great boiled ham in the dining room, and with the warm comfort of the kitchen wholly reserved for us youngsters, Yetmercy and Ishmael. I had always thought of Emilie as a manner of angel, but, holy prophets, how after that cold ride my angel could eat! She surpassed Tabitha (never backward) and at length Yetmercy avowed she outvied the leanest and hungriest of the three clergymen.

Before long all the constraint and affectation which had perchance colored my last visits upon Emilie, had gone up the cavernous chimney. I was as ready to state my full mind to her as to Tabitha—almost. And I thought the evening had only begun, when we heard the convicting voice of mother, "Children, it's past ten now. Stop chattering and get to bed."

What a week of joy it was! Every dawn I would dive down from my icy bedroom with the blood tingling from crown to heels, to stir the smouldering embers in the kitchen. It was my pride to pile in the massive back log and forestick, grizzled and bearded, then feed on the best splittings of last year's hickory until the great flames fairly raced up the chimney, and the whole kitchen was warm and glowing when my lady came down to do her share with the smoking brown bread and hot sausage. We had been merry enough before in the summer at Redford, but somehow I began to like winter the best. The second day after Emilie's arrival came a great New England tempest, a gift of the wind gods far up in Canada; when all the landscape was whirling snow, when the great elms tossed and groaned, and when as we sat and told stories in the firelight, the whole parsonage seemed laboring on its foundations like a ship in the gale and we rejoiced that its builders had indeed "founded it upon a rock," and wrought its frame of mighty timbers. The next morning all was for hours a white and whirling gloom, then at last the upper boughs grew still, an unaccustomed hush reigned in the heavens and we gazed forth into such intense, such artificial brightness that the eye turned away dazzled as with an unearthly beauty.

How Emilie loved the snow, and the battle we had to clear to the gate; and that other battle we had to break as far as the tavern! It was three days before a post rider floundered through from Woburn and then he had no Boston papers. King George might have sent over frigates and regiments and hanged every Mohawk saving myself, and I become never the wiser for a week. What matter? Through all those days of icy brightness, Boston, Samuel Adams, tea duty, the debate with England seemed things of another and distant world. I was far more proud because I could drive the four-yoke chebbobin bringing down the big log timbers for the new parsonage barn voted at the last parish meeting, than because I knew the inner sentiments of Dr. Warren. When I marched upstairs in the evenings with the great warming pans to take the chill from the icy bed-linen, I was happier than when a monseigneur was bidden to carry the candles before the Queen at Versailles. On Sunday what if the meeting house was the temperature of the arctic outside, and poor father had to take refuge in heavy knit gloves, long camlet cloak and skull cap while he pounded for hours the enormous Bible? Mother and Tabitha and "my sister's friend" had each at their feet snug little brass stoves, filled with hot coals at the parsonage, and brought thither by a certain Harvard student who never felt the cold—his veins glowed so warm on account of some one in the pew beside him.

Emilie had come for ten days. The *grand-père* was lonely without her, Berte was getting very stubborn and old, and "hired help" (Emilie had learned our Yankee term) was costly and bad in Boston. She had done wrong, she said, to listen to Tabitha at all.—The week was over and in three days the sleigh from Concord which served as winter stage-chaise would again swing north from the Lexington road, call at the parsonage—and my golden hours would be ended.

Could I ever pluck up courage?—I would sometimes steal away from the girls and stand shivering in the "best room" gazing upon Great-uncle Waitstill's sword and wondering why it seemed so much easier to run through a battle-worthy redskin than to say a few plain words to the most beautiful woman in the universe? I knew I had lately joined in a deed which would make the King himself speed me to the hangman—and I was sleeping the sleep of the healthy righteous. "Gilman," I said to myself, as on the seventh night after Emilie's arrival I dove under the bed-clothes, "You will do that thing to-morrow or go through the ice in Concord river. Cold drowning's the only fate for blind kittens and cowards such as you.—If she won't have you, bear your denial like a man."

. . . It was the eighth morning. It had turned a trifle warmer. The night before rain had fallen and changed to ice upon all the branches. Every twig had been given a casing of diamonds. The next day it was slightly colder again. The sun shone upon a world like a palace of fabled genii. The cathedral arches of the elms flashed like the gates of the Heavenly City—jasper and sapphire, chalced-ony and emerald, topaz and amethyst. Father at morning prayers dwelt affectionately upon the verse: "This is the day which the Lord hath made, we will rejoice and be glad in it." Then hardly was his "Amen!" uttered as he stood leaning upon the back of his tall praying chair, before Amos Tyler (a harmless and respectable admirer of Tabby's) came knocking to say that the sap had begun to run well over in his father's maples and did we care to come over? "They probably would boil."

Would we come? The snowshoes, which Tabitha and I had been teaching Emilie to wear, could not carry us fast enough over the fairy country. The Tyler sugar camp was about four miles into the Carlisle woods. Over the frozen river we flew and up one dazzling slope after another. Then we found the Tylers, father and sons and hired hands, with their shacks and big fires, buckets, troughs and axes. They had been out two nights, rising to empty the troughs, then turning in again after piling dry logs upon the embers. Now all the pails and troughs were filling with the clear pure sap, the forked sticks were being forced into the frozen ground, the green sticks were being set from fork to fork and we came just in time to help with the "sugaring-off kettles" and heap on wood, wood and ever more wood upon the enormous fires.

The Tylers were hospitable folk; besides their guests of honor "the minister's children," there was a great coming and going, scrambling and frolicking of sled-loads of lads and girls, all with enormous quantities of edibles. For a long time I was too busy helping with the kettles to have much to say to Emilie, but at last when we stopped to drop a little hot sugar in the snow and see it turn to candy, I caught her licking her fingers and could remark to her, "They tell me great things of the pleasures in France, but where have even your great folk anything like this?"

"Where have they?" she echoed cocking her pretty head, opening the whitest teeth and letting the sugar string between them. I could have eaten her then and there, except that about twenty witnesses would have cried out against my cannibalism. It was a "very good run" said the Tylers, and as usual when the trees responded freely the weather turned quite mild; just cold enough not to melt. We could throw off our heavier wraps and romp around delightfully. Then when the last sausages had been stowed down; the big sled laden with the kettles and buckets, the fires raked low for safety, and the trees were casting long shadows, our snowshoes must go on again, and away we fared toward the parsonage.

Tabitha and Amos were just ahead of us. They were talking very fast. I envied Tabitha's vast ability to make her tongue clapper. Emilie for a while talked very fast too, somehow talking much yet saying nothing. Then of a sudden she lapsed into silence, and I as promptly realized that for a long time I had been walking beside her as dumb as the tall beeches that glittered icy and white around us under the evening sun, while we struck the long smooth descent to the river. Equally suddenly a great resentment began welling up in my breast; resentment against all those flowery-tongued men of gallantry who could ripple off compliments by the yard, and cover the most important thing in life with a mountain of fine phrases. Something at length seemed surging within me mastering reason, mastering cowardice, commanding my speech.

Day and night for weeks I had rehearsed for this ordeal, but now my voice rattled in my throat, harsh, clanking as the sugar kettles. Tabitha and Amos had glided far to the front. Nobody was in sight behind. Only the snow and the trees and the frozen river it seemed could eavesdrop. I had selected a smooth little bit of the road much nearer the village for my great adventure, but I could no more have kept silent at the place we were that moment than I could have commanded those black twigs "Bud forth green," and seen them all obey me.

All of itself, speaking, it seemed, directly against my will, I could hear my own voice, not with the fine speech so long prepared but only the stammering blurting of a schoolboy.

"Emilie, I have something I've got to say—before we get home."

"Yes, Roger," looking down into the snow.

"Emilie, you are French—can never understand—I've no right—not Uncle Peleg's heir—poor minister's son—no settlement—no property—just two honest hands—but I——"

Doubtless I said more, but before I clearly knew more,

some one was crying right in my arms, and a voice was answering close, so close, "Oh Roger, stupid, cowardly *garçon*—we knew all that. *Why* have you not said this long before?"

. . . Out of the darkening boughs above us scurried a great white owl, flapping off with a hoot that went echoing far along the icebound river, crying "Scandal!" to all the black avenues of the trees.

"What shall we say to your grandfather, dearest," said I, and Emilie looking up into my eyes replied, "My beloved, we will simply come to him hand in hand and say *'Roger and I have resolved to make the new America together.'*"

We did not reach home very early that evening. Since we had only the rest of our lives to plan about, we found the snowshoeing excellent and followed the line of the river far along into Billerica. When at last we turned back and came down to Redford high street, the lights in each one of the paternal old farmhouses seemed blinking "Welcome! welcome!" while all the youth in our veins cried out "Joy! joy!"—That an angry king afar off could reach forth to distract our happiness was the last of our dancing, glowing thoughts.

At last we realized that we were at the parsonage and were actually inside the gate. Most unaccountably it was well past supper time. Emilie and I looked at each other, tried to compose our features and go in completely self-possessed. As I threw back the door whom should I come plump upon but Yetmercy.

"Are we late?" I queried innocently; "we lost our way by the river."

Yetmercy regarded us with perfect composure, then, grave as the meeting house, shut one eye. "I *expected* you to lose your way;" was all that she said.

Nobody spoke to us with reproof or curiosity when we

sat down to a very late supper. Mother helped Yetmercy
with the dishes; father spread out his *Gazette* and fumed
over a labored Tory reply to one of Warren's letters.
Tabitha and Darius were very quiet, although once or twice
I caught my sister looking at us out of the corner of her
eye. At last when our own supper was over, and father
had given his much delayed evening thanks, I took Emilie
by the hand, and proud as an emperor and empress we went
straight over to mother, where she sat by the betty lamp,
a great basket of darnable stockings in her lap and her
needle plying steadily.

"Mother," said I, in my firmest tones, "we have something to tell you."

Mother rose, very carefully laid down the basket, took
Emilie in her embrace and kissed her. Then she opened
her arms to me, and kissed me also.

"Dear new daughter of my love," she said, "this is what
I have prayed and ached for."

Then father had to be told, and he had to lay his hands
upon our heads in the good old Apostolic benediction; next
mother, Emilie and Tabitha all cried hard together, and
father and I did much hard blinking. Following that we
all felt still more happy.

"And when did you first know that you cared?" I whispered, before Emilie went up the stairs to Tabitha's room.

"Since that night in Queen Street," came back softly in
my ear, "and, *bon Dieu*, what years of torment you have
given me!"

. . . I gave Tabby a great suffocating hug when I saw
her next morning. "I think I managed very well, brother,"
she observed demurely, and I did not contradict her.

. . . The Concord stage sleigh three days later received
a young lady handed in at Redford by a young gentleman
who took extraordinarily elaborate and ceremonious leave

of her, quite to the admiration of the farmerish passengers who were delighted to see how young Mr. Roger Gilman could "tech it off Boston fashion." The sleigh bells went jingling away down the Lexington road. It was still white winter around us. But the spring robins were already singing in my heart.

CHAPTER XXVII

IN WHICH I CLEAN A FIRELOCK

MONSIEUR GEORGES looked at me very hard when I told him what Emilie and I had determined.

"Marriage is a solemn matter, my friend," said he, "it often concerns many others besides the giddy young. What will you do if I oppose?"

I met him eye to eye, for all that his gaze was so terrible; "You will never force me to tell, sir."

Whereat he seized me in almost as close an embrace as my mother had vouchsafed Emilie. "If we were in France," he spoke, "if we were in France, *mon fils*, I would have to say, 'Send me your father. Let him make formal proposals. Let him name a sufficient settlement.' But since we are in Massachusetts,—may the God of the Puritan and Huguenot make glad your lives!"

After that he talked to me very affectionately and sagely, saying that he had long since determined that I was worthy of Emilie if she cared for me, but knowing our New England pride feared to give the least formal encouragement lest he seem to be buying a husband for his granddaughter with his fortune. It was agreed that I should complete my work at Harvard, and that after I graduated in '75 there would be time enough for the wedding, and for finding some business which would make me a gentleman by the New World and not the Old World formula. Emilie was in all things discreet and practical; made me promise that I would not spoil my college work by too many visits to Boston, nor buy

her foolish presents out of a deplorably small allowance.
The next day I learned in a roundabout manner that M.
Rivoire had bought up several of Mr. Peleg Fifield's more
dangerous bills, and had informed my uncle with his best
native delicacy that he hoped he would use no inconvenient
haste in discharging them.—For some time therefore, after
my return to Boston, I walked about as if the Dock Square
cobble-stones were air bubbles; indeed except for Emilie's
good sense I would probably have done some outrageous
thing just to show how delightfully crazed an accepted lover
can be.

What drew me down to earth was no unkind trick by
Cupid, but the very formidable and prosaic news that now
began coming from England. Every mail bag, even before
the tale of the Tea Party had crossed, brought home the
inveterate purpose of King and ministers to force us to
the wall. We knew that Chatham had at the time of the
Stamp Act declared his belief that no minister would ever
be found "who would dare to dip the royal ermine in the
blood of Americans," but everything pointed to the fact that
this hope was becoming vain. St. James and Westminster
were precisely in a mood to dare the worst. Once more
the Committee of Correspondence became very busy.

Before, however, the official reaction to the deeds of the
Mohawks could reach us, I perforce had returned to Harvard, albeit not entirely to study. Cambridge was beginning to boil and bubble in its smaller way almost as fiercely
as Boston. Although the fine houses along the Watertown
road, where Vassals took off their hats to Lechmeres and
Lees played cards with Fayerweathers, were already known
as "Tory Row," the college and the bulk of the village were
Whiggish enough to warm Sam Adams' inner heart.

I saw Adams once when he came out to the Blue Anchor
for a consultation with the local committee, and asked him

whether it was not still right to hope that in the face of the unmistakable warnings Crown and ministers would not at last recede with dignity. He pulled out a letter just received reciting how at a hearing of the Lords of the Committee for Plantation Affairs, Solicitor General Wedderburn had covered Dr. Franklin with inconceivable villification and ridicule before an audience of councillors and peers which applauded every coarse denunciation. This had been followed by the summary dismissal of Dr. Franklin as postmaster-general for America.

It took me a fair minute to realize all that this deed implied. Franklin had been mediator betwixt Britain and America. He had been the most distinguished citizen of the New World. He had been treated with high respect even by those Englishmen to whom Samuel Adams was a candidate for Tyburn.

"What does this mean?" I asked blankly.

"What does it mean when any king flings out of his court the ambassador of a country with which he has vowed to pick a quarrel?"

"A declaration of war?"

Adams nodded; "Wait for the next ship."

And that "next ship" brought news which sent the messengers fling inland as swift as horseflesh and spur could carry them.

. . . Other pens than mine must tell at length how his Majesty blew out against the act of Boston as a "subversion of the constitution"; how my Lord North warned British that here was the culmination of years of riot and confusion; how the orators in the Commons raged against us, often in the words of the insolent and arrogant Venn; "The offense of America is flagitious, the town of Boston ought to be knocked about its inhabitants' ears and destroyed. *Delenda est Carthago!* You will never meet with proper obedience to the laws of this country until you have destroyed that nest of locusts."

"Alas! poor Americans," wrote Herbert Dunmore in another long and pathetic letter; "you seem to have no friends left. Even Lord Chatham frowns on your rash act, and Colonel Barre says there must be punishment. At three thousand miles distance I at least will keep from judging harshly. General Gage fresh from New York, I know has advised His Majesty that four regiments can hold down Boston, while saying concerning your people 'They will be lions while we are lambs, but if we take the resolute part, they will be very meek.' Ministers think that Boston will be left to bear her punishment alone—the other colonies never will stand by her."

"Not stand by her"? Having seen the Virginia and Pennsylvania letters I had my doubts; but that the first blows would fall on the head of Boston and Massachusetts, who could question? Weeks before the ponderous process of legislation could be completed at London we knew the fate in store for us;—the port of Boston was to be declared closed to all commerce, her wharves and shipping left to rot, her inhabitants to migrate or starve, her custom house withdrawn to Marblehead,—until the East India Company should be reimbursed for the tea now steeping in the harbor. No preliminary demand was made on Boston for reparation; no avenue permitted for compromise and conciliation; no separation in penalty between the Mohawks and the High Tories.

Circumstance had made Boston the center for the resistance to royal policy. The Port Act told all America what resistance to royal policy would cost. It would be Boston to-day, Philadelphia to-morrow, Charleston soon after. We went to a common doom together. And right soon we heard how far up and down the Colonies the blackbordered copies of the Port Act were being burned by the common hangmen upon the scaffolds before huge cursing and raging mobs.

Against Massachusetts were aiming other blows. Our charter was to be upset. The right to name councillors was to be reserved for the King, likewise the choice of all peace officers and sheriffs. More devastating still, the precious right to hold town meetings, the warp and woof of the old freedom of New England, was put stiffly under the control of the royal governor. Last but not least there was now pending the "murder act," whereby any British officer or soldier who might be chargeable with high crimes against our citizens, could have his case with all the witnesses transferred to England where conviction before a native jury was the last thing possible. These first arrows were aimed at Massachusetts, but what of the other colonies? Spring had not run its course before we learned how the Virginia House of Burgesses was voting Mr. Thomas Jefferson's resolutions, making the day the port of Boston was closed "a day of fasting, humiliation and prayer" for the averting of "the heavy calamity which threatens the destruction of our civil rights and the evils of civil war."

Before that spring was ended I had likewise begun to think personally upon a sufficiently serious matter; namely whether I might become obligated to die for my country.

Now "dying for one's country" seems an extremely pretty thing, and is often commended in books. Nowadays Fourth of July orators often talk about the men of the 1770's as if they were inordinately very fond of this perilous but praiseworthy avocation. But I assure you that there was *one* perfectly normal youth of military age who was not in the least anxious for this form of patriotic service. On the contrary (public interruptions aside) my methodical Yankee brain had mapped out a very peaceful and non-military career for myself. I was to marry Emilie as soon

as I was graduated. We were to be blessed of course with
a fine houseful of children. With Uncle Peleg's and M.
Rivoire's joint assistance I was to enjoy unbroken progress
as an eminently distinguished merchant, with every cocked
hat coming off as I went down lower King Street to get
the reports of my captains when they made fast to Long
or to Wentworth's Wharf. All this seemed very plain and
simple except for the one small item of the news from England, and what it clearly implied.

Nevertheless here I was sitting in my room high in old
Stoughton, and upon my table directly beside lexicon and
chrestomathy there rested that most unacademic of instruments—a long musket. And close beside it lay that most
unacademic of books *The Manual Exercise of 1764 as
ordered by His Majesty*, the official treatise upon infantry
tactics. I had banged away with father's lumbering fowl-
ing-piece since I became old enough to level at the crows,
but as for this firelock—it was different. And here again
I was taking off a blue and white coat boasting the chevrons
of the first sergeant of the Harvard company.

We had maintained a college military company since
1769, but it had been a laughable, disorderly affair, joined
mainly because of the non-disciplinary custom of passing
around several buckets of toddy when the men broke ranks
after drill. But now nearly a hundred of us were marching
up and down Cambridge common with solemn purpose;
and I had had the greatness of the first sergeantship thrust
upon me, probably more because the upper officers were all
seniors and I was a prominent junior than from the slightest degree of military fitness.

Day after day we donned our "buff and blue" regimentals (a uniform later to be worn with more effect by
a decidedly larger army) and struggled together with the
"file right," "file left," "in column by fours," and all the

intricacies of the manual of arms. Many is the time I bawled my orders to a platoon of sophomores, and saw them all grinning and watching to see if their first sergeant could get his own firelock upon his shoulder without some egregious error. Many is the time when a knotty sentence of Thucydides seemed infinitely less complex than the eight "orders" and twelve "movements" for priming and loading, as laid down in the misnamed "simplified" manual.

For the whole science of martial evolutions I seemed to have no more aptitude than for flying without wings;—and yet master it I apparently must, master it all the other youth of America very possibly must, or all the fine speeches of Samuel Adams and Patrick Henry were like to prove merely so much sounding brass and tinkling cymbals.

The whole business was utterly unreal to me. The musket (which I kept in my room and struggled with privately) seemed so harmless, so impersonal. Nevertheless I knew what "the last appeal," which we had come to whisper about would mean, and so, I think, did many of my classmates who took the crisis intelligently. It meant (in very plain terms) for me that I must be ready to go out to kill fine British lads perhaps as fine as Herbert Dunmore, and never flinch while they tried to kill me. It meant too that with a mere smattering of a science, which all our little drilling now had at least taught was a grim and intricate science indeed, we must go forth to face regiments boasting long traditions of victory, and on whose banners were blazoned the battles that had broken the power of France and of Spain. It was like entrusting a frigate to queasy farmers and commanding, "Sail forth, and carry safe through the howling gale."—You can understand then why I did more than laugh with my mates, when I oiled the barrel and knapped the flint of that musket.

Likewise another thing came home. Grievous as were the wrongs under which we suffered, abominable as were the oppressions by King and ministers, none of us could conquer the old, old love for England. What if she had been a stern, harsh parent indeed; was she not our parent still? Had we not been born and bred to rejoice that we were Englishmen; settled in a new land, shaping our own provincial laws, but Englishmen still, and sharers in that national heritage which made the English the proudest race on God's earth?

Was there no peaceful way? Would not the King at the last awful moment recede? Would not the wisdom of our chiefs find some outlet aside from that fearful one before which the heart shuddered? They were talking now a more sweeping and rigid non-intercourse pact against Britain, as the final means for bringing London to terms—unless? But I knew in my heart of hearts, and so did many another that the measure would not succeed. After that if we called to heaven for aid, it must be to the Lord of battles.

Hitherto for years we had divided ourselves into Whigs and Tories, using the good old English party names; neighbors could still argue without passion; vigorous words could fly, and then the most belligerent disputant close politely with "Will you favor me, sir, with a pinch of snuff?"—Now there came crowding new terms, "Patriot," "Loyalist," and the issues were cutting deeper. Many an honest man who had denounced the Stamp Act, shuddered over the Massacre and cried out against the Tea duty, murmured when he found himself on the mortal brink—"England is very wrong —but I cannot bring myself to this." Many a loud-mouthed, brawling Son of Liberty flung out the most bellicose counsels simply because he had never counted the cost, and would prove a chicken-hearted scoundrel at the "whing" of the first bullet.

I blame not the better Loyalists—*almost* their arguments convinced me, as they convinced wiser men. Yet this I say —and no insult to them; the best of the Loyalists never rose above the vision of America as in perpetual tutelage to Britain; a tall boy forever tied to his mother's apron strings, and dutifully accepting the scoldings and cuffings of her more peevish moods. Would the mother have learned wisdom; have presently cut the tall boy adrift under conditions of amity; have suffered an upstanding nation and not a rich dependency to spread across North America? I doubt it; and the more I read the story of the Britain of George III the more my doubts grow stronger.

The one thing certain is that King and ministers did not relent. Through Commons and Lords advanced the Boston Port Bill, and thence to the royal signature—voted by great majorities after perfunctory debate; to be embalmed on the statute books of 1774, along with acts for paving London streets and widening English country roads. We all read how Lord Mansfield had congratulated the House of Lords on its chance now at last to undo the calamitous results of "lenity" toward America—"The sword is drawn and you must throw away the scabbard."—The Harvard company drilled very hard the day after the *Gazette* carried this and other "important intelligence," and the first sergeant found the manual of arms coming materially easier.

So another winter and spring jogged along—Roger Gilman trying his best to accomplish the impossible, namely, to serve two masters—Harvard College and the cause of the United Colonies (as we were coming to call them). Fortunately the first of these masters was very lenient. As often as Emilie would let me I went to Boston. Our betrothal had not been formally announced to that arrogant little world calling itself "genteel society—," but of course

Hope Fifield and Lucy Flucker had to be told "under pledges of absolute secrecy." And in an amazingly short time the whole business miraculously leaked out—Hope and Lucy both denying passionately "that they ever had breathed a word."

As a result there was a great falling off in fashionable swains at North Square; and Emilie got fewer sleigh rides and chaise rides; went to fewer assemblies; was less often toasted over the punch-bowls. On which treatment she throve exceedingly, never was in better health, and looked ten times more beautiful. Tabby came down for a visit to Boston, and Aunt Mercy piloted the pair over to view the placid glories of Cambridge. I had therefore the conspicuous honor of being permitted to parade the yard in company with two of "the most elegant of their sex" as one of my friends enviously assured me; while half a dozen others the next day wished me joy and vowed that "Gilman's a lucky rascal."

After Tabby was gone, however, one afternoon I had Emilie all to myself. We went strolling down to Battery March below the South Battery and Fort Hill. It was a perfect April day, the nineteenth as I later remembered, and all nature seemed leaping out of its cold chrysalis. There was a warm, balmy smell to the air. All around the southern slopes of the parapet of the fortress were the first dear green things growing. We stood at an unfrequented spot watching two bluebirds busy over a new nest. They were both so happy about it, working in the twigs and old twine, and twittering to and fro out of sheer love of their performance. Emilie's hand on my arm tightened a little. She did not need to utter the thought that was dancing in the minds of us both; "Only a little over a year now—and we—and what joy it will be——"

Then while we watched the birds, and saw them jointly

drag a particularly heavy wad of lintage toward the new mansion—"Boom!" the report of a ship's gun startled us, and made the home builders drop their burden with a frightened flurry. We looked toward the harbor. A very large troopship had dropped anchor by Castle Island. Even in the distance we could see the swarms of red jackets leaning over the bulwarks for their first sight of that town and country which the regiment had come three thousand miles to coerce. Emilie's hand tightened again, but not in the former manner. I could feel the dread sent tingling through every nerve of her dear body.

"There they are," she said at length.

"A few days sooner than expected," I tried to say lightly. "It's well known that the new governor is to have several regiments to back him."

"Four years ago," she pursued with the barest quiver, "we saw the red coats depart from Boston. When—when will they go again?"

"When heaven helps us to drive them out," I said soberly.

"Drive them out? Oh, *mon cher ami,* will there be no other way?"

"Emilie," we were quite alone save for the birds, my arm stole around her, "you are nearer to God than I. Perhaps *your* prayers may open to us some other way. The wisest and most peaceful of us see none."

"You will do nothing rash?"

"Nothing; the promise has gone to all our friends throughout America that the Massachusetts patriots will endure to the uttermost, will exhaust all resources before— 'The final appeal.'"

"But there is no hope of success? You stand silent. I know there is no hope of success. O my beloved!"

"Cursed be they," I cried in rising anger, "cursed be those

fools and tyrants in England who send this cloud betwixt
us and our right to happiness!——"

But she touched my cheek very gently, and when I ceased
storming, she asked with troubled lips, "If all we dread, if
war really comes, could you,—tell me, *ma vie*—could you
with honor stand aloof? Would it be right?"

Whereat my eyes shot sparks, even before my dearest.
"Honor? Right? You know I have wrought for the Committee justifying the patriot cause. Of all the young men
in Massachusetts, I least could refuse the summons—if summons came. I could not touch your hand and say aught
else."

The birds were again fluttering about the new nest, busy
and joyous. Emilie looked upon them with a little sigh,
then lifted her eyes with a glorious attempt to seem brave-
hearted, "We are not birds, and our happiness is not for a
summer. How can I receive your hand into mine, unless
I know that all the strength behind it belongs first to that
precious thing I learn to call America?"

Back we walked very soberly, albeit talking rapidly of
many things. Both of us saw not the cobbled streets all
the way to North Square, but only that stately ship
crowded with red-coated men. We knew the clouds were
drawing on apace after our dazzling sunlight.

On May thirteenth, 1774, the frigate *Lively* glided up
Boston fairway. She brought the new military governor,
General Gage. The punishment of Massachusetts for vin-
dicating the liberties of America had begun.

CHAPTER XXVIII

HOW THE DOOR WAS LOCKED IN SALEM

Now I suppose that some day certain good people will rise and assert that if George of Windsor and George of Mt. Vernon had only sat down together and conversed for a while amiably, our American independence would have been established without a sniff of burnt powder or a pin prick. I suppose something like this, because, as Yetmercy used to say, "The fools ain't all dead yet." But if you care to study the character of that George of Windsor and the then condition of England, you will probably agree that notwithstanding all the persuasiveness of George of Mt. Vernon or any other American we might to this day be accepting broken-down noblemen for our governors, be forbidden to manufacture iron goods or hats, or to trade direct with France, and be dutifully teaching our sons to praise the British constitution and to sing "Rule Britannia."

No doubt somebody will tell me that George III was personally a "good man." And "good" he was,—a faithful husband, a kind father, and well-intentioned by his subjects. But it is your ignorant, obstinate, "good men," pitifully convinced that God has told them exactly how to make their fellow mortals virtuous and happy, that have set more cannons to thundering and women to weeping than all your remorseless tyrants,—in all lands at least where men speak English.

However, too much ink has been wasted here on moralizing, and so let me relate merely what I saw or heard.

Upon Tuesday, May seventeenth, amid a terrific downpour of rain, his new Excellency, Thomas Gage, landed at Long Wharf. He was more than our governor. He was major general, and behind him was all the military power of Britain, assembling to crush that "faction" which was defying the wise laws of the King. General Gage was nevertheless escorted in state to Faneuil Hall by the Boston Cadets led by no less a personage than their commander, John Hancock. There were also huge banquets, loyal toasts and all the fuss and clattering becoming an exchange of potentates at Province House.

The festivities were the more genuine because the coming of Gage at least betokened the exit of Hutchinson. Since the Tea Party that magistrate's power had sunk to a contemptible nullity. He had been summoned to England "to advise the King," and thither he soon departed, execrated by the great part of his fellow citizens, and destined for a time to be caressed in Britain by his patrons, and then to die straitened and pining for the land of his birth, like many another Loyalist who made the Great Miscalculation.

Nevertheless although Gage was a man of genial manners and easy approach he had been sent to tyrannize over us, and in a few days Boston felt the clamping of the irons. On the first of June all vessels were forbidden to enter the port even with the most needed supplies. After the fourteenth none could depart. The shotted guns of the Castle were trained on the ship channel; directly across the fairway with springs on their cables and batteries cleared rode heavy men-of-war. No anchor could be weighed, no sail unfurled along the most thriving water front in America.

The ship yards perforce grew silent, spiders and not artisans spun in the great rope-walks. No scow could so much as bring in a sheep or a truss of hay from the islands. No provisions could enter Boston save by the long dreary wagon route along Roxbury Neck. The streets were soon full of idle, angry, and even somewhat hungry men, sailors, fishermen, longshoremen and mechanics; while once more the cobbles reechoed with the tramp of regiments sent back now with grim purpose. Lord North had pledged that Boston should be put "seventeen miles from the sea." He seemed twice as good as his word.

A few days after the port was closed I revisited Boston. The Charlestown passenger ferry was still running, but a red-coated sergeant stood by the ship to see that not a quintal of fish, not a bag of potatoes came across. Except where little knots of idle men stood sullen and silent, it was like traversing a city of tombs. Boston had been famed for its intense bustle and activity. The contrast now was all the more startling.

When I called at North Square I found Paul Revere deep in converse with M. Georges. The friendly silversmith had with him the plate of one of his old engravings published at the time of the Stamp Act. He had been consulting about some matters of retouching, but now with hardly a word, he pointed to the verses upon the legend:

"O thou, whom next the heaven we must revere,
Fair Liberty! Thou heavenly Goddess hear!
Have we not woo'd thee, won thee, held thee long,
Lain in thy lap and melted on thy tongue?
Thro' death and danger rugged paths pursued,
And led thee smiling to this solitude.
Hid thee within our hearts most golden cell
And braved the powers of Earth, and powers of Hell?
Goddess! We cannot part, thou must not fly,
'Be slaves?' We dare to scorn it,—dare to die!" *

"Orthodox doctrine, eh, Roger?" demanded Paul, and when I nodded, he put his hands deep in his pockets, hummed a bar, then added, " 'Dare to die'? They say

*The editor has been unable to determine the original authorship of these verses, well-known from their use upon the engraving of Paul Revere.

nasty things about clergymen who don't live up to their preaching. So I guess that for us——"

He did not complete the sentence but M. Georges looked at him with a very significant smile, "There is a great deal to be dared first besides merely dying, my friend;" and then to me, "Have you received Mr. Adams' message, *mon* Roger?"

I had not; but a few words more sent me almost on the run over to Hanover Street, and into Warren's office; and a little later, after a single precious hour with Emilie, I was headed off, not toward Cambridge, but toward no less a place than Salem, leaving it to the doctor to patch matters for me with Harvard, and having under me a very good horse loaned by Paul's Charlestown crony, Deacon Larkin.

"Mr. Samuel Adams needed me at Salem," to which town, as a further token of the degradation of Boston, Gage had transferred the legislature. All the taverns and hospitable residences of the Essex town were now alive with councillors and representatives, and to the general public grievances were now being added the personal ones of being obliged to skirmish suddenly for quarters in a strange and overcrowded town.

It went out that ministers had fondly imagined that Salem would rejoice at this honor thrust upon her, and that the merchants along Derby Street would be rubbing their hands at the opportunity for prospering at the expense of ancient rivals, but I admired the few Tories who were bold enough to stalk along Essex Street those days and to try to ignore the mutterings all around them; and as for the wharves they were crowded with shipping, but nigh every foremast flew a Boston houseflag, the Salem traders putting all their docks gratis at the disposal of their one-time adversaries.

My own lodgings I easily resumed at Mr. Truswell's, the good people of the house having lived down the scandal of my last year's exit; and after being warmly welcomed and leaving my bag I hunted up Mr. Adams, whom I found —just as I might have expected, down by Becket's ship yard, talking in earnest, homely language to a half-dozen iron-handed calkers, and assuring them of his great joy. "At finding that you understand the case precisely as I do."

When he saw me out of the corner of his eye, he broke off politely, and soon his arm was in mine and we strolled back into the town.

"Well," demanded I, as we walked past the big white mansions, "all ways become closed for us; when must we begin to fight?"

"Fight? Young blood, boy, young blood!" he began to laugh, which was often a sign that he had something important to impart. "Why, 'pon my soul you are not turning twenty, and you have fifty years before you during which, as Warren wished for himself the other day, bedeviling the British, 'You can wade up to your knees in blood.' Fight we must—as long ago I told you, but just now must do a harder thing—far harder."

"And what is that, sir?"

"Wait, sit meek after insult and bullying, give the rascals their tow. America is like a big vessel—it takes time for her to swing around. Boston is not all America, nor does every lad of spirit see the papers of the Committee on Correspondence. Here are the good folk in Philadelphia advising us to pay for the tea and so take ourselves legally out of the wrong. Poor Franklin, still trying to say his 'Peace, peace,' over in Britain writes the same thing. In Boston there'll be a town meeting soon with all the Tory respectables putting it to vote whether to compensate the

India Company—the Tories offering to pay their share. And I don't want," his glance was that of a father, and his tone had more than its wonted trembling: "I don't want to feel that lads like you walk up against the fire-locks, until not only poor Sam Adams, but all the conscience of America says, 'There is no other way but this one, hard and bitter.'"

"The sight of that dead port of Boston makes my blood boil."

"There be a lot more 'boiling' coming pretty soon, and over worse things than a silent port. We'll take that thing which God first sends to hand, and that (thanks be!) doesn't call for bloodshed. Yet, come peace, come war, we need this thing, and I need help to put it through. Committees of Correspondence have done their work. Massachusetts shall vote her delegates to a Continental Congress which will either face down the King or fight him, and vote them now before Sam Adams quits Salem."

"The day that scheme is rumored won't the governor dissolve the legislature?"

"The day that scheme is rumored, the deed is already done."

Thus began one of the most ticklish, anxious weeks in all my life.

.   .   .   .   .   .

As clerk of the legislature Mr. Adams was entitled to name a temporary assistant, and Mr. Roger Gilman was more than delighted to serve in such capacity. The representatives met in the big bare court room of Salem Town House. Here I met the farmer members from the inland counties, big-limbed, heavy-handed men, keen with their axes, rough in manner, but brisk in zeal. Most of my work seemed to be buttonholing one double-fisted member after another and imploring: "Mr. Adams entreats you not to touch up the governor. Don't slam back at the Tories."

The Tories certainly were there, some twenty of the Very Respectables, gold-laced coats, nankeen breeches, gold-headed canes and all to match, who day after day took bold delight extolling ministers and scolding Boston. Their courage had risen because not merely was his new Excellency now at his friend "King" Hooper's house at Danvers only three miles away, but camped near him were picked companies of the sixty-fourth, ready, at least so their swaggering ensigns boasted, "to clear the Assembly Hall with the bayonet."

The Tories therefore were arrogant, while Sam Adams was remarkably meek. He was in fact absent so much from his clerk's desk that the Tories sneered "where's your leader?" and threw out that he had skulked back to Boston. But the claws of the lion suddenly reappeared when Mr. Eli Gorton, the most portly Loyalist member, planted himself in the clerk's seat right under the speaker's nose. The next thing we knew Mr. Adams, suddenly as if by magic, was standing right at the trespasser's elbow.

"Mr. Speaker," rose his voice in the crowded hall, "where is the place for your clerk?" Under his official wig Speaker Cushing rose and pointed toward Gorton, whereupon Adams' tones sounded with even clearer emphasis, "Sir, my company will not be pleasant to the gentleman now in my seat. I trust he will remove to another part of the house." —And remove Gorton did, nor did another Loyalist desecrate the clerk's chair.

All this on the surface. What behind the scenes? Who told me that "smart politics" was only imported to America on a kind of second *Mayflower* after adopting our glorious Constitution? Every day the committee "On the State of the Province," Mr. Samuel Adams, chairman, met

and deliberated, talked, split hairs, did nothing. Every
day Daniel Leonard of Taunton, its zealous and watchful
Tory member, was more than ever convinced that the Whigs
were scared and divided, and at last he drove out to Danvers and told General Gage how there was little to be
dreaded at *that* session. Every night little groups of members met at Adams' rooms at the Pickering house for conferences long and whispered. Then the groups increased,
five visitors upon the first nights, then ten, then thirty.
Next I sought Adams myself behind a bolted door.

"News," I announced, right gleefully, "Leonard's land-
lady has been buttered—never mind how. She says Mr.
Leonard thinks things are all quiet and he's gone home to
Taunton on a lawsuit."

Sparks almost snapped from my chieftain's eyes, "An
old Roman would say of you, Roger, 'You have deserved
well of the Republic.' Now use your ears to-morrow!"

. . . A very full meeting it was, a hundred and twenty-
nine members present. The little bunch of Tories looked
isolated and uncomfortable. Mr. Clerk sat in his usual
place, the last minutes were droned off and approved, a
member from Greenfield cleared his throat and began a
meandering speech about fishing rights in the Connecticut.
While he rattled a pile of papers, few noted how Samuel
Adams, with feline tread, went down a side aisle and whispered to the doorkeeper. Somebody near the front blew
his nose like a trumpet, otherwise you might have heard
the faint clicking of a lock. Forthwith in a most astonishing manner the member from Greenfield requested that his
bill might be allowed to lie over, and with still more astonishing suddenness Mr. Speaker was announcing that "Mr.
Samuel Adams of Boston had the floor."

The elder Adams could be solemn as the grave, but
élan and joyousness were in his tones when now he stood

forth. The Tory members were fingering their big hats nervously. Those in the secret—a good majority now of the house—were grinning at their consternation. For there was the chairman of the all-important committee reading its report "signed by all members present—with the regrettable absence of Mr. Leonard" that the house proceed to name five delegates to meet other like delegations from all the other colonies, upon the first of September at Philadelphia in a "Continental Congress" to determine concerning the common weal of America.

You could see the Tory benchers turning white and red; you could see Mr. Eli Gorton's great body go fidgeting down to the door, and his hands flying like a windmill as the keeper seemed denying exit, then came the voice of Mr. Speaker: "Mr. Adams has taken upon himself to lock the door, and to direct the keeper to permit none to depart until the close of the session. All in favor of sustaining Mr. Adams say 'Aye!'"

The "Ayes" made the brass wall sconces rattle, and the debate swept on.

Fierce and furious was that debate. Mr. Cushing's gavel almost drew splinters from the solid desk before him. I resigned all attempt to take notes, and simply listened, while all the passions lit by a long, bitter struggle blazed up in the arsenal. After the mine had been exploded and the Tory minority realized the odds against them, they plunged into the fray like men—sparring for time, exhausting every dilatory motion, taunting their foes to make them waste precious minutes in retorting, and bullying and threatening the doorkeeper. Everybody knew the purpose of *that*, but the keeper, an elderly, friendly old functionary who above all things "hated a fuss" was manifestly getting uneasy. At the height of the debate I edged up beside Adams.

"Despite the vote of the house," I whispered, "he's going to let them out."

While his lieutenants fought the battle on the floor, Adams, in person, strode down to the exit.

"Mr. Keeper," he commanded, "the responsibility is mine not yours—give me that key." And back he came, the key reposing safely in his pocket, while verbal thrust and counter-thrust raged on.

Outside the June sun was beating pitilessly and if the honorable members that day were not shedding their blood, heaven knows how they shed quarts of perspiration. Many a sweltering patriot prayed inwardly for that blessed word —"Adjourn!" After one parliamentary battle after another had ended in the rout of the Tories, pity perforce had to be extended to one or two panting reddening members, Adams himself unlocking the door for their departure. Hardly had he done this than I, who had moved near a window, saw a horse flying down the Danvers road as fast as whip and spur could send him. When I took the tidings to my chief, he met it with one of those silent chuckles, characteristic when all went well.

"I knew they would, but it's three good miles to the Hooper house and three miles back. We are nearing the vote. Go outside and be witness to all that happens."

The key therefore turned for me also, and I waited outside the Court Room for the last scene in the summer comedy. Already Salem was charged with rumors. The lobbies of the Town House, the streets outside, were beginning to buzz with merchants, shopkeepers, sea-captains, factor's clerks, and all the lesser fry of a busy harbor. The upraised voices of the orators came in angry gusts through the open windows. Not half an hour had sped since I left the chamber when we saw a chariot tearing in from Danvers, the horses in foam, the negro coachman standing and lashing them. Before the wheels ceased grinding Mr. Secretary Flucker had leaped upon the curb flourishing an official paper: "Way! Way in the King's name!" was his command. He went up the stairs two steps at a bound to the court room, then recoiled blankly before the solid bolted door. I was at his heels, and half of Salem seemed trampling close behind us.

The crowd was none too friendly, but Flucker swung about with a flushed face and his eye lit on me:

"Young Mr. Gilman, you are known here. Have that door opened instantly.—Governor's orders."

"I am no member of the house, sir," rejoined I, bowing politely. "My understanding, however, is that the door has been ordered locked, and the key is in Mr. Samuel Adams' pocket.

His Majesty's secretary delivered himself of an oath: "Zounds, my fine dabbler in treason! Get in word to your ring-leaders that I bring an official mandate from his Excellency the Governor."

"I have no power, sir, to open that door. If you have aught to say it must be through the keyhole."

Mr. Flucker cursed again, pocketed his dignity and bawled as I suggested. In reply the door was opened the narrowest crevice, and a voice announced that "the clerk's assistant" might come in alone to carry the message for his Honor the Secretary. It took me not over two minutes to enter, receive my answer and emerge. I fear there was swagger in my manner when I gave Mr. Flucker a yet deeper congé:

"May it please your Honor, Mr. Speaker Cushing informs you that the pleasure of the House is that no communications of however high a character are to be received until adjournment."

Flucker's face was that of a man in an apoplexy, but he drew himself together: "There'll be a reckoning for this, my fine lad," he cast at me darkly. Then readjusting his waistcoat and wig he turned toward the tittering jostling crowd in the lobby, pulled out a paper, bawled at the top of his voice, "Oyez, oyez! A proclamation of his Excellency the Governor," and shouted off an extremely abrupt order for the immediate dissolution of the legislature, ending by fairly trumpeting down the corridor, *"God save the King!"*

A clash of doors, a rush of feet, a babel of voices answered him. Out poured the assemblymen, wiping their foreheads, laughing, gesticulating.—Carried with only twelve dissenting votes, that five delegates staunch and true be named to a Continental Congress and all the towns be assessed for their charges. Carried also the solemn resolution to sustain to the uttermost Boston now suffering for American liberty. Carried again, that all imports from Britain ought forthwith to cease. Carried finally that Mr. Speaker should notify these actions to all the sister colonies.—If his Excellency was now pleased to discharge the members, why the weather was warm and their duties were completed!

Mr. Flucker stood so dumbfounded that I nigh could pity him, but when Samuel Adams walked calmly forth the secretary's kettle fairly boiled over.

"You've spun long upon your halter, Sammy, and now you've spliced up the nose. If ministers haven't turned poltroons, a voyage at last to England and to execution dock——"

Adams imperturbably fanned himself with a newspaper, but I stepped forward:

"The day is very hot, Mr. Flucker, and I trust Government will remember how you have now put private interest beneath public duty. Of course you know what's by this time happened?"

"Happened to me, sirrah?—What?"

"Oh, nothing calamitous your Honor. Merely that just before the House opened this morning I had a letter from Boston. By this time you should possess a fine son-in-law, Henry Knox."

. . . Two of the Tory members helped poor Mr. Flucker into the chariot. They all lumbered away toward Danvers. A few hours later the members of the legislature had dispersed, the soldiers of the sixty-fourth were harmlessly strolling around the Salem shops and the seventeenth of June, 1774, had slipped into history.

CHAPTER XXIX

THE WEDDING AT KING'S CHAPEL

STILL again I must tell of the passing world as viewed through the eyes of Emilie Rivoire.

. . . What though Boston Common was whitened with the marquees of the incoming regiments, though in Boston thousands idled, fretted and tightened their belts, though General Gage fulmined his proclamation against "hypocrisy" to castigate the day of prayer and fasting enjoined by the patriots, not all this could lessen the activity of the little household on North Square. Quietly, effectively, Emilie was beginning her preparations for the founding of her own and Roger's happiness.

Fortunate among their co-religionists the Rivoires had kept most of their wealth during the long persecutions, but it had been a reticent wealth in movables and intangibles. Georges Rivoire had accustomed his children to a home of refinement but also of studious modesty. Now alike he and Emilie discovered that the habits of a life-time were needless. Come King, come patriots, the Rivoire thrift seemed about to reap its due reward. Emilie held her head a trifle higher when she told herself that nought should prevent her future husband from closing the gate of a tall North End mansion, and planning for his seat on the council. The Old World with its old wrongs and forbiddings was far, far behind her. She opened both of her strong young arms, for the hopes, freedom and honest loves of the New.

Georges Rivoire too had renewed a departed youth. His heart had almost sunk in the grave of his children, but now in his grandchild's happiness he had recovered his own. His step was resilient, his eyes alight with more than their wonted fire. With pride he could say to his expected son-in-law: "Trusting you, here is no mean heritage—the gift of France to New England." In such a mood for the first time in his life he loosed his purse-strings, gave with liberality to the funds for the Boston poor, nor was Peleg Fifield the only Whig merchant who suddenly found an unimpeachable credit turning back protested bills.

As for Emilie's friends there was for a while a constant coming and going to eye those treasures of lace and tapestry, glass, porcelain and silver wherewith the little house suddenly abounded. Paul Revere found that nearly all his time, when he was not riding post for the patriot committees, was bespoken for that great service of plate, blazoned with the Rivoire and Gilman arms, which was to adorn one of the most splendid sideboards in Boston.

Yet with it all Emilie moved as in an uncomfortable dream. What if her love for Roger was perfect, and her trust in his love for her? What if every day her grandfather told of some readjustment of properties, shifting his wealth to America, and putting it into lands and farms not easily shaken by any financial tempest? Every morning she woke to hear the bugles blowing down the streets, and the clank and the tramping of the marines and grenadiers as the soldiery changed guard—and every evening she knew herself a stage nearer to a fearful "something"—with Roger Gilman in the center of that fiery calamity.

Being a child of the Huguenots she would steal away to her little bedroom, to read her big lettered Geneva Bible and run over in mind the long dark history of her people; persecutions and massacres, fitful gleams of sunlight; more

persecutions, confiscations, exilings, dungeons, death. But
through it all had run the unfaltering faith that a good
God was making the wrath of man to praise Him. There
had survived the French geniality, grace and fire, with the
confidence that at the last there should come some age of
gold. And here in New England and in Roger's love there
had seemed vouchsafed to Emilie that long recompense
earned by her ancestors. Could it all prove deceit and
mockery? Could a "good God" ruin her happiness even
now?

If, however, Mlle. Rivoire had these moments alone, not
even her most devoted gossips ever knew thereof; and of
one particular friend, be it said, she was far too engrossed
in her own affairs to have two thoughts left for anybody
who seemed just then to have no great troubles at all.
Not in vain had Roger Gilman been informed that the self-
same day Mr. Secretary Flucker shouted his proclamation
in Salem, Miss Lucy Flucker had changed her name to
Mrs. Henry Knox.

Lucy had been subjected since the encounter between
her father and Henry at Redford to just enough family
persecution to make her determination sure. Henry had
enjoyed the solid Scotch sense to refuse to hasten matters,
to keep out of public broils with his prospective father-in-
law, to tuck away the profits from the bookstore, and
finally, after timely waiting to strike when the iron was
hot. It had been impossible to forbid Lucy to enter the
bookstore, when all the Very Respectables made it a genteel rendezvous. It had been impossible to forbid her to
visit "her dear friend, the Mam'sel," or to control said
"Mam'sel's" male visitors. Mr. Flucker stormed, Mrs.
Flucker had wrung her hands, Brother Thomas (who wore
the King's uniform as lieutenant in a marching regiment)
had vowed that sooner than see sister of his join hands

with a damned Whig, he'd see her dead!—And they all
had cried out that Henry Knox would lead her from the
altar to the poor house. To all of which Lucy had tossed
her large and not unshapely head, laughed a strong, competent laugh and reminded them "that she greatly understood her own business."

Thus it had come to pass that almost at the hour when
Speaker Cushing put the question at Salem, and while the
better part of Boston surged toward yet another huge town
meeting to listen to John Adams fling more defiance to the
Tories, Emilie and Hope Fifield and a very few others
made their way toward King's Chapel. "No wedding for
a Flucker," scolded the censors of genteel conduct, no bib-
bing and bobbing of fashionable bonnets, no organ solemnly
rumbling old "Wells" as the bride came down a close-
packed aisle, no fluttering of fans, nor rustling of silks, nor
subdued creaking of whalebone stays from a crowded
church. It was all deplorably simple.

The morning before the wedding Lucy had calmly entered
the Rivoire parlor, and announced in perfectly matter-of-
fact tones: "Henry and I are to be married by Dr. Caner.
Mother is in a spasm. I'm glad father's away. You will
let me dress here and help me?"

And "helped" she was, although M. Georges lifted his
shaggy white brows very high, muttering something about
—"In France 'twould trouble my conscience."

Dr. Caner, the fine, gentle Church of England rector of
King's Chapel, whom all Boston respected despite his Tory-
ism, also looked very blank when the circumstances were
told him, but Mr. Flucker was in Salem, and the good man
comforted himself that if such a wedding had indeed to be,
it were better out of the Prayer Book than under the dubious auspices of Non-Conformity. At least he could assure
his supper table that never had the chancel of his chastely

beautiful Christopher Wren church arched over a handsomer bridal couple, what with Henry Knox looming manfully in his militia lieutenant's uniform, and Lucy Flucker in her massive beauty with the Rivoire needlepoint falling in a drift of snow from her black hair, and with Emilie herself, the rose beside the tall lily, standing at her side.

The "Amens" were said, each of the little party kissed the bride, the guinea was pressed in Dr. Caner's hand along with the gloves to take Mrs. Caner; the bride and groom swung into the hired chaise that was to bear them to the placid honeymoon in Redford. And so was consummated that marriage which caused all censoresses of Boston to shake their heads and predict black ruin, and which was to make Lucy Knox the honored intimate of Martha Washington in the years when her exiled parents were sorrowing out their lives in shabby London boarding houses.

But Emilie enjoyed no prophetic vision that day in June while she watched the chaise rattling away down Long Acre. A deep resentment filled her at the authors of a quarrel which could set the Fluckers against so worthy a son-in-law as Henry Knox. It seemed a personal forewarning. For the moment she felt perplexed and forsaken.

She was therefore more than glad when Hope proposed that she return with her to Sudbury Street for a cup of that chocolate wherewith Whigs and Tories still could compound their intercourse. Eleazer Fifield was at his office and the big house was nearly empty. Nero was just being bidden to prepare to serve in the garden, when there was a polite banging on the knocker and "A naval gemman wished to pay respects to Miss Fifield." Whereupon with his hat in one hand and his other clapped to his heart there stood bowing in the doorway none other than the gallant Captain Prothero.

No ordinary crisis stopped the heartbeats of Mlle. Rivoire. If at all she showed heightened color, its effect was broken by an unwontedly elaborate curtsey. The visitor on his part went through his congés, with the profusion of a Parisian dancing master. Hope Fifield, nothing if not self-possessed, began at once her regrets that her father was absent, while Captain Prothero on his part was "sensibly affected with pleasure to be able to enjoy this intercourse only with Miss Fifield and her most charming friend."

In short he invited himself into a chair, took off his gloves with polite deliberation, gave the least touch to the set of his carefully craped wig, and assured Miss Fifield that here already was recompense for the salt food and vinegar-sprinkled cabins of a long and irksome voyage. To Mademoiselle he addressed as many remarks as strict etiquette demanded, and not one more. The call lasted a proper interval. For the sake of her hostess Emilie addressed him with formal politeness. If Hope for once failed to be voluble in her entreaties "not to go," the officer certainly did not take his departure abruptly.

At length after much talk about generalities Prothero was gone, and Hope urgently entreated her friend to spend the night, but Emilie shook her head, her grandfather needed her, and the sooner he knew that Prothero was in Boston the better for all. "She could take care of herself." This was all very bravely said, but it was far less bravely felt when at the turn of Cold Lane and Hanover Street a very resplendent naval uniform came out of an alley and moved straight toward her. Prothero again bowed, with precisely the proper inclination for saluting a lady for whom one had deep respect. Emilie's pace quickened, but he was instantly beside her. Thanks to the closing of the port half the shops and offices were now shuttered, and Hanover Street was almost empty. Unless she had wished to make a scene she had no means of shaking off the escort which he thrust upon her.

"You honor strangely the pledge which you gave in Maine, Captain Prothero," spoke she at last, growing hot and cold, "that saved you from a judge and jury."

"Jove laughs at lover's promises," he replied coolly.

"That bond you gave Judge Gamage will be forfeited."

"It will take more than your Yankee constables to collect it to-day in the face of the regiments now in Boston, Mademoiselle."

She walked on rapidly with averted face. "If you call yourself a British officer and gentleman—" at last she cast over her shoulder.

"Being a British officer and gentleman, I crave the liberty to sue out my pardon for surrender to a delicious folly. My intentions, I swear were honorable, if my manner of wooing rude."

"I will not hear you," and Emilie walked still faster.

"Miss Rivoire will not say that whereof she may repent. My new ship the *Argus* rides in Nantasket Roads, but for three days now I have been in Boston. The coffee-room gossip of course is open to me. If report does not do him wrong, I have the honor of a rival."

They were approaching Union Street. The town meeting had ended. Crowds of citizens were coming from Faneuil Hall. Emboldened by the sight Emilie turned with heightened color and sparkling eyes: "A rival you never had, sir. For to have a 'rival' one must possess chance of victory. But that all may be plain between us, I am betrothed to Mr. Roger Gilman—I believe of your acquaintance."

The officer bowed again, this time with an unconcealed sneer: "Oh, I cannot push my poor claims against your mohair nobility." Then he showed all his large teeth in a smile: "Your pardon, Mademoiselle, but this was already

known to me. I have not failed to use my ears. Mr. Gilman, I may add, is said to have mixed deeply, (considering
his youth) in practices which his Majesty's law officers
advise are treasonable. I must actually some day crave
your forgiveness if I perhaps have to escort him to
England."

Emilie was not easily disconcerted, but her cheeks were
turning ashen, while Prothero pursued his advantage: "I
find that his assistance to Samuel Adams is common talk.
This perhaps must wait until we can deal with his chief,
but testimony comes also to Province House that he was
identified in a certain band of 'Mohawks,' in which
case——"

His companion cut him short by a little sobbing cry and
by darting straight toward a scarlet-and-white army captain who was emerging from Cross Street. Emilie almost
embraced the stranger: "Herbert Dunmore!—God has sent
you. Take me away from that man!"

Prothero's countenance was a study. Dunmore's figure
was a trifle less boyish than of old. He wore a captain's
straps and slashings with easy pride. Without a word he
passed Emilie's arm within his own, then turned sternly
upon the other officer: "Reckon this lady as my sister,
sir. I will escort her home."

The naval captain gnawed his lip an instant, then burst
forth: "Don't presume on your new rank, Dunmore. I
can call you out."

Herbert gave the military salute: "You can call me
out, Captain Prothero, but I am not bound to favor you.
McVitie is still on the coast to bear witness. Come, Emilie."

Back to North Square they went and each had so much
to tell! Dunmore's voice trembled with rage as he spoke
of Prothero's reappearance in the navy: "Heaven must
reserve great things for England, or the realm would perish

with such ministers. This is another of Jemmy Twitcher's doings, I mean of my Lord Sandwich's. When Prothero flung down his commission half the navy rejoiced.—But what happened? He tired of London clubs and his brother persisted in living and keeping the property, so our gentleman makes interest with Miss Martha Ray (no person for decent mention, but out it must) the standing 'friend' of the First Lord of the Admiralty. Though certain rear admirals stormed like Biscay gales the twirk of her finger was too much for them.—So there's a new commission and a bigger ship to America for Prothero.—I had hoped to forestall him hither, but 'tis enough to damn the honor of England."

Emilie's adventure was soon told; when she spoke of Roger as her betrothed Dunmore's pleasure beamed from his honest face: "Such news makes my journey seem less vain." Then he added with manifest anxiety, "But is it true that Roger was among the Mohawks?"

"Captain Dunmore," she answered archly, "is too fine a gentleman ever to ask me *that!*"

"Captain Dunmore understands," was the smiling response, "but if Prothero is in Boston and colorable suspicions have reached Province House, Roger Gilman is much safer on the other side of Roxbury Neck. The governor has been ordered to be cautious in his moves against the Whigs, but a little over-zeal would only be praised in London. Thank Heaven, we've now ample warning."

Why, however, was Captain Dunmore himself, thus suddenly in Boston? Because, he admitted with one of his doleful whistles, of "that unpleasant thing called 'Duty.'" Then vowing Emilie to secrecy he became more particular. —Despite sparks and fury the ministry was still groping for an American policy. Even his Majesty had moments of wavering. And a great personage was now on his way to Boston, none other than the noble Hugh, Earl Percy, heir of the Duke of Northumberland. Nominally Gates' lieutenant, he actually bore orders to treat privately with our Whigs and to report if even in the eleventh hour there was healing for the quarrel.

"Was his Lordship wisely chosen as a peacemaker?"— Another long whistle from Herbert: "The appointments of God and of the King are unsearchable. Percy is a young man of courage, honor, generosity, magnanimity to inferiors. But as for treating with Massachusetts Yankees" (Dunmore fingered his sword knot) "well—you'll doubtless see him, and I shall hope for the best."

Concerning Herbert's own mission, all was soon told. If St. James could send one emissary, Chatham House could dispatch another. The Whig lords had agreed to send a reliable agent to New England, to report the situation confidentially, to work for peace and to try to make Percy see the truth through undimmed eyes. So the august Chatham himself had laid it on Herbert to quit Peggy, to desert all the joys of England, to risk much upon a despairing errand, "in order that whatever horror might befall, *one* Englishman can say to himself, 'I have done my little to keep the fairest jewels of King George's crown from being lost forever.'"

Dunmore had his captain's commission, but was on a long leave of absence. He would pay his respects at Province House, but his mails were at the Vernon's Head. A tavern, however, being but a dreary place, his old friend Major Pitcairn of the Marines had already asked him to share his lodgings in the Shaw House upon North Square. After the events of the day it gave Emilie no small comfort to know that near at hand was such a friend in need.

CHAPTER XXX

HOW THE PERCYS CAUTIONED THE GILMANS

THE day after the Assembly dispersed, I was leading my horse upon the penny ferry from Malden to Charlestown, when suddenly I knew that a strong, friendly hand had slipped into mine. If the skies had opened I could not have been more astonished—and then delighted, for next to sight of Emilie, my heart had hungered for Herbert Dunmore, and there he stood, handsome and hearty.

"Whither now?" were his first words, after we had ceased shaking and laughing, and got ourselves back to speech.

"To Charlestown to return this horse, then to Boston."

"Don't go to Boston," he advised gravely, "Emilie will bless heaven that I caught you here in time."

Then leading me aside he told me of recent events and especially of the threats of Prothero. I ground my teeth at knowing Emilie was in the same town with that villain.

"A dirty rotter," he admitted, "but she's in no danger. Boston is not the *Comet* nor is North Square the same as Cape Newagen. Curse our red coats if you please, but there are decent men under most of them. I've said enough to two or three of Gage's staff to see that a friendly eye is kept on Mlle. Rivoire. Your own risk's another matter."

"My own risk," seemed very small compared with the disappointment of not meeting a certain young lady. It was only after Dunmore gave me a scrap of paper *"Obey Herbert and do not come. X X X! E."*, that I listened to argument, crossed the ferry with him, then gave my horse

to a boy to take to Charlestown and walked slowly with
my friend along Milk Row toward Cambridge.

Herbert talked so much about "Peggy" and "my wife,"
that I was obliged to tell him that I never had imagined
a young husband could become so gone a fool, at which
he most unreasonably taxed me with over-frequent mention
of Emilie,—something of course entirely different. However, he succeeded at last in bringing home my own case.
Gage had been ordered (my friend felt certain) to arrest
Samuel Adams and John Hancock, and ship them to England—but not just yet at the price of a bloody crisis, and
he had wisely stayed his hand. But it would be indeed a
sweet morsel to the mighty if one of the "incendiaries' "
assistants suddenly disappeared from Boston and appeared
as suddenly for trial at the Old Bailey for something that
could easily be warped from riot into treason. No doubt
somebody around the Green Dragon had blabbed in his
cups about us Mohawks.—Really it did not matter. In
any case for Emilie's sake I must keep out of Boston.

This was no great hardship while college was in session
and Emilie could come over once or twice to Cambridge
under her grandfather's convoy. Herbert also could ride
out frequently for a long chat. He was stunned and sad-
dened by the situation he had found in America. "It is
stemming the avalanche," he confessed. "But here I am!
And I can but try."

Interviews with the Adamses and Warrens he gained
easily. They were charmed with his friendly manner, but
he could only entreat them to pay for the tea, get the port
reopened, and then wait gropingly until North and his
coarse cabal had run their course and made way for the
Whigs.

If any good could have come from these vague counsels
it was undone in a twinkling by Gage. This was the time

when his Excellency, less knowing than Hutchinson, had the folly to send Colonel Fenton to none other than Samuel Adams, to expand upon his peril and upon his vast gains from prompt submission, "whereby he would not only receive great personal advantages, but would make his peace with the King." At which Adams had risen in his wrath, "Sir, I have long since made my peace with the King of Kings. Tell General Gage it is the advice of Samuel Adams no longer to insult the feelings of an exasperated people!"

Very soon after this, however, while the Harvard year was closing amid utter informality, public commencement ceremonies being actually omitted, Herbert came again galloping out to Cambridge. This time there was a little glow about him, despite his pained glance at my blue and buff uniform as I came in from our drill.

"*He* has come," he announced, and I knew that by "he" was meant Percy. "I waited on him at his quarters. My hopes were largely justified. Before quitting England he had an interview at St. James—well, with his Majesty, himself. He is directed to sound out your leaders and try to find room for passing the olive branch."

"Good," spoke I, unbelting my cartridge box, "take him straight around to Purchase Street, or he'll discover that Warren has a civil tongue in his head."

"Why so I proposed. But the Earl distrusts your chiefs. His only hope is through their 'misguided followers.'"

"Try Boston town meeting then." I fear that Noble Lords did not impress me over-much, but Herbert laid hold on my arm and his face showed real distress.

"Before heaven, 'tis no laughing matter. Percy is the last chance of peace, if you'd not brave the whole power of England. You must help in this."

"I help you?"

"They have it at St. James that Boston cannot speak for New England. All your chiefs seem to come from Boston. The Earl would hear from the inland towns. Before holding a wider conference he would talk with that man who, he learns, wields a mighty influence across the province. You must arrange that he meet this man.—He is your father."

.   .   .   .

Father and I rode down from Redford in the parsonage chaise, leaving Herbert to conduct up his noble friend upon horseback. We had pitched upon Wetherby's Black Horse Tavern at Menotomy as the rendezvous. This was convenient enough for us, and also for his Lordship, who desired to have the interview decidedly private, as well as to enjoy a ride through our famous green Middlesex country, glorious with the bursting summer.

Reading and hearing are not the same as seeing, and I had never beheld an actual flesh-and-blood lord. If the latter now displayed three hands or four eyes I was resolved not to seem in the least startled. Father had consented to the interview readily enough, although I knew from his manner that he was not sanguine. At morning prayers he had specifically requested for himself "help for duties which may gravely concern the weal of the people of God here in New England." Upon the drive he spoke very little. We broke our fast at the Monroe Tavern at Lexington, and the afternoon was well started before Mr. Wetherby threw open his door for us. In the big tap-room, lounging on the huge settle over their kill-devil was a pair of extraordinarily spick and span orderlies. I saw one of them stare hard at father's over-shiny, well-brushed coat and old-fashioned wig, nudge his comrade and whisper something which made the other snicker while he tugged at his leg-lacings.

I was giving them one subduing frown, when from a

private room emerged Herbert in his best uniform. Of course he knew father well and bowed very respectfully, then more at our ease we passed inside, where a slight, youngish man with more gold lace than red upon his coat rose from the big armchair.

Lord Percy looked even as Dunmore had praised him to Emilie. "Courage, honor, generosity, magnanimity to inferiors" he seemed all to possess. His figure was slight, but his military tailor set it off to advantage. His hawk-like nose was worthy of a Roman senator. The other features, and especially his delicate mouth and eyes were small, almost feminine. Across his face would flit shades of sentiment, now humorous, now cynical. His delicate hands seemed very fit for dealing the cards at Whites, with a royal duke sitting beyond the pile of gold upon the table. Here, in short, was the heir to perchance the greatest non-royal title in England, and from the motion of the lace upon his wrists to the manner whereby he opened his teeth he showed the part.

Herbert played the master of ceremonies: "Your Lordship, this is Dr. Gilman, that distinguished clergyman you have desired to meet."

The great man smiled, bowed slightly and waited as if expecting an elaborate congé. Father merely nodded stiffly and held out his hand. There was an awkward moment before Percy took a forward step and their hands clasped.

"Pleased to see you, sir," spoke his Lordship with constraint.

"Pleased also, your Excellency," rejoined father, then seeing the Englishman's brows go up, "Bear with our New England titles, sir. None save the King can rank above our governor.—Allow me to present my son, Mr. Roger Gilman, of late clerical helper to Mr. Samuel Adams of whom (with a little cough) you have possibly heard."

His Lordship smiled again. Apparently the game pleased
him. He proffered me his hand also, and made some civil
remark about the beauties of his ride through North Cambridge. We were soon seated with long pipes around the
table, and then Dunmore, whose anxiety was pathetic,
broached the issue with: "You understand, Dr. Gilman,
that personages of great rank in London have desired his
Lordship to converse with your leaders in America with a
view to a friendly adjustment of the present deplorable
issues."

"Even so," assented father warily. "My influence is over-
estimated, but what has his Excellency here to propose?"

"Dr. Gilman," opened his Lordship with a manifest eoffrt
to conciliate, "I will deal frankly. Ere quitting London, I
was admitted to the cabinet of his Gracious Majesty himself. The confidences of a King are not to be repeated,
but upon my honor I assure you that no father ever felt
such Christian tenderness toward erring children——"

"Toward *erring* children, do I hear?" interposed father
solemnly.

"That, sir, is simply a form the King and ministers are
at present compelled to use officially.—But to pass to particulars,—his Majesty is all compassion toward America
in general and especially toward your Massachusetts. In
his paternal wisdom he constantly studies your welfare.
The same is equally true of his ministers and all our upper
classes. We look upon our colonists as we do upon our
personal tenantry, to be counselled and assisted in every
reasonable manner. The increase and enrichment of the
colonies, so far of course as is compatible with the necessary interests of England, lie close to our hearts."

"You mention the interests of England, your Excellency?"

"Why, naturally, tender consideration has to begin nearest

home. In return for our protection the Colonies should yield some items to our advantage, but they will prove the merest trifles I do assure you."

The minister deliberately produced from his coat-tails a well-born silver snuff box, extended it to his Lordship, who repulsed it gracefully, then took snuff himself, blew his nose and rejoined: "We are fortunate then beyond our fathers. *They* found the rulers of England so little concerned with their welfare they were even constrained to flee thither across seas, for the mere right to serve God after their consciences."

"Let me avow," returned Percy with a little heat, "that no idea of religious interference enters any present designs. Your worthy Chapel-people, Non-Conformists I mean, though not of course partaking of our nobility and gentry, form an esteemed part of our lower middle classes. And although it could be devoutly wished your colonies had all their regular Episcopal establishment, there are no active plans to that effect."

Father's jaw was going down steadily, but he merely said, "I thank your Excellency for the assurance."

His Lordship smiled and pursued, "As a man, we are told, of great influence among your colonial yeomanry and peasantry, I will actually open the royal mind to you— First of all, complete pardon for all past offenses,——"

Father's jaw went lower still, but he did not interrupt.

"In the necessary alterations of your laws and charters, tender attention will be paid to the needs of your substantial classes. It cannot, of course, but be irksome to your men of breeding to have clerks, shopkeepers and even lower down express themselves against their betters in what you call 'town meeting.' This inevitable causes many disorders. Just before I sailed, Lord George Germain expressed himself very justly, I'm sure you must agree with him, 'I would not have men of a mercantile cast every day collecting themselves together and debating about political matters. I would have them follow their occupation as merchants and not consider themselves as ministers of the country.' "

"Lord Germain's opinions are already in our gazettes," observed his listener dryly.

But here Herbert Dunmore with plainly troubled countenance interposed, "But of course your Lordship is merely suggesting Lord Germain's views by the side. You were explaining the intentions of his Majesty."

Percy hemmed and cleared his throat, "Quite correct, Captain Dunmore.—And I pass over also the creation of an American peerage and gentry, to which second order I flatter myself that Dr. Gilman's family might perhaps hope to belong. But for the healing of present discontents I am empowered to say the royal government is prepared for extremely large concessions. Lord North (I will betray) will soon lay before Parliament a bill omitting the taxation of any colony imposing its own taxes in a manner satisfactory to the purposes of his Majesty. After this we can take up with complete benevolence the smaller questions of the alteration of your charters, and the affectionate subordination of the Colonies to England."

Father's hand was playing nervously with his lapel, his lips moved slowly, but ere he could speak Mr. Wetherby entered to plant before us four tall toddy glasses, rattled the sticks to crush the sugar, smiled politely for "orders" and closed the door. Percy sampled the mixture, licked his lips and resumed, "You cannot but be aware, Dr. Gilman, that the royal law-officers advise that recent acts and combinations in Massachusetts undoubtedly constitute treason. Nevertheless the reluctance of the King before harsh measures—how can I express it! Therefore I beseech you to counsel your friends to hasten to make loyal submission ere the patience of the Crown be exhausted."

Father had rested his large hands on the table during this last appeal; now he sat bolt upright and his fingers came together hard!

"Your Excellency. Some language I am too old, too provincial (you would say) to understand. You tell me the King loves his children: he has proved a very stern father to us. That he shuns harsh measures: he has closed our port and brought thousands to poverty. That he desires our welfare: he aims to destroy those institutions under which for a hundred and forty years we have dwelt in our own peace, asking of England no blessing but her neglect. If this country is become a good land, meet for the Lord's high purposes, it is not because of any benevolence of your Kings. We, we and our fathers have made this country, English in speech, but no more, I fear me, English in mind. Grievous though the question be, stand we not at the parting of the ways?—If the love of peace possess your King and his ministers, let England, if she would keep America, keep her only by the silken thread of freedom and affection. If not—without a heritage of war hatred let us be suffered to tread our separate path among the nations."

Percy reddened to his hair and plucked at his sword knot. Herbert's face grew piteous with dismay, but the nobleman by an obvious effort controlled his speech, and kept a conciliatory tone.

"Of course, Dr. Gilman, I understand that you speak half in pleasantry. 'Twill be admitted that if the supremacy of the King and Parliament over the Colonies be denied the Empire falls to pieces. That supremacy once loyally granted, very liberal concessions (upon my word of honor) will follow."

"Concessions?" repeated father rising slowly, walking to

a window, and pointing to the broad fields rolling away behind the tavern. "See you those stone walls, your Excellency, (Percy nodded) marking our New England boundaries? Not shaped and mortared as in your Old World, but piled rough as they came from the soul. There they stand, token of the clearing and taming of the land, and likewise perhaps of the rough men who laid them."

His Lordship gazed forth, a little bewildered by the argument.

"These walls," the speaker pursued, "hewn by nature, held firm by their own weight, stretch as memorials of how our fathers fought with beast and savage and ruthless winter, and out of the forest fashioned this New England. The good rights they passed to us we keep. The attack upon those rights we resist. The attackers we must count our enemies. From England we ask not one thing but the freedom enjoyed by our fathers. 'Concessions' we do not seek. Guiltless of crime, for pardon we will not sue. Therefore unto blood we will defend our heritage."

The clergyman had spoken deliberately, solemnly, even gently, as if merely stating the inevitable rather than matching warning with warning. At the first interval Herbert Dunmore broke in passionately: "Gentlemen, gentlemen, if a younger man may speak, you address one another in two strange languages. In the name of the peace you both desire, I pray you to strive for some accommodation."

"You are right," asserted father very calmly. He resumed his seat, whereupon Percy, not without winsome sincerity, set forth again at length the British desire to benefit "our subjects in America," the reluctance to seek stern measures, the entire willingness to condone the past, but father only sat looking fixedly and sadly, and I could predict the end.

"In sum then, your Excellency," at last he returned, "I

should call together a sufficient group of our inland clergy and civil leaders to deal with you as to accommodation?"

"Such is my hope," assented his Lordship.

"To us you would pledge the speedy opening of Boston and oblivion for acts of treason in return for submission to the alteration of our charter and the limitation of our town meetings? Also as a matter of favor there will be some review of the present taxes?"

"I can pledge this for his Majesty," Percy's eye had kindled, while Dunmore's eager countenance lighted with hope. "Once let there be proper submission, and every dutiful petition will be almost certainly granted."

Father rose yet again, put back his chair, rattled the toddy stick and drank off the glass slowly. Then he looked squarely upon the quizzical face of the nobleman:

"We are a rude people, your Excellency. Our rocks and forests teach no courtly speech. The kindness of your own intentions, the benignity of the King I doubt not. He is only a man, and can know little more of America than I, who have never seen your vast city, know of London. And benevolent ignorance can, alas! work more mischief than scheming tyranny. What have I then to lay before my friends?—Pardons which we do not crave, and the recall of an act of brutal power. In return we surrender those dearest rights which touch every village in New England. —I must thank your Excellency therefore, for your good intent, and desire you an agreeable return to Boston."

His Lordship's color had mounted. Now he stood erect facing father, his cheeks as red as his scarlet coat. "Before Heaven, sir," cried he, "will you not even assemble your friends?"

"Knowing your proposals I know the meeting were useless."

"But are you sensible of all implied? The King's mind

is fixed. The English nation sustains him in crushing stark rebellion. Our dignity will not suffer another retreat."

"Then the King's wrath must be braved, your Excellency."

Percy's lips became twisted: "You are a man of sermons and books, sir. War to you is only a name. Yet be advised. Where will your untrained peasants be, when they face that armed power that has just given the law to the House of Bourbon?"

"Where the God of Battles desires them!" Father had seemed growing taller and taller as he stood in that little room. His voice, without becoming strident, took on power as when he swayed the meeting-house. "Let us not bandy words, your Excellency. 'Cromwellian saints' you may reckon us, yet suffer me to answer you now as once spoke Cotton Mather, numbered among the pillars of New England, 'Let all mankind know that we came into this wilderness because we would have our posterity settled under the pure gospel *defended by rulers who shall be of ourselves.*' Tell therefore even the highest of England, tell even your King that we will hold fast this right as dearer than life itself."

Dunmore's eyes were wet. Across Percy's pale lips came mutterings. "Insolent gospeller, clownish rustics!" one seemed to catch, but yet again he compelled himself, put one hand upon his breast and made a bow faultless if ironical:

"Then I regret the report I must bear back to Boston. At least I have not dissembled. In days to come the difference will be taught between royal benevolence and the potence of Tower muskets and six pounders." Then seeing that father stood unmovable, he bowed still another time. "Sir, I am a Percy, and the Percys do not give their caution lightly. Remember you are warned."

Father's well brushed coat bent with the dignity of a chief justice, "Sir, I am a Gilman, and the Gilmans thank the Percys for their warning."

.   .   .   .

My heart bled for Herbert. Percy, who now manifestly distrusted him, consented with an abrupt gesture when he asked leave to ride with us to Redford. My friend blamed neither the nobleman nor father. "I knew it would so end," he continued repeating bitterly, "from the moment I set foot on Boston dock I knew my mission was impossible. Oh! Ocean, ocean—made to set men of English speech apart, what power can bridge you!"

"All is not lost," I consoled. "Not all the Britons are like Percy or King George. Americans know that."

"No," he returned, tightening his fingers, "but why deceive ourselves. We Britons of better minds are helpless."

"Will you at once go back?"

He shook his head; "God knows my heart is hungry for the sight of Peggy, but, as you say, all's not quite lost. Till blood is shed, I'll strive and hope against hope. Then if the worst comes, I'll face the truth like an Englishman; and if home I go, I go with clear conscience."

"Your heart is in the right place, my son," said father, very gently, with a hand upon his shoulder.

. . . A very few days later my Lord Percy was writing thus to Britain: "Till you make their Committees of Correspondence high treason and try them for it in England you must never expect perfect obedience to the mother country. Everything is quiet, but the people threaten much. —Not that I believe they dare to act."

Almost at that same hour Colonel George Washington at Williamsburg in Virginia was delivering perchance the briefest yet most important speech in the history of America: "*I will raise one thousand men for the relief of Boston and subsist them at my own expense.*"

CHAPTER XXXI

THE presence of Prothero in Boston put a stop to my visits thither from Cambridge, but from the most excellent sources I know of what passed in the capital of Massachusetts.

Privation enough there was in Boston while 1774 drew toward its end. All America seemed pouring out its bounty to relieve "the first victim on the altar of Tyranny." Israel Putnam drove up his hundred and thirty sheep from Connecticut, and the great Carolina planters sent up their cargo of rice. But no charity could relax British severity while North was receiving such admonitions from his King as "The die is now cast, the colonies must either submit or triumph."

Whig families moved away. Idleness and hardship among the poorer classes increased. The white tents on the Common multiplied.

If, however, Whigs were quitting Boston, Tories were moving in. It was no safe thing now in Massachusetts villages to toast the King and be suspected of tea-drinking. Doubtless many a peaceful household found itself outrageously mobbed just because of the honest conviction of its head that he ought not to join in the Liberty Song. There was a disgraceful amount of tarring and feathering of harmless persons. Your good Loyalists of the interior counties therefore crammed the Boston boarding houses or the spare-rooms of their friends, drank "Damnation to traitors" in the taverns, and scolded the governor because "hanging work" had not begun already. In the streets brawls betwixt townsmen and soldiers multiplied. Boston was becoming no place wherein women-folk could range the streets at night.

In August had come a little excitement when the Massachusetts delegates set forth for Philadelphia to that Continental Congress which was to talk or to coerce his Majesty into a better mind. Not being in Boston Roger Gilman had had no share in those remarkable transactions upon Purchase Street, when alike for the honor of the cause and the love which his friends bore him, a surprising series of donations were showered upon Samuel Adams; he being in fact presented by his admirers with a new broadcloth suit, new wig and hat, a dozen pair of fine hose, half a dozen pair of shoes, and other outfit to boot, along with the "loan" of no light purse of travel money. Which gifts the patriot received with a perfect thankfulness and simplicity of heart, being entirely willing to wear the fine clothes of Philadelphia, yet equally doubtful of the needfulness of discarding the old red coat now approaching its last mending.

Emilie walked forth with many another girl of Boston to wave her farewell when, on the afternoon of August tenth, the coach with the four Boston delegates rumbled slowly down Tremont Street and Long Acre toward the Neck, the two Adamses, Cushing and Paine within, and outside an enormous mass of cheering townmen, muttering Tories and scowling, wondering redcoats. If the appeal to the King, which would be issued from Philadelphia, failed, there was only one recourse awaiting—and Emilie with all those thousands knew it. Foreboding and high resolve were behind all that handkerchief fluttering and cheering. She felt useless and sad as she strolled homeward at the side of Lucy Knox now beginning a very modest housekeeping.

They were turning again toward Queen Street when, hat in hand, pleasant young Dr. Eustis accosted them:

"A request from Dr. Warren, Mlle. Rivoire. Will you have the goodness to wait on him after his patients depart to-morrow morning?"

Not without curiosity was the summons obeyed. When the last shipwright with a mysteriously blackened eye, had been salved and sent away, Warren in his most gracious manner showed Emilie to a chair in the little surgery, fastened the door, took his own seat and then pushed back the vials before him.

"Mademoiselle," spoke he, ingratiatingly, "I trust it is no vain report which links your name with Roger Gilman's."

Emilie reddened, but answered not without pride, "We are to be married next summer, Dr. Warren."

"Another time," he answered, not without a glance at a portrait of a beautiful and gracious woman above his table, "I should indulge in congratulations—to you both. We have proved Roger Gilman. You are fortunate, Mlle. Rivoire. But of course I have not invited you merely to say this."

"What is it, doctor?"

"You are aware that we must wait, must wait however our heart burns, to teach these condescending gentlemen from Britain that cold steel can eke out flouted petitions. Massachusetts is not all of America. Time must do its work in Pennsylvania, Virginia and the Carolinas to justify our cause. So the hardest months are before us."

"How long will they be?"

"Autumn, winter and springtime. At Philadelphia we will frame a last petition to the King. It will be sent to England and then flung back in our faces. A greater and more stringent non-intercourse resolve will be passed, the last refuge of the friends of peace. It will merely leave the old tyranny more intolerable than ever. Meantime we must arm quietly. A peaceable unwarlike people, we must learn the horrid art of butchering our fellow men. It will take all of the respite given us."

Emilie raised a face kindling with desire: "Oh! Doctor Warren, would to God I were a man!—Roger can fight. Roger can risk his life in what becomes for us the noblest cause in the world. I—I can only sit and grieve upon my uselessness. Perhaps later, if this dreadful thing must be, I can nurse the sick, I can run bullets; but to sit waiting, waiting, when for the cause I would proudly shed my blood—it is intolerable."

"For that reason, I have sent for you, dear lady."

"I am all eager. I am entranced."

Warren's tone became that of an elder brother: "After the conflict joins there will be work and to spare for every woman who loves America. Let the future care for that. But there is now a service which not one of the Committee, not one of the Sons of Liberty can render. It is a service not without peril and doubtless 'twill prove repugnant to those fine instincts which Mlle. Rivoire proclaims by every glance."

"Oh! speak not of that."

"Listen then. Here in Boston, Tories and King's officers surround us. Despite many threats, the fear lest the Loyalists throughout the province should be imperilled by any rash move, probably keeps us safe for the present. But lines are tightening. Secret plans are maturing at Province House. General Gage in a feeble way desires peace, but the pressure upon him for some violent stroke may become irresistible—Do you begin to follow me?"

Emilie shook her head, "I am still wondering."

"Clearer then. A young woman of social grace, beauty, intelligence, love for America, can render a service not to be reckoned in all the gold of Spain."

Emilie's eyes began to dilate, but she threw out half demurely: "There is Hope Fifield."

"Miss Fifield has rendered great services. She will render them again. But Mlle. Rivoire (with the least smile) has *certain advantages* over Miss Fifield."

"Then you would have me—" with gaze now upon her lap, "be friends to—our enemies?"

"Dear Mlle. Rivoire," cried Warren gallantly, "how should a mere man force particulars upon a lady gifted beyond question with one of the wisest heads as well as the warmest hearts in the world? What you must do I fear will cost you keenly. It will cost much to Roger Gilman. I shall endeavor to lessen his anxieties, but a certain sacrifice there must be by both of you. It must be part of the sacrifice that as few of your friends must know of your service as possible, and this may earn you the black frowns of many of the rest. Your grandfather of course is to be trusted, and Hope Fifield. No other, barring myself, must know in Boston. Me you must meet as seldom as possible."

Emilie rose and gave him her hand. Her face was glowing: "It will be hard. It will hurt Roger. *Bon Dieu!* 'tis so much easier to drill and fight. But it is for America."

. . . A few days later Roger Gilman, then in Redford, took a letter out of the tavern post office which sent him away with his heart swirling in chaos and black night.

"My beloved: Dismiss all thoughts of coming to Boston even should you believe it safe. Do not be angry with me if I see you seldom for many months, and if my letters are secret and few. Believe it not even if strange stories are told concerning me, not although Herbert Dunmore himself confirms them. If our love is pure and unfailing, equally unfailing is our trust in one another. 'America' is greater than even the joy of the sight of your face. When another summer comes I am awaiting you. As always your own E. R."

With these came lines in a familiar hand.

"Mr. Roger Gilman—Draw no conclusions as to any letter from Miss E. R. until we have conversed. Public interest takes me to the Wright Tavern in Concord on Thursday. Yr. obdt. etc. JOSEPH WARREN."

An anxious young man drove over to Concord that Thursday. He spent an hour alone with Warren and emerged a little comforted. Nevertheless rumor was soon going from one Redford back-kitchen to another, "That French girl has thrown over the minister's son." Mrs. Gilman of course preserved proud silence. Yetmercy avowed, "She *could* talk but she wouldn't. Ishmael however asserted, "They jest quarrelled, and she warn't good 'nuf for him no-how." This seemed the official version. Since Roger Gilman was well liked in Redford, everybody voted that "He had had a lucky escape," and soon settled on the eldest Tyler girl as a very suitable candidate.

. . . .

The story spread in Boston a trifle more slowly. First it was whispered that young Mr. Gilman had stopped calling at North Square. M. Rivoire stated, with a significant hesitation, "He regretted that he could say nothing." Then Lucy Knox made some mention of Emilie's coming marriage, whereupon that young lady burst into tears. Before September advanced all the Very Respectables knew the affair was off. The reasons? A black chapter of Harvard escapades was at first hinted by the malicious, but soon another version spread without denial. Mr. Gilman had compromised himself so completely with the desperate Whigs that M. Rivoire, whatever his mild political sympathies, simply could not permit his granddaughter to take a husband headed straight toward the gallows.

All this caused a grand reshuffling of friendships. Lucy

Knox angrily ceased calling. Paul Revere as suddenly practically broke intercourse with his kinsmen. The Peleg
Fifields boiled angrily: "Of course those Rivoires were
French; couldn't be expected to risk much for America;
still if she had really *cared* for Roger, etc., etc." And all
the genteel and fashionable shook their laces and curls
while they stirred their gentian tea and agreed, "There must
be something behind it."

If, however, Mademoiselle lost one set of friends, she was
instantly embraced by another. The Tories welcomed her
with open arms. The mere fact that she had jilted a
Whig was enough to make Vassals, Faneuils, Olivers and
Auchmutys all rediscover her extreme respectability. The
town also swarmed now with splendiferous young officers.
The Whig houses were socially barricaded, but every Tory
miss was having her head turned by the incessant beauings
and flattery. And when "the great Mademoiselle" stepped
out of the Sewells' calash on the night of a Province House
ball, the Sir Walter Raleighs would have lined all the steps
for her with scarlet coats if only the steps had been con-
veniently muddy!

First it was ensigns who squabbled for the right to knot
her ribbons in their sword hilts after dinner; next it was
the lieutenants; but after the third ball disconsolate subalterns scolded, "That French puss is a proud minx. She
hasn't an eye for a poor devil below a captain."

All this might have been very diverting to Mlle. Rivoire
(she was very human—Roger or no Roger) except for certain unpleasant incidents. Herbert Dunmore presently made
an unwelcome scene:

"I am Roger Gilman's best friend. What has happened?
I have the right to know."

"I cannot tell you, Herbert. Alas! I can tell nobody."

"We are old friends, Emilie. If it hadn't been for Peggy I might even have envied Roger. I cannot endure to have your happiness and his so ruined."

"A King's officer would not wish me to marry a rebel?" she attempted banteringly.

"Do not play with me. You know my opinions. If I were Roger Gilman I would do exactly as he is doing."

"Dr. Warren will welcome your services then."

Herbert's courtesy nearly dissolved: "I'll never fight against my King be his cause however bad. But you evade me. No politics separate you from Roger. When I landed you were a ranker Whig than he."

"No," confessed Emilie drearily, "it is not entirely *that* which separates us.—Oh! I am so miserable." And not ill-advisedly she delivered the feminine ultimatum, tears: "Please, please do not question more. Not even to you, dear Herbert, can I tell what has come between us!"

Whereupon the officer went out of the Rivoire parlor with a *"Varium et mutabile semper femina"* upon his lips, and dark questionings in his heart even as to the constancy of Peggy.

He relieved the situation, however, by taking himself off to Virginia. It was upon another of those brave, hopeless peacemaking expeditions, an effort to work upon his very unworthy namesake Lord Dunmore, there governor, and try to get him to take counsel with Messrs. Henry, Washington, Jefferson and their friends as to means for halting the hurricane. "Probably a vain quest," he admitted ere leaving Boston, "still he would try."

So Herbert went, and Emilie had need to cultivate other friends if only to fight off persistent and not easily repelled attentions by Prothero. The naval officer freely admitted to his equals, "I was a d—— fool at Newagen. But the devils roast me, if I won't even things up with her." It was in fact at a great rout at the Frankland house, the mansion full of candles, cut glass and plate, white powder and silks, civilian velvet, military scarlet and naval blue, that the captain of the *Argus* edged her aside behind a great palm stand, offered himself with all propriety;—and received an answer lacking nothing in emphasis and clearness.

After that the very need of competent protectors led Mlle. Rivoire to encourage certain gentlemen whom even Prothero was fain to admit were somewhat formidable rivals. There was a young baronet in the Fusileers, Sir Francis Claypool, who suddenly became amazingly pleased with Boston society. But, then, Major Upson, heir to an old Staffordshire house, was equally devoted and equally in favor, while one of the Vassals ("sure to be at least lieutenant governor some day") was almost wearing out his curricle driving about a delightful lady.

As the winter advanced and the province muttered and armed, as outside of Boston Gage's power sank to a shadow, the little refugee-military aristocracy was flung even more completely upon itself. Since idle brains demanded occupation Mlle. Rivoire became the subject of an enormous quantity of bad sonnets. She innocently caused two affairs of honor—neither fatal. My Lord Percy (although his countess had already been picked for him at home) was far too gallant an officer to leave Mlle. Rivoire entirely to the mercies of the subalterns. He was seen sometimes riding out with her toward Dorchester, he upon a fine white horse already conspicuous at the reviews, she upon a bay jennet loaned by the governor himself.

During these three months Dr. Joseph Warren continued about town, despite the steady Whig exodus, visited his Tory patients and maintained correct social relations with even his Excellency. When, however, he met Miss Rivoire upon the streets his bow was cold and distant, precisely as was proper from a gentleman to a lady who had fallen away from the patriot cause.

From time to time indeed there were angry conferences at Province House as to how prime secrets had leaked. How came it to pass that when careful plans had been laid for the quiet transfer to Boston of the powder at the fort at Portsmouth, the local Sons of Libery had suddenly pounced down upon the feeble garrison and hurried away a hundred barrels of the precious explosive to their fastnesses at Exeter? Or how, when Colonel Leslie with a strong draft of the sixty-fourth stealthily landed at Marblehead, and advanced to Salem to seize the cannon there secreted, behold! he found the drawbridge over North River up, and so many homespun-clad men with muskets just beyond that he was fain to compound for an ignominious retreat? To these problems and to others like them, this authentic history supplies no answer. The one thing certain is that General Gage scolded his lower officers at length, and formally warned that the first detected indiscretion meant an instant trip back to England.

All this of course in nowise concerned Mlle. Rivoire. It was commonly said that she could be Lady Claypool for the least hinting; but then, what of the Vassals when provincial loyalty has its sure reward? In the meantime she seemed to find life exciting, enjoyable and extremely occupied, being almost incessantly now at Province House as the favorite and bosom companion of no less a personage than Mrs. Gage.

Was Emilie at ease amid all this tense, exotic gaiety; gaiety all the more frantic because the shadow of coming tragedy lurked in every mind? One dare not write quite the contrary. The vibrant youthful life of a woman of France surged strong within her. Every day, her devotees vowed, she came forth to them more vivacious, more beautiful. But no one, not even her grandfather, knew how at some hour daily, she found time to steal alone down the narrow streets past Christ Church to Copp's Hill, below which stretched the narrow river, Charlestown village, and beyond that, graying into the distance the rolling contours of Middlesex toward Cambridge, Lexington—and Redford.

One red winter evening she held out her hands toward the icebound waters and snowbound hills, then spoke aloud with only the stones of the solemn old burial ground for her auditors: "*Hélas*, my new friend called America! How could I know my love for you would cost so much?"

CHAPTER XXXII

IN WHICH I DRILL A COMPANY

ON my desk lies a small pamphlet, yellowing now with the years and poorly printed. How crowded are the memories that troop back as I turn its crumbling leaves! *"A Collection of Faithful Testimonies to the Cause of God and His New England People"*; a compilation from *"the sermons of memorable divines who have gone to a heavenly country,"* setting forth the high purposes for which these colonies were planted *"that the rising generation might count it their glory and their duty to continue the right ways of the Lord wherein their fathers walked before them."*

For now were the days of the girding of loins and the strengthening of hearts; and if one assistant to the Massachusetts Committee of Safety was very young to be compiling such pamphlets, he was not so young as a certain Alexander Hamilton, whose patriotic tracts already were confounding the New York Tories.

We had our Provincial Congress at length and our Committee of Safety, all through that tense dark winter while the old Bay Colony was arming. If a few Quakerish souls still said their "peace, peace," for all that, mothers were looking upon their sons, young wives upon their husbands, and the minutemen's companies were trampling the snow on every village common. For we knew that Britain would not relent and the spring must bring the crisis.

All through that autumn and winter I had eaten my heart out longing for a sight of Emilie. The mandate from

382

Warren that I must do nothing to destroy the belief in our quarrel barely kept me out of Boston. How gladly by some daredevil charge upon a smoking battery would I have purchased the right to one glimpse of that dear face. At rare intervals Warren brought out to me letters, letters breathing of trust and love, and drawing a blissful future, but they were poor substitutes for those golden hours which are a lover's eternal prerogative.

Through those months I had been again nominally at Harvard. Nominally I say, for if the college had been demoralized the year earlier who can describe the poor dying rate at which faculty and students tried to wrestle with languages and philosophies in 1774-75! I kept my old room at Stoughton, but half the time I was either at the Cambridge meeting house, where the Provincial Congress (heir to the dissolved legislature) convened, or at Concord, where the Committee of Safety was painfully collecting those twenty field-pieces, five thousand muskets, one thousand wooden mess-bowls and sundry other appurtenances for defying the greatest power in Christendom.

Then late in February came my partial reward. A great ball had been held at Province House. It had been in honor of the Queen's birthday, the twenty-second, a day somewhat regularly observed in America in later years, although not in commemoration of her Majesty. Mlle. Rivoire had led the grand promenade hand-in-hand with a lieutenant colonel, advancing under an archway of crossed swords.

The next morning incidentally (when he had slept off his burgundy) Sir Francis Claypool imparted to his closest friends that "she" had promised to give him a definite answer on or before May-day. But that same morning the young lady's gallants were all too dampish and dozy to dance attendance upon her, or for anybody in fact to make a particular note that she had arisen crisp and smiling, had dressed with unusual pains and driven out in a sleigh with her grandfather, past the new fortification on the Neck, to Roxbury where M. Georges wished to examine a tannery offered him for purchase.

There in a quiet little inn kept by a sound Whig, while her grandfather traded shrewdly near the bar, Emilie threw back her sables in a private dining room, and miraculously found herself being embraced by a young gentleman just ridden out from Cambridge.

Oh! the pure joy of that meeting:—but there are some things whereof I am not fool enough to write. And after our feet again were touching earth, what a budget of news to exchange!—I told how Uncle Peleg, who had withdrawn to Newburyport, had arranged such a connection with the Dutch at Eustatius Island that Mem Watchhorn was running in enough of French and Holland goods to pay off all M. Georges' notes. Emilie related how Uncle Eleazer was nigh insane over the ruin of his rum and black ivory trade, and went whining around Province House for some compromise whereby to open the port. Also the dear girl gave me her solemn vow that with the summer (come what might) her pact with Warren would end, and we could be married—if only to start life in the old cabin on the parsonage wood lot by Concord River.

After that we were exchanging tid-bits as to the preparation of the province and the garrison in Boston (our tongues going like magpies), when we heard the pounding of drums and also fifes screaming out that "Yankee Doodle," which the British fifers had pounced upon in derision of us Provincials. "The fifty-ninth," announced Emilie, now very army-wise, "on a practice march through Dorchester."

The troops tramped by the tavern harmlessly, never heeding two watchers from a window. It was almost my first

sight since 1770 of a large body of regulars. The sun was
pouring over the winter landscape, and the moving mass
of scarlet and flashing steel made my blood tingle. The
platoons of tall-hatted, six-foot grenadiers all moving with
clock-work rhythm, the snappy stride of the light companies, the magnificent figures of the tightly laced and
gaitered young officers showed forth all the splendor and
pageantry of war without its tragedy. But I could recognize the discipline and deadly power behind those glittering
files. Bayonets had been fixed and rose above the white
belts and swaying hats in a bristling hedge, menacing and
defiant.—We had seen a little, a very little of the might
of Old England. As the last file-closer disappeared I ven-
tured:

"Well—we see our task! How much more time is given
us?"

Emilie shook her head: "General Gage does not know
himself. The Tories and younger officers rage around Province House, but the general is in a sorry plight. He's a
kindly man who dreamed one flash of the sword would
bring Massachusetts under.—*Eh! bien!*—It has not. His
power stops at Roxbury Neck as you quit Boston. London
writes, 'Seize the Whig chiefs.' Gage answers, 'Do that and
you declare war.' Weak and dilatory, he puts off the last
decision. Some day it comes suddenly. *Pouf!*"——

"Is it true he has sent out his spies?"

She nodded, "Ensign De Berniere told me at the ball how
he and Captain Brown put on your Yankee brown coats
and red-checked neckerchiefs, tried to talk through their
noses, and went clear out to Worcester. They made sketches,
noted crossroads, watched your minutemen drill at a place
named Framingham. How the ensign laughed over a speech
by the militia captain quoting Cæsar, Pompey and your
generals Putnam and Ward!"

"I could tell your fine friend something," I began; when in came M. Rivoire with a tactfully cautioning rattle of the latch, and warned us his business was over: "Having spun it out as long as possible, *mes enfants*," he added with a smile. "We must be going back immediately. Roxbury is a pleasant ride from Boston and officers often halt at the tavern."

Therefore after a tantalizingly blissful farewell, with "summer" repeated many times, I heard the sleigh jingling off to the long causeway, and although the sun still glittered on the snows of Dorchester, I fear that for me the whole landscape was sadly darkened.

Nevertheless as I made my solitary way back to Brighton Bridge and Cambridge I really felt much happier, and on my table I found a letter from John Hancock which sent me hurrying to Lancaster after an offer of flints to the Committee, then off to Medfield to interview a wheelwright who thought he could build gun carriages. Hard work is a sovereign specific for restless thoughts. As for Harvard my attendance gradually faded into thin air. I never knew when they ceased calling my name at chapel roll. So February advanced well into March, and then on a flying trip to Redford I found that greatness had been thrust upon me.

So busy had I been for the Committee that I had given little heed to my personal part in the ordeal before us. I expected to fight, and I drilled as I could with the Harvard company, but inwardly the whole military process seemed to me very uncongenial. By an effort I had mastered the manual of arms and the simpler marching tactics, yet I felt no craving for the honors of a leader. An uneasy suspicion in fact often came to me that when once under fire my legs would feel a great impulse to run away. How could I be an example to a command! I fully intended to enlist at first as a private and trust the rest to Heaven.

Destiny ruled otherwise. I had just turned from the meeting-house door, where I had nailed up the fiat of the Committee that every minuteman should be provided with thirty-six rounds of powder and ball, when Job Twitchell, arch-busybody of Redford, came running up to me.

"You're elected," quoth he with a friendly grin.

"Tarnation," I vowed. The high office of a hog-reeve was vacant, and it was a standing jest to vote it to some finicky young man who delighted in many things other than the duty of seeing that every porker was ringed, marked and kept within bounds.

"Not by town meeting," he explained, "by the minute-men. Lieutenant Foster says he's too old and rheumatic to be counted on."

"Sergeants Hooper and Purdy are both aching to jump into his shoes, and they're both very proper men."

"Why so they both kind o' threw out, and their friends hinted still broader. There's just the rub. They're jealous as Lucifer and Satan and neither'll take orders from t'other. 'So' says I, 'boys, let's compromise. If Roger Gilman's good enough to go to Harvard and write Johnny Han-cock's letters for him he's good enough for a lieutenant.'— And they all cum round to that opinion. Cap'n Harter's more'n willing. So the notice for your commission went down to the Committee at Menotomy this morning."

Honest Job was sadly puzzled because I did not thank him heartily. I pled with Harter and the selectmen to be excused: "My time so belonged to the Committee." But everybody said, "Hooper won't serve under Purdy and Purdy won't under Hooper—it's you or old Bill Sedgwick, whose a clown at giving orders." So reluctantly I consented; especially as I could see that mother felt that I ought.

Tabitha at least was in glee; she introduced me to girl friends as "Lieutenant Gilman" and made me a uniform with fine epaulets, very magnificent but equally unmilitary. My own comfort was that the captain was responsible for the company and my own first duties would probably be near headquarters.

But my office was no sinecure. Harter at once had me aside and confessed relief at my election: "Fact is, Roger, I've bitten off more'n I can chaw. They made me cap'n because I moved those awfully hot resolves in town meeting roasting the British. Now, oh, Lordy! I'm in a mess; served a bit as corporal of militia when I was in my teens, and had a cousin who fought at Ti'—and that's the limit of my sojering! You must help me out."

Ours was a small company. Only forty-five averaged at the four-hour drill each week. The first day I faced that line of gawky men and youths, clad in everything from tattered broadcloth to leathern jackets, and some with fowling piece on left shoulder, some on right, my first impulse was to laugh in their faces, my second to shed tears.—To stand such men against the glittering scarlet regiments!

That night after our so-called "drill" I was in such a mood that I actually drafted an outrageous letter to Hancock urging long temporizing with Gage rather than risk sending our lads not to a battle but a slaughter-pen.

The next day, however, the letter went into the kitchen fire. Many companies, with abler captains, I knew were drilling better than ours. Then my stay at Redford being prolonged, I threw myself into the task, and got the selectmen to offer extra bounty for extra drill. The weather was luckily fine and the men turned out readily. Before

April was fairly opened we had drills on the Common that would not have been sneered at by any one short of a King's officer. All the girls came out, and their open comments upon the more awkward lads did far more good than all my official reproof. Tabby and her intimates made us a fine red flag blazoned with an arm bearing a drawn sword. The banner floated grandly when little Eph Tucker marched with it at the head of the column.

The men, I must say, took their duty seriously, and Harter backed me up steadfastly in a case of discipline when certain fellows began to snicker at my youth. Thanks to my Committee connections I procured furthermore six half-kegs of that most precious substance in New England—gunpowder. We kept them, as per custom, in the great recess under the meeting-house pulpit, and partly to encourage morale, I had three men take turns guarding our treasure.

All this, with constant drives to Concord, Lexington and Menotomy, where the Committee of Safety often sat, left me little enough time for moping about Emilie. Then at last after an open winter, came the warm touches of spring; the cat-tails swelled, the brooks opened, the roads became for a while simply founderous wallows. And with this new spring air came the inward assurance, stronger than any words, that our armistice with Gage was nearing the end.

For months now George III had been "King" over Massachusetts only in name. All the new "mandamus" councillors, appointed by Gates under the mutilated charter, had either resigned at the behest of enormous mobs or slunk away to safety in Boston. No judge sat higher than the justice of the peace, yet never had the Bay Colony been more free from crime. In lieu of taxes, "contributions" came in to the Committee of Safety. Town meetings convened everywhere despite the royal prohibition. While over in Britain, we knew Parliament was preparing to order the exclusion of our fishermen and our traders from the high seas, coercion being piled upon coercion, defiance upon defiance.

. . . Yet as the imminence of the peril came crowding home what wonder that good men and better women, good patriots all, had to question hard whether or not that cruel thing called "war" must really be? Was there no escape? Were the wrongs from Britain so intolerable that gallant young men by thousands must march away to die? In Redford as in all Middlesex there was no wavering, but we all caught the murmurs and the drawn looks, and could not quite ignore them.

All this father carried on his heart. Never at family prayers did he fail to ask for "guidance to justify to the people the grievous necessities of the times." Then upon a Saturday mother came home quite upset. Hannah Davis had ridden down from Acton. Her husband, Isaac, a hale young farmer-blacksmith there and captain of the local company, had brought her along with him while he stayed over at Gilpin's to dicker for some hogs. And something (so mother said) had started Hannah off before a lot of Redford women. She had wept and vowed that no matter what England did and Sam Adams said, "It didn't seem right," and "She could never bring herself to let Isaac go and be shot by the redcoats." She had stirred all the other women up; some actually chimed in "They felt like Hannah. They just *couldn't* let their men go." Mother had said what she could; but "she was terribly afraid, if such talk went round the parish."

Whereupon father very solemnly sifted the sheets of a nearly completed sermon on "The Vicarious Atonement" into the fireplace and sat up most of the night; while Yetmercy, an unsurpassed news medium, gave out that "There'd be something worth hearing at the meeting house."

. . . Sunday morning dawned blustery and cold as April mornings can, but the roads were all beaten out to the meeting-house. Women came in on pillions behind their husbands. Chaises crowded the long shed. It seemed as if the pew doors would never cease banging for the families shutting themselves into their hereditary castles. Father prayed, read scripture non-committally, and made the congregation drone through a very unpolitical psalm. Then at last I saw him shake out his great wig,—sure sign that he was ready for action. The wind whistled and roared through all the big rafters overhead, but the upturned faces of assembled Redford heeded it not. Their law was again about to be handed down from Sinai.

Father took for his text, *"My thoughts are not your thoughts, neither are your ways my ways, saith the Lord."* He began very mildly, saying that he would not have his people imagine that they alone were the true patriots. Colonel George Washington worshipped devoutly in the Church of England, and Charles Carroll, the Whig chief for all Maryland, was a pious Catholic. Nevertheless Heaven had so ordered things that the honor of the first burden of this crisis fell upon New England and upon the men of its Faith, and of the New England heritage he would speak.

Then he read from the last ordinance of our Massachusetts Congress proclaiming that our forefathers had "fled from oppression for the sake of civil and religious liberty for themselves and their offspring. . . . And we do think it our indispensable duty to recover, maintain, defend and preserve the free exercise of all those rights and liberties for which many of our forefathers bled and died."

Next he recited gravely and clearly the helpless state of Massachusetts if we endured the present tyranny—Boston full of troops, with a standing camp upon the Common; our old charter swept away; our old councillors replaced with government nominees, our criminal and civil suits tried before judges paid by the Crown and juries picked by Crown officers; our respectful petitions flung back at us as almost treason.

Whereupon, throwing out his voice with greater power, father dwelt on the many things which were worse than death; how nigh every gain for mankind had been purchased at a price unspeakable, by those who endured to the uttermost. Next leaping from theme to theme he rehearsed all the story of those who across the ages had battled for their freedom and their faith; the story of the Swiss cantons, of the Dutch cities, of the Scottish Covenanters, of the Puritans of England. At length, leaning across the great Bible, he stretched forth his arms like a prophet:

"And for us of New England, was this land founded on hope of gain, on nice calculation, on delicate seeking the paths of safety? I say to you, my brethren, this New England came into being *by great acts of faith;* and by faith alone shall it be perpetuated.

"*By faith* Brewster and Robinson fled to Holland from Scrooby, rather than abandon the service of their conscience.

"*By faith* their company made its way across the solitary sea and pitched on the winter shores at Plymouth.

"*By faith* Winthrop and Dudley and the men who prayed with them forsook the honors of England, that they might here found a Commonwealth more pleasing unto God.

"*By faith* Thomas Hooker and his following went forth across the naked wilderness, and carried the bounds of New England into Connecticut.

"*By faith* the men of Massachusetts dared greatly, and

flung from power the tyrant Andros who was undoing all that holy sacrifice had wrought.

"*By faith* Pepperell led forth his untaught host against Louisburg, and took that great fortress against which the power of Britain had raged in vain.

"And now, people of Redford," father's voice held the drowsiest pew rigid, "*by faith*, we of New England will take up the birthright inherited from our fathers, and pass to our children a heritage which never, as the years blend into the centuries, shall scorners and defilers rend away!"

Then clearly and sensibly he spoke of the present task. Like all our leaders he said we must never force the battle with the British; the first shots of aggression must be theirs. Nor did he make small the military power confronting us. Some there were—he said it openly—doubtless then before him, who would in the struggle be summoned to yield up life itself. They could know that forever their memories would be kept sacred, numbered among the great army of just men made perfect, so long as America endured as America.

So through two hours—while the tithing man stood motionless by his unneeded rod, and the silence in the packed meeting house was broken only by the approving of the gale. At last when the cord was nearly drawn to breaking, father bent again from the pulpit:

"We shall go forth together, O my people. We shall suffer together. We shall glory together. I ask no sacrifice from any which I do not proffer from among those I love. And for those of you who reckon up the power of England, and cry, 'This hard thing is too great for us!' let me pray for you after the manner of Elisha of old: '*O Lord open their eyes, that they may see that the mountain is full of horses and chariots of fire; for they that be with us, are more than they that be with them!*' "

In the ensuing hush yet again he sent his voice across the church:

"Stand all now, and sing the seventy-eighth psalm."

Whereat box pews, rear stalls, high galleries rose together, and to venerable St. Martin's notes, thundered to the huge rafters that psalm which aright has been called the national hymn of Puritan New England:

> "Give list'ning care unto my words
>   Ye people that are mine.
> Unto the sayings of my mouth
>   Do ye your ears incline.
>
> "My mouth I'll ope in parables,
>   I'll speak hid things of old,
> Which we have heard and known and which
>   Our fathers us have told.
>
> "In Jacob God a witness set
>   And put in Israel
> A law which He our fathers charged
>   They should their children tell:
>
> That age to come and children which
>   Are to be born might know
> That they might rise up and the same
>   Unto their children show." . . . .

After the "Amen" of the benediction, as the people turned to open the pew doors, father's hand detained them for the last time:

"Twice each Sabbath do we worship God in this our Redford, but is it not written 'To everything there is a season' and again 'There is a time of war and a time of peace'?—This afternoon we worship best by witnessing our company at drill before the meeting house, 'For the Sabbath was made for man, and not man for the Sabbath.' "

. . . . After the service, while the folk from a distance stood around the "Sabba' day house," warmed themselves, ate their baskets of victuals and conversed, Isaac Davis hearty and wholesome came up and took father's hand: "You done us a world of good, doctor," spoke he unaffectedly, "and my wife most of all. As we went out I said to her, '*Now* will you let me lead the company, Hannah?' and she came back, 'You've just *got* to, Isaac.' "

We had the best drill of the season that afternoon.*

*The authenticity of this report of Dr. Gilman's sermon is greatly strengthened by the fact that it resembles even in details very many other sermons preached in Massachusetts in April, 1775. (Editor.)

YET again to see Boston through other eyes than mine.
. . . If tension there had been in wide Massachusetts,
what in her chief town? Four thousand redcoats idled in
Boston streets, in the harbor rode many men-of-war.
Despite the earnest efforts of the better officers to control
their men, ill feeling with the not lamb-like townsfolk ran
high. Jem and Jock, Thomas and Andy, as well as their
company officers, were grinding their teeth because not yet
had they been suffered to give "the lousy rebels" a bloody
lesson.

The crisis came nearer when on March fifth, under the
very eyes of the garrison, with British officers sitting on
the pulpit steps to shout their "Oh, fie!" at the speaker,
Joseph Warren had stood before the crowded Old South
and cast defiance against "our most inveterate enemies" in
an oration commemorating the Massacre. In every Tory
parlor, every regimental mess-hall there were curses against
the governor who suffered treason still to stalk unscathed.
Was Gage asleep? Had he taken "King Hancock's" gold?
Had that devilishly elegant Warren bewitched him? Was
he a poltroon? Was he anything (save what was the
case) a weak, well-meaning man recoiling before a fearful
responsibility?

It was soon after this when Warren was walking along
the Neck where the public gibbet stood, that three officers
bawled after him, "Go on, Warren, you will soon come to
the gallows"; at which the doctor turned sharply with a

"Who said that?" and meeting only sheepish faces calmly continued his walk. But other incidents soon came after. The fence of the Hancock house was hacked by the swords of officers. Regimental bands brayed outside the churches when pious citizens gathered for evening lecture. The tombs on Copp's Hill burial ground were outrageously shivered by being made practice targets for the regulars. On the other hand, despite all search at the Neck and the Ferry, Yankee ingenuity was smuggling forth saltpeter, powder, musket balls and even actual cannon to those grotesque minutemen who were the butt of every loyal gathering.

Emilie had watched and waited with beating heart even if, as yet, with untroubled eyes. Hope Fifield and her grandfather were her only confidants, save when she contrived stealthy interviews with Warren. Paul Revere turned his face from her now when they met on North Street. The excitement of the game was overwhelming, but she dared not dwell upon the stakes.

Hourly a move might come from Province House. Warren himself was becoming anxious, "Could she learn nothing?" Emilie could only answer, "From Percy downward the officers fume and curse, but the general gives no word." Every day she looked west from Copp's Hill; every day she told herself, "If I fail or blunder, the forfeit may be paid by the jeopardy of the man I love."

Thus the grass grew green along the Common. The majestic Boston elms began to bud. The first warm days proclaimed the coming victory of the spring. With them came a packet from England with tidings that Parliament had pledged to the King "life and fortune for the reduction of America," that New England was prohibited the fisheries, that more troops were on the way. At which there was much loud talk and sword clattering at Province House, and very soon after that John Hancock and the two

Adamses suddenly withdrew from Boston. Possibly Mlle.
Rivoire knew somewhat of their departure. But if they
went, Warren remained. "I am turning soldier," he had said
to Emilie, "yet my post is still here; and a soldier should
be no more afraid of a halter than of a bullet."

The buds swelled. The purple crocus and grape-hyacinths
pushed forth in the stately North End gardens and along
the slopes of Beacon Hill. It was afternoon of April the
seventeenth.

.   .   .   .

The cabinet of General Gage in Province House was a
deep wainscoted, gilt and mahogany room, before which
was an ante-room with chairs for his Excellency's orderlies.
Here there was lounging a self-sufficient young Lieutenant
Gould of the "King's Own," when he was awakened from
day-dreams by the entrance of four gentlemen who brought
him upon his feet with a very deferential salute. They
were none other than Mr. Eleazer Fifield, accepted spokesman for the Boston Loyalists, Captain Prothero in his best
naval blue, Lieutenant Colonel Smith, ranking regimental
officer in Boston, and my Lord Percy himself. There was
something about the four which made Gould tell his friends
immediately afterward, "He knew they had come for a
purpose."

"General Gage is within?" panted Smith; he was a fat
and heavy man, and the long flight of stone steps to the
door had been almost too much for him.

"He is, sir," returned Gould respectfully, "but he is momentarily closeted with Captain Dunmore just returned
from Virginia."

"The devil he is!" ejaculated Prothero under breath;
while Fifield muttered, "Praises be, we didn't come a bit
later,—or the old coward's mind would have been pumped
full of more poison!"

Percy pointed toward the door with an imperious gesture: "Captain Dunmore can wait, Lieutenant Gould. Go in to the general and tell him this deputation would see him immediately."

Gould disappeared, returned in an instant, saluted again and reported, "His Excellency will see you, gentlemen"; then threw wide the door and the deputation was in the presence of the royal governor.

Thomas Gage arose from behind his desk and bowed. He was a large florid personage, with a countenance open and pleasant but lacking a firm chin. "More than welcome, my friends," spoke he affably, "for you can share the report of Captain Dunmore. He brings us the good news that Lord Fairfax is sure the Virginians will remain entirely quiet unless our Massachusetts Whigs actually force the fighting."

"Captain Dunmore," rejoined Percy with a frown, "is an excellent young officer, whose ardor for a peaceful settlement sometimes blinds him to the unhappy realities. We trust he has not been again misled. Our mission, however, General, concerns not Virginia but the present plight of all loyal subjects in Massachusetts."

Gage looked uncomfortable, but resumed his seat, motioned his guests to chairs, and began to twiddle his thumbs nervously. He was in manifest awe of his Lordship. Herbert had flushed, then demanded, "Shall I withdraw, your Excellency?"

"Remain, Captain," ordered Gage, not anxious to face the deputation alone, "perhaps your report from the other colonies can assist these gentlemen in what they may propose."

Percy glanced at Fifield, and the old Tory cleared his throat and began: "The loyal people of Massachusetts, Gov'ner, are getting sour and impatient. Hard words, mobbings, and now a state of things where no man dares so much as cry 'God save the King!' except behind the regiments here in Boston. Our trade is tumbling to pieces. The ministers clamp tight this port, and the Whigs tar and feather any man in Salem or Newburyport who dares bring in a bale of goods from England. I'm not as bad off as most; won't speak of my own losses. But I say this for all the Loyalists in Boston—where's it going to end, Gov'ner? Where's it going to end?"

Gage's thumbs continued chasing one another: "I feel for your hardships, Mr. Fifield, before Heaven I do. The wrongs done all his Majesty's friends lie on my heart. Your admirable patience——"

"Patience be damned!" Eleazer's fist banged on the table, "I've not come for a sermon. I speak for the Vassals and the Olivers, the Lechmeres and the Faneuils, and all of those poor Hutchinsons that haven't been chased yet to England. Ten regiments here in Boston, and yet Sam and the two Johns now flit out of town right under your nose. 'Tain't to be endured!"

"Your feelings are very natural, good Mr. Fifield," deprecated Gage, "but consider my responsibility. 'Twas impossible to risk driving the province into bloody revolt by seizing those rebels on the day of Warren's incendiary speech. Better too much leniency than rashness."

"We are not here, your Excellency," interposed Prothero in his blandest manner, "to question the former wisdom of a policy doubtless admirable until recently. Conditions, however, have changed. I am present in behalf of the naval officers now in port to urge a more vigorous policy. My Lord Percy and Colonel Smith can speak for the army. Loyalty to the King will excuse our plain speech."

Gage looked uneasily upon his visitors, while Percy nodded and Smith both nodded and grunted. The general was becoming red, and acted as if he would gladly have shown the deputation the door, but he only fidgeted in his chair.

"What are your suggestions, gentlemen?" spoke he, after an awkward pause.

"Merely," said Prothero, quietly, "that this unnatural truce, or rather condoning of rebellion should end, and some effective blow be struck to bring back Massachusetts Province under royal authority."

"It must be done, gentlemen, it must be done," assented Gage, "but remember, in a little more than a month the garrison of Boston will be doubled. We can then make such a show of power that these misguided men will be glad to forsake their ringleaders and sue out their own pardons."

"Four thousand troops are in Boston now," spoke Smith, in his slow, dry manner. "My own ensigns and lieutenants swear that it will be a blot on the fair name of the tenth if we must wait reënforcements before teaching these canting Cromwellian Mohairs what it means to defy the regulars."

"General Gage," interrupted Dunmore, not without heat, "is not bound by the grumblings of the mess-halls. These Mohairs may poise their firelocks very ill, but they are neither fools nor cowards. Officers who served beside them at Ticonderoga do not speak as does Colonel Smith. If the worst comes, I pray there be no lessons learned by his own regiment."

"Don't asperse the tenth, Captain Dunmore," retorted Smith testily, "Why, with seven hundred good infantry I engage to march from Boston to Albany in the face of all New England."

"No wrangling, gentlemen," pleaded the uneasy general; "We are all loyal servants of his Majesty. 'Tis merely a matter of policy. I agree with Smith,—the military value of the Provincials is contemptible; my beloved chief, the

brave if unfortunate General Braddock always said so
But to return to the question. The King's honor will hardly
suffer if, after enduring so long, we wait now for Sir William Howe and the reënforcements. Then without firing a
shot——"

"Has your Excellency heard the latest from Concord?"
thrust in Percy who had been sitting silently with his quizzical smile.

"What is that, my Lord?"

"Simply that the Provincial Congress which usurps your
place has finally ordained the actual embodiment of an
army to withstand the King; 'generals,' as they are pleased
to style them, have been named, and all the forms of a
military establishment, so far as peasants can burlesque
them, are now to be improvised. When Sir William comes
we shall have to deal, not with a disloyal province, but with
a veritable rebel army."

The color partly left Gage's face; "I have not interviewed
our spies to-day," he said hurriedly. "Is that news possibly
correct?"

"Indubitably, your Excellency; I have seen them myself."

"This is serious, your Lordship," admitted the governor,
with knit brows. "And yet, as I wrote lately to England,
we deal with people incapable of enduring command or
discipline. One firm push will disperse them."

"Very true, General," affirmed Smith, "but the push must
be given. The honor of the army demands it."

Gage looked perplexedly from one face to another. "I'm
the judge of that," he spoke almost peevishly. "If the rebels
scatter at the first bayonet charge—well. If not—we have
war. Victorious war I grant—but war with our fellow
subjects. I like not the alternative."

"Only a few volleys at the worst. One lesson will finish
them," rejoined Percy.

Dunmore leaped to his feet. He looked very young and boyish, his tones were almost shrill from anxiety. With almost a supplicatory gesture he turned to Gage: "I'm but an intruder at this debate, but for God's sake, harken! I've just traversed the provinces as far as Virginia. This will not prove an affair for Massachusetts only. The first spark will explode the magazine. These Provincials you depreciate are of British blood like ourselves. They know the use of arms, they know the country, they are desperately in earnest. This is not a question of law nor of regimental honor.—So long as no blow is struck there is still hope of conciliation. I entreat the general not to be persuaded into deeds which at best can only recover the Colonies after making them shambles, at worst can lose them to Britain forever."

"Spoken like an Adams!" sneered Prothero openly, but Gage's countenance registered a certain approval.

"Captain Dunmore," said he, "has expressed, over-vigorously perhaps, but not unjustly, sentiments which I cannot ignore. You see the responsibility which I am under."

"Then," rejoined the naval captain with a bantering glance toward Dunmore, "permit me to write to Lord Sandwich, that the commanding general in Boston allows the King's enemies to array an army, but fears the responsibility of lifting a hand to check them."

"This is intolerable, sir," cried Gage, with rising anger. "Lord Sandwich is in nowise my superior. Your own intrusion here is unwelcomed."

"Your pardon, General," spoke Prothero with a bow of ill-concealed sarcasm, "I observe that his Lordship and Colonel Smith, your own officers, do not contradict me. Of course you have seen Earl Chatham's last speech in Parliament?"

"He has said many things derogatory to his Majesty's

policy," protested Gage. "With all respect for his greatness
he cannot speak for Government."

"He assuredly speaks the minds of very many, however.
Suffer me to read his words as reported in the *London Post*,
'General Gage and his troops are penned up, pining in an
inglorious captivity. You may call them an army of safety
and guard, but they are in truth an army of impotence,
and to make the folly equal the disgrace they are an
army of irritation.'"

"Zounds!" swore the general, half-leaping from his seat.
"Had I no champions among ministers to defend me?"

"Very lame champions, please your Excellency. A little
later Lord Sandwich told the Peers that the Provincials
were 'raw undisciplined men,' and that the more of their
'brave fellows' who confronted us, the easier would be the
conquest."

"My Lord Percy, Colonel Smith," appealed Gage, "are
you here to sustain this naval captain in his abuse of your
general?"

Smith looked solemnly upon the parquet floor. Percy's
feminine, aristocratic lips opened slowly: "Captain Prothero has not stated the case as I would desire. Chatham
and Sandwich of course spoke without local knowledge.
But I cannot dissemble from your Excellency that our
royal master himself begins to feel that the time for inac-
tion has passed."

The aspect of Gage was almost pitiful. He had plumped
down in his chair white and muttering: "You have certain
knowledge of this, my Lord?" he spoke audibly at last.

"Permit me, your Excellency, to read a few words from
my last letters." Percy unfolded a fine, crackling sheet,
taking pains to betray the armorial stamping: "'*Yesterday
I was graciously received in the royal closet at Richmond.
H—— M——y unburdened himself freely to me*

concerning America.   He stated unreservedly that he
felt there was a grievous lack of energy in dealing with the
rebels.   Said he feared a certain appointment to office there
was a sad mistake, but would wait until Sir William Howe
arrived before any pronounced action.' "

"Before God," burst from Gage thickly, "was ever loyal
servant of the Crown treated thus!—Meddlesome ignorant
curs in London to slander me to his Majesty!" Then his
own fist banged the table; his form straightened while his
voice quivered. "If 'tis war they want, war let them have—
I'll show them enough energy. I'll smash these Massachusetts rebels. For the rest of America let others answer.
The blame won't be mine.—But you might have told me
this alone, my Lord Percy (his tone became chiding); to
bring this deputation thither was not over civil of you."

"I had hoped my final words would not be needful,"
answered the nobleman mildly.

"They were not—before Heaven they were not! I merely
resented Captain Prothero's manner—understand.   The
rebels must be broken up. We'll teach 'em what it means
to defy the King.—I was just about to say this. Action'll
be taken promptly. You have my promise."

"I beseech the general," Dunmore was now even whiter
than Gage; "do not be hastened against calmer judgment
into some fearful act. Consider—if only for an hour."

"The time is past, Captain Dunmore," ordered Gage
with an impatient gesture (being a very shaken man, he
was glad of some victim for his feelings). "Your intervention has become untimely. Cease interference with what has
become a merciful severity."

The young officer stood gnawing his lips for very despair,
while the general with a heavy attempt at dignity motioned
toward the door; "I have given my word, gentlemen. Action
shall be speedily taken. But to serve, it must be careful

and secret. Therefore will all you others retire while I deliberate with my Lord Percy."

Herbert went out with the others. He was too stunned by this crowning calamity to heed the triumphant glances and muttered boasts of Prothero. In the ante-room he stood to recover from his daze, while the other three walked contentedly away. The lobby was now filled with young officers gathered for routine reports at Province House, and Smith had sent them into a joyous mood by winks and whispers that the deputation had not been in vain. When Dunmore came to himself, several subalterns were standing about him, eyeing him in no friendly manner.

"Well, Captain Dunmore," spoke Gould, by whom Herbert's peacemaking activities had been particularly unwelcomed, "I imagine you'll soon be tossing over your commission here to get a better one among your friends the Mohairs. Ought to be a colonelcy, or even a generalship (they need a man who can drill two files of their clodhoppers) : then you can be saluted as 'Excellency.'"

"A very forced jest, Lieutenant Gould," answered Dunmore, fingering his sword knot, while several onlookers snickered audibly.

"Why, jest of course it is, for no man can wear the King's uniform and not know that after one good stroke by us the best fellow in Massachusetts will be the clown with the fastest legs."

"I've put ten guineas to two with Creswell of the thirty-eighth," piped up a very small ensign, "that the rebels won't stand a second volley."

"You'll best have the sum ready, sir," spoke Dunmore, pale but steadfast, whereat Gould instantly sprang before him.

"You, a King's officer, imply that these Yankee militiamen, traders, yokels from the plow, canting, whining Non-

Conformists, without honor, order or discipline, can stand
ten minutes before the regulars?"

"If we elect war," spoke the other gravely, "let us not
commit the prime blunder of despising our enemy. I have
seen much of this provincial militia. There's a hard military task awaiting you at the very best."

"Gad, sir!" cried Gould, "this is unendurable. You
almost throw dirt upon the uniform. I've a mind to call
you out."

"Do it, Gould, or I will," urged the very small ensign."

"Do ye' hear, Dunmore," bawled Gould, red now himself
and his voice rising, "I tell you the honor of the service
is insulted by your vile suggestion. Will you name a second, sir, for that; or must I flip my glove across your
face?"

Herbert had recovered himself completely. He bowed
with stiff dignity to the lieutenant. "If Captain Prothero
were still here, he would testify that I do not shun my
part in affairs of honor.—If within two weeks the Americans
themselves have not answered this point to Lieutenant
Gould's full satisfaction, let him send his second to my
friend Major Pitcairn of the Marines. He will arrange."

Dunmore bowed again, walking out of Province House
with a face that glowed, but never by word or gesture
acknowledging the buzz and titter which was going behind
him.

.   .   .   .

My Lord Percy, being a gentleman as well as a nobleman,
and having seen his mission prosper, went next to no small
pains to soothe the wounded feelings of his military chief,
and to convince General Gage that the latter had been
himself just on the edge of a summary blow against the
rebels. The two high officers continued closeted for over
an hour. They turned over many confidential reports, con-

sulted maps, drew up and modified several lists of officers—all the time conversing in so low a tone that any traitorous eavesdropper could have caught nothing.

When the business had been concluded, and Gage had drafted certain orders in his own hand to avoid calling in a secretary, he unlocked a private door in the rear of the office, saying, "Pass out this way, my Lord, without having to face the questioning of all those subalterns in the ante-room." However, just as the two stepped into a secluded corridor, there was a flutter of silks and crinoline, and the passage was darkened by the ample figure of a woman. Instantly Percy's hand went to his breast as he made a genteel London congé, and the lady responded with an unusually deep curtsy.

"Oh! la, my Lord," she ejaculated, in a slightly affected voice. "You and the general have been closeted together in that murky cabinet until your heads must swim. Now I can hold you to your promise."

"Promise, promise, my dear Mrs. Gage?" spoke Percy with another profound salutation. "I do not wholly recollect."

"Your Lordship is like all other men," she giggled. "Who can complain of broken lovers' oaths when easier pledges are slipped so lightly?—Why, I mean the promise you gave me last week when you left us in such haste,—that at your next visit to Province House you would honor my tea table."

The nobleman frowned slightly, "For proper reasons, dear Madam, I must not mingle in company this afternoon. The general will confirm me. I cannot dally in a crowded parlor."

Mrs. Gage repeated her laugh, "Oh la! my Lord:—then this is the best possible time. I am quite alone—not even my inseparable Mlle. Rivoire, no one present. I can have you all to myself—only half an hour please?"

His Lordship glanced toward his Excellency. Truth to tell, there was nothing more to be done immediately. Mrs. Gage's tea was always refreshing. He felt a trifle tired. A third time his hand pressed his breast: "In that case your wish is my pleasure. Egad! Those rebels deserve double halters for wasting so good a thing as good tea."

So in a few moments the inner dining room witnessed Mrs. Gage, a stoutish, puffy, graying-blonde woman of uncertain age and a perpetual smile, enjoying the extreme satisfaction of sitting tête-à-tête with a great English nobleman. Not that she was anything but a lady born, for her father, Peter Kemble had been President of the Council of New Jersey; but then, heirs to the Northumberlands do not grace American tea tables every day. She was in a happy mood therefore when the resplendently liveried black brought in a tall silver tea-urn, dropped within it a red-hot weight, and forthwith produced the noise of a jovial boiling.

Soon his Lordship's India-china cup was in his hand, and he was professing that Province House hyson was "equal to any he had drunk at Marlborough House," while the general was saying, "You may fill again, my dear." All three in fact were feeling somewhat happy, Mrs. Gage because of her aristocratic company, her husband because he had finally screwed himself to a firm decision and believed he had found a way for a remarkable blow against the rebels, Percy because he had finally induced the senior general to resolve on that which for months all the rest of Loyalist Boston had counted necessary.

The talk therefore was merry. Much badinage passed between the noble lord and the lady as to the certainty that Mlle. Rivoire would finally accept Claypool—Major Upson's attentions had been dauntless and constant. Finally, however, Mrs. Gage brought the subject around to the rebels, the stories of their musters, and the great pity that nothing had been done to stop them:

"Oh! do you, my Lord, try *your* eloquence upon the general to get to order something to end this disgraceful truce. *I've* said all that *I* can—and you see how little power we poor wives have!"

. . . . The tea, I repeat, was very good. Even the negro had disappeared from the room. His Lordship, to repeat once more, was somewhat happy and in a mood for a little harmless boasting. He let his cup be filled a third time, and partook of some excellent seed cakes. Across the table Gage now was smiling complacently.

"Ah! dear Madam," confessed Percy with a polite sigh, "now I have the secret of my good fortune to-day. It was your argument that had prepared the way for me. Something *shall* be done against the rebels.—Of course I can trust to your absolute discretion."

"Absolute discretion," avowed the lady, toying no longer with the silver tea-caddy.

"Then, my dear Mrs. Gage, as a great state secret—a little event is being prepared for our Whig friends to-morrow night."

Mrs. Gage gave a great giggle, and leaned across the table, with a face of delighted inquiry. . . .

. . . The next morning a packet from General Gage, endorsed *"Highly confidential, to be opened only after sunset,"* was placed in the hands of Colonel Francis Smith of the Tenth Regiment.

CHAPTER XXXIV

ABOUT eleven o'clock upon April the eighteenth, two adjutants of Paul Revere, jobless ship-carpenters now putting in their time in somewhat desultory spying, witnessed Hope Fifield descending from the paternal chariot at the door of M. Georges Rivoire.

They had sought their chief at the Green Dragon, and missing him there were loitering before his residence. Both scowled as they saw the daughter of the great Tory alighting.

"I'd like to get that father of hers," growled the one, "near the tar bucket and feather-bed."

"And I'd like to get that big-eyed French gossip of hers on the old ducking stool," added the other. "Them 'ere frog-eating parleyvousers can't be patriots no-how. A gushy Whig until the scarlet-coats struck the town, and *then* see how she's made the epaulets all run a'ter her!—But we've got to find Paul. Real news. All the warships' boats are lowered and trailing under their sterns. Don't that mean a moving of troops? And a lot of grenadier and infantry companies are being called off regular duty."

Heedless of sour looks Hope Fifield was soon past Berthe and up into her friend's little boudoir. Emilie had been washing her hair, cleansing it of that great mass of white powder that fashion demanded for all formal gatherings. Now it spread out in a confusion of red gold all over her shoulders as she moved about in cloudy dishabille. Hope, as a passionately adoring friend was fain to embrace and kiss her, and make her standard remark—that the young

men would be more desperate about her than ever after the
coming drum; which was to be given this time by the Fusileers at Hancock House, a mansion promptly commandeered
as Lord Percy's as soon as its owner disappeared from
Boston.

Emilie flung down the bracelet which she had been testing upon her arm, in disgust; "Oh, if you love me give a
truce to such speeches! Is it not bad enough to have poor
Sir Francis and all the others vaporing compliments in my
ear and know the emptiness of it all, and how I am deceiv-
ing them? I can't endure another assembly. I'll get up a
headache and go to bed; I vow I will. I can never last
until the summer. The fun and excitement are all *fini*.
I am *fatigué* to death. I've told Dr. Warren enough. I'll
escape to Redford, and cry to Roger, 'Marry me!'—After
that——"

"Hist!" ordered Hope, her black eyes like sparks; "you'll
not drop the game now—when we've got to play for the
greatest stakes of all?"

"Greatest of all, *ma chère*—What's befallen?"

"Know then," pursued Hope, "that something big, very
big, is in the air. Last night father had Captain Prothero
home to supper. They talked much, drank much, boasted
much. It seems that they both, along with Colonel Smith
and Lord Percy himself had waited on the general. They
urged a great blow against the rebels. The general hesitated. Dear Herbert Dunmore was present and pleaded
desperately for delay, but at last Gage was overborne by
Percy's avowing that even the King was angered at the
present inactivity. Then the general promised a stroke of
'merciful severity' against the rebels—to be taken right
away."

Emilie was plaiting her hair with swift, nervous fingers.

"Right away? You make my heart turn over—But what is this stroke?"

"That, father and Prothero do not know themselves. They left the general in private conference with Percy."

Emilie was thrusting in pins, and settling a great carved comb with desperate precision, "So many things could be done! Perhaps to seize Salem, Marblehead and the other ports and quite seal up the province. I've heard that talked of.—Perhaps to rush all the Boston Whigs on shipboard as hostages for the loyalty of their friends outside."

"Either of these things, or even a march on Concord where the patriot supplies are gathered. Or something else. Oh, you must help, right away!" In her fears and excitement Hope found herself clinging fast to her companion's arm.

The other put her by with a laugh and a kiss; "If it were only a matter of silly boys like Claypool or Upson I could twist it all out of them in half an hour. But the general and his Lordship—very different. I cannot promise.—With time, perhaps; but 'right away'?—The words are bad."

"The fate of the cause, of America.—I know by father's words the general has resolved upon some fearful, cruel thing. You are so wise, so clever! You *must* find out."

Emilie administered what was almost a savage shake. "Hope Fifield," she commanded, speaking rapidly, "dry your eyes like a Christian girl. Tears don't help my brain to work. Get word to Dr. Warren that something serious seems afoot, and for Paul and all the rest to be alert.—I'd not planned to go to Province House to-day. I'd promised the boys of the forty-third that if the weather was fine I'd watch their bowling on the Common.—I've changed my mind. There's one chance, a poor one, but a chance. I'll go to Province House.—Now leave me. I need all my time."

Mrs. Gage loved to play the gracious hostess at the seat of power. The general was extremely busy that afternoon, but a good fraction of the officers' corps attended her levee, along with a large sprinkling of the Tory Very Respectables. It did not lessen the pleasures of the gathering that the beautiful Mlle. Rivoire herself (in a close-fitting, blue walking toilette, adorably plain and envied by all the women), sat behind one of the huge tea-urns. Flip, arrack or punch were duly provided, but all the holders of his Majesty's commissions for once preferred hyson. There was, however, a hardly suppressed groan of dissatisfaction from a dozen resplendent subalterns when a good half hour before the usual time Mademoiselle arose, smiled, curtsied, made room for a much more elaborately gowned young lady, and followed Mrs. Gage up the great staircase of Province House.

"My dear," spoke that gentlewoman, the instant they were in her private withdrawing room, "what good fortune! I *had* to get you away as quickly as possible. You told me your new French patterns would not come for another two weeks."

"They were sent by a droll mistake to New York," said Emilie, unwrapping a large paper packet, "but the ship made an excellent passage thither. So yesterday they came up with the post-rider."

"My dear," continued Mrs. Gage, "every day my wonder at your talent grows. Even for a French woman you are a marvel. To think that to all your other accomplishments you should add 'paper-cutting'—papyrotamia I think they call it."

Emilie smiled demurely: "My mother was favored with

the friendship of Madame Delaney, so famous for her sil-
houettes. As a young girl once I learned a little."

"A little!—Which means that you do it marvelously."

Emilie merely spread out her patterns upon the broad
table, produced a pair of very sharp scissors, and saying
that next time she would bring the projecting machine,
which by candle-light cast a sitter's profile upon a sheet of
paper, she next began initiating the older lady into the art
of producing "spruce trees twined with roses," and land-
scapes showing whole farmsteads, with foliage, persons and
cattle. Mrs. Gage was delighted. She proved a reasonably apt pupil, and before long began blessing Emilie
afresh for "giving her something to occupy her mind on a
terribly anxious, nervous day."

"Anxious and nervous, dear Mrs. Gage? I'm sure you
startle me. The general surely is well; no bad news, I hope,
from England?"

"Oh, no, my dear; nothing like that I promise you."

"Then no doubt some other family of poor, peaceful
Loyalists has been forced to flee into Boston to escape the
Whig mobs. Your heart always bleeds for them."

"None came to-day. A great relief."

"Then I'm afraid that still another nice young officer
ruined himself last night at hazard. *Ma foi!*—if I only
could make them heed my sermons. I know how both you
and the general are distressed at such disasters."

"No, something very different. Something you could
never guess."

Mrs. Gage looked at her visitor as if expecting the pleasure of answering a curious question with a mysterious "I
can't tell you." Emilie calmly began, however, on a design
of a dancing girl leaping over a flower-chain, with the
shading brought out by finely cut lines. Mrs. Gage admired,
interfered, imitated awkwardly, fidgeted:

"It's terrible to have something on your mind which you must not tell. Not that it would matter now probably if I told—still I said to his Lordship——"

Emilie burst into a laugh like a musical brook. *"Oh, ma chère madame!*—Lord Percy has told you 'in the strictest confidence' that his aide Captain Bedlow is engaged to Sally Oliver.—Why, all we youngsters have known it for a good three weeks. How droll of his Lordship to pretend any secrecy about *that!"*

Mrs. Gage fidgeted still more, and kept glancing at the tall clock ticking solemnly in a corner of the withdrawing room. "Half past five," she presently mused aloud, "and Colonel Smith will begin calling out his grenadiers and light infantry as soon as it gets fairly dark."

"I never knew them to drill before after sundown," submitted Emilie between her snippings; "still no doubt it's sometimes necessary."

The older lady's countenance must have greatly resembled an amiable petard determined to explode: "Of course you are quite one of us. That is you are as good as contracted to Frank Claypool. I'd tell his Lordship if he taxed me——"

"Pray, don't indulge in confidences, dear Mrs. Gage,—that is, if you really feel it would be wrong."

"Well, you really have the right to know. It now makes very little difference. In a few hours the troops are well off and the thing's done.—Botheration—all the servants, everybody else is out of hearing—I can't hold in any longer. —Have been dying to tell some one all day."

"Of course if confiding in me makes you happier, I'd not mind hearing; but pray don't think me inquisitive." Emilie laid down her scissors and began inspecting the pattern of a girl driving a flock of geese.

"Well then—here it is. All Boston will rattle about it

to-morrow morning, anyway. To-night, after it gets real dark, Colonel Smith and Major Pitcairn will take most of the grenadier and light infantry companies from the different regiments, some seven or eight hundred men, and start for Concord. Some officers in disguise have already been sent out to watch the roads. The rebel supplies are there and they'll of course seize and burn 'em. Then Lexington's on the way, and the general has got word that those dreadful scoundrels, Sam Adams and John Hancock, are staying at Mr. Clark the minister's house. They're to be snapped up and persuaded back to Boston.—You see the whole thing's so sudden and secret the rebels won't know what's happened until their leaders are ironed and their arms destroyed. His Lordship assured me there could be no real fighting. 'Just a little push of bayonets,' said he, 'or at worst a few volleys in the air—then the whole thing is mercifully over. These Yankee peasants have no discipline.' "

Emilie's scissors made a false snip as she tried the new pattern, but she continued her work unremittingly and replied with even accents; "Very interesting. Our young friends, the infantry officers, surely ought now to be happy. What an exciting march for some of them! Of course they'll run no danger."

"None in the least, so the general vowed to me. Your special gallants Claypool and Upson won't go, but there'll be Captain Lowrie and Lieutenant Gould and two or three other of your devoted cavaliers. They'll all be back to-morrow evening to tell their adventures."

"And the Whigs here in Boston," Emilie held her eyes close to the design and puckered her lips with her scrutiny of the papers; "are they going to be left alone?"

"Why, probably not," observed Mrs. Gage, "but I think that Lord Percy and the general agreed there was no hurry about seizing them, until well into to-morrow when the expedition was getting back."

"So kind of you to tell me; that ought to make things here in Boston easier." Mrs. Gage was rather disappointed her friend took her own revelation so much as a matter of course, but Emilie had never seemed to care for politics. And here Mlle. Rivoire laid down her pattern and sighed, "I'm afraid the light has begun to fail—and really I cannot do these properly by candles. If what you've just said doesn't interrupt, to-morrow I must watch the forty-third's bowling. But the day after to-morrow if you do not mind——"

"The day after to-morrow bring all the patterns, my dear, without fail. Then we can hear all about the march to Concord, and perhaps we can see that dreadful Adams and Hancock when they hale them to Province House for examination."

Mlle. Rivoire wrapped up her packet of designs and papers very neatly, declined an urgent invitation to stay for supper, kissed Mrs. Gage deliberately and affectionately. Next she walked with calm dignity past the bowing negro footmen through the entrance of the residence, and passed down the gravel path to Marlborough Street. Then she turned abruptly, looked up through the budding arches of the elms to the fading sunlight beyond, gulped deep, and uttered two words,—*"Grand Dieu!"*

.   .   .   .

Emilie's first impulse, after her heart had ceased leaping, was to run at random, somewhere, anywhere, merely to give respite to her struggling thoughts. She controlled herself enough merely to walk very rapidly toward Hanover Street; so rapidly in fact that she never noticed two fine lieutenants in service uniform, who saluted her ceremoniously while on their way to Colonel Smith's headquarters. Her intercourse with Warren had been of a most clandestine nature, but now everything must be dared. Soon she was beating the knocker to his door, but there opened to her not young Dr. Eustis, as she had hoped, but only the kitchen-faced domestic who cared for the four children and prepared the meals in Warren's widower household.

"Was Dr. Warren at home?"

"No, he had gone out half an hour ago. Sudden call from Mrs. Plimpton over on Pond Street. Dropsy much worse. He took Dr. Eustis with him to help him tap her."

Emilie regretted that feminine prohibitions kept back the luxury of an oath. She knew that Warren had carefully maintained his practice, partly out of duty to his patients, partly to blind the British. Pond Street was well down toward the Neck—Of all places in Boston!

"Would the young lady wait? Would she leave a message?"

"No, there is a chance of catching his curricle upon the streets. I'll leave no message."

But as the door fairly closed, and whilst Emilie stood considering whether to walk to the Plimptons' or to risk some other expedient, a very elegant white-and-blue naval uniform came jauntily along Hanover Street and quite uninvited attached itself to her arm.

"Fie on the army," Prothero's smoothest voice was saying, "to let Miss Rivoire tread Boston highways without escort! What can Upson, Claypool and the rest be doing? —Yet why should I rally them?—The soldier's loss is the sailor's gain!—But do I actually see your ladyship leaving the house of that most equivocal subject of the King, Dr. Warren?"

"My grandfather is very indisposed," Emilie lied bravely. "Dr. Lloyd is in Charlestown on a case and Whig medicine will not poison M. Georges."

"You obtained a remedy then?"

"The vial is in my reticule."

"I congratulate M. Rivoire. They say that Warren is the best physician in the provinces for all his vile principles. And now I also congratulate myself. I can escort a certain estimable lady to her home while she conveys the medicine."

Emilie's sigh of vexation was barely quenched in her throat. Policy absolutely forbade making a scene with him. Prothero hung himself to her despite all efforts to draw away. All the way furthermore she had visions of the old Frenchman himself, brisk and hearty, greeting them at the door. Prothero's talk was sentimental, insinuating, charged with highfalutin gallantry, which was never daunted by his companion's coldness. He improved his opportunity furthermore by walking very slowly despite her attempts to hasten. M. Rivoire, however, was luckily nowhere around his entrance, and Emilie in sheer desperation got rid of her escort by consenting to honor a little supper which he was arranging Saturday upon the *Argus* for various Boston ladies and army gentlemen of her acquaintance.

It was now almost dark. Providence alone knew how long the doctors would be working upon poor Mrs. Plimpton! Even as Emilie listened to Berthe grumbling over her supper tasks in the kitchen, she caught the click of a well-shod charger in the street. Away from his door at the Shaws' rode Major Pitcairn. There was just enough light to know that he had on his service sword, and that the pistol butts were sticking from his hostlers. From North Street came the tramp and rattling arms of little squads of marines, going apparently toward some rendezvous nearer the center of the town.

Time was creeping. Her grandfather was still, presumably, at his office on King Street. Berthe was perfectly

terrified at being abroad in the troop-infested town after
dark, and was an impossible messenger. There was nothing
for it therefore, but for Emilie to go back herself. Taking
a big gray pelisse, pulling up her hood to shield her face,
and telling Berthe (who wondered and sputtered vainly)
that "She hoped to return in about an hour," forth she
went again into the now gloomy ways.

Fortunately by this time she knew all the North End
alleys like a cat. Fortunately, too, better discipline than
sometimes obtained prevailed that night among the soldiery—so many men were being quietly summoned for duty.
Fortunately likewise, Boston folk had learned lately to
keep much within doors after dark. Emilie therefore
reached the Warren house without incident, but her heart
went down again when she noticed only a single light in
a rear window. Her furious knocking brought the old
woman once more to the door.

"No, the doctor had not returned. Was the sickness so
serious? Would not the lady wait this time?"

Mlle. Rivoire this time had no alternative save to wait.
She sat long in semi-darkness, while the enormous Holland
clock by the door to the surgery sounded forth its solemn
"Tick, tick, tick," telling off the transit of mortals through
eternity. What if the doctor had been seized already,
despite Gage's contemptuous dallying? What if the ferry
and the Neck were alike so guarded that no word could
slip out of Boston? What if to-morrow Samuel Adams and
John Hancock lay in Queen Street jail? What if—— A
clatter of hoofs, a rattle of wheels, the sound of a clumsy
carriage stopping at the door; then the hearty voice of
Warren himself, "Put up the horse, Eustis, and meet me
in the surgery."

The voice of an angel could not have been more welcome
to Emilie Rivoire. Warren came leisurely up the steps,

turned to take a glance at the clouds sliding across the newly risen moon, called back to Eustis something about "good weather to-morrow," stepped inside. Emilie had risen to her feet, yet for an instant, thanks to the stress, all her English seemed to forsake her.

"*Vite! Vite! Vite!*" was all she could get across her lips. Warren paused upon his own threshold, pulled off his hat, peered for a moment curiously, then answered with one of his reassuring laughs: " 'Pon my soul 'tis Mlle. Rivoire!—And something tells me with news."

"This way," ordered Emilie, her English tongue returned; "the surgery." And without waiting for candle she dragged him into the little darkened room, and poured out a torrent of words. "Am I too late?" she knew she was demanding at the end.

"Late, but not too late, please God," came Warren's voice, seemingly afar off; then for an instant all turned black around her.

Her next consciousness was that of sitting limply upon a sofa, while Warren with a candle in one hand and a small glass in the other was ordering, "Drink this—you will feel better." Then Eustis was entering, not without wonder, and his superior was commanding, "Go to the Green Dragon and hasten hither with William Dawes and Paul Revere."

. . . Emilie sat in the parlor at Hanover Street while around her moved a sudden, if secretive activity. Her sensations were those of a person who upon pulling some tiny lever sees a vast mechanism beginning its intricate motion, and passing at once beyond all his power and control.

William Dawes came first, a strong-limbed, broad-shouldered fellow turned thirty, with a wide intelligent face. Warren simply told him the news just imparted, and bade him, "Get through the lines at the Neck and do his end

of the business." Out Dawes went into the street and the
night devoured him. He was well known to the sentries at
the Neck and would take his chance of finding a friend upon
sentinel duty. If any could smuggle out by the land route,
he was the man.

But Warren continued pacing the narrow floor of the surgery, until another guarded tap brought through the door
the stalwart form and open countenance of Paul Revere.
The candle-light fell clearly upon the face of the girl as
he entered, and the silversmith recoiled with sheer surprise:
"Emilie Rivoire—that Tory turncoat; and here of all places!
—I'll be damned!"

"Your fair kinswoman," spoke Warren with all his wonted
elegance, "need no longer labor under the distrust of good
Americans. Her service to the cause can be acknowledged
later."

Paul wiped his brow in unfeigned astonishment. "Thank
God, cousin," came from him at last; then gravely he
listened to the doctor's recital of Emilie's story, confirmed
now by many incidental facts collected through the day.

The moment Warren halted, Revere, awaiting no directions, began tightening his belt. "The real call at last,"
he announced composedly, "home now for boots and sur-
tout, and then for Charlestown. Conant there'll be alert for
the signals, and'll have ready Larkin's fast horses."

"All the ferryboats are drawn alongside the *Somerset* in
the fairway, at nine," cautioned Warren.

"I've a skiff against just that tied under Freeman's
wharf. Richardson and Bentley will take the oars, and
we'll risk a shot in the dark from the man-of-war."

It was all spoken as coolly as about an appointment for
clock-repairing, but at the door Revere suddenly turned
about upon his heel; "Cousin Emilie, 'fore God I've been
a blockhead about you.—In proof that I'm forgiven, let me

buss you." And waiting for no consent of hers, he bent and kissed her forehead resoundingly. "Take *that* from an honest kinsman!" Then recollecting further added, "Now shall I convey you back to North Square?"

Warren bowed gallantly, "That, Paul, is now *my* privilege." Whereat Revere with only a "Good luck then to all!" in his turn strode out into the dark.

After that, however, there was still more coming and going. A sea-captain, bluff and burly John Pulling, appeared. To him Warren entrusted the task of ascertaining (what Emilie had been unable to report) whether the troops were departing by the long land route around the Neck, or were being conveyed more directly by boat nearer to Cambridge. It made much difference in the measures taken against them. The great clock ticked calmly on; Emilie sitting in a kind of stupor knew it was stroking half-past ten when Pulling stamped in with his report, "Boats from foot of the Common, I guess to Lechmere Point."

Warren nodded approval, next gave his last order, "To Sexton Newman then, he knows all about the signals." After which he asked "if Mlle. Rivoire felt she now had the strength to walk out in his company?"

Mlle. Rivoire had strength, oh! decided strength. With Pulling hastening on ahead, soon she found herself in the completely deserted streets, flanked only by Warren and Eustis.

The point for the embarkation of the troops was far away. The rest of the garrison presumably were slumbering like gallant warriors. Only before a few of the barracks there was pacing a sleepy sentinel. Most of the scattered street lights had now burned out, but the moon cast its pale yellow panels through the budding trees and athwart the tall chimneys. The three traversed Hanover and Middle Streets

with no greater alarm than from the fleeting shadows of
two chasing cats. At Princess Street Warren momentarily
paused; "You are now near home, dear lady," he stated
politely.

"Home? Now?" returned Emilie, as if home and bed
were the last things she then desired in all the world.

The three therefore turned into the black passages of Hull
Street until before them spread the slopes of Copp's Hill
Burial Ground. The tall slabs stood outlined before them,
as without a word they ascended the peaceful avenues of
the dead. At the highest point they halted. Before their
gaze, with gleaming clearness spread the Charlestown fairway, and in the very center of the channel, swinging slowly
in the young flood tide, with its tracery of spars clearly
silhouetted above the further shores, swung the hull of a
heavy man-of-war, the *Somerset;* a few lanterns glinting
here and there from the black mass of her mighty batteries.
Behind the three watchers rose the houses of the town,
ghostly and calm. Around were the silent graves, wherein
slept the Mathers and many another of the great and good
of Massachusetts.

The glance of the three went next to the lofty tower of
Christ Church, a prime landmark of Boston. There it
stood with upward pointing finger,—a monument to the
peace that reigned in the silent, star-spread heavens. Its
entire tall fabric was dark. Warren looked well about him,
then dropped his eyes to the serried array of graves. "Be
witness, Saints of New England," he spoke so softly that
Emilie barely heard him, *"we, your children, keep the
Faith."*

Dimly across the stretch of the waters came the sentry's
call from the poop of the *Somerset:* "Eleven o'clock and all
is well." Even as the clock bells from the different Boston
churches came through the darkness in different cadence

answering him, Emilie clutched Warren's arm, "See!" and they all pointed together to the fairway; a boat was gliding with swift, vigorous strokes directly across to Charlestown. The oars apparently had been muffled, but either the sentinel was dozing again or he had received no orders to halt such navigation.* Contrary to what the three dreaded, there was neither hail nor musket-shot when the skiff sped over a peculiarly bright spot in the steel blue water. The craft glided onward as silently as the moonbeams.

Presently the skiff faded into the safety of the Charlestown shore, and their eyes went back to the dim, still tower. Without the signals Revere went upon a crippled errand. They stood in constrained silence for some minutes, Eustis muttering at length that, "Newman had British officers quartered upon him, and couldn't get away from them," and even Warren was making his long delicate hands clinch and unclinch nervously; then from them all issued the simultaneous "Ah!"—High up in the black tower, well above the glorious chimes there was a gleam; now beside it, distinct, separate, flashed a second gleam. The sexton had done his work.

Warren heaved a deep sigh, and again drew off his hat; "We of Boston have now done that which we can," he spoke now firmly aloud. "The future belongs to God and to America."

. . Two little candle dips winking, winking out into the chill April night. No throngs to witness, only a few tense watchers below, and perchance a few more unseen in distant Charlestown. Yet there will be those to say that the tiny fires will never be put out; through year and decade and century their light will gleam, will brighten, will pass

*Later tradition affirmed that five minutes after Revere's skiff passed the *Somerset*, orders were sent aboard the warship to stop all boats going to Charlestown.

over Middlesex, over Massachusetts, southward, westward,
across warm savannahs and teeming prairies, across august
rivers and imperial mountains, until their beams glitter
with noon-day strength at last upon that western ocean
whereof the folk of Old Boston had barely heard the name.
—Since the star of the Magi hung above Bethlehem has
ever shone beacon charged with more fateful portent!

.   .   .   .

Emilie let the others escort her home at length, but in
no wise to sleep. The immensity of the thing she had been
permitted to do, the dim vastness of the deeds invoked overwhelmed her. Despite vivid talk overheard between Warren and his friends, many of the things pending were still
wrapped in awful mystery. She knew that Revere had sped
on no errand of peace, and that Roger Gilman might any
hour be standing face to face with those gallant, boyish
officers whereof she had learned to like so many, if her love
had gone to none.—The night passed amid one procession
of lurid, waking dreams.

Very early she was in the streets, telling her grandfather
and Berthe frankly how she had spent the night, for all
her subterfuge at last was gone. The ways were full of
troops on quick-step toward the Common. "An expedition had set out during the night," everybody was telling
everybody else, "and now my Lord Percy was mustering
to take out reënforcements—of course only a precaution."
Civilians were flurrying about distractedly. There was a
story that somebody had arrived from Lexington with
"fearful news." "Fearful," but nobody knew precisely
what it was.

Instinct took her to the Charlestown ferry. It was again
running, despite the *Somerset* in the stream and a corporal
and six men hitching their belts and shifting their muskets
nervously upon the dock. A boat was ready, and many

passengers were stepping aboard. Women were taking anxious leave of husbands or brothers, who were tense and excited: *"Something had happened."* As Emilie approached a rider came down the slip upon horseback, leaped down nimbly, and approached the ferry leading his steed. The craft was already well loaded, but at sight of the newcomer there was a general squeezing and making of room. Warren guided his horse aboard, then lingered for a last word with Eustis.

"Look to my patients and get out when you can," she heard him saying in his most collected manner. "My duty is no more in Boston. The Lexington tidings are just confirmed. Keep up brave hearts. They have begun it—either side can do that. We will end it—that only one can do."

Heedless of witnesses Emilie forced her way to the doctor's side. "You are going to my betrothed," she said, all red but speaking steadily. "Tell him—tell him I have done all I can for our America, and I will come to him as soon as it is the good God's will."

Warren without a word, bent, lifted her hand and kissed it. So might a duke have saluted a princess. His hat swept off to his friends, then he leaped upon the ferryboat just as the hawser plashed into the harbor. The big sail promptly caught the wind, and the heavy craft was beyond musket shot from the quay when a mounted subaltern pounded down over the cobbles and planking, flourishing a paper before the idling corporal: "Orders from Province House, the general himself—to seize that rebel doctor, Warren, if he tried to take the ferry!"

"The devil!" swore the corporal, waving his fist toward the boat. "There he goes now. Three minutes earlier, sir —but they're clean across now before we can get word out to the *Somerset.*"

"Not my fault," growled the ensign, "I rode my best.

Everything's delayed this cursed morning. Seems as if Percy never would get started. But it's all the same. The troops will nip Warren and every other vile Whig by nightfall."

Emilie saw the boat touch the Charlestown ferry slip and scatter her living freight. A moment later a platoon of marines swung down upon the quay, ejecting the bystanders with their musket butts. The Charlestown ferry had been closed for a twelve month.

. . . Rumor on rumor, and never had Boston seen day like this.—The shops were barricaded, the schools were closed with a "War's begun and school's done," proclaimed by pale and excited masters to even more pale and excited pupils. Women alternately shivered behind barred doors, or raced in reckless bevies along the streets.

About noon the fell stories became more definite: "Yes, there certainly had been firing at Lexington and many persons killed. Of course the regulars had swept all before them." Yet the feeling was getting out that not all the killing had been done by the regulars, although how could there be the least doubt of the result, seeing that at nine o'clock Lord Percy himself had led out nearly the entire first brigade to reënforce Colonel Smith?

"Needless precaution," avowed young Claypool in Mlle. Rivoire's presence. "Damme, if Smith isn't a fat old woman to send back for help just because he heard a bit of noise which showed that the peasants were stirring. But it'll be a jolly march outside this stupid town, and perhaps just a sniff of powder.—Cursed luck that our company was ordered to stay in garrison!"

Emilie never remembered how she answered or bore herself. She knew, as certainly as she knew that it was a very fine April day, that her mask was about to fall, her part in the jumbled drama about to be discovered. Her mood was utterly reckless. For her personally nothing mattered now, nothing. She felt herself a part, a very small part in some mighty, impersonal force which was hurrying Claypool, his comrades, Gage's army, Boston, the Provincials, America, onward, ever onward, toward a goal which she could only glimpse dimly, and with a potence which made them all helpless as the pebbles swept down by the avalanche.

There was no bowling upon the Common that afternoon by the officers of the forty-third. Most of them had marched away with Percy. Another part of the army was standing to its arms by Roxbury Neck. The warships were warping in from the outer harbor. The *Somerset* was being reënforced by several lighter vessels. Emilie saw the *Argus* gliding slowly up to position opposite Charlestown. Her ports were open, her guns run out and her people bustling about their batteries. It was the same with the *Falcon* and the *Lively*.

Presumably Mlle. Rivoire returned home during the day, ate food, conversed with the absolutely demoralized Berthe, and her less terrified but none the less excited grandfather. An armed party called at the house of Paul Revere, flourished a warrant before poor Mrs. Rachel and the squalling children, searched and rummaged shop and dwelling, but went away at last convinced that the desired bird had flown. Emilie fully expected that a patrol would call for her also, but as yet nothing befell. Meeting Eustis upon the street, he assured her that a Province House official was at Warren's dwelling, ransacking desks and bureaus for letters, but was being rewarded only by a great heap of ashes in the fireplace. Newman, the church sexton, had been dragged out of bed and taken to jail. "How came those lanterns?" But his face had been guileless, his protests of ignorance fervent. Before the day was out he was free upon the streets, elbowing with all the news-hungry crowd.

Afternoon wasted into evening. Once more Emilie sought the view toward Charlestown. This time she made for Beacon Hill, going up the slope behind Hancock House. Hundreds of people, townsmen, women, army men off duty, were pushing toward the old beacon where it rose high above the last dwelling. There, after a scramble up cowpaths amid the small cedars and shrubbery, at length before the onlookers stood out Charlestown, the Charles estuary toward Cambridge, and all the retreating slopes of Middlesex against the pellucid April sky.

Emilie found herself yet again with young officers of her acquaintance.—"Yes, there had been something like a skirmish. Not merely at Lexington, but something had befallen nearer Concord. Evidently the peasants had dared to stand their ground a second time.—Just as well.—A thorough lesson was what they needed.—Now the troops were well through with it.—Trust Percy for a proper job.— But what a damned pity to have it all finished, and so many fine fellows of their mess never get even the chance to hear a shot!—Nothing at all to brag about when the rebels have taken their whipping and the regiments all go back to England!"

"And had 'King' Hancock and Mr. Sam Adams been seized?" inquired Mlle. Rivoire very artlessly.

"Why it's uncertain still at Province House," confessed Claypool, "but something seems to have slipped. There's no report at least that they're taken."

"We'll get an express soon," explained a lieutenant at his side. "Of course having dispersed the rebels, Percy will need only to march back slowly. I've heard he intended to halt in Cambridge, and barrack in that ramshackle college there. It's getting dark, and I at least am ready now for supper.—Egad! All've been so cursedly excited that we could hardly eat a bit all day."

"Look!" intervened Claypool, his finger going out toward Milk Row, the low causeway joining Charlestown to the mainland, where Prospect Hill was outlined now against the dimming sky, "What are those? Musket flashes?— But the rebels were dispersed long ago——"

A sullen rattle of what seemed undeniably musketry, now in heavy platoon volleys, now in more scattering but well sustained firing came down over the shallow waters upon the land breeze. The crowds upon the hill suddenly became almost as silent as the tombs below in the Old Burial Ground.—More flashes, more rattling. "Company firing, as I'm a sinner," muttered Claypool through gritted teeth, "and, by gad, something is answering steadily!"

Emilie, like all near her, stood as in a trance, when a hand suddenly touched her shoulder. She turned to see a Captain Osterly, whom she knew very slightly, and behind him were three soldiers.

"Mlle. Rivoire?" Emilie nodded. "My duty is—ahem! —an unpleasant one. Certain suspicions connect you with the traitor Warren. The rebels were evidently alarmed betimes. I'm compelled to conduct you to Province House. Captain Prothero of the navy avers that last night——"

"Before heaven, Osterly," cried Claypool with a clap on his hilt, "what nonsense is this with Mademoiselle? Understand that——"

"That Captain Osterly," completed Emilie, with perfect composure, "is doing his duty as a Briton, as I have done mine as an American.—What was that?"

The flash of a cannon lit the air beyond Charlestown Neck, then a second, followed by the unmistakable roar of two field-pieces. From all the group, Emilie's predicament was momentarily banished by the new quiver of excitement.

"Percy is using his guns," spoke Osterly, unconsciously drawing one of his own pistols, while again the two cannon thundered above the diapason of the muskets. "Can—can it be possible that he's not going to Cambridge? That he's forced to fight his way homeward?"

"Preposterous, the peasants——" began the lieutenant.

"Are impertinent to his Lordship," completed the lady, her countenance glowing.

"A boat is coming from Charlestown," called Claypool, trembling as he gazed. "A man-of-war boat. Pulls as if devils were chasing her. She makes for Barton's Point just at our feet. What can she bring?"

Had Emilie wished to flee her chance was open. Osterly and his three men were hurrying toward the slip with all the others. Her only impulse was to hasten with them. They raced past the long rope-walks and crowded out upon the little quay just as the boat shot up beside it. From across the waters to Charlestown and Cambridge there rolled near and ever nearer the tumult of the running battle, while two sailors lifted upon the dock a portly officer. His regimentals were mud-splashed, his forehead scratched and bloody. The sailors upheld him as he tried to stand despite a gunshot through the leg.

"Colonel Smith!" shouted Claypool and Osterly together, as their ranking officer gazed about dazedly. "What has happened?"

"Get to Province House," spoke Smith thickly, "tell the general—my ammunition and Percy's too is nearly spent. —Another three miles would have done us all.—And for God's sake hurry the gun-boats down Charlestown Neck, and rush a strong relief over to cover the retreat!"

He collapsed in sheer faint from weariness and loss of

blood. The din of a thousand muskets pealing across the still waters drowned the horrified murmurs of those who heard him. Osterly at length recovered himself enough to touch Emilie's arm again: "My painful duty still remains. Will you go with me to Province House?"

Emilie held her head high, her eyes burned with fearless excitement, her voice was shrill. "My part is done, henceforth my friends *over there*," she pointed to the spits of fire all along Milk Row, "will speak for me!"

CHAPTER XXXV

MID-APRIL had come and gone and still no clash of arms. The Provincial Congress had adjourned from Concord on the fifteenth, apparently expecting a long, desperate war with Britain, yet with no real treasury but the good will of the people, not a soldier in actual service, only sixteen poor cannon, and hardly powder enough for a decent sham battle, no executive but the Committee of Public Safety, no military staff, no commander-in-chief for the campaign.— A supreme act of faith, you say? Yes, I assent, and in addition *too* great a trust in the mercy of Providence for America's safety unless Providence were extraordinarily good humored!

Nevertheless certain extra precautions were being taken. The possibility of a raid upon Concord against all our precious stores was rising in many minds. After all, the supplies were within half a day's march from Boston, and Lancaster or Worcester would be a great deal safer. I attended the last meeting of the Committee upon the seventeenth, and when it adjourned to Menotomy the removal of the stores had already begun. A great mass of papers needed recopying, and I could do this best on my own table at Redford. So I drove in Mr. Hancock's chariot as far as Lexington, left that gentleman and Samuel Adams at the Clarke house, and walked alone, with my big portfolio, home to the parsonage.

The work had been close and unemotional. Hancock had yawned many times as the carriage lumbered over the bad road. Adams had tried to tell a rather pointless story of a very verbose minister. We were all still very zealous for the cause, but then again we were equally human. The truce with Gage in Boston had lasted so long that somehow almost every one of us hugged halfway the fond notion that no fool would break it. Every order, every sermon addressed to us had enjoined, "The British must fire the first." An attack upon Boston nobody planned. And now as time stretched on, plenty of good Whigs whispered at work, at the tavern, on the return from the meeting house, "Gage won't dare do a thing. We'll face him down without a shot." The advices Warren sent out from Boston hardly confirmed this, nevertheless the lull had relaxed a little the thews of everybody.

At Redford on the eighteenth I found myself vexed with a horrid headache—too many of Yetmercy's doughnuts, perhaps, for supper after arrival. In the morning I sat over my table until my head reeled, then concluded that Massachusetts could survive until my brain cleared. It was an ideal April day in an unwontedly early season. The maples were very red, the grass was springing tall, the frost had long fled the ground, the great Redford trees were musical with birds. I would have given the gold of the Indies for a walk with Emilie through the green fairyland down to the river.

That being impossible, notwithstanding my headache I devoted myself to mother. She, dear soul, despite wars and rumors of wars, had just indulged in the neighborhood excitement of a "Whang,"—namely a cooperative housecleaning up and down our part of the village, when all the good women got together, and cleaned house by house seriatim, like so many hostile castles to be wrenched from the moth and spider, working from cellar to garret as might a well trained army. I had remonstrated earlier, but she

had said that, "If anything dreadful *should* happen, to know
the spring cleaning was over with would be a great relief
to her mind." And the "Whang" had proceeded with all
its dusty energy.

This fortunately had been while I was at Concord, but
now mother was indefatigably attacking her garden. Ishmael being very busy with a new calf, I went to her assistance, and weeded and scratched and grubbed for her, helping her to prepare new beds for white satin, hollyhocks and
gilly-flowers, and to cultivate her sweet briars and patience
roses.

All this made mother very happy. She toiled and dug
beside Tabby and me, humming little catches from "Old Sir
Simon the King" and "Bobbing Joan" and like songs, and
enjoying herself so much that I got her to laughing merrily
by insisting that she looked so young and fetching that
everybody would take her merely for Tabby's elder sister.
Then late that afternoon an enormous flock of pigeons
darkened the sky, and presently we had all to run down
into the back pasture where they were alighting in such
numbers as veritably to break down the limbs of the trees.
What a whirring, and screaming and shouting when we
routed them off; and without a gun Darius and I knocked
down enough to make Yetmercy promise us an enormous
pigeon pie!

Next some of the young Tylers and Griggses came over,
and I left the last remnants of my headache as we sat
around the dying fire and killed time harmlessly with passing a shilling at up-Jenkins. Finally I walked home with
Martha Tyler, trying to be very polite to her, although
nothing more.—In two months that cursed compact Emilie
had made with Warren would end, and after that, come
peace, come war, I intended to do all the spy-work needful
for the family.

Thanks to the violent housecleaning, his bedroom had been changed about, and Darius slept upon the little trundle-bed that was thrust in the daytime under my own. I had a long brotherly altercation with him that night as to why he was too young to 'list in the company, although he was much taller than the Updike twins who were three years his senior. Unconvinced by my dicta he at last climbed under his sheets muttering.

As for me after the candle was out, I lay awake some time going over a certain paper which Mr. Hancock had asked me to draft the next day. Then it seemed as if I were presently out in a sunny meadow watching two cats. They were creeping through the grass nearer, nearer, their eyes fastened upon each other, until within striking distance each poised for a spring. I could see the coiling energy all through their frames as they crouched motionless save for the least wriggling of their tails. They waited and waited, and presently one cat seemed to wear a red coat, the other a blue checked shirt and homespun. Out of their paws protruded muskets. Then of a sudden the red-coated tabby flung herself in the air, the homespun flew to meet her. They grappled amid a rending yowl and din—and din there was, and Darius was tugging at my nightgown.

"Roger—Roger—the bell—something has happened!"

I sat bolt upright in the bed. Chill bars of moonlight were falling across the counterpane. Beyond a doubt the meeting-house bell was fairly tumbling around its wheel.

"There may be a fire," cried I, "but it may be——"

Outside in the street we heard a horse coming on at speed. He swung into the yard and the rider, not quitting the saddle, bawled out like a trumpet: "It's I, Ben Tidd from Lexington. Cap'n Parker sent us up. Revere and Dawes are in from Boston. The regulars are out—seven

hundred for Concord. Get the word through the village.
I'm on to Merriam's Corner."

"Are Adams and Hancock safe?" called father's voice
from his window.

"Safe and sound," came back from Tidd. "We're getting
'em off to Burlington."

The hoofs clattered away in the distance. I was out of
bed while Darius fumbled around and struck a light.
Candles were already shining in the windows across the
street. The bell continued to clash and boom like mad,
while from the tavern came loud reports as Landlord Fitch
was evidently letting off his big horse pistol. Mechanically
I was putting on my clothes, quite properly I imagined,
until Darius suddenly humiliated me by remarking, "Your
shirt's on hindside before." I was too dumbfounded even
to fetch him a blow for his rudeness. Downstairs I heard
Yetmercy stirring the fire with fury, clattering about and
hurling shrill mandates to Ishmael, and then at length
mother's firm voice directing her, "Don't act so like a hen
with her head cut off," and next arranging everything composedly and bringing calm out of the tempest.

It still lacked an hour of the first dawn. I took up a
candle and waved it about the room. *My* room with all the
dear, homely, familiar things I had accumulated since I was
a little boy. For no particular reason whatever my glance
fell upon an excellent fish-line wherewith I had once caught
an unusually large perch directly under the eyes of Emilie.
Somebody seemed to be saying right across my shoulder,
"Perhaps you will never see that fish-line again!" The
whole thing seemed unearthly, like a walking dream.

I fully expected to wake a second time and find myself
still in bed, with Darius ordering, "Stop that nightmare!"
—Nothing of the kind. I went down stairs, and found the
house for once lit brightly with a profusion of candles.

Even the august "best room" was ablaze. Tabby had lighted every taper, because (as she later confessed) "She felt she simply *had* to do something."

Mother and father were dressed and waiting for me. My knapsack was already on the chair by the door and Yetmercy kept running in and explaining, "We'll pack it just as soon as those eggs boil hard." Father himself brought out my gun,* snapped the lock several times, cleaned the hole to the pan with a splinter and said, "I'll screw in a new flint." The cartridges had been made up, but were to be distributed from the meeting house.—And all the time the bell kept clanging as if possessed, while far away now, from the direction of Carlisle, came the sound of signal guns—passing the summons from farm to farm.

I slung the musket over my back and began to buckle on my belt. A great comfort was possessing me, after all I was simply the lieutenant. Ours was a small company. Harter was a brave cool man, and well able to command now without assistance. The responsibility for the day's work must be his. I need answer only for myself.

"You'd better go to the muster," mother said with perfect steadiness. "Of course we'll all come to see you off—we won't talk now."

But hereupon up the gravel we heard a running, and into the door scurried little Sim Harter, the captain's eldest. "Where,—where's Lootenant Gilman?" he demanded, panting for breath, and blinking at the candles.

"Here I am, Sim," spoke I, "but what's the message?"

"Please, oh, please, sir. Father's powerful sorry, but he split his foot yesterday afternoon chopping. It's all swelled. Tried hard, but can't get on his boot. *You've got to lead the company.*"

*In the 1770's British and American officers of the lower ranks carried muskets very much as did the privates.

I saw all those candles going round and round. Doubtless I turned ghastly. The next thing I knew mother's hand was tight in mine, and her head was on my shoulder. "You can do it, boy," she said in her brightest voice. "No Gilman ever shirked a responsibility. You can do it. Now you go and answer that big Percy."

My vision cleared. I did not try to speak, but while I stood by the door Tabby made a dreadful clatter in the best room, then came flurrying out with Uncle Waitstill's great sword, and snapped its rings upon my belt. "A captain wore it before," cried she, "and a captain shall wear it again!" And with that, and with one hard glance to right and left around the old house, I strode out to the rendezvous.

It was still pitch dark with only the slightest hinting of light in the east, but overhead the birds were now awake and robin was calling to robin. All Redford, man, woman and child, seemed headed toward the rallying spot at the great oak by the road, where the Concord way branches off from that to Billerica. There were plenty of torches, much forced laughter, much loud talking, and somewhere out of sight a girl was weeping violently. About half of the minutemen were already standing in an irregular line, and the rest were straggling in, one by one, from the more distant farms. I strode out before them, unslung and grounded my firelock, then in the best tones which I could summon, announced that Captain Harter being unfortunately disabled, and another leader impossible to obtain at such short notice, the command necessarily fell to me, and therefore, " 'Tention company, Sergeant Hooper will call the roll!"

The darkness was to me a blessing. It concealed any pallor in my cheeks. If my knees were quivering strangely I alone knew it. Hooper doubtless sought relief by calling off his list with more than his wonted energy. He stopped from time to time as one man after another came running out of the darkness.

No hanging back. Barring the captain, every one of the five-and-forty was at last in the line which faced me under the torches and lanterns. Behind, peering out of the gloom, shone the faces of the older men and women, doubly pale now from the dimness and excitement. In this respite I recovered myself. My knees ceased quivering. In better voice than before I ordered, "File right to the meeting house," and off we marched, escorted by the lanterns and the great trailing crowd.

Before us, sepulchral and dim, with the black glare coming back from its broadsides of windows rose the huge bulk of the meeting house. The door was already open, and Purdy, the second sergeant, stood on the horseblock beside a great basket. Everybody knew what he was passing out to each man of the company; six-and-thirty precious cartridges, to be sent ere nightfall against King George's troops, or all Redford would rise to learn the reason why. The forced laughter had ceased. There had been plenty of "alarm musters" before but this was different—so different!

Now the light was strengthening in the east. The tracery of the elms, the long ridge-pole of the meeting house stood out against a cloudless sky which was fast changing from black violet to dim blue. Purdy handed to me my own cartridges last of all. I placed them in my pouch as he slung his firelock, then he made his best salute, "All distributed, Cap'n." While Hooper saluted likewise with "All present or accounted for."

"Break ranks," I ordered.

. . . In a voice needlessly gruff, I commanded Darius (scowling with vexation because he could not go) to "get

mother and the cows down into the woods if the British
went back through Redford." I told Yetmercy to be very
kind to the new family of kittens. I enjoined Tabby to
help mother finish the garden. But to father and mother,
somehow I could say not one word. Father laid his hand
on my head and spoke gently, "Would God I could go with
you, my son." Mother touched my face once, and whispered, "You've always been a good boy, Roger, and I know
you'll be a good boy to-day." Then I was brought back to
my duty by hearing low a "boohoo" from somewhere among
the women. The old sword slid out of its sheath, and I
strode out before the meeting house with a strident, "Fall
in, company!"

If ever man strove, I strove then to stand straight, tall
and collected before the little files which broke from the
crowd behind and stepped into place before me. Hooper
and Purdy saluted again with a "Company ready for duty,
sir," then Toby Emmet ruffled the drum, and I tried to
make a dignified flourish with the sword. "The men of the
company know me," spoke I, "and I know them. The
time for fine speeches is past. We go to Concord for the
honor and safety of Redford, of Massachusetts, of America.
Those whom we leave here will never be ashamed of the
account we shall give.—Now Dr. Gilman."

Father stepped to my side. The men grounded their arms
and pulled off their hats. Father's prayers had been
counted marvels of eloquence through the countryside—
great resonant words, which must have beaten open the
portals of Heaven however they shot over the heads of
men. But now he chose the simplest words and very few.
Twice his voice broke and he ended quite abruptly: "And
the God of Abraham, Isaac and Jacob, of Gideon and
David, of the Prophets, the Apostles and the Saints who

builded New England, be with you all and make strong your hands,—and bring you back to us. Amen."

. . . "Shoulder arms! March!" I ordered, just as the first bars of dawn shot up behind the meeting house. A kind of murmur and sighing came from all the watching people, but we turned neither to the right hand nor the left. Emmet began pounding with the drum. "Must! must! —must! must must!" it seemed to go. We went down the dear familiar street, and past all the great solemn houses, not one man speaking a word. Then Horace Trimble commenced squealing with his fife. He played very poorly but even his disastrous notes took our minds from weightier matters.

We got fairly out of the village and everybody breathed a sigh of relief. The worst seemed over. It was six good miles to Concord and we must not be too tired when we got there. I therefore allowed the men to break ranks and march at ease. The fifer used up his breath presently, but the drum continued its monotonous "Must! must! must!" and so we marched on into the dawn.

What a morning it was, and how fair can be a New England April when in its gracious moods! The air was warming rapidly, and told of the joy of living. All around was youthful light and youthful greenery. Now we were tramping along one of the brooks fairly wakened from its winter bondage, and very fussy, purling and chattering. The water maples were flinging out their crimson tassels; the catkins had puffed huge on all the willows, and out of the dancing water were just peeping the green blades of the sweet flag. I saw the bobolinks rising from their new homes out in the meadows, and the other birds seemed passing us along from one choir within the green archways to another.—Never a day of more surpassing beauty, and here we were marching forth to stake our all—even life itself, in mortal combat with the soldiers of the greatest government upon the earth.

I looked upon the men. They were marching doggedly, with a set look and hardly talking at all. I knew every one of them they were friends, neighbors, playmates, not waifs and idlers as so many in the Boston garrison, who had taken the King's shilling and tossed off the enlistment cup at the Crown and Mitre, because peaceful life had looked very dubious; but quiet, toiling farmers, who had never heard a shot fired in anger, to whom "war" was still only a horrid name, and whose women-folk were just left behind them.

I was their captain now. They were bound (if discipline held) to obey even if I ordered them to certain death. Their mothers, wives and sweethearts all would demand of the "how" if any failed to come back.—And we untrained, pacific men were marching straight against those steel-and-scarlet regiments which had humbled the proudest of France·and Spain. We had got to face them, defeat them, accomplish "the impossible." If we failed therein, all the proud words touching "American liberty" were like the thin mists then dissolving over the meadows.—The inequity, the iniquity of the thing almost made me cry out with pain.

On, on we went, by the farms of Shady Hill, with the big, peaceful cows gazing curiously over the fences at the unwonted sight of forty-five men marching rapidly along the Concord road. As we advanced a cart met us, an old white horse was being driven by a very old man, and an equally old woman was beside him. The cart was piled with hastily collected family gear, and the woman clutched a bag whence projected the head of an enormous gander. The driver pulled up to let us pass, and we saw that he was Sol Mason of North Lexington. "Awful stories from the Center," he flung after us, as we trudged past.

"Didn't you hear them volleys a while ago? We jest hustied all we could upon the cart, turned the cattle loose and are putting for Carlisle." And as we passed, the frightened old woman, holding her head down over the gander, began blubbering big tears.

I slid the sword back into the sheath, unslung my firelock and for the sixth time looked to the priming. A kind of slow, sullen anger was coming up within me.—Were we not a peaceable, home-loving people? Had we asked one boon from England, save to be let alone under the laws our fathers and grandfathers had enjoyed before us? Wherefore should our women be made to weep and we young men to march away to face a thing we hated? Should the offenders escape fearful requital?—Not so if God was just.

"Must! must! must!" again seemed to go the drum.

At last to break the monotony Ozra Bowman (accustomed to lead in church) struck up a psalm-tune. Ozra never had the least discretion. His choice would have dashed the courage of Michael the Archangel:

> "My thoughts on awful subjects roll—
> Damnation and the dead:
> What horrors seize the guilty soul
> Upon a dying bed.
>
> "Then swift and dreadful she descends
> Down to the fiery coast——"

"Hold your jaw," thundered Purdy. "I want some stomach left for fighting." "Give us old seventy-sixth," called somebody from the rear ranks, "that's the real thing now!"

Whereupon, with better wisdom, Bowman resumed to the resonant notes of "Bedford," and we at once began heartily singing together:

"In Judah, God of old is known,
His name in Israel great;
In Salem stood his holy throne,
And Zion was his seat.

From Zion went His dreadful word
And broke the threat'ning spear,
The bow, the arrows and the sword,
And stopped th' Assyrian war.

At Thy rebuke, O Jacob's God,
Both horse and chariot fell!
Who knows the terrors of Thy rod?
Thy vengeance who can tell?

When God in His own sovran ways
Goes down to save th' oppressed,
The wrath of man shall work His praise
And He'll restrain the rest.

The thunders of His sharp rebuke
Our haughty foes shall feel:
For Jacob's God hath not forsook,
But dwells in Zion still."

With the "Amen!" we all felt better. We were getting
over the ground. The morning was beginning to advance;
the warmth to strengthen. Presently the farms were coming more numerous again, but no children scampered now
to the gates to stare at us. The houses looked strangely
deserted—the men we knew had already gone to Concord
with their guns, the women and children were hiding in the
woods. I beckoned the two sergeants nearer to me and
was just asking them how we had better swing the march,
when down the road upon a piebald horse came Corporal
Hunt of Dave Brown's Concord company. He was flourishing a huge pistol, ready cocked, galloped straight up to
us, took a glance at our Redford flag, and then demanded,
"Who's your captain?"

I put my hand on his pommel, and met question with question, "Are the British in Concord?"

"They are," came the answer, "and too many of 'em for us yet to tackle. But Cunnell Barrett sends me to order you to hustle your company across the river and join the muster on the Butterick farm. And after that—the Lord march with us!"

"Must! must! must!" went the drum, while our strides grew longer and longer.

CHAPTER XXXVI

WE mustered upon the little hill about a quarter of a mile beyond the North Bridge by Concord. The British were in the village, seven hundred strong, and for the two hundred mil¹⁺ia of that town to have faced them unaided would have been throwing good lives away.

However, already other companies, besides our little Redford band, had marched in, such as Billy Smith's from Lincoln and a good three companies from Acton, whereof one was led by that hale and hearty Isaac Davis who had listened to father's great sermon. As our numbers grew steadily, Jo Hosmer, Colonel Barrett's adjutant, formed us into line, as a kind of battalion. Soon after our arrival we were also gladdened to see the small Carlisle company come puffing and muddy with their last mile upon the double-quick, and by still smaller bands of men with firelocks, you could not call them companies, from Westford, Chelmsford and Littleton.

Almost everybody knew everybody else at that rallying spot. There was a silent nodding all along the line as each reënforcement marched past to its place. Had the order "break ranks" sounded, easily enough the whole gathering might have dissolved into little neighboring, gossiping, chattering groups just as on court days or at cattle shows.

But the order came not. Instead a dreadful muttering went down the ranks. The Lincoln men had brought it —a story not quite confirmed, but still they thought it true —"Eight men killed by Pitcairn's troops at Lexington."

At which there was a silent gritting of teeth, and the blood of at least one acting captain, who had had his quavers, went pulsing faster. And now over toward Concord village a mile away across the meadows dense smoke was rising, while right below us by the North Bridge, standing to their arms or moving in platoons with a mechanical precision wonderful to behold, were soldiers in white and red with their gun-barrels flashing in the sunlight. "Three companies," somebody told us, "guarding the bridge, while three more had crossed the river and gone down the road on the Acton side, to raid Colonel Barrett's house in search of military stores."

Barrett himself, a plain, heavy farmer of sixty-five, who had pulled a blue and white coat over his hickory shirt and who strode a very knock-kneed horse, looked like anything but the commander of a forlorn hope, but he was giving us his orders in a calm, steadying way, twisted often in his military terms but strong in common sense. On foot beside him was Major Butterick, also of Concord, a younger man of the same kidney. They had quitted the town because, as they frankly told us, "The British seemed too many for them." But that did not mean they were going to stand still forever.

Almost nine o'clock. At first we were glad of the halt and rest. Some men twitched around their knapsacks and began to gnaw their rye bread and cold meat, but most of us were too tense for that. Presently we could see the red-coats, as if a little afraid of our growing numbers, retiring for the most part to the farther-side of the bridge. Yet there they were, King George's men, past masters in that school of war wherein we were the gawky lads on the rear benches. Nevertheless four hundred of us now had gathered on that hill slope upon the Butterick farm, and the smoke from Concord was rising in a vast gray column.

I stood with the Redford company. In fact, we all liked
to keep together. Left entirely to myself and my own
thoughts it is quite possible I might have done something
utterly unmanly. In desperation I tried to recall the proper
orders for putting the company through the evolution
"change front to rear." My mind seemed a blank; the
only words that would rattle through my head were student
jargon, utterly senseless:

> "Finis circumsistula, popularum gig——
> A man without a head has no need of a wig."

As I looked along our Redford lads, I could see that many
of them were getting white in the gills. If action was not
taken pretty soon, there was no answering for the action
of the company.

Just as I was worrying concerning this, however, Hosmer,
the adjutant, began calling, "Officers this way," and I edged
up to the little group which was already gathered about
Barrett as he sat upon his horse. Beside him stood two or
three elderly men, selectmen, I took it, of Concord. They
were pointing toward the village and the great pyramid of
smoke that was rising near the court house. Of course the
British were rummaging for the stores, but had they fired
the buildings? And if they had, what of the women, the
children and the old people abandoned to their power?
After the story from Lexington any horrid thing seemed
possible.

I nudged up close beside Davis who greeted me with his
heartening grip and smile: "Fine morning, Roger, glad to
see Redford's ready for her duty just as Acton's ready for
hers.—I just told Hannah, 'Take good care of the children.'
And off I come."

Not a council of war. It was a friendly committee meeting. Nobody bandied military titles. The lieutenants
sometimes contradicted the majors. Everybody called

everybody else by his first name. I have read in old Herodotus about a famous council of the Athenians, when Miltiades talked his fellow generals into risking the battle of Marathon against the Persians—and so made a deal of history. When the last scroll is written, will it have been more important history than was shaped by the little knot of homespun, plain featured, earnest men who pressed together on the green hillslope under an April sun?

No holding back, although a little honest questioning. A word was dropped about "waiting till some more companies came up." Whereupon Hosmer swept his hand toward the huge smoke column then hanging over Concord, "Will you let them burn the town down?"—That was the clinching argument. Old Barrett leaned from his saddle and put the vote, "Are you willing?" Every one of us nodded.—We would march down upon that bridge in the teeth of the regulars, cross it come what might, and know the fate of Concord, be the British few or many.

I walked back to my company, called the men around near me, told them what we had to do, and they received the tidings, not with cheers, but with that glint in the eyes which to those who know the Yankee means more than any brawling courage. Hosmer helped us again to dress the lines, and I heard Davis say, "I haven't a man that's afraid to go," as he marched his Acton company through to the head of the column, the post of honor. Concord came second, Redford third, then Lincoln and the others. We marched by twos, a long slim column, with the Acton and Concord fifers screaming "The White Cockade," but I could only hear the drums of all the companies now pounding together, "Must! must!—must! must! must!"

Down that green hillslope we went and toward the causeway approaching the narrow bridge. Barrett sat on his horse giving fatherly exhortation as we all passed, "Don't fire first, don't fire first!" not being sure of the story from Lexington. Then we started on the longest quarter of a mile which ever I traversed in my life.

. . . A few Harvard commencements ago, when I had to bottom one of the Overseers' chairs, a young exhibitioner spouted about a German pundit named Kant and his "Categorical Imperative" which makes frail men do that which is too great for them. It must have been a "Categorical Imperative" or his very near cousin which sent us over that quarter mile. I marched just ahead of the men with Tabby's banner shadowing my shoulders. The bridge was getting nearer and nearer. Most of the British were beyond it, standing in beautifully ordered ranks to see what we would do. Over them floated the cross of St. George, the flag which until only the other day I had reverenced as the noblest in all the world, the emblem of all that men of English speech held dear.

And I was marching straight against that flag, was about to kill or be killed by its soldiers. For one instant the thought overwhelmed me. I could almost have dropped from the march. Then suddenly a kind of barrier in my head seemed to snap. *I was not English.* That was a hostile banner. The men beneath it had no more right than Spaniards or Russians to despoil our Concord and distress our countryside. I was advancing against them as a holy duty and with perfect conscience. "MUST! MUST! MUST!" went all the drums.

Whereupon I knew, and every man in that silent, tense four hundred knew, that fortune, life, death, nothing in heaven or hell mattered at that moment save to cross that bridge before us, cost whatever it might.

We reached the bottom of the slope and turned out upon the causeway leading straight toward the bridge. Out in the river I saw a fish leap up with a splash amid the clumps of greening flags and cat-tails. The British were drawing together in fighting array, and an officer (Captain Lowrie, later I heard) was waving his sword and shouting orders. Their three companies fell into solid platoons, the front rank kneeling down, the second and third aiming above their comrades' heads—a bristling array of bayonets pointing straight toward us.

Our column moved directly toward the bridge, not a stride faltering. Major Butterick was at the head, Lieutenant-Colonel Robinson (a gallant volunteer merely) at his side, and a step behind went Isaac Davis, poising his gun, then all the Acton company. A few British with axes and crowbars had lingered on the bridge and when they fairly saw, what they may have doubted, that we were fully determined to cross, began to tear up the planking. Butterick raised his voice with a loud "Stop that!" whereupon not liking the way we came on, with no waste heroics they scampered back behind their own ranks. The Acton men were only seventy-five yards from the head of the bridge, and from van to last file-closer there was no halting. "MUST! MUST! MUST!" thundered all the drums.

Directly from across the river came next a puff of smoke, a musket crackled, a shot spat in the water beside the drifting sedges. A little cloud of dust leaped up in the road near me. Something whistled overhead; many necks ducked but the march was only faster. Whereat the British officer gave his sword a sweeping flourish; his shout came over the river, and instantly the whole array of bayonets was blotted out in smoke, while the air was filled with things screeching, but more than that, right under our eyes Isaac Davis, just raising his gun, sprang high in the air, then fell in a motionless heap down on the road, while Abner Hosmer, another Acton man, was lying almost beside him.

One fleeting instant we stopped to take this in, then Butterick nearest the bridge, leaping himself as he thundered his order, called down to our farthest files, "Fire, fellow soldiers, for God's sake fire!" "Fire!" cried I to our Redford men, and next, almost to my own astonishment, I found my own firelock going off automatically in my hands. All up and down our line went the crashing of the muskets. More balls were tearing overhead; I heeded them no more than the drift of leaves from October maples. Entirely as a matter of course, I saw through the smoke a young officer across the river clap his hand to his side and totter into the arms of a corporal. I loaded and fired mechanically, and so did every one of us.

Then all of a sudden a great silence possessed the bridgeway. The British, those splendid white-and-red regulars, were no longer standing in line. There were three heaps on the grass just beyond the river. Some of the scarlet coats were making off at an unmistakable run. Some were scattering in frightened little groups, with their officers vainly waving their swords before them. Some were hobbling wounded, and gesturing to comrades to help them to escape.

And the passage of the bridge was open. And we, the victors, marched over!

Done! done! done!—We had achieved "the impossible." We had seen the backs of the regulars.

What if our triumph had demoralized us almost as much as a defeat? We had won the bridge but knew not what to do next. The force in the village still far outnumbered us. The smoke now rising was less dense. Concord was not burning down. Some of the companies, having proved their courage, actually marched back to the rear of the bridge—wholly puzzled at the proper moves in our fearful game. We of Redford, with others under Butterick, ascended the little hill by the Elisha Jones place and flung ourselves behind the stone wall, expecting to be attacked by the force in the village.

We saw a strong column of the invaders tramping out toward us, and cocked our firelocks! But perhaps they had learned something about our doings at the bridge, for just before they came in good musket range lo! they suddenly halted, and then as suddenly marched back into Concord. And while we waited their next move, the inner man began to speak to us.—It was nearly noon, haversacks swung around and home victuals surrendered to appetite. We were so content for that instant with our glory, and our bread and cheese, that we let the British companies which had been raiding the Butterick farm, and which were now recalled pell-mell by the firing, march straight over the bridge and into Concord in our plain sight with never a gunlock flashing.

But now the sun was at height and we had at last sure tidings of bloody work at Lexington. Over the roads from south and west were streaming the homespun companies. Up to our station panted the Sudbury men. The Framingham men, said they, were hurrying close behind. We could count soon on Woburn, Billerica and even Reading. Up to our station too came scurrying white-faced women, with stories of coarse work and brutality by the raiders as they ransacked the town. Then at last directly under our gaze we saw British filing out in the road, and two men on tall horses—Smith and Pitcairn, so the women said,—dashing back and forth and hustling the columns in order. For an instant we braced ourselves. Would they charge up our hill with the bayonet? Not at all. The long lines swung slowly out into the Lexington road, and began marching slowly, steadily, without fife or drum, but with their faces set toward Boston. And one common impulse shot through us all—though no officer spoke it, few privates even muttered it—never, never must those columns see Boston again without paying a price which would teach forever what it meant to dishonor the towns of Massachusetts.

Almost without orders we rose and hastened along the ridge, at first parallel with the British, not a ball being fired. Parties of flankers from the regulars marched across the fields on a line with the road, to keep us from pressing too close to the main body. But we who knew every farm, knew well our goal. Right by Merriam's Corner the ridge north of the high road fell away, and the flankers were forced to draw closer in. We were all on the double-quick, and as we ran the men even from distant Stowe and Westford came cutting across the fences and fields to join us.

We beat the slow-moving redcoats at the fork, racing as we did over the "Great Meadow," and there from behind our walls and trees and thickets we had the tall hats of the grenadiers right against the skyline. The road narrowed down for a little bridge across a brook. When it was crowded all our hillslope burst into smoke and flame. And when the smoke cleared there were scarlet heaps all over the bridge, and in the brook and upon the young grass beside it.

. . . There is a devil in the meekest, mildest of us all; a gentle, subdued, harmless devil through most of our days, but once in a life-time he gets unchained—he was unchained now. There were we, farmers of Redford, shouting, cheering, firing, while red death danced all among us. There was Peter Armstrong, the kindest most piteous tinker in the land, who made his wife kill all the chickens, standing from cover, waving his gun in defiance and bawling like mad, "I got him! He's down, he's down—that officer. Glory be, I got him!"

And what of that strange creature called "myself"?—I had made a great discovery. I was letting the bullets sing past with never a tremble to my own aim, or the least summons to run away. Young Levi Porter lay white and still at my feet, with a scarlet froth on his lips. I lifted him back against a tree, called, "We'll avenge him, boys," and rammed home another cartridge. I was giving commands clearly, firmly. I seemed to remember every move in our fearful game. The men were obeying me, looking to me for guidance. I wondered at myself, and the fight went on—it all seemed proper and natural.

The British column advanced, but no longer in its old arrogant parade array. The men could be seen hastening nervously and the officers running back and forth to keep them in some kind of order. Every now and then a company would halt, fire a volley at us, and sometimes a farmer would drop. Sometimes a squad of flankers would come crashing through the thicket and drive us from our cover, but the bullets usually flew high, and a charge against our shelters was like a hand dashed against a swarm of angry bees—who scatter and return to sting.

Five miles from Merriam's Corner to Lexington and no man ever could tell all of the tale. We kept under cover all we might, and got as near the road as the flankers and platoon firing of the troops would let us. Very brave were the British officers striving to hold their men to their discipline. The last thing they seemed to fear was death, but not so their rank and file. The retreat at last became so fast we could barely keep pace with it. The flankers seemed weary and demoralized themselves. The platoon volleys were scattering and almost at random. All up and down the column were men hobbling and groaning with wounds, while more were dropping by the roadside, their comrades forsaking them (if they still lived) to the mercy of those "peasants" who had been unworthy of regulars' balls or steel.

Some of the minutemen who had set forth with us were already being left behind, winded or out of ammunition; but others took their places steadily. We had just reached Fiske Hill when the British were rallying again. I glanced about and momentarily our Redford company seemed all alone, without supports before the full power of the enemy, when along the slope came a long file of homespun men striding up to the wall to join us.

"They shot my youngest like a dog, while he ran unarmed from the meeting house," spoke the lantern-jawed farmer nearest. "And so—I told his mother," he cocked and primed very deliberately, "I guessed I'd better come here." And he levelled a seven-foot fowling piece.—It was the Lexington company.

Here it was that the British made their best stand and reformed, and well they might, or their men would have broken and flung down their muskets. A mounted officer made them halt and reorganize, the subalterns running up and down the files and pricking the faltering privates into place with their swords. It was bravely and coolly done as became their nation's honor. Our own fire was very hot, and soon I beheld the officer's horse leap as a ball grazed him, throw his rider and tear straight toward our lines. You can see Pitcairn's pistols in Lexington even to-day.

The British gave us another fierce volley, but they were not firing as they had at first. I knew they must be nearly out of cartridges, while soon their retreat was more disorderly than ever. Straight across Lexington village we chased them, across that common where they had spilled innocent blood. As the running fight raged along, old men and women peered from the barns and woodpiles, shook their fists at the foe and cheered us on. Then half a mile more we heard another deeper cheering, and knew that the expected had happened—a strong reënforcement had come out from Boston to save Smith's seven hundred from sure destruction. There was a flash and a roar, and a six-pound ball went crashing through the meeting house. Percy was using his cannon to win respite for his countrymen.

No shame to us if we could not get close enough to see whether in truth Smith's men were so spent (as British writers affirmed) that "their tongues hung from their mouths like dogs," when they dropped in the hollow square formed by the troops of Percy. The artillery kept us back for a time. We were getting used to the hum of musket balls, but it takes practice to stand under the screech of a cannon shot. Besides, the British were nearly two thousand now, more than half of them fresh, unshaken men.

We stood our ground, breathed, waited, let more companies come up, watched to see what the enemy might do. Farmhouses and barns were burning, terrified country folk flying in every direction, the British were getting scared and reckless. Doubtless their better officers tried to restrain from wanton deeds, but war is a miserable sport at best. I myself picked up the body of poor John Raymond, the unarmed cripple, shot in cold blood when he tried to flee from the garden of the Monroe Tavern after serving Percy's officers with grog.

At length the guns were limbered up. It was now about half-past three when the British set forth again, Smith's demoralized companies in the van, Percy's fresh Fusileers covering the rear. The moment the columns were out in the road we were after them. Men from the remote corners of Middlesex and all nearer Essex were crouching by the wayside now, and as the battle raged along, the smoke of the burning farmsteads quickened the pace, and pointed the way for all the breathless companies.

I forget all the places where we gave fair volleys, or where the cannon had to be set down to give a little respite for the hard pressed infantry. We Redford men were lucky beyond our comrades. We came on a little extra powder at Lexington and could keep in the chase long after many of our comrades at the Bridge had turned honorably away. It was near the "Foot of the Rocks" * in Menotomy when we came up again close to the road, and if we paid a price, we took good quittance. Here it was that just as I pointed our men to a good ditch and hedgerows which would afford fair cover from the brisk volleys of the regulars, I saw a figure I knew well standing out in the thickest storm of the bullets. It was Warren, a little dusty perchance, but as always his collected, elegant self. As I ran to drag him back, a ball struck the pin out of the hair of his earlock. "Rough surgery," laughed he, "and professionally unsound, but do you think that after all my brave talk I can rightly keep away?"

Nevertheless he let me shelter him, and I pledge you that the next hour gave him sufficient sample of the hum of bullets so that he learned that a good soldier does not let himself be killed before it is strictly needful. We were still on Percy's flank and rear. The field-pieces were ceasing to frighten us, and still the companies were always coming up—Dedham, Medford, Watertown, Lynn, Salem and many more. All Norfolk and Essex were pouring in to avenge Middlesex.

In that running fight at Menotomy came nearly half the loss, both British and American, of the entire day. The British were using the torch recklessly now, and shooting non-combatants often at sight, but still the puffs of smoke were coming from left and right of their long swerving column. The Fusileers had had enough of it in the rear.

* "Arlington Heights" by a later nomenclature.

They had to be relieved by the Marines. The prisoners we took had their pouches nearly empty. We knew that Percy's own cartridges were beginning to fail—and we pressed more boldly.

Stone walls, stone walls, little did your builders in the Old Colony know that along the waysides they were setting up a bulwark of life for their grandsons on that day of Massachusetts' greatest need! We all fought for ourselves and by ourselves, only the abler captains holding even their companies together. No colonels in command; no regiments. Once or twice I saw a mounted officer galloping bravely through the smoke—General Heath, but he had no power to sway the battle; only here and there could he get a few squads to follow him. Yet with it all we nearly stopped the British; and if Nat Greene, or Mad Anthony or the Marquis had been there to rule the fight—I need not name the Virginian—I vow not one of that force from his Lordship down would ever have seen Boston, save perchance as a paroled prisoner.

As it was I hung on until after that second great fight on the verge of Cambridge, when Percy yet again had to unlimber the guns to blast through a way. Still the battle rolled eastward with Percy's men going almost as fast as Smith's near Lexington. I saw a high officer on a white horse dashing hither and thither in the fight, waving, ordering, forcing his troops into line. I was sure it was his Lordship and I was glad he did not fall—there was a tale for him to tell in England.

By this time our second supply of cartridges was nearly spent and as the sun slipped lower we began to know that since before gray dawn we had been marching or fighting like men possessed. Then somewhere by Winter Hill, while the Americans were still crowding in and the forty-seventh was facing them (the Marines too had become played out),

directly by the road where the column had passed, there
swirled a little group of shouting, gesticulating minutemen:
"A prisoner! A prisoner!" Down to them I ran, and pale
as death, gripping a fence-post as he dropped an empty
pistol was Herbert Dunmore himself, with a ball somewhere
near his foot.

I thanked heaven for being able to pass as a captain;
ordered the others (Newton men) away, and called my Redford lads to drop out of the battle (which now they did
gladly) and help me take the dear fellow to the nearest
farm. Good luck had spared the dwelling. The conflict
was roaring away in the distance. As we burst into the
kitchen a very stern-faced old Yankee and his frightened
but firm-lipped wife confronted us. "A British captain," I
declared, touching my own epaulets, "a prisoner."

The farmer looked at Herbert strangely, torn manifestly
by conflicting questionings whether duty required him to
cut the enemy's throat or to invite him to supper.

"Treat him well," I ordered. "He's a hostage. Precious—
for all our people now trapped in Boston."

The old man grunted in a kind of relief; his wife spoke,
"I'll get hot water," and between us we had off Herbert's
boot, and found to my great joy that the ball had not
touched the bone. Our new hosts gave him a swig from a
certain black bottle which made him feel steadier, and we
improvised a dressing for the wound. But before I could
ask him how he came to be on the expedition, into the
kitchen stamped a second party with a second wounded
prisoner, taken (said our men) from a chaise caught in the
rear of the British.

"Lieutenant Gould!" exclaimed Dunmore, lifting his
head with a queer smile which he explained only afterward.
The other, painfully wounded, was gesticulating wildly and
moaning, "What have we done? What have we done?"

"Done, son?" answered the farmer grimly, again uncorking the bottle, "done? You've only done what fools I guess will do six generations hence, then count the cost. *You've made New England fighting mad!*"

"Herbert," said I, while Gould was being clumsily attended, "for God's sake, were you at Lexington? What really happened?"

He shook his head sadly, "I went with Smith as a volunteer, in the vain hope of fending off some deviltry. Your militia faced Pitcairn's companies on the Lexington green. I suppose they thought they had the right to stand their ground by their own dooryards. Pitcairn ordered them to 'Lay down their arms and disperse.' He's a decent man, and I don't think would have shed blood wantonly, but the troops and subalterns were mad for revenge upon your Boston insolents. Some fool behind Pitcairn flashed off a pistol, somebody else roared, 'Fire.' After that every platoon shot straight into the militia. It was like the King Street massacre only worse. It lasted only a minute."

"A minute," said I passionately, "yes, one of those minutes which sets enmity between nations. Your grandchildren and mine, and those to come after will find 'Lexington' rising up between them." Then seeing the tears in his honest eyes, I repented my frankness and did my best to comfort him. We were all limp now, conscious of a fearful weariness, and glad when our hostess set food before us, saying bluntly to the prisoners, "If thine enemy hunger feed him"; and telling them that her own boy was out with the Cambridge companies, although they said he was still "Safe from your ruffians, thank God."

I got Herbert and Gould into the chaise and led it myself into Cambridge, where at the Henry Vassal house (emptied of its Tory owners) they were setting up a hospital. It was now dark but the yard around the college was aglow

with campfires; the college buildings were opened, hundreds
of minutemen were pouring into the town. It was said
headquarters would be there for pushing the siege of Boston.

I thrust open the entrance of deserted Harvard Hall and
bade the Redford men who still followed me to make their
bunks anywhere and find rest. For myself I stumbled
upstairs in Stoughton to my old room. The key was still
in my pocket. I pushed back the door and cast myself
upon the mattress. I was weary, more weary than ever
before in my life. My face was caked with dirt, begrimed
with powder. A ball had just edged my forehead with a
red furrow. My brain was one mass of whirling, struggling
emotions. I had no power of connected thought. But I
was happy, diabolically happy. Outside to eastward came
the dull booming of the warships covering the redcoats as
they panted in Charlestown waiting to be ferried to refuge
in Boston.

The Gilmans had answered the Percys.

CHAPTER XXXVII

EMILIE RIVOIRE carried herself like the Queen of France when brought into the presence of Gage that evening after Concord Battle. The general was manifestly a shaken man. The thunders of the warships making a brave noise to protect Percy, while his troops were being hurried into the boats back to Boston, were still jarring Province House. Already carts and chaises were clattering up from the ferry laden with the groaning wounded. All the spare forces of the garrison were hastening to Roxbury Neck, where a rebel attack seemed any moment possible; while as harbingers of the onrushing gale the last Tory families in the adjacent towns were scurrying into Boston with fearsome stories of the fury of the people.

Mlle. Rivoire affirmed nothing, denied nothing, when they questioned her. Prothero had reported her call at the Warren house. A little inquiry had disclosed that her grandfather had seemed in excellent health and needed no medicine, while Warren himself had been visiting a distant patient when she gave out that she had just seen him. A score of witnesses could testify as to the particular farewell she had taken of the doctor at the ferry-slip. One or two also could swear that a woman resembling her had been seen in his company upon the streets the night preceding. As for Revere's ride and the rousing of Middlesex, they were already common talk in Boston. That sturdy rebel and his even more treasonable chief were momentarily

466

beyond the grasp of vengeance. All the more cause for
following diligently the case of any one who had perhaps
transmitted to them a great military secret.

When, however, Captain Osterley, who had conducted
most of the examination, put to the prisoner the question,
"It being plain, Mademoiselle, that you conveyed to Warren
news of the first importance, whence did you get it yourself?" Emilie looked fixedly upon the general.

"Does his Excellency absolutely require an answer?"

Whereupon Gage, turned very red though beneath the
gaze of a dozen officers, then to the surprise of many
held up his hand, "We will not press for an immediate
reply. Mlle. Rivoire will require time to consider her
extraordinarily serious situation."

Osterly bowed, but bit his lip. The examination had
been unsatisfactory. He had hated his own part in it, and
was glad of a decent excuse for relaxing with the prisoner.
"Then, sir, I can go no further. Perhaps Mlle. Rivoire will
give her parole not to quit Boston nor communicate with the
rebels. She can then return to her home."

But the general forbade even sternly. He was extremely
nervous and again kept playing with his hands: "I regret
this cannot be. A great disaster has come to the King's
forces. The case has its intricacies which I cannot reveal.—
Let the prisoner be held under close guard, and communi-
cated with only on my personal authority, pending complete
examination."

"You order well," spoke Emilie with rising voice, "I
would have given no parole."

Thus the scene ended, and the prisoner was soon taken
to the Hutchinson house, then filling with Tory refugees,
and confined in a couple of second-story rooms in the ell,
with a sergeant's wife to play her jailor, and a private with
a bayonet killing time before her door. Her grandfather

had been arrested already, but the provost-marshal's wits were soon blunted by the sharp replies of the old Frenchman; nothing could be established against him.

Most naturally after all this, Emilie's old mess-room admirers had looked strangely at one another. Percy actually had to admonish certain ill-friends of Claypool and Upson that they were not to make "cutting remarks." This was no time to lose valuable officers over affairs of honor. But about the third day, when the keenness of the thing had worn off a little, several of the old rivals had met in the British Coffee House (where liquid comforts abounded, even if the town was now on salt provisions) and after toasting the King, and turning down a well-filled "Damnation to the rebels," young Sir Francis stood again, and held up his glass; "And now another toast—to the girl that fooled us all."

His voice was unsteady, but not from drinking; and Upson stood up beside him with "I'll drink that, Frank." Their glasses clinked; the others imitated, and all the gallant circle felt better.

"We've been to see her," pursued Sir Francis. "Had some trouble to get in but managed it. Gad! she was glorious. 'My heart's aching for you boys,' said she. 'It's been aching for a long time. Don't think me a sinful coquette. If it's right for you to toss your lives into the cannon's mouth, it's right for me to fight with all the weapons I had. It was for America. An English girl would do as much for England. If I can be wife to none of you, I beg you let me part friends with all.'"

"They say there's a Mohair captain out there who claims her," spoke a lieutenant angrily. "Curse him, that she should throw herself thus away!"

"He may be the best of us all," returned Upson. "My

mind's greatly changed about those Whigs. Fight them we will, but malign them we won't. She has a right to her own choice."

"She'll make her own choice, that I warrant," answered Claypool with a very sorry smile. "No fear of that. But one thing she shan't say,—to her Yankee captain, to King Hancock, nor to any of the rest of the rebellious pack— that British officers do not know a brave lass, or are not gallant losers. Yet that's not what's now plaguing us most. —What's to become of her?"

"Turn her loose," vowed Upson. "Drive her down to the Neck with a ruffle of drums and a platoon presenting arms; hand her over to her Whigs—After that God bless her! and henceforth ho! for the girls of Old England."

"So say I," quoth Sir Francis, "but you'd better take the advice to Province House. Damme, but the lass has played with fire. Percy and Smith are hot as fiends against her; keep swearing, 'If that Revere hadn't been slipped off, Hancock and Adams would be snug in jail with iron ruffles, and the Concord supplies would have been found and burned without loss of a man.'"

"Does she know her danger?" queried a captain.

"Knows it too well. Zounds!—If I could only talk as she does. Asked us point blank, 'If woman spies were shot or hanged?'"

"No danger of that, thank God!" swore the captain.

"We trust not.—But if you knew what we think as to what—hem!—his Excellency thinks concerning how the secret leaked—well, there might be a fine story. Percy in irritation told me, 'The general assured me that he had revealed the plans of the march only to himself and one other.' Who was that 'other'? Not the great Mademoiselle herself!"

"His Excellency," observed a very small subaltern, between pulls upon his pipe, "is in no enviable case. And what about *her* Excellency?"

"Mrs. Gage," returned Upson with an unconcealed sneer, "is 'very much indisposed' these days. Doubtless from the shock of the battle, poor lady."

"But what has that to do with the divine Emilie?" vigorously demanded Claypool.

. . . The result of this conclave was a formal call by Upson, Claypool and two others at Province House, with the request that Mlle. Rivoire be immediately set at liberty, and passed out of town in exchange for certain Tories in the clutches of the rebels. The refusal for once, however, was very firm.

"We are at war, gentlemen," spoke Gage with all his frowning dignity. "This unfortunate young woman for whom you intercede is charged with conveying precious military information to the King's enemies. Thanks to her alleged act the royal arms have been humiliated. Her treatment must be duly determined by court martial."

"Before heaven, sir," broke out the distracted Claypool, "you won't treat that splendid creature like a common spy? After so long a policy of leniency——"

"A policy pursued, I fear, too long," replied his unbending commander. "I confess with chagrin my laxness. Examples must be made. Ringleaders must not be spared. Captain Prothero of the navy has urged me, in the name of our sister service, not to discourage the King's friends by condoning disloyalty. A proclamation is now being drafted, proffering pardon to the lesser rebels, but denouncing the rigors of the law against John Hancock and Samuel Adams whose 'offenses are too flagitious to be condoned.' In like manner must we deal with this young woman.—The interview is over, gentlemen."

After which the four went out of Province House with scowls and flushed faces, Claypool vowing, "If she goes to a court martial I throw up my commission and join the rebels." But Upson, a little older and wiser, bade him not to talk rashly; "The old man is covering his own plight with a great rub-a-dub of courage. Twenty guineas to fourpence that she never sees a court martial. It's not *that* which she has to dread."

"No," confessed Sir Francis, "a court martial can order a rope or a file of muskets; but not before hearing evidence,— and there's *some* evidence that'll never be heard, not at least while Tom Gage commands in Boston."

The little band therefore swallowed its rebuff and waited. They were not permitted to see Emilie again, but contrived to get to her books, fresh edibles (now becoming desperately scarce in cooped-up Boston), and not a few flowers. April crept into May, and May was verging upon June, and still the sentry yawned before the door, and still there was no court martial.

. . . .

Let no man say that these were joyous weeks for Emilie. The two rooms wherein she was confined were of respectable size; her food (the gifts apart) was tolerable; but activity had hitherto been her life. Now she was indeed the wild bird in the cage, and, what was worse, was denied all forms of information as to external events, save only such distorted scraps as were doled out by Mrs. Nevins, the grumpy and frowsy woman who tended her.

Emilie was indeed permitted one interview with her grandfather in the presence of a suspicious corporal. M. Rivoire could do little more than assure her that he and Berthe were well, and bid her keep up a good heart for "We Huguenots are accustomed to prison for a good cause." Another attempt by Claypool to visit her had, however, been forbidden "on direct orders from Province House," and after that Emilie was largely left to her own devices. She was permitted needlework and books, but they were pitiful substitutes for freedom. For some days she had expected to be brought out before some military tribunal, but the ruling powers seemed to have forgotten her. In her heart she knew well why his Excellency was in no hurry to force the disposal of her case.

The Hutchinsons' house faced on Garden Court Street near the Old North Meeting House, but Emilie's chambers looked down upon a closely-walled garden, once a thing of tender care and beauty, although this year, thanks to the disorders of the times, allowed to grow up somewhat wild. Heavy bars had been placed on her windows, but these could not shut out the soft light, greenery and the calls of the birds. It gave Emilie vast pleasure that one of her windows opened toward the west. The west meant Charlestown, Cambridge, America. Somewhere beyond the chimney stacks and treetops that barred her vision was Roger Gilman.

What was he doing? How often could he find thoughts of her as he learned that fierce new trade of war? Would he—? But Emilie always (she had to do this ten times each day) had to fight back the awful query, "How did he come through the battle?" The heavy British losses had become known to her. But there had been American losses too. And Redford was so near to Concord and to Lexington;—Emilie knew that her betrothed had been in the thick of the fighting as certainly as she knew that she was being held within four walls.

One thing comforted her mightily;—the intermittent roaring of the cannon. The British had a battery now on Copp's Hill close at hand. On the thirteenth of May there had been a fearful belching and bellowing. Mrs. Nevins said later that a great force of rebels had in sheer defiance marched from Cambridge into Charlestown and then marched back again.

On the twenty-seventh there had been a more distant thunder from the harbor. All the warships seemed in a fury. Mrs. Nevins could not tell the cause, but that evening, when the sentry was changed, Private Jenkins told Private Simpson that there had been a real battle along the flats by Noddle Island, and that "the cursed rebels had had the best of it," had burned a schooner and won all the glory. On other days the firing had been toward Roxbury Neck or toward Cambridge, and whenever the windows rattled and the houses jarred, Emilie had taken courage, *"My* Americans are still there, pressing in upon Boston." She schooled herself to resist the constant question, "Did that last cannon shot speed death to the man I love?"

Then May fairly disappeared into June, and the air in the garden below became heavy with the perfume of the great lilacs, when Mrs. Nevins, who became more communicative the longer she fell under the spell of Emilie, made a remark when she brought in a very simple supper, "New sentries by the door to-day."

"Indeed, and who are they?" Anything was of interest in Emilie's unchanging state.

"Why I think the fellows of the tenth are needed for more active service. The new ones are 'Loyal Colonials,'— Mr. Ruggles' enlistment. You know he's getting up a force of royalist volunteers."

Emilie turned with disgust; "Ruggles? A Tory traitor to America! Give me honest British lads instead."

"I didn't order them here, Miss," mollified the woman, lighting the candle and leaving the dishes. After her footsteps had died away, Emilie at length became conscious of a certain fumbling near the door, and that something white had been thrust beneath it. A moment later she was back by the candle holding a paper to be read in a twinkling:

"Friends will be near you at last. Look well at the sentries but speak not unless they speak to you. Time must be taken or all is ruined. Keep courage. R. G. is safe."

No signature, but Emilie hugged the paper to her heart, then dipped it in the water pot until the writing was obliterated and the whole became one harmless pulp ball.

Almost instantly she had cause to rejoice that she had done this. Outside came the steps of Mrs. Nevins and those of a man behind her. The sentry banged his musket butt upon the floor as the jailoress thrust a paper before him. Emilie could not of course see how the soldier was suddenly holding down his head, and seemed to have a sudden need of readjusting his hat.

"It's all right," Mrs. Nevins was saying. "The pass is signed by the general himself."

What the officer behind her might have added if he had taken the least interest in the sentinel appears not in this history, but he was only anxious to have the door unlocked. This Mrs. Nevins did very promptly, announcing to her prisoner, "The gentleman has permission to see you, miss," and retired immediately. Whereupon Emilie found herself looking straight upon the naval buttons of Bernard Prothero.

The captain of the *Argus* held back nothing of a very elaborate salutation.

The prisoner on her part, white and staring, retired before him toward the entrance to her inner room, but Prothero with his mildest manner pointed toward a chair.

"Mlle. Rivoire has nothing to dread—to-night," spoke he in suave accents, and Emilie halted, obeyed, bit her lip and collected her wits.

"Permit me to add," he continued, "that this confinement

is not improving a complexion which has been the praise
or envy of every genteel circle in Boston. I hope your
imprisonment may soon end."

"And by whom was it begun, pray?"

"My duty as an officer overrode every personal consideration. Besides, what is the saying about 'All's fair in love
and war'? Since we are alone, however, permit me, as a
member of the rival service, to congratulate you on a piece
of intelligence work against the army, which, if you had
been acting for our accustomed foes would have won a
patent of nobility from the King of France or of Spain.
That we are confined so uncomfortably to this town, that
our American friends are not to-day broken and leaderless,
I ascribe very largely to a certain lady whom I have the
honor now to meet again."

Emilie's coolness had returned, her lips drew in tightly;
"Captain Prothero did not come to-night solely to say this."

"Egad!" he cried, his mood changing in a twinkling, "I
did not. Mademoiselle, Emilie, I'm a desperate man. I've
been misjudged, maligned, toyed with, cuffed aside. I'll
make no boasts of whining Methodistical virtue, but I'm as
good as Upson, as Claypool, as that gawky rebel of yours."

"You will please not mention 'that rebel' before his affi-
anced wife," Emilie stood now, and seemed six inches taller.

He gazed on her with undisguised admiration. "Curse
my tongue—let it pass! I barely got out of Gage this permission to see you. Got it only by swinging over him the
threat of disclosing something which I more than guess.
Now I'm here to save you—understand?"

"To save me before the court martial do you mean?"

"Court martial to the devil. Gage, Percy and Smith
would all like to see you on the gibbet—Gage don't dare it
in Boston—you well know why. But there's one thing he
can do—send you to England. The King's bigwigs would

gloat over the chance to stand a woman rebel in Old Bailey dock.—Or at best it would be a long, hard imprisonment,—with your fine America three thousand miles of rough water away."

Emilie's cheeks were extremely pale, but she eyed him steadily; "That may be as you say, but Captain Prothero neither commands the Boston garrison, nor issues King's pardons."

"Damme," he blurted in louder voice, "I'll whisk you out to the *Argus*. The ship sails home soon. Once you are my wife, let me say one word to Earl Sandwich at the Admiralty and we can snap fingers at all the charges these army fools can hint against you. I'm the chief King's witness. A husband cannot testify against——"

"Bernard Prothero," spoke the prisoner, sifting out her answer slowly, "if I had wished to sell my soul I'd have sold it earlier to kind, brave Frank Claypool on friendlier terms. If your London Tyburn were before me, I pray God to give me strength not to buy reprieve by wedding you. Let us not bandy words. When my betrothed can brave your cannon I can brave your threats. Begone—or I call the sentry to protect me." She took three steps toward the door.

The sailor cast forth an oath unprintable. At last he returned to coherent speech: "The devils seize me if again I proffer fair terms to a woman!—Very good, mistress! You may have your voyage to England. And I swear that I'll see that you pray for nothing worse than rebels' law before it's ended."

Out he flung, leaving Emilie chilled and shivering in her chair. The noise of his footsteps died away. Mrs. Nevins had disappeared. She was alone. Terribly, horribly alone; the fact came home as never before during her imprisonment. Then came the relief of a great rush of tears. After her weeping ceased she felt a little stronger. Directly under the candle upon the table her eye fell upon the innocent little ball of paper. Outside the door the sentinel was again pacing and rattling his musket and Emilie sprang to the large keyhole from which her custodian had withdrawn the key. In the corridor hung a lantern, and as if of set purpose the sentinel stopped directly beneath it, removing his hat and turning his profile.

"A close call," he soliloquized aloud in melodious Yankee, "but a miss is as good as a mile, and next time I'm prepared for him. I wonder why that fellow had to talk so tarnation loud?—He hurt my ears."

That profile Emilie had seen before.

CHAPTER XXXVIII

THIS is a personal story. Other pens than mine must tell of the mustering before Boston of that army the like whereof had never earlier been upon sea or land. While even we chased Percy through Menotomy, the messenger had spurred into Worcester. "To arms!" he called at the town house; then on a fresh horse away he sped. Before next daybreak all the little villages betwixt Worcester and the Connecticut had been awakened by the tramp of men, the rumbling of wagons hurrying eastward. All the ferries over the Merrimac had long since been crammed with the strength of New Hampshire, like those minutemen of Nottingham who raced fifty-five miles in twenty hours.

A little later we in Cambridge stood wondering at the long, rangy lads in buckskin leather, who tramped in from the Winnepesaukee and the mighty hills beyond. Nat Greene was up from Rhode Island with a thousand men boasting tents, uniforms and something like a real military array. Spencer and Putnam were come with over two thousand from Connecticut. Of course Massachusetts had sent the most; and thus from Dorchester to Chelsea in a great sprawling half-moon, hemming in the British lay the "grand American army" of sixteen thousand.

The most remarkable fighting force no doubt it was in the world, for it had neither proper commissariat nor magazines, neither artillery worthy of the name nor recognized staff officers nor commanding general. The men from the other colonies took directions from our nominal leader,

478

General Ward; yet he, the senior Massachusetts general, infirm and elderly, shut himself up in his Cambridge headquarters, arbitrated squabbles thrust before him as might a justice of the peace, and was anything but the dashing, tireless leader to bring order out of chaos and to hearten the wavering.

Bayonets and powder, horses and uniforms, cannon and tents, these were only a *few* of the things whereof there was an amazing lack. The Harvard buildings (the college was practically suspended) were crammed with troops and so were all the houses of Cambridge and Roxbury; for the rest of the mustering thousands there were huts of boughs, turf or sail cloth, or often only the hay mows and the barns. The weather was unusually fine, and many spread their blankets in the open. Yet with it all, with the incessant coming and going, captains being mistaken for privates, and much worse things to astound the martinets, there was ingenuity, good comradeship, good courage and a passionate desire to get at the British.

We who had arrived first stood to our arms in the earlier days, expecting an instant attack, for it passed belief that Gage would swallow his defeat. Only slowly did it filter in from Boston, how complete had been the impression wrought by the twelve mile running battle, and how "the scalded cat fears cold water"; nay, that Gage had actually dreaded lest he should not have enough troops to hold the town until heavy reënforcements reached him. Late in May we knew that large bodies of troops had at last made harbor, as well as three self-important generals,—Howe, Clinton and Burgoyne (all suffering from indigestion when they left America) but now full of confidence that one bold push would disperse the "peasants" and give plenty of that "elbow room," which Burgoyne had demanded ere he fairly touched the wharf.

But by that time something like order was emerging from utter confusion. If we did not have a great commander, we had a levelheaded Committee of Safety, and upon it we had Joseph Warren who never shone to nobler advantage than in those eight-and-fifty days following Concord Battle, while Hancock and Adams were in Philadelphia, and before Warren's own star was dimmed forever.

I was constantly with Warren. Harter's foot had recovered; he appeared in camp and I was glad to hand the company over to him, especially as there was little now for it to do save to go through routine drills and grumble about hit-or-miss rations. Thanks to the doctor I received in due form a Massachusetts captain's commission, and was attached to him as his personal aide, inasmuch as he was clearly marked for a major-generalship the moment that high appointment could be ratified by the Provincial Congress. Never shall I forget his disgust and scorn when some busybody proposed that he be made "physician-general" to the army: "We'll win this war by breaking bones, not by setting them. How can I look a wounded private in the eye if I've not been hearing the balls whistle myself?" And so it went into the formal record that "preferring a more active and hazardous employment he accepted a major-general's commission."

On more than one afternoon to forbid constant interruption at his own quarters at the Hill house, he would come over to my chamber at Stoughton, lock the door, take down my little pile of military books, and sit studying them for hours. "A long, hard game we've got to play, Roger," once said he, closing *The Manual Exercises* with a snap; "and it's no small thing to sit at chess against past masters, when we can hardly tell castles from bishops—*but we'll do it!*"—Giving one of those laughs that always sent us from his presence firmer and braver men.

However, my duties left me plenty of time for personal worriment. Herbert's wound fortunately yielded to proper treatment; he was soon able to hobble upon parole, and was often over at my old room while waiting for exchange negotiations to be completed. The absolute failure of his peace mission of course he confessed with sorrow. "But it was a good fight," he would add courageously, "and I go back to England with honest conscience as soon as I can with honor."

Thanks to Warren he was permitted to write to his friends in the town, and they to him; and the word which he transmitted concerning Emilie set me to grinding my teeth and pacing the floor almost in a mood to storm the British works with my own bare hands. At my entreaty her name was added to the list of Whigs whose release was demanded in exchange for our own prisoners. The reply soon came that Mlle. Rivoire was not an ordinary captive of war and that her exchange could not be considered. At which I was anxious to halt the whole exchange and threaten every prisoner in our hands (barring Herbert) with a gallows high as Haman's if she were not released. Of course I was overruled; it being hard enough indeed to get Gage to acknowledge that our officers should be exchanged for British officers rank for rank.

Yet Warren went over Emilie's case with me patiently and earnestly, with that little pursing of his lips which told his friends much. "Officially," spoke he, "I am nigh helpless. Unofficially perhaps not quite so helpless. But time is required—wait." And presently I learned that he had been closeted with a certain small, sharp-featured fellow, who stole into and out of his quarters, and had a most uncanny way of retailing all the news from Boston.

This was as far as I got by the sixth of June when, Gage having at last quitted his high horse, the exchange pact was

ratified, and I took farewell of Herbert when he rode out
under the white flag with Warren, Putnam and the
exchanged Britishers to meet his own countrymen in
Charlestown.

Possibly it relieved us both a trifle to part then, notwithstanding we made a solemn agreement to meet again if
possible before his return to England. The sight of our
furious if unscientific preparations against his nation pained
him daily, although once and again I caught him suppressing
a smile at our clumsy efforts to imitate the King's service.

"I can't fight for you, and I won't fight against you,"
were almost his final words, "so what have I to do in
America?"

"And Emilie?" said I.

"To the limits of my honor," said he, with a last
clasp; and with that upon the road to Charlestown I left
him.

The third day after I was very busy copying letters for
Warren to the delegates at the Continental Congress in Philadelphia, adding his personal entreaty to the request of the
Massachusetts Congress that a commander-in-chief be
named for the army, and that this officer be none other
than "the beloved Colonel Washington." When I brought
in the papers, Warren laid another in my hand:

"This is for you," he said, "I won't tell now how I
received it." Then, seeing that the address was in the hand
of Herbert himself, you can tell how quickly the seal was
broken.

"Captain Roger Gilman, in the Army of Rebels auda-
ciously arrayed against the Forces of his Majesty—Sir:
otherwise Dear Roger:

"On our ride to Charlestown Dr. Warren had much talk
with me, and we entered into a kind of treaty, it being
understood that all things done should hurt the public cause
neither of our King nor of your Congress. Perhaps it was

owing to this talk that I can get this message to you speedily.

"Emilie Rivoire is confined in the upper rooms in the rear of the Hutchinson house. She suffers for little but the denial of friends and of liberty; 'Not quite trifles,' of course I hear you say. My known friendship for your party makes my own representations at Province House worthless, but Claypool (the most magnanimous fellow in the army) has moved heaven and earth in her behalf.

"She will never (I may affirm) be brought to a trial, for reasons which I can hardly hint upon paper. I think in fact that a certain Major General would be very happy to send her fairly out of Boston, provided he were sure no fleck of scandal would spatter back upon a certain lady. 'The deed's done. Spilled milk can't be regathered,' declare some of us, 'but Mlle. Rivoire will at least politely engage to repay mercy with silence.' This has been said most earnestly to the Major General. Unfortunately another tongue perhaps can chatter in the case. We fear lest Bernard Prothero has guessed the truth and uses his power over Gage, who is (you know) weak as water and like most weak men terribly touchy in his pride.

"The report is that the *Argus* needs complete repairs, and also that her commander is getting very tired of Boston salt-victuals and hard cider. A relief ship arrived last week. Another story that gets out is that evil pressure has been brought to bear on Gage to order Mlle. Rivoire to England. He is ordinarily a man of honor, but Prothero may swing the lash over him. The *Argus* is to sail home upon the eighteenth. All her better officers and seamen have been drafted off upon the *Cerberus* and *Glasgow*. The officers remaining aboard will be after their captain's own kidney.

"We have no more to go upon than this, but Claypool, Upson and myself are resolved that the honor of the service and our own honor as Englishmen, forbids that any female prisoner should be sent on such a vessel. We do not think Gage dare to issue formal orders to that effect, but he might be browbeaten into closing his eyes to strange practices. That may justify us also in closing our eyes to yet other irregular deeds to counter them.

"Arrange your affairs therefore, if your 'rebellious and

traitorous cause' will permit, so that you can answer a
summons into Boston instantly. Your aid may be needed.
Yr. most obedient H. D.

"P. S. I hear your uncle Eleazer Fifield is very far gone
with a pleurisy."

This came on the ninth. I have had an easier seven days
than the span which followed.

On the morning of the sixteenth I woke with a rap on my
door, and opened to Warren himself. He held again a billet
in his hand, which he stretched toward me, but I saluted
very deferentially. He was in his new general's uniform,
donned for the first time, and the blue and buff with a
proper splendor of gold braid became his supple figure
rarely. A slim gilt scabbard clicked at his side. Heaven
had intended him to look the perfect soldier.

"I salute Major General Warren," said I, with my hand
at my forehead.

His laugh was that of a playful,boy: "You may salute a
barber's prentice about to trepan some poor devil's skull—
the appointment would be nigh as fitting." Then his won-
derfully mobile face grew graver. "Ah! Roger, Roger, what
times we have to live in. 'Tis just as in 'Measure for
Measure,'

> The baby beats the nurses, and quite athwart
> Goes all decorum.

I don't think I'll wear these gay feathers very long."

"You will perhaps be summoned to the Philadelphia Congress then?"

He shook his head; "No, merely that we are playing a
game of great forfeits, and something whispers I'll have to
pass out of mine right quickly.—No matter; the game's
worth the hazard, and we at least will play it fairly.—Now
give ear. I know you'll never blab. There'll be something
more to write in the books in a few days. It has lately
come to us how, now that Gage has his reënforcement, he's

squeezing up enough courage for another move to teach a
lesson to us 'peasants.' He'll seize Charlestown or perhaps
Dorchester Heights, unless somebody forestalls him. The
majority of the Committee are hot for action. I have
resisted—no heavy cannon, pitifully little powder, worst of
all no commanding general. But old Put from Connecticut
swung the vote against me. He can never forgive us Massachusetts men for chasing back Percy before his regiment
could arrive.—The decision's made, and I like an honest
fellow will do my part.—I think I know what's in the
message I give you. I'll not need you, but get back to-morrow—*if you can.*" Then his hand slipped into mine, as he
added, "Tell Emilie Rivoire that if Major General Warren
could only be plain Doctor Warren again, you'd not go to
this 'genteel assembly' without one good Yankee friend to
share the dancing with you."

Down the rickety stairs he went, then turned at the landing and shot over his shoulder, "Take your pistols." Next
from the window I saw him going across Harvard yard,
amid the salutes and admiring glances of a throng of militiamen.

I tore open the packet:

"Be at the Little Cove on Charles River at eleven
to-night. A boat will be waiting. The password to-night
is 'Charlotte Amelia.' Of course we trust your honor to
make no military use of this or other like knowledge that
may come to you. All is provided unless fate turns fickle.
E. is well. H. D."

You can vow my pistols were well primed.

CHAPTER XXXIX

THE GUNS OF THE "LIVELY"

I DRESSED carefully that night, putting on a tight-fitting civilian dress instead of my own very unsoldierly captain's blue. The business of course would be hazardous and if I were taken I would most probably be hanged as a spy, but about the last thing in my mind then was the chance of danger. About ten o'clock I went out across Harvard yard. The camp fires around Cambridge Court House had burned low; the air seemed heavy, there were no stars nor moon. I passed the huts of many men snoring the snores of the patriotic just, but as I turned down the dark foliage-hung avenues of Braintree Street, the clicking, tramping and low murmur of a considerable body of troops came up from the north, as if a force were mustering at the corner of the Common nearest the Charlestown road.

Another time I would have been racking my wits to find excuse for joining those regiments, but now I only turned my head once, then hastened down Braintree Street. Presently the houses were farther apart, farms replaced the garden patches, and I struck down the lane over the low land extending toward Little Cove on the Charles River. The way was known to me, and although stumbling a trifle on the rutty wagon road, I made good speed. Once or twice I was challenged by sentries on their lookout for General Ward's pet bugbear—a surprise attack upon Cambridge; but I had all our own passwords, and went by with hardly a halt.

At last I was down by the level marsh land. The tide was creeping in across the flats. It was a warm, dark night;

486

the south wind was causing the heavy boughs to creak and the shutters of a ghostly farmhouse to rattle. I could just tell the difference between the sandy wastes in the Charles and the widening reaches now being covered by the water. The masts and hull of a man-of-war riding on guard without lights were barely distinguishable. To eastward, rather more than a mile away, spread a dark outline still marked by a few scattered lamps—foe-gripped Boston. Next I passed along what I knew was a small inlet now filling with the tide, and caught the whiff of marsh-grass, kelp and half dry seaweed, and once more a sentinel challenged me. Again I gave him our password and he let me out upon a stubby wharf.

"Is there a skiff here?" I asked.

"Came ten minutes ago," returned the fellow. "Just slipped in out of the dark. I was about to fire on her, when the man aboard gave the word and the countersign. Said he was waiting for some one."

"Probably I am he."

Against the spiling could just be discerned something floating and a human figure within it. "Who are you?" I questioned. "I am Roger Gilman."

"Give the British password," came back in a whisper too low for the sentinel.

"Charlotte Amelia," also in whisper.

The stranger stood upright in the skiff. "Sit down quiet-like in the stern," he ordered. The instant I had obeyed a mighty shove sent us out over the black water, whereupon the boatman fitted carefully muffled oars; then with steady, noiseless strokes sent us onward until the wharf was blotted out behind us.

"Guess you know me," the rower confided at length.

"Mem Watchhorn, as I'm a mortal man."

"Yep—" he confessed, "we'd ha' done it three nights

ago, but had to get the tide jest right, no moon and Shrimpton sairtainly on as sentry. Him and me've been outside your Mam'sel's door about half the time now for two weeks; but we had to pry ourselves well into that bed-bug Tory Ruggles' confidence to make positive sure the guard wouldn't be changed at last minute. Shrimp thought we could do it all alone; but I said 'Three'll be absolootly needed if things should suddenly get to a pinch.' . . . So we sent for you."

"Where are you going?"

"To the slip by Fox Hill, foot of the Common; makes a long walk but that 'ere Sir Claypool's cap'n there to-night. Nice white young feller he is—not like most o' them top-gallant officers. Herby Dunmore (Mem was never wasteful with titles) got him to pass us out and back."

I thought that the man-of-war might spy us, but my rower kept well in the gloom of the Cambridge shore until close by the Brookline sandflats, then struck across the shallows where only a very light skiff pulled by a master boatman could have escaped grounding. As we approached the Boston shore Watchhorn again became very uncommunicative and worked his rowlocks in profound silence, until a second small wharf emerged from the dark ahead. To this we shot up boldly, a sentinel with a dimly flashing bayonet ran out to meet us, whereat my guide promptly gave the British password, and we both scrambled ashore, being promptly greeted by two officers whose figures were barely revealed by a carefully shielded lantern. Instantly I was gripping the hand of Herbert Dunmore and he was introducing me to "Captain Sir Francis Claypool, one of the most honest of fellows in all the service."

Claypool's hand also went into mine, "You may call us 'tyrants,' but you must call us 'brave losers' to boot. If you are Captain Roger Gilman you are a happy man. And may you make *her* more happy than ever I could have done."

There was something sticking in my throat when I tried to answer him, then they explained to me the plot. It was extremely simple. Watchhorn and I were to proceed to the Hutchinson house. Shrimpton on sentry would admit us by the rear garden door. While one of us stood guard the other two must bind and gag Mrs. Nevins (who slept in the room outside Emilie's inner chamber). Emilie then would have to don some manner of male costume and return with us to Fox Hill. The walk would cover Boston, but the password ought to get us by all the guardhouses. Claypool would be on duty until four, and would permit Watchhorn to row us back.

"Honor's a queer jade," laughed Herbert, as he walked a few steps with us, away from the pitch-dark landing. "She lets us close our eyes to your comings and goings. She forbids us to help bind that Nevins woman. Anyway the King's the gainer, for it's in the bargain that now Watchhorn and Shrimpton will have to quit Boston for good, to the detriment I fear of Dr. Warren's intelligence service; though I doubt not that pleasant gentleman has other strings to his fiddle."

Watchhorn piloted me swiftly and silently across the Common where artillery and marines were tenting under the sultry night, and thanks to our perfect knowledge of every back alley and dog-run we were only challenged once, and then by a half-sleeping sentinel near King Street, who gave never a second glance when we satisfied his summons. I knew the vicinage of the Hutchinson house almost as well as I knew the barn at Redford. We slipped down Middle Street, turned at the angle of Fleet Street, then glided along the wall eastward until Watchhorn halted suddenly and pushed at a door in the garden gate.

From this entrance we routed a couple of romantic cats who made off with a yowling flurry, but nothing stirred in the great black house above us. The door yielded promptly, and walking across the dirt garden path on tiptoes my guide led straight to a second door in the ell of the mansion itself. This portal was set with glass, through which the dim radiance of a night lantern in the passage above was discernible. Watchhorn gave two barely audible taps, then three more. We saw a figure coming down the stairs, and immediately a soldier in uniform was unlocking to us. Shrimpton's hard, wiry fist was proffered me; "All's safe and snug as a December night. Old woman's puffing hard. Hardly need do a thing to her.—Glad to see the cap'n, but he's scarcely necessary. Still something *might* happen."

His whispers ceased as he piloted us upstairs. My own heart beat faster, for I knew the climax of the adventure was nearing. One moment more, and then!—The two Marblehead men were significantly preparing some cords and a solid muffler. Shrimpton had also flung over his arm some nondescript male garments. It almost seemed that he had been right,—there was no necessity for me to have come at all. As if Heaven could have forgiven me for letting the rescue of my darling belong entirely to others!

Mrs. Nevins had turned the key, but Watchhorn at once produced some implement which readily seized and revolved it from the outside. The oiled hinges swung back, we crept within. Somebody was breathing heavily upon a cot, and my two escorts were beside it in a twinkling. I caught the noise of a stirring in the blankets, one smothered scream, one hoarsely whispered warning, "Quiet now, missus, and no hurt will touch ye," then Watchhorn spoke a shade louder; "All right, miss. We've got her, and here *he* is." He swung the key in the inner door, whereat it simply flew

open to meet us, and something marvelously alive went
straight into my arms.

. . . By the time Emilie and I could know anything
else, Watchhorn and his comrade had carried Mrs.
Nevins into Emilie's chamber, and were binding her, feebly gasping
and struggling, to the bedstead. "Triced and tight, till
morning," commented Shrimpton approving the knots professionally, "when they'll make a to-do, find ye, and cut
ye loose." Then he brought a lantern, and Emilie and I
very suddenly disengaged ourselves. "Coast seems clear
and everything nice," he assured us. "Still, 'tain't no time
now for—sociables. And now the Mam'sel had better see
how she likes these ere coat and small-clothes."

Emilie gave me one glance of utter seriousness. It never
occurred to either of us that there was anything laughable
in Shrimpton's command, or in the worthy sailor's acting
as costumer. The two Marblehead men discreetly glided
into the corridor. I turned my head while Emilie panted,
tugged a little, ejaculated a mild *"Ciel!"* when some strange
adjustment failed to yield. She had just whispered, "Almost
ready"; when we heard a gasp from Shrimpton outside,
"Lord Jehovah, what's that?"

"That" was the sound of several men entering directly
by the garden gate and lower door, and far less quietly than
had we. Before an instant was given us for council the
lower door was opened. "Unlocked! Thank the devils,"
sounded a voice I recognized in a twinkling, "up then and
out with her."

"Prothero!" spoke Emilie, and even by that poor lantern
I knew that she had turned white as a sheet.

At least four men were coming up the stairs. I knew then
precisely the feelings of a trapped animal, but my wits did
not forsake me.

"Are the windows barred?" I demanded.

"Oui, oui! No escape there. But they're only after me. Save yourself while I keep them in play."

"Saving is *my* work," spoke I, with every fiber tingling. One pistol was already in my hand, the second loose in my belt. "Lie down on Mrs. Nevins' bed. Keep quiet."

Emilie obeyed, too stunned for argument. I crouched in the opposite dark corner. Never had I fired a shot in anger save at Concord Battle, but the few seconds of respite steadied my nerves; not in my whole remaining life did I think so fast, so clearly as in that moment. Outside I knew that Watchhorn and Shrimpton had pulled themselves together, the former was biding his time at the end of the darkened corridor, the second had resumed his place as sentinel, apparently just shaking off a fit of dozing. They would help me if I gave them the least chance.

The four had mounted the stairs all together. Shrimpton's voice sounded challenging:

"Who goes there!"

"Charlotte Amelia," came back from Prothero in harsh whisper. "Stand aside, sirrah. If you can read it, here's a paper from Province House to cover you.—Let us alone. Ho! The door's unlocked already—All the handier. What guard you scoundrels must keep. In with you, men. You, Atkins will take her in hand. As little squealing as possible."

The hinges swung again. A second lantern was being flashed up and down the chamber by a tightly cloaked officer. As he did so three other men, sailors apparently, entered, headed by one of enormous size and brutish countenance. The lantern swung this way and that, but I was glued to the wall in one shadowy corner and Emilie lay motionless upon the cot in the other. All four might have stalked across and tried the inner door, when a beam fell athwart the cot. The huge seaman paused for an instant puzzled, when his chief gave a sudden start and "Damnation!" which sent the burly giant straight over to Emilie. But before one finger could touch the white skin that shrank before him, my pistol blazed out from the dark. The giant tossed his arms wildly, gave a shrill cry like a child's and tumbled directly across the cot.

Instantly the report was followed by a rush from the door. I had planned the second shot for Prothero, but one of his myrmidons swung across the muzzle just in time to take the full charge in his stomach. The fellow went crashing to the floor precisely as Watchhorn and Shrimpton bounded into the room, and we all went whirling round and round in a common mêlée. I knew that I was hammering something with a pistol butt; also that another pistol (Prothero's possibly) was being fired so close to my face that my ears almost burst with the discharge, while the powder grains seemed burning through my cheeks. The next I really knew we were all in the corridor. On the floor of the room we had just quitted forms were groaning and struggling, and Watchhorn was muttering hoarsely beside me:

"We've got her, Shrimp and I; and now to run for it. Those shots will rouse the North End. There's all the devils to pay!"

Both lanterns had been dashed out, but our eyes were well wonted to the dark. Somebody in the room behind us was cursing now and trying to stagger to his feet. I feared that it was Prothero and turned back with "I'll finish him off," but Watchhorn dragged me around by the arm. "Don't be a fool. Come!" he ordered, and he was right. In the main body of the big house women were screaming, children bawling with dread, men with nightcaps throwing up windows and shouting "Thieves! Robbers!" Lights were flashing up by the time we reached the garden. We knew the barracks of the marines were only a few turns away by North Square. In a few minutes anything might happen.

Our two sailors had borne Emilie between them down the stairs and through the garden gate, but by that time the blessed girl was again her courageous self. "Put me down!" she commanded, and I thrust my arm into hers.

"Come what may," I spoke in her ear, "after this Prothero never can get you. If we are hard pressed go quietly to your grandfather's house. Surrender only to an officer you can trust, and on his word of honor that you shall have a formal examination."

"My beloved," answered she, and even in that gloom-wrapped street I could see the flash of her eyes, "to-night God will let us either escape or die together."

Small time had we left, however, for romancing. It was already far past midnight. We were at the shortest day of the year; there would be light speedily. To traverse Boston now in the face of the hue and cry sure to be raised in a few minutes, and reach Fox Hill before Claypool was relieved from his post was impossible. The clamor would make every sentinel alert, and even with the password we would be stopped and questioned long enough to make over-taking certain. While the noise yet rose and swelled in the Hutchinson house, we whisked into Fleet Street, and there even Watchhorn stood for an instant irresolute. Five minutes' respite we had at the very best. More from sheer confusion than design we all halted under a doorway and deliberated.

"We might cut up toward Back Street," I urged. "That'll take us round to Hanover Street, and there'd be a chance."

"Mighty poor one," whispered back Mem, "they'll know we're making toward the Common and the Neck—only way out of town without a boat. The guard over Mill Creek'll never do for us."

"It must be risked," I pleaded, "the only way. Beggar's can't be choosers."

"Mebbe not—hist!"

A noise had sounded from another garden gate, directly at our side where we stood huddled by the brick wall. The gate had opened, a small figure had emerged, then came a little scream:

"Henry—somebody's here!" But before that figure could push back those behind her and slam fast, I had put my foot across the lintel.

"Hope Fifield, as I'm a sinner!" cried I in incautious astonishment. And standing now in the little area behind the gate I saw three forms, one short, two larger, and the bulk of the largest could belong to only one man. "Henry Knox—and Lucy."

We had all pressed inside that protecting wall and gate, and if ever whispering tongues went fast, those were ours and theirs. Our story at last they grasped. Their own plight so far was only a little less desperate. Hope summed it up in a very few words; "Father died a week ago. I went straight to Lucy's. But Gage won't give Henry a pass out of Boston, so we had bribed the sergeant at Freeman's wharf. There's a boat there. We were about to slip off to-night."

"Take Emilie," I ordered, "the rest of us can shift."

Henry's big frame could almost be seen to quiver in the darkness; "Shift? You've made it all or none for us. Hear that alarm rising? I can never get the girls off now without aid. With you three men, perhaps——"

"Quick," ordered Watchhorn, pulling at us again, "Hear 'em at the Square, 'Turn out the guard! Turn out the guard!'—If they'll only let us on the wharf where there's a boat, Shrimp and I can risk hell.—The one chance."

"*Oui!* Quick," commanded Emilie, and I knew the others were right. The clamor at the Hutchinson house was increasing. A lantern flashed out from the angle of Garden Court Street. Our only hope was to reach Freeman's wharf, force our way past the sentinels, and get the boat beyond musket range before all was too late. Many townspeople, I knew, had escaped by mercenary connivance of the guards, though not with such hot pursuit at their heels; but other choice we had none. Just as we heard a rattle of scabbards and a heavy tramp around the corner, we darted from our temporary shelter behind the Knoxes' lodgings and charged out into the night.

. . . If roads can be measured in heart-beats that journey took us the length of the world. If ever I blessed Heaven it was for the great house on the corner of North Street, which made that wide thoroughfare one murk of gloom where we had to cross it. We sped up Bennet Street, almost pitching over the cobbles as we raced. Emilie was upon one of my arms, Hope upon the other, but neither of the dear creatures faltered. For a moment I thought we would evade pursuit altogether; then as we neared Salem Street a fearsome glance over my shoulder caught a lantern speeding along to the angle of Fleet and North Streets, and behind it I saw the gleam of bayonets. However, at the crossroads the lantern stopped, we knew that the party was halting to make sure whether we had continued ahead, or had swung toward Middle Street, the shortest route to the Common.

Possibly we might have got away entirely had not some fool in a nightcap (startled probably by the approaching uproar) thrust his head from an upper window and bawled down, "What's the matter?" Answer we never gave him, but his shout put our pursuers on the scent. However, we were now fairly down Salem Street, with the memorable tower of Christ Church looking benignantly upon us. The next turn was upon Charter Street, with only the fleeting thought for me that I was passing, hunted in the dark, that second home where I had passed happy years.

We knew the pursuit was well after us; but now at last came the sniff from the water-front, of old hemp and oakum, rotting chips, drying seaweed, and it gave fresh courage. Both Hope and Emilie were beginning to drag upon my arms now, when Shrimpton and Watchhorn each seized them respectively upon the other side, almost plucking them from their feet.

"Brave heart. Almost there. We can beat 'em, the dog-fish!" adjured Watchhorn, though the marines were clattering behind with increasing noise along Charter Street. We were reckless at last and made no attempt at quiet. People were everywhere throwing up sashes and shouting questions. Nevertheless we were almost holding our own to the little turn at Sliding Alley which cut down to the wharves, when Shrimpton stumbled over a bit of timber and went down with a curse and a howl, nearly dragging Emilie with him. He was on his feet instantly, but the noise told the chase that again we had swung aside, and not held on (as we might) to the old ferry slip. We dashed past dim storehouses, then saw the gleam of another lantern,—the sentry post upon Freeman's wharf. Of necessity our pace slackened, and Henry, who had led the way with the untiring Lucy, strove to approach the head watchman with an unruffled manner:

"Here's my party, sergeant."

"Your party? Zounds!—Seven. You bargained to pass three. Not all those for five guineas."

"Offer five more," I was whispering, when there came a veritable trumpeting from our rear.

"Hold in the King's name!—Stop 'em all!" while one

pursuer discharged a musket to put the wharf party upon the qui vive.

Once more my head was going around, but Watchhorn had dropped Emilie's arm and bounded straight ahead. "It's for life or death," he called, then sent a pistol into the wondering sergeant's face. As the man went down a comrade loomed behind him, only to meet the swing of Knox's great paw which swept him over with one blow. We clattered out upon the pier, almost tumbling in the water at the end.

Left to myself I would have been lost. The least delay in finding the boat would have left us trapped, but the same darkness which bewildered me, halted also our pursuers. They groped about, banging and cursing, while our two Marblehead men must have seen in the gloom like cats. The tide (thank Heaven) was now high, and a dory bobbed close beside the spiling upon the inky water.

A shot whistled by us, then a second while we tumbled into the craft. A calmer moment would have made us hesitate, for the dory, if large for three, went down almost to her gunwale with seven. I knew that I flung rather than lifted first Emilie, then Hope upon her slimy bottom, next piled over the side myself. The same instant Watchhorn's sheathknife was through the painter, and the dory under a mighty thrust shot out into the void.

Shrimpton had one oar, Watchhorn a second, but our kind genius had laid a second pair along the bottom boards. Knox and I scrambled upon the same thwart and flung ourselves into our task. The final ounce in my power went into that ashen butt, but I could feel the nose of the craft leap around at every one of Henry's titanic strokes. Figures had chased us to the end of the wharf, then came a bellowed "Halt" followed instantly by the crash of four or five muskets. The balls sang by us, and spat up white foam ahead

in the harbor, but somewhere in the dory I heard a scream
from Lucy; "They've hit the boat. Oh! the water." "My
handkerchief's in the hole," almost instantly announced
Hope; and Emilie as calmly added, "I've found the bailing
bucket."

That young gentlewomen should be attending to such nice
matters appeared at that instant eminently conventional.
My life seemed going into that oar. A second volley after
reloading followed the first from the wharf, but the distance
was now so great that the shots all flew harmless. Nevertheless Shrimpton gave out a good maritime curse, "That
raises 'em, at the guard boat by North Battery. We can't
do it."

"Do what?" I demanded.

"Make Noddle Island to north'ard—our best landing.
Now it'll have to be Charlestown, and in the teeth of the
warships.—The Lord aid us."

From the line of wharves to southward was rising now
the sound of men rummaging about, shouting commands,
clattering oars; then more shouting. I knew that the waves
were almost surging over the gunwale of the perilously
loaded dory; whether we shipped the water across the side
or through the bullet hole I knew not. Emilie was bailing
furiously; Lucy had plucked off her husband's cap (my own
had long since disappeared in those black alleys), and was
bailing also. Right across the horizon to the east—never
was dawn so unwelcomed—had spread a strong yellow bar.
To the westward where Charlestown reached out toward
Boston, rode the hull of a warship; "The *Lively*," Shrimpton
cast at me. That the commotion we caused should fail to
attract her attention seemed of all things impossible, but
every stroke was bringing us fairly under her broadside.

Watchhorn and Shrimpton were rowing as seamen row
when the fiend is close behind them. Knox could not mend

his earlier pace. If my oar did not snap in the water it was because mountain ash had a sturdy pliance. Presently a light gun boomed off from the battery on land, as if signal to the *Lively*. The heavy boat which had started after us was gaining, although not rapidly. She pulled ten oars, but the people behind them had no lives at stake, and possibly were a little uncertain as to our course.

When I spared a glance over my shoulder the Charlestown shores were clearly outlined now—blessedly nearer. Yet we were at length absolutely athwart the *Lively*—two hundred fathoms and less from her battery. We could hear the trampling of many feet upon her decks, bosun's whistles, strident commands, creak of tackling, the rumbling of guns running out through portholes. We seemed due for the entire broadside. If so all would be over in a twinkling, the dory matchwood, our troubles stilled forever.

Somehow, I knew not clearly, I found myself rowing with only one hand; Emilie was clasping the other. Her thought was even as mine, that by a merciful decree we were about to pass from this life undivided. Nevertheless I was a fair swimmer. The impulse was almost irresistible to seize Emilie, leap overboard, and trust that the tide was not running too swiftly to forbid us a chance of making land. Watchhorn, apparently reading my thoughts, panted across, "Not yet! No chance! We're in the Lord's hands." Then his voice died, as across the dark waters we heard the trumpeted, "Now lads, all together."

In answer came a flash of livid light from every porthole of the man-of-war. Our cars throbbed with an unchained thunder. Instinctively our oars trailed in the water, while overhead seemed rushing the giants of a fiery gale. The noise ended, the tempest passed, and yet we drifted unscathed. While yet we marvelled in the throbbing silence, Lucy from the stern and looking toward Charles-

town gave a hysterical "See!"—And lo! directly upon the
hill above the village, clearly marked now against the
strengthening skyline, was a long irregular tracing and
above it wafted a flag.

The *Lively* had seen the American earthwork, had taken
the shore signals and guns as directions to fire upon it, and
had ignored our insignificant boat to turn the King's thunders upon this newest audacity of the rebels.

We drifted a good minute blinking at the amazing situation. This star-gazing nigh cost us dear. The pursuing
boat was pulling up perilously, the warship's battery fired
again and heavy shot even if flying overhead make no
games for parlors. Again we rowed; rowed and bailed,
the water gaining almost more ominously than the craft
behind us. The light was increasing steadily, and every
instant might bring a lower aim with the cannon. Watchhorn, however, kept shouting directions for steering our rud-
derless craft, and at last after a panting eternity I felt
the joyous tingle when my blade hit down upon the sand.

Thirty yards of water sundered us still from the shore
when we grounded, but the deep-keeled guard-boat had
already abandoned the chase. Just as we slid into the sands,
her people dropped oars with a yell of fury, stood erect
and crackled off a dozen musket and pistols. More splinters
flew from the dory. Shrimpton clapped his hand to his side,
growled, " 'Tain't nothing!" and leaped into the water, we
all following. As my feet sunk in the ooze, something fell and
floundered beside me. I made a grasp for it; it was not
Emilie but poor little Hope whom I slung into my arms
as one might lift a bale. The others I sensed rather than
knew were running and struggling beside me.

Presently (I was far past the stage of asking "how" and
"how long") the dry ground seemed to be under us. Muskets were still rattling. It was now light enough to take in

that men in homespun were firing from behind rocks and stumps toward the retreating guard-boat. A cannon-shot went somewhere tearing over the sands and crashing through some timbers. Nevertheless everything seemed relatively safe and peaceful. Emilie, her hair all covering her face, was clinging tightly to my arm while still I carried Hope. And then of a sudden a voice, a friendly pleasant voice, sounded in my ears: "We saw you coming and tried to cover you.—Lieutenant Lakin of Colonel Prescott's regiment—your most obedient. And 'pon my honor, do I recognize Captain Gilman, the aide of General Warren?"

We made our way across Charlestown causeway, with the fire of the men-of-war still screaming above us. The three miles into Cambridge were through a scene of utter confusion. Mounted officers were tearing hither and thither; militiamen hunting desperately for their companies; some regiments standing to their arms as if to meet instant attack; other regiments digging frantically upon earthworks where no attack could have been possible. All the warships in the Charles were bellowing, and the British batteries on Copp's and Beacon Hills were joining their sulphurous chorus. A great battle, a pitched battle, and not merely a running fight as in April manifestly was about to commence.

Yet momentarily it seemed as if all our troubles were fading far behind.—What mattered artillery roar and human clangor when I walked through the gold of that June morning, with the hand of Emilie Rivoire fast clasped in mine?

We were utterly shameless about it. Emilie's strange masculine garb should have been all the more for wonderment, because her hair was now tangled all over her back—a great mass of red gold. If every company we passed had shouted "Fie!" we would never have known, nor cared. Henry and Lucy were also walking hand in hand, Lucy's

dark head likewise all dishevelled, and never a thought by
either if curious looks went chasing. Shrimpton walked
stolidly along, now and then touching his side where the
ball had streaked a rib, but Watchhorn, capless, coatless,
perfect figure of a ragged sailor, had taken little Hope out
of my arms as he might lift a kitten, flung her over his
broad shoulder, and so laden veritably led our march. I
swear that seven stranger appearing mortals than we never
crossed Cambridge Common.

. . . I left Emilie with Lucy and Hope at the home of
Mrs. Compton, an old friend of mother's, upon the Watertown road. The good woman gasped at the sudden visita-
tion, but Cambridge homes were becoming used to war
crises, and I knew her resources. The dear creatures would
be in excellent hands. Watchhorn and Shrimpton had left
us; Henry had taken momentary leave; Lucy and Hope
had disappeared up the wide staircase amid female "oh-ing"
and fluttering, but Emilie turned toward me as we stood in
the spacious hall with the open door bringing in the scents
of the great rose garden. A wondrous knight-errant no
doubt I looked to make adieus to a wondrously dressed
lady. Fearing the place I tried to bend over her hands and
pretend that I was not anxious for anything else, but with a
little cry she went straight into my arms, and if anybody
witnessed, much harm did it do us!

The cannon toward Charlestown were roaring now like
furies unloosed. Perhaps I was very weary, but at that
time I did not know it. Emilie put back her cloud of hair,
and looked straight into my face.

"There is about to be a battle, *mon* Roger?"

"I believe so."

"You have told me Dr. Warren asked you to join him if
you could."

"So he said," suddenly my speech came hard.

"Then, my beloved, if God could carry us through the gates of death last night, He can carry you through the lesser perils this day. You belong to America."

No Yankee girl could have done it thus, but with perfect nobility and simplicity, she laid her hand thrice firmly upon my shoulder: "I have no sword for that quaint thing they call the accolade. But you are now my *chevalier*. I send you out my champion. Whatever befalls I shall be eternally proud of you, *mon cher ami*—and God will not deny that soon we shall be joined forever."

I kissed her hands, then again her face, and sped to the Hill house in search of Warren. The cannon were pealing louder, louder, louder.

Note. The escape of Henry and Lucy Knox by stealth from Boston upon the eve of the battle of Bunker Hill rests on very reliable evidence beyond the narrative of Colonel Gilman. (Editor.)

CHAPTER XL

DULCE ET DECORUM EST

APPROACHING three o'clock I went up Breed's Hill side by side with Dr. Warren. At Charlestown Neck the guns of four British men-of-war and two floating batteries as well as the more distant cannon upon Beacon Hill were rending the air, and flinging up dense clouds of sods and sand. We had traversed Bunker Hill and the half-finished earthworks begun by Putnam, then come to that rail fence, breastwork and redoubt which shall endure in the empire of the mind while America remains America. Warren was in his general's uniform, but over his shoulder was slung a musket. I stood near him when Prescott proffered him the command, and when he answered modestly, "I come as a volunteer to serve under you, and shall be happy to learn from a soldier of your experience."

The men huzzaed and waved their caps when they saw Warren. His coming seemed earnest for those reënforcements which the trembling Ward, shut up in Hastings House by Cambridge Common all through that day of thunders, ordered too late and never got into the battle. "The men," I say—should I not say, "The lads"? For there is one term, used now by our stock orators which sticks in my craw, 'tis so misleading,—"Revolutionary sires."—Doubtless as years stole on, those of us who survived *did* beget families and our hairs turned white, but doddering old men then we were not, and the right to say this is mine—only in my seventies still and glorying in the morning.

There were more lads in their teens than men in twenties
along those trenches; broad-freckled, blue-shirted farmer
lads, who if they dressed ill in their march knew how to
ply the spade. No graybeards could have made that fortress spring up overnight. It was the young men rejoicing
in the fullness of life, who went forth to the Charlestown
hills that day, as on every day when the story of the
Republic was traced with fire and steel. And if I was a
youthful captain myself, my years were not less than those
of full many of the homespun officers who thought of sweethearts or young wives, whilst they strove to hold their men
steady through those hard hours while the British were mustering just below.

Warren moved about, calm and smiling, sometimes imitat-
ing Prescott by walking on the parapet of the earthworks
to encourage their defenders. A heavy shot screamed over
him, the wind thereof half lifting his hat. "Come down,
General!" I entreated. "Your life is precious." He laughed
at me, not in bravado but as one might in a friendly talk;
"Why, that's just what Elbridge Gerry said when we were
leaving Cambridge, and I gave him back the old *'Dulce et
decorum est pro patria mori.'* The peril's not so great, it
heartens the men, and taking a mortal chance is part of the
lawful fees of an officer."

The clouds had blown clear. It had come on one of those
mortal hot days which Providence can send as warning to
sinners. The shovel work and the cannon balls between
them had created enormous clouds of dust, and every one
was sweltering. A few pails of switchel were passed about,
but there was a direful lack even of tepid water. The fifteen
hundred odd men holding the works had dined meagerly
upon the cold provisions in their knapsacks, sitting most of
them behind the crumbling parapets, ill shaded from the
broiling sun.

There was much grumbling, much muttering, "Why aren't we reënforced?" many glances back toward Bunker Hill and the causeway to Cambridge, but no flinching. I was present at the consultation of Prescott with Warren and Putnam when it was agreed not to ask to have the men relieved. Tired as they all were, they possessed one quality priceless for the coming ordeal, they had become used to the British fire and had learned to let cannon balls crash by without quavering. "They had done the work and they should have the honor," spoke Prescott, with Warren nodding "Amen!"

The intrenchments had been completed, rude platforms set up for the musketeers, and for a trying interval there was little to do but to keep a stout heart and to watch the British. Never since firearms drove out arrows could be a more spectacular battle. Rough and sheer on the summit of Breed's, with the fresh yellow earth marking its front of eight rods, rose Prescott's redoubt. At right angles down the slope toward the north ran a breastwork, open at flank and rear, but covering the retreat from the redoubt toward Bunker Hill. Striking from the breastwork, first diagonally, and then parallel with the falling land almost over to the Mystic ran yet another work; but it was little better than a blind, a rail fence hastily made double and with the spaces stuffed with hard-rammed hay, barely able to turn musket balls.

Six small cannon, very indifferently served, were casting defiance at the British; perhaps their ineffective uproar helped to steady our men. Over the earthworks floated the "New England" flag, a blue banner with the red cross of St. George in one corner quartering a white field, and with a green pine tree set in the upper angle. I recall wondering how long that red cross would remain upon an American ensign, but a halt was given to day-dreaming when Lakin,

the friendly lieutenant who had greeted us earlier, touched
my elbow: "There!"—The regulars had started.

Even without Prescott's good spyglass I could see nigh
everything. Since one o'clock the flower of Gage's army
had been ferrying to Charlestown. Landing at Moulton's
Point in plain sight at our feet they had been drawing up
leisurely, deliberately, as for dress parade. No scurrying
from dusty bivouacs. From their quarters officers and men
had marched forth oiled, powdered and laced as if fit for
inspection.

All the regiments were forming now in three long lines.
It was a delight to watch the far-stretching ranks of white,
scarlet and burnished steel undulating together, the officers
moving about watchfully, gesturing for perfect alignment.
Behind the troops rode the warships, five in all, out on
the sparkling Charles. As the smoke blew aside there could
be seen the decks alive with the blue figures of the seamen
bustling like ants, as they tugged on the ropes of their
leaping and recoiling cannon. Beyond the dazzling stretch
of the waters spread Boston itself; every roof dark with
the people, human figures lining the belfries, and masses
upon Beacon and Copp's Hills almost crowding around the
batteries.

From these the flashes of fire and bursts of smoke came
incessantly. As the gray vapor lifted, upon Copp's Hill I
caught even the gleam of the scabbards and the scarlet of
a knot of officers, Gage and his retinue doubtless looking
forth to see how the "peasants" would endure the ordeal of
fire.—And we all knew that it mattered never a whit who
that night possessed those Charlestown hills; it mattered
eternally how the men in homespun stood before the men in
red. I looked to my firelock. This was to be no Concord
volleying. If it was youth that afternoon that dared to do
battle for America, that evening youth would have passed
to manhood.

At Concord we had been ever advancing. Now we had to endure the harder testing of sitting tensely under the dust flung up by the ceaseless cannon. The balls ploughed into the earth, but only rarely making a dangerous hit. More harmful was the fire sweeping the causeway behind us, daunting all but the most firmly-led regiments, and checking all but a dribble of reënforcements.

The British ranks formed slowly, very slowly. At last, however, some signal apparently waved from Moulton's Point which told all the Boston batteries to double their fury, while even the distant guns at Roxbury Neck began roaring—to scare our men by the landward gate to Boston. Simultaneously we saw groups of cannoneers running field-pieces along the shore by the Mystic. "To enfilade the entrenchment," I caught Prescott muttering to Warren; but speedily they stopped. A bit of soft land nearly foundered them. Then the eight guns unlimbered, and their grape-shot began rattling over our parapets, now and then striking a man and greatly discouraging any rash adventure.

With the first salvo of the guns the infantry went forward, a sight to rejoice the war-gods. They were advancing in two large bodies, the artillery firing between them; one moving along the lower ground to the north near the Mystic to force the rail fence; the other straight up the hill to the redoubt. The men wore their heavy knapsacks and came on slowly, regiment stretching beyond regiment, each three in lines, the officers walking proudly alone in the intervals, and the drummers and fifers pounding and screaming in the rear.

There were many fences, stone or rail, to cross, but the troops surmounted each obstacle deliberately and always resumed alignment. Over each regiment blew the great banner of the cross of St. George, carried by some veteran of Minden or Quebec. The sight was magnificent. It was more than magnificent. Every swaying of the long, symmetrical lines, every flash from the serried gunbarrels and bayonets, the very swing of the officers told the contempt which the advancing two thousand bore for us; how a few moments would tell what it meant to stand before British regulars; how our tatterdemalion companies would be sent flying toward Charlestown Neck.

Before the enemy started our men had been chattering nervously. Now they were amazingly still, but the sight of those bayonets moving as with a perfect mechanism straight upon us was almost more than flesh and blood could stand. A few firelocks went off from the redoubt, despite the stringent orders, "Hold fire till within ten rods." I helped to kick up the guns of some nervous lads who seemed deaf to shouted entreaty.

As for some of us, for a little space it seemed almost as a thing hellish and impossible to fire point-blank into those splendidly marching regiments, that seemed teaching us the pageantry of war. The British themselves dissolved the spell. To give a foretaste of their coming, suddenly one rank after another fired upon us; reloaded and fired again. The balls sang over the earthworks with amazingly little damage. Vaguely I remembered a saying that uphill firing was often high, but there was no time for any nice philosophy.

Behind the works now our men were crouching like arrows upon taut-drawn bows. In the redoubt where I stood to bear messages for Prescott or Warren, I saw the former, a tall blue figure, standing calmly upon a timber, head and shoulders above the earthwork, his eyes riveted upon a stake driven on the slope before him. A white-belted color bearer reached it. Prescott's hand went down in a signal which every watching officer sent on with one great shout, *"Now!"*

From redoubt, breastwork, and rail fence there answered one long ripple of flame. Never had firelocks hurled death more fast. Through the murky clouds as I loaded and primed could be had glimpses of the red and white lines now almost at the foot of the redoubt. Gaps were being torn in them. The foe were so close we could witness the handsome officers stepping about coolly as at their cricket or bowls, pointing, ordering, pricking faltering privates with their sabers. "Close up like Englishmen!" came clearly through one awful lull in the pandemonium.

They stood in line under the redoubt and gave us volley for volley. Men dropped inside our works, but all our fear was gone. The firelocks never slackened. The British were so close that their own artillery perforce was stayed lest it strike friend as well as foe, but our own few guns swept bloody avenues through the lines confronting.

Five minutes, ten, or was it a century?—At last no more balls were coming across to us. The smoke cloud lifted. Our own fire went down, just as my gun became hot within my hands. The field before us was clearing, save for the multitudinous red and white patches upon the greensward, some scattered, some in long windrows. Masses of men were hurrying down the hillslope, here in orderly squads, there in headlong crowds, racing to clear the range of that musketry. The attackers upon the rail fence were in equally scattering flight. Our own men were leaping on the parapets, cheering, waving; and some fools would have sprung down and pursued save as they were vigorously restrained by their officers.

My own sight of that hillslope was sickening. God forbid that I pen some things among the wounded; but it was no hour for qualmishness. Prescott and Warren had passed among the men, praising their steadfastness, and bidding them await another onset. As I came up for orders I congratulated Warren upon the outlook. "Surely we can do it again."

"Surely," said he, as always smiling, "that is if they can be stopped with twelve cartridges." Then he bade me, "Go to Colonel Stark at the rail fence, and tell him to hold fire until within six rods, or we shall lack powder to turn the next attack."

I found the New Hampshire men and Knowlton's Connecticut companies at the rail fence running down to the Mystic. All were in good courage for militia who had crossed the Neck in the teeth of the British cross-fire. Whilst I was looking for Stark, who was senior officer, a sudden grunt halted me, and I beheld none other than Watchhorn leaning upon a firelock.

"You are hungry for fighting," said I, rejoicing to see him.

"Shrimp's wound was getting nasty," spoke he coolly, drawing out a tinder box and lighting a pipe, "so I took him to Vassal House horspital, then hoofed it back here. That poor old Ward's shut up in headquarters, and too dog-sick to issue a straight order, but one of his aides gave me something to carry." And nobly indifferent to his pipe, he tapped a half barrel of powder.

"And glad we're to get it," vowed a lean Merrimac country sergeant; "sent out to talk with the devil with only a gill a piece, and that's half gone."

I found Stark, a straight mountain-ranger, hard as nails, giving orders to Captain Trevett in charge of one of our few cannon, and he took my message with a shrug, "It shall be *five* rods at the fence. Let the redoubt do its business and we'll do ours. But O Lord, why were we sent out here if they didn't mean to back us up!"

My duty was again with Prescott and Warren, but before I could remount the slope the grape from the British field-pieces reopened, making the space betwixt the fence and the breastwork one highway for death. Without desperate reason no man had right to cross it. Then while I hesitated Mem's finger went out, "See Charlestown!"—

Right under the turn of the hill that deserted town, caught in the focus of war, was one mass of smoke and flame. Doubtless it was the proper military thing to do, to clear out a possible refuge for our flanking parties, but it made knotted fists from all our works shake toward the fire-scaled roofs and belfry. The smoke from four hundred buildings went up in an awful pyramid which the wind bore mercifully slowly to seaward, leaving our own view clear toward the rallying enemy. The steeple of the church was presently traced in flame. The crash of falling timbers sounded through the din of the unwearying cannon. But we were conscious again of only one thing—again the British were advancing.

The lines were not dressed quite so precisely as before. A wounded prisoner, who had been brought in, said that while Pigot was leading against the redoubt, the very resplendent officer who, with a knot of aides could be seen directing the advance on the rail fence, was none other than the great Sir William Howe himself. Whoever he was, he and his men came on gallantly, more gallantly than before —for now the troops had to step directly across the bodies of their fallen comrades. It was all done coolly—without the slightest faltering. Once again they next began volleying at us, the balls rattling through the hay or sending white chips flying from the railings. It was hard enough as a result to keep Stark's men from firing, especially when the redcoats went fairly past the mark for the former death blasts. "Aim at the waistbands," "Till you see the whites of their eyes," "Pick off the officers"—such things we all kept shouting just to steady one another.

Nine rods, eight, seven, six, five. The British volleys had ceased, their cannon were silent to spare their own files. Directly before me, every button on his scarlet coat glittering, a tall captain gave his flourish and shout, "With the bayonet, men!" Before us danced one line of gleaming points poised for the final onset; when in answer from the hillcrest to the Mystic there was one rending crash from the firelocks.

It was the first attack over again, with the British closer, our own musket work hotter. The regulars were toppling like blocks, but for long moments our foes plied ramrod and gunlock, firing almost into our faces, while officers would push them forward with halberds and swords. Our own lines were a continuous stream of fire, as the red battalions surged up to six paces of the works,—six paces but no farther, for no man could cross that awful interval and live.

I saw a fine young ensign levelling his fusee toward us. The ball sang between Watchhorn and myself, and the ensign, not a man now standing near him, walked away from us in cold disgust. "Damn the rebels!" I caught his tribute, *"They won't flinch."* A high officer all alone was waving his sword, trying to rally the men. It was Howe, every one of his aides shot down. The balls must have hailed around but fate was with him,—he turned away unscathed.

Already through our din came the cheering above from the hill. Pigot's lines had shivered before the redoubt, and just when Howe's regiments broke also.—A real flight this time. The redcoats ran into the smoke and some we could glimpse even making for their boats. The slaughter had been greater than at the first onset; mere handfuls had fled back of some companies. The officers were striking the privates with their swords to make them form again into line.

New Hampshire and Connecticut were cheering from the
rail fence; Massachusetts from the breastwork and the
redoubt. "The battle's over!" the thoughtless were shouting. "We can whip 'em again and again." But Stark came
up to me with a smoke-grimed face.

"Reach Prescott and Warren if you can," he ordered, "tell
them that thanks to this 'ere Watchhorn we've still got five
rounds apiece at the fence. But if they are provided at
the redoubt as I fear they are, the battle's good as over.
We must think of saving the men."

I made my way again up to the redoubt. The British
field-pieces were being dragged forward by desperate efforts
across the soft land, but momentarily they had ceased
firing. At the boats the regulars were forming once more,
and we could see heavy drafts of marines and men in blue
—armed seamen, landing to reënforce them. I found our
troops in the redoubt still cheering and taunting the
redcoats, "Come another time!" but Prescott, Warren
and a little group of higher officers were apart in anxious
debate.

"I have besought powder from Ward by repeated messengers. He sends nothing," Prescott was affirming solemnly.
"Not fifty of my men have bayonets. Few have three
rounds left apiece, most have only one. The next attack
ends everything."

"Shall we then retire?" asked a sober-lipped major.

"Honor forbids," spoke Prescott and Warren together,
and Warren added, "This hill shall be sold for the uttermost. Tell Colonel Stark that we will hold the redoubt to
the last cartridge and beyond. When all fails let him shield
our retreat."

Prescott nodded and I turned to go, but Warren walked
with me a few steps toward the exit from the redoubt. His
eyes shone preternaturally bright: "I'm learning this black

trade fast, Roger. Righteous Heaven, but 'tis a day to
have lived for! Come next what may, 'rebels' we can be
in Boston still, but 'peasants' never more." Then his hand
slid into mine, and his grip tightened. "God bless us all."

Thus I left him, flecking the dust from his fine blue uniform and quietly ordering an artillery charge to be broken
open and doled out for the muskets. As I passed from the
redoubt the men were gathering piles of stone for the last
defense. The breastwork had been abandoned already, for
now the British guns were beyond the soft ground and
raking the whole open end of the intrenchment, driving its
defenders into the redoubt. My own path was sufficiently
perilous and I made the long interval upon the run, wondering if the howl of demons was worse than the whir of grape-
shot. Somewhere about midway I vaguely knew that something had struck me, but it might have been only a pebble
flung up by the cannon. I felt neither pain nor wound as
Watchhorn dragged me behind the feeble shelter of the rail
fence.

It was nigh half-past four when thus I reported again to
Stark. He received the orders, but everything possible had
been done already. The New Hampshire men were tensely
waiting, but for the moment we could only stand and witness. Taught wisdom at fearful price, Howe had now made
his infantry doff knapsacks and form up in huge columns.
Toward the rail fence a few companies merely offered a
feint; the whole onset was toward the redoubt.

We watched the long columns mounting higher, higher,
solid masses of advancing bayonets, past the ten-rod line,
the five; but till within fifteen yards was there not a shot
fired. Then indeed the redoubt was clouded with a deadly
volley, the heads of the columns went down in heaps, and
the assault wavered. Three more good discharges would
have sent the attackers flying again to their boats; but the

fire died away to an ineffectual crackling, and soon the crests of the redoubt were swarming with the bayonets.

The British were cheering now and firing, as a great dust rose from the mêlée behind the parapets. Out of this dust presently we saw forms running down to us, Prescott's men, clubbing their muskets to dash aside the bayonets. The British were chasing but were also in a scattered confusion, while figures alike in red and in homespun were being bowled over like tenpins.

One glance I took of the men about me. They were forming in solid ranks behind the still sheltering rail fence. There were strained faces in those New Hampshire and Connecticut companies but no wavering. Thank God they had still a little powder! Fire for the moment they could not, with their friends streaming down right toward them, but there was a silent screwing of flints and snapping of priming pans for the instant soon to come. The tall figure of Prescott was now descending the slope, striking back bayonets with his sword; by every mortal chance he should have fallen, but he came steadily toward us through the bloody murk that now spread far down the hill.

Having no command I knew my business.—Where was Warren? One of my pistols cleared from my path a grenadier corporal who had almost pinked me. The flat of my sword bowled over another. Up past pursuers and pursued I ran, until before me there were not redcoats but the blue of sailors from the warships.

That instant my sight lit upon Warren. He had dropped his gun, and sword in hand was striving to cover some raw lads from the seamen. One moment more and I would have been beside him for life or for death, when out of the swirling eddy came Prothero leading his sailors. He must have recognized Warren instantly, for under my mortal eyes I saw him snatch a musket from a seaman, and fire almost

in the American's face. Warren clapped one hand to the
side of his head, turned mechanically, fell without cry or
pang.

Sight, hearing, for me almost ceased as I sprang over him.
Vaguely I knew that Prothero was shouting words of triumph, was leveling something at me also, while my least
effort now was to resist; then right across my shoulder
blazed a firelock, *"Starn all!"* bellowed a great voice, and
the captain of the *Argus* went down beside the man he had
slaughtered. Watchhorn's giant paw hustled me to my feet:
"God has him and the devil's got his slayer. Off! You're
needed!"

Stunned and groping I let him drag rather than lead me
away through that raging hell. The fall of their leader
halted instant pursuit by the seamen, and we regained the
rail fence. Powderless and leaderless now, the men from
the redoubt were breaking into a run toward Bunker Hill
and the causeway, but the battle was not yet over. The redcoats were cheering and charging to cut off all retreat, when
we heard Stark's shout above the raging tumult: *"Abide the
shock! For the honor of New Hampshire!"* Whereat our
men of the North stood out before the onrushing regiments
like the granite of their hills. We were barely within their
lines before the British onslaught halted before a blast of
fire like the fiercest from the redoubt. No breastworks now;
we were facing the regulars clean in the open, volley answering to volley, while Prescott's men streamed to safety.

In a red daze I saw Trevett trying to turn a cannon to
help check the pursuit. It seemed a thing very ordinary
at that moment for one of the gunners to fall sprawling,
whereupon Watchhorn with a single gigantic thrust shifted
the piece to position. I helped to cram home the scrap iron
till it dropped from the muzzle, when the sulphurous
charge crashed by me into the advancing column.

Nothing was clear to me after that. The cannon blast gave the New Hampshire companies a welcome respite. They yielded ground at length, albeit stubbornly and in good order, although heavily outnumbered now and their pouches nearly emptied. The pursuit nevertheless was slow and respectful. Howe had paid too much for his hill to have stomach for recklessness.

We tugged together at the ropes of that cannon, Watchhorn drawing like an ox, assisted by others who had shot their last round. Back we retired over Bunker Hill, where brave old Putnam and Pomeroy were adjuring, "Make another stand!" their fighting blood too fevered to let them know that men without powder or bayonets would be throwing their lives away.

. . . The sun was sliding down in the heavens one ball of fire, with that redness which tells when one torrid day must follow another. The warships and floating batteries were still flinging their shot across Charlestown Neck. At times a gray-puffing mortar shell would arch over the waters from Beacon Hill. They seemed harmless as thistledown after what we had lived through. On the causeway we met the troops at last ordered out by the feckless Ward. Their volleys stopped the cautious advance of the British, and they cheered us roundly when they saw us march past with Trevett's cannon. Alone of the guns sent out from camp we had tugged back the six-pounder.

. . . Thus for a second time that day of decision I trudged those mortal three miles into Cambridge. That we had done anything memorable, worthy of fame and glory was the last thing then in my thoughts. Watchhorn, as his giant sinews strained and cracked, was cursing bitterly to himself: "One minute too late to save him—Oh, Lord, Lord!" While before me one fact stared out blackly before everything, *"Warren is gone! Warren is gone!"*

And a kind of dull rage possessed me that Prothero had escaped into the grave, eternally baffling my studied vengeance.

Our regiments were around us now, standing to their arms at last; ready for that assault upon Cambridge which Gage and Howe were only too thankful to hold back. The sultry air was growing still; the warships and the batteries had calmed. As I came into the village, the clock was striking seven amid what seemed an unnatural silence under the elms. We cast off the gun ropes. Somebody was offering me food and drink; I dimly knew that it was Harter from Redford. My own voice rattled in my throat while remarking something about "At Mrs. Compton's and *she* ought to know." Then all the houses and trees spun around, while friendly voices, seeming very far away, were saying, "Loosen his shirt. There's where it grazed him."

After that I saw nothing, felt nothing until a candle was gleaming near my eyes. I opened them upon my own rough, plain little room in Stoughton,—the carpetless plank floor, the stiff chairs, the paintless deal table, the familiar row of books, with the old flock-bed under me. Everything was peaceful. Holy God, how peaceful! Eustis (out under exchange) was saying, "Thanks be, it was not an artery!" Harter was answering, "She's been sent for."—And I, who had conversed with fire and death all day, suddenly knew that I was weak and helpless, and with one impulse began sobbing and sobbing as once in Yetmercy's arms while yet a little child.

. . . How could I know that on that day America had become of age?

CHAPTER XLI

EMILIE and I were married upon July the third. An honest man, however prolix by nature, will be brief about his own wedding, and I always try to be honest.

It was somewhat this way. I had collapsed more from exhaustion than the scraping of a grape-shot, but for a good week during that diabolically hot weather I was compelled to lie in bed while Emilie, Hope and the Comptons tended me most absurdly. Strange stories, outrageously adorned by Watchhorn, about my part on the hill had gone back to Redford, and down to camp came mother and father and all the rest of the tribe. Warren, whose aide I had been, slept on the field of honor, but General Heath himself came up to my little attic chamber, and assured me that a captain's commission in the new Continental army now organizing, was waiting the moment I could report for duty.

That moment I assumed would be immediately, but at the first step I took upon the floor everything went wobbling, and Eustis informed me it would be a good six weeks still before I could do any more real fire-eating. All that brought up the question of Emilie. What in the Lord's name was it right to do with her? I put the question to the lady herself squarely the next afternoon, when I was propped up on the mattress, and mother very thoughtfully was looking after a wounded fellow in the next chamber.

"There's a long war ahead," I remarked presently, after we had been holding hands in silence for quite a time.

"A long hard war, Roger. The soul of England is not in

it, but it may take years, years to teach that hard, stubborn King and the Tories like him, their fault."

"What will you do, sweetheart? Will you not go back to Redford with mother?"

"Alone? Must I go alone?"

"What will you? Is it right that we should be married? You know the chances of battle?"

Her face came down very close to mine: "Better a soldier's widow than never my true love's wife."

Thus I consented, and in my innocency I imagined that father would be called in to say his words immediately; but you should have heard the protests and uproar among the women when "I spoke of such a thing." Even with the British guns booming again along the Charles, and with our nine thousand men in Cambridge working like mad to throw up intrenchments to stop a sortie over Charlestown Neck, I was so overwhelmed with reproaches that I asked mother "Whether I had stumbled into the unpardonable sin?" To which she answered, "Almost," and left me to my bewilderment.

Another long week therefore went by, which was perhaps as well, because I was at last able to stroll around a bit with comfort, with Henry Knox, or Harter, or Darius at elbow to steady me, although of Emilie, as thus I grew better, I saw deplorably little. Lucy Knox was in her majestic glory "arranging things," Tabby seemed beside herself, and even mother had once to say to Yetmercy, "Don't act so like a fool."

Henry was often over at good old Ward's headquarters at the Hastings house, where brisk young officers cooled their heels, fretted, and planned great things "when the real general comes." I understood that a large convoy of fat Tories fleeing from the interior, had been stopped in Cambridge; and that Henry had seen to it that they should not be passed through the Roxbury lines, until a flag had been sent into Boston telling Gage that if he wanted to see his friends they must be exchanged against certain personages such as M. Rivoire.

Day therefore slipped into day, and I grew stronger. At length it was the afternoon of the second. I had been walking with Harter among the tents and turf huts which now covered the Common, when we caught a great clattering of hoofs, and swaying of cocked hats, and a party of horsemen in better uniform than most of our strangely clad regiments came up the Watertown road. Men near at hand were waving their caps and cheering; and we caught the "There he is," as some notable figure passed.

The squadron stopped before Wadsworth House, politely evacuated by President Langdon; there was a ruffle of drums while certain personages dismounted and passed inside. We approached, however, too late to see anything more remarkable than a magnificent bay horse with embossed leather housing being held at the entrance by an affable negro, resplendently liveried in blue and scarlet. "Yes, sahs," the African was complacently declaiming as we edged up in turn; "*the Gineral,* and Gineral Lee and Gineral Ward are all in there, but this am Nelson, the best hoss in Virginy, and I'm Billy, the Gineral's own body servant."

Further great news, however, I heard not, for that instant something was coming around the turn from Brighton bridge. "A redcoat in Cambridge?" cried Harter, starting to chase me, "Hi, there! Hi!" But he could not overtake me before I had given one hand to Herbert Dunmore, and the other to Georges Rivoire, both under the pilotage of Henry Knox.

M. Georges must needs haste to the Comptons after words to me that set my eyes to winking hard, but what a good chat Herbert and I had together! He greatly comforted me by reporting that Claypool, although desperately wounded in the second charge, was pulling through, "And sends you the friendliest greetings as from one good enemy to another. And between ourselves I think there is already a little Tory in Boston who will help him to mend a cracked but in no wise broken heart." Then he told of how Gage was being toasted ironically as "Lord Lexington, Baron of Bunker Hill" in all the officers' messes, and that probably he would soon be on his way back to England.

"But not without consolation," Herbert added; "first, because among all the good men fallen, the world also was rid of one knave. Mem Watchhorn can have a commission, I think, if he will turn redcoat, for doing Prothero. The hold that villain won over the poor governor will never be cleared up. And second, because of that letter which I know Henry Knox sent in with the flag, 'Mlle. Rivoire assures General and Mrs. Gage that what she did was for the public interest, and the cause of America having been served, henceforth her lips are sealed.'"

"And yourself?" I asked, after we had talked of nigh everything else.

"I am one of the many in the army and navy who will never draw sword against America. Lord Chatham's eldest son now in Canada has flung up his commission. Lord Effingham threw back his the moment his regiment was ordered overseas. Keppel, at the very top of the admirals, has begged not to be used against you. There are dozens more.—If we cannot stay the wrong at least our hands will be fouled by no blood. Some day the King, and that North and Germain, will know the truth—pray God before they have ruined Old England in Europe as well as in America. Then we, when they're brushed aside, shall pick up the wreck and try to build a better Empire.—But don't deceive yourselves. All Britain is not Whig—there's a fearsome work before you."

Then we talked about Peggy and how he soon would be

back with her, and I promised my small aid in getting
certain harmless Loyalist families passed through our lines
into Boston—the business which had brought him out under
the cartel.

Of course this business kept him lawfully in Cambridge
until next day, and I think one of the Compton girls would
have turned Tory after the way he handed her about on the
floor that night—if he had not been unfortunately a firmly
married man. Emilie seemed to have time to say fine things
to everybody but myself, and made me wonder whether
after we were married I would still see so little of her. Yet
the next morning it was my turn to make her vexed, for I
could not come to the Comptons until just before the wedding. "Wedding or no wedding," I made her comprehend,
"war was around us and I had a military duty." I had
promised the Redford men to stand beside Harter when they
paraded on Cambridge Common.

It was about nine when we mustered; our Middlesex
companies who had won honor at the Bridge were rewarded
by being stationed nearest to that monarch elm that flung
out its vast shade on the southern side of the Common. We
were all spruced up in our best, and if our uniforms lacked
much, the poise of our firelocks and the even swing of our
march drew out the admiration from the unkempt, raw
militia who gaped in uncertain ranks from behind.

It was a typical July day, warm, a little dusty, with a
steady wind that made the great boughs move like so many
slow green pendulums. Presently after an impressive delay,
cornets and trumpets blew; there came the prancing of a
troop of brightly furbished horse, then a smaller group of
mounted colonels and generals, then a single figure upon
Nelson. The rider was well over six feet and built accordingly. He strode his steed like a centaur. We saw a figure
in blue and buff with large gilt epaulets. Under the black
cockade of the hat were features bold yet symmetrical,

cheerful, deliberate, firm. The whole man spoke of bound-
less vigor under masterful control.

The cavalcade halted under the huge tree. The charger
pawed the turf, while the slighter figure of Ward rode out,
his white head uncovered. All our drums sounded. The
long files presented arms.

"General Washington," spoke Ward, "I transmit to you
the command of the army."

The cocked hat was raised to us, slowly, gracefully. From
all our regiments went up the cheering. The hat was
replaced, then a strong hand flashed out a glittering saber.
The shouting was great, but I heard the clear reply:

"I ACCEPT THE COMMAND."

With perfect horsemanship, sword on shoulder, the rider
went down our lines, the deep blue eyes taking in everything.

. . . A greater than Joseph Warren was in Cambridge.
The War of New England had become the War of America.

. . . .

Father married Emilie and myself at the Comptons' about
noon. I could never understand her dress, but despite the
war it was white and billowy and very wonderful.

Bradish chased enough officers out of the Blue Anchor
for a dinner which, if it fell short of some of his triumphs,
taught us that wedded life begins the best without starva-
tion.

Herbert gave me a last hug as we climbed into the parsonage chaise. The old horse knew the road; without touch
of rein or whip he took the way to Redford. There we
were together for one month in the cabin by Concord river,
living for the present and trying to forget that fifteen miles
away there still were sounding the guns.

After that I belonged to the War.

CHAPTER XLII

HERBERT DUNMORE I saw not again until December 7th, 1782, and thus it came about.

Once more I was in Boston, for a longer sojourn than of wont during seven years of war. Heaven had spared my life when better men than I had died for the independence of the Republic. I had played my part in things not to be forgotten though my days be lengthened to those of the Patriarchs. I had shared the flight from Long Island. I had been in the boats amid the ice of the Delaware that Christmas night when under God George Washington had saved the whole Revolution at Trenton. It had been mine to see Fraser fall at Saratoga, to hear the Virginian curse out the caitiff Lee at Monmouth, and to reach West Point just after the mask fell from the Great Treason. Wounds and hardship had been mine, but in no greater measure than to any in the great comradeship for which "America" became across those years a mistress to whom it was a glad and holy thing to proffer life.

Then had come our crowning mercy. I had charged at Alex Hamilton's side when we went over Number Ten Redoubt at Yorktown. There I won that clip on the thigh which makes me limp a little to this day, and which caused his Excellency to tell me that I could serve best the next year by commanding the Continental Infantry stationed in Boston. War there still was in name, a few naval raids and privateering; but North had been flung out of office at last, and despite the sulks of their master the new Whig ministers now had their envoys at Paris wrestling with

Franklin and John Adams over the peace terms. At New York the magnanimous Carlton was tacitly at truce with Washington, and any ship from France might bring the news of the formal end of all warfare.

Days there are when sorrows behind and troubles advancing seem all forgotten, when one great glad fact will come home to the hearts of men. What though our paper money was worth only its rags? Our Confederation a makeshift ramshackle? Our burden of debt and demoralization everywhere heavy?—Thanks to Heaven, to the French alliance, to the genius of the Virginian, we had carried through. The United States of America was made.—And we of Massachusetts, if we had sent forth no Washington to command, had sent him more men than any other state, and had vexed him with the fewest of Tories. To the God of New England, to the graves of the Saints gone before us, to the sacrifice of Joseph Warren and those who slumbered with him *we had kept the Faith*.

. . . On this day Boston opened her gates to a foreign army, albeit one that she welcomed with wide-flung arms. The French who had fought by our side at Yorktown had come marching up from the south to Boston to embark for their own lands, after duty bravely done. A fine long column they made, the men under perfect discipline, and so aloof from deeds of license that Britons and Americans alike might have imitated. On a bright, mild day, such as can favor Boston even in December, they had entered the town along Roxbury Neck, their regimental bands playing, and all in their bravest uniforms:—the Royal Deux Ponts regiment in its shining white, the Saint-Onge in white and green, the Bourbonnais in black and red, and all the rest. The gaiters, queues, and huge cocked hats, the white cockades of the officers, alike spoke of Fontenoy and all the

great wars where the fleur-de-lis flags had been borne to
glory.

My duty would not suffer me to linger along the streets,
where the walls were lined with cheering men, the windows
with waving women, while the bayonets went gleaming past.
Nor could I go with the committee, chosen by town meeting, when Samuel Adams headed the deputation to welcome
General Vioménil and his gallant men to Hancock House,
where Governor John Hancock and the Honorable Council
of the State of Massachusetts arranged for a noble feast in
compliment to our visitors and to the officers of the great
French fleet riding peacefully in the harbor.

My own troops lined the ways and did the military
honors, and if our uniforms were less gay than our guests',
our discipline less mechanical, I promise you that our Massachusetts Line was very different from the band of minutemen that crossed the Bridge or stood in the Redoubt. I was
nowise ashamed to have all the fine vicomtes and barons
exchange salutes with them. Everywhere across the march
floated the thirteen stripes and the thirteen stars, with the
biggest banner right over the State House where the column
swung down King Street (State Street, I meant to write),
almost shadowing that pavement where twelve years before
had crashed out the muskets of the Boston Massacre.

I was on service most of the day; but at last came a
lull in the bowing and scraping, saluting and complimenting,
and I was glad enough to mount and ride back to Charter
Street. Since Aunt Mercy's death, Emilie and I had dwelt
there, for Uncle Peleg was growing old, and needed to be
made comfortable, even if (lucky in war's grand lottery)
Watchhorn and his other captains had made him a snug
fortune privateering. When I had tossed my reins to my
orderly, through the door I could see the parlor full of the

rose-and-white of the Soissonaise regiment, and in the center of the group stood Emilie herself, a little rounder than once, a little more matronly, and a great deal more beautiful. She was just permitting the colonel, M. le Comte de Segur, to kiss the hand of "Madame, the wife of *mon brave camarade*." But before I could go in to them, my own aide touched my elbow: "A British officer in Boston on exchange business thinks that Colonel Gilman might be glad to see him."—And there in the private office I found Herbert Dunmore.

He wore a major's regimentals. There was a scar over one eye, reminiscent (it came out) of a Spanish bomb that burst at the siege of Gibraltar. Like many another Whig officer, he had donned his uniform again after Spain joined France in the war, and the volley that had sounded at Concord had multiplied its echoes until Kent and Devonshire trembled for their own safety. I do not know how we got through that first five minutes, what we said, how we acted. I was dimly glad that none of my young ensigns and lieutenants could see then how their colonel bore himself. We managed to get word at length to Emilie; and she with her perfect ease passed the honors of the parlor over to Mrs. Bowdoin, then came charging out in all her velvet and lace, towered hair and crinoline, giving Herbert such an ardent, sisterly kiss that I ought to have been jealous, but stubbornly refused.

We had to hear all about Peggy, and admire the miniatures of the two children; and then George, and Sabra and Debby had to be brought in,—the first two quite old enough to shrink with amazed horror at seeing their parents in friendly converse with something that Yetmercy had taught them to hate a little worse than the devil—an officer in a red coat.

One might have thought by our talk that the war was the

least important thing in the world, when for Herbert we had to pick up all the loose threads.—Yes, father and mother were still in Redford, both grayer no doubt, but mother ruling the house as usual, and father warning sinners in general when he was not warning tall boys even now to follow their brothers into the army. Lucy Knox was a great lady at the camp with her husband the major general; I had last seen her at Newburgh playing loo with Martha Washington. Hope Fifield was Hope Blanchard; her husband, a state councillor down in Connecticut, thought her the handsomest woman in North America, and was hopelessly wound around her little finger. They were at Philadelphia now, where Blanchard had public business with Congress. Darius had got a smart wound at Stillwater, but emerged as a lieutenant, and was now in garrison at Ticonderoga.

And Tabby had fulfilled her heart's desire. She had married a young minister up in the Vermont Grants just before the battle of Bennington, had nursed him through his wound after he had led out his parishioners to join Stark, and now they were (as she had lately written) "very poor but very happy—especially since the coming of twins." Shrimpton had passed to the good sailor's reward whilst he fought beside Paul Jones on the deck of the *Bon Homme Richard*, but Mem Watchhorn had been more lucky; after long tempting the fates as privateersman, he had won more legitimate glory as lieutenant on the *Winthrop*, when that sloop-of-war only ten weeks earlier had cleaned out a whole nest of Canadian gunboats and raiders in the Penobscot, and so had won the thanks of all the coasts of Maine and Massachusetts. He was on another cruise now—or what would not he have given to see Herbert?

Only Georges Rivoire was gone. He had been cheerful and hale, until that day, just after the consummation of the

French alliance, when Emilie had gone to his chamber and found him forever sleeping. It had given him joy unutterable that France had taken her open part in making what he always called "The New America."

Herbert gave us assurances of the survival of most of Emilie's old flames among the regulars. Poor Upson had been knocked in the head at the Brandywine, but Claypool, having found a Roxbury Auchmuty willing to heal his bruised affections, had sold out his commission after Princeton, and was now famous through Yorkshire for his pack of beagles. Dunmore had lately come upon McVitie commanding a frigate, "as gallant a captain as the navy boasts, but not likely to get a seventy-four, thanks to over-much love for usquebaugh." Then with a grim laugh he added, "I can also testify to the 'exaltation' if not the glory of another of your acquaintance. Elnathan Hirst somehow slipped from his marooner's island and got to New York. Howe and Clinton let him do some ineffectual spying, but after Yorktown (when the public wind had veered) Carleton caught him spying in turn on us. Perhaps your General Knox, perhaps his Excellency himself had passed us the word that neither Britain nor America needed him longer.— I saw him neatly hanged a week before I quitted New York."

At last we got the French officers politely swept out of the house, all but Comte de Segur and that delightful Chevalier de Lameth who had won such glory at Yorktown. We had them to supper with Herbert and Paul Revere, who was still in his coat as lieutenant-colonel of militia. Paul was again, as always, full of schemes—this time for casting bells, since cannon would be out of fashion, and for opening some copper works down at Canton. We had all to eat and drink that was good for us, and the Frenchmen delighted the rest by assuring them that their own great country was on the eve of a remarkable but wholly benevolent revolution; wherein, without loss of life or even the kindling of base passions, the victory of benevolence, philosophy and reason would somehow make the stupid wise, the corrupt virtuous, and cause France to be admired across the world as a reconciler of peace and liberty.

We chattered thus late into the evening, sometimes in English, sometimes in French (which Herbert spoke perfectly and I now tolerably), and at last the talk became more piquant as Segur began to touch upon the future of America.

"Voilà!" spoke he, not without a glance toward Dunmore, "you Americans are a people that are English in speech and foundation, *peut-être:* but after the severance by war from Britain, the ties that will henceforth bind you to Paris, the irresistible conquest by our civilization—will you not become another France?"

Herbert's color mounted the least bit. "Pardon me, M. le Comte," he returned firmly, "kinship, speech and traditions are not to be thus lightly effaced. What makes us English grieve the less because our rulers played the fool is this—that in our muddling way we have now made another, a greater England."

Both looked toward Emilie, and she gave back her most impenetrable smile; then neither in French nor in London English but with the accent of purest Yankee, she answered them together: "No, no, my friends. Wrong both of you.— And if across the years the Old World would remain happy as our New World waxes strong, remember this: We have not made another France. We have not made another England. *We have made another nation.*"